NEAL'S HOMECOMING

A Second Historical Novel by the Author of *"Faded Tracks"*

Based on the Narratives of Ruben McNair

This Second Novel is

of

Ruben McNair's Brother
Beginning with the Battle of Franklin, Tennessee
and continuing after the American Civil War

BY JIM L. McALPIN

Edited by Merl R. Wilson

HHI

HHI
P.O. Box 2280
Verona, Mississippi 38879

Library of Congress Catalog Card Number: 97-95116

Cover by Author

First Printing

ISBN 0-9658220-1-X

Printed in the USA by

MORRIS PUBLISHING

3212 East Highway 30 • Kearney, NE 68847 • 1-800-650-7888

THE AUTHOR

Jim L. McAlpin, born and reared in the deep south, finished high school at Magee, Mississippi in May of 1967. He went to Mississippi State University on a football scholarship and while there started three years as a defensive end. In January, 1972, he finished college with a B. S. Degree and in June of the same year, received his Master of Education Degree. He coached and taught school for six years after graduating and worked on his doctoral degree.

Jim has been in retail lumber and construction business now for the past twenty years. He is married and has two sons. Becoming a writer seemed inevitable for him. Being a history major, and having several relatives who fought in the Civil War, he has acquired a vast store of authentic information on this period of history. His ability to tell a good story, plus the knowledge he gained from history books and extensive personal research, equipped him rather well for writing. Also, he had first hand from his mother, accurate accounts, both verbal and written, of his ancestors' involvement in the war between the states. With all of the above, he proceeded to write his first book, "Faded Tracks," which was published in the later part of 1996. This book covered a period beginning one year before the war, and continuing until his great grandfather came home in July 1865. (1860-1865)

"Neal's Homecoming," which begins at the battle of Franklin, Tennessee, is the second book by the author and is an exceptionally good account of Ruben's story about his brother, Neal.

Having read both books, I appreciate Jim's ability as a writer and the way he lets us see history unfold in a realistic, day by day story. He writes about his family, the McNairs, who were real people who lived, loved, and were happy, with only the simplest things of life.

You'll find it interesting, to read answers to some of the question we were left wondering about, in his first book. When you see the demanding work schedule Jim maintains daily in the work place, you wonder how he ever finds time to write. I feel the books he has written, came right from his heart, where a storehouse of treasured memories were placed by his mother. She gleaned them from her grandfather, Ruben McNair, who was there before the Civil War, during the war, and for many years after this conflict. All of this makes the author a writer with a real, or maybe many real stories to tell. I appreciate him and the wholesome books he writes very much. I trust you too, will enjoy both books and look forward, as I do for the next one by this author.

Rivers M. Wilson

DEDICATION

This book is dedicated to the Sons of Confederate Veterans and the Order of the Confederate Rose, for their work in striving to preserve American History accurately.

Jim L. McAlpin
Author

To our Beloved Friend & Brother in christ, David Bruce
I give this book that is authentic History of Neal McNair and the Battle of Franklin, Tenn. The Story of Neal McNair's experience and final Home coming.
Lovingly,
[illegible] Wells

NEAL'S HOMECOMING

OUTLINE

GRANDPA RUBEN TELLS ANOTHER STORY

• • • • • • • • • • • • • • • • • •

April, 1932

There is a sure sound of excitement in Ethel's voice when she runs into her home on the last day of school and yells, "Grandpa! Grandpa!"

"What's got you so fired up now Child?" asks Grandpa Ruben as he walks into the front room, where his excited granddaughter is calling him.

"Grandpa, I finally have made it out of Mize school and I'll be graduating next week."

"Then what Child? You know that you need to go on with your education."

"I know Grandpa, and I will, I've just got to decide what I'm going to do."

"Well you let me know what it is, when you decide Girl," smiles Ruben as he turns to leave the room.

"Aw Grandpa, you're not even going to ask me what I made on our paper? — You know, Faded Tracks."

"Well, I figure you'll tell me when you get good and ready," laughs Grandpa Ruben.

"Well, I'm ready, I got an A+, and no other kid came even close with their paper. The teacher said we should make a book out of it, whatcha think about that?"

"Aw Girl, everyone has a story to tell, some are just better than others, I guess."

"Yeah, well yours was the best Grandpa, and you ought to know it," argues Ethel.

"Well, that was a long time ago, and not too pleasing to remember," sighs Ruben, with a sad, distant look on his face.

"Well Grandpa, you did tell me that you would tell me what happened to Uncle Neal. You do remember saying it was another story for another night, don't you?"

"Yeah Child I do, and after supper I'll tell you all I know of what happened to Neal, and about him coming home."

"That will be great Grandpa, I'll get my chores done, and after supper I'll be ready to take it all down."

"That's fine by me Girl because I ain't got nothin' else to do tonight. Now off with you, go do your chores."

After the chores are done and the supper dishes are put away, Ethel gets her pads and pencils. She then goes into the front room where her grandfather is smoking his pipe while he waits for her to join him. When she enters the room, Ruben asks if she has everything she needs with her.

"I think so Grandpa, besides, if we don't get it all done tonight we've got all summer to finish it," she answers, with a smile.

"Think so, huh Girl?" grins Ruben.

"Yes Sir. Just let me fix the lamp and you can start when you are ready," answers Ethel, eager to hear this story about her Uncle Neal.

With the lamp placed to suit Ethel, Ruben begins telling the story of Neal's Homecoming.

"Now you remember when we lost Thompson, don't you Girl?"

"Yes Sir."

THE BATTLE OF FRANKLIN, TENNESSEE

• • • • • • • • • • • • • • • •

November, 1864

"The four McNair brothers had joined the Confederate Army almost at the beginning of the war between the states. Neal, the oldest, and Thompson, next to him in age, joined the 8th Regiment, Mississippi Volunteers, Captain William T. Ward's Company, back in **June of 1861**. Melton and Ruben joined the same regiment, in **January of 1862**. Ruben is the youngest of the four brothers and Melton is one year older.

Ruben is sixteen, Melton is seventeen, Thompson is nineteen, and Neal is twenty, when all of them are enlisted together in **1862**. These four brothers, in the years that followed, saw their share of the Civil War, and a whole lot more.

When **November 1864** comes around, these brothers have been in fourteen continuous months of fighting, dating back to **September 1863,** and the Battle of Chickamauga.

Neal is a lieutenant, Thompson is a sergeant, while Melton and Ruben are both privates. The only way Hilton and Lilly McNair would agree to let Ruben, their youngest son, go to the war so young, was if the older three boys would promise to care for him.

Through the months of combat, the brothers watched out for each other, with each one taking care of the others. They have seen places and things that boys from Smith County, Mississippi up until then, have only dreamed about. Oranges from Florida, the ocean at the Gulf of Mexico, are just two of the things they have seen in the many places the army has taken them. They have traveled through the mountains of Tennessee and Georgia, guarding the trains.

For a while, early in the war, when they trained and moved around from place to place, there was an itching to get into the action of the war. When the action for the 8th Mississippi did come, the boys from Smith County, turned into fine soldiers and fought well.

Neal was the Assistant Company Commander to Captain Ward, and Thompson had his squad, which was called "McNair's Squad." The 8th Mississippi was assigned to General Hood's Army of Tennessee. He had started his Tennessee Campaign in **October of 1864**.

The place now is Franklin, Tennessee, **November 30, 1864. It's 3:00 in the afternoon**.

The boys in the 8th Mississippi have their doubts about attacking so late in the day, across the vast open ground in front of them.

The Yankees, unknown to the Commanders of the Confederate Army, have reinforced and built a strong defense around Franklin. The Mississippi boys just follow orders, as good soldiers do, and the attack is on.

With the skirmish lines formed and the cannoneers ready, the big guns begin firing at a little past 3:00. At this time the gray line begins to move forward, toward Franklin. They move out at a standard march, with their own guns firing over their heads, into the defensives at Franklin, a mile or so away. The shells are hitting the edge of the city and after a little bit, the smoke from the shells hides the city from sight of the advancing Confederates. When twenty minutes have past, the Confederates are halfway across the field, with what appears an easy task of taking Franklin, ahead. At this point, no shells have been fired in return to the Confederate artillery.

At midpoint across the open ground, the gray line is put at the double time and the Rebel yells begin to sound. Just then, General Schofield, the Commander of the Union forces, has his own artillery open up on the exposed Confederate infantry, as it is crossing the open ground. As fast as the Yankee cannoneers can load and fire, the shells are coming from Schofield's battery.

The shells hit and explode, leaving voids in the once solid line of the charging Rebs.

"Run! Run!" yells Thompson, to his squad, as he encourages his men on. The smoke from the shells is drifting across the field, and it is getting harder to see.

"Faster! Faster!" encourages Thompson, to his tiring men, as they run into the face of death.

While the Yankees keep a steady stream of fire coming at them, Neal runs up behind Thompson and yells, "Can I run along here with ya'll, Sergeant?"

"Suit yourself Lieutenant," smiles Thompson in reply to his brother, "But I wish I had a great big hole to run in."

"Ya'll stop your jawing and keep up with me," yells Ruben as he picks up his gait and passes his two older brothers.

"Slow down Ruben!" yells Thompson as Ruben disappears into the smoke. "That fool kid is gonna get himself killed," yells Thompson to Neal and Melton as he starts running faster toward the enemy. Neal, Melton and the rest of the squad see Thompson and Ruben running faster and they pick it up too.

Having no targets to shoot in the smoke, the Rebs have loaded weapons as the Union trenches come into view. Thompson and the rest of the squad are running after Ruben. Dan Curry, Norris Bryant, Royce Foster, Chris and Luke Tyler, make up the rest of McNair's Squad, along with Ruben, Melton and Thompson. Neal is still with his brother's squad as they hit the Union lines. As the charging Rebs come into view of the Yankee line, the Yankees put up a volley of rifle fire, when the squad is about sixty yards out. To the amazement of the Rebel squad, not a single one of their own goes down in the face of the flying lead.

Before the Union soldiers can reload, Ruben, who is about ten yards in front of the rest of the squad, is on the edge of the Yankee trench. He fires his rifle at close range, into the nearest blue coat, and the Yankee boy is blown to the back of the trench, dead before he hits the ground. Moving quickly, Ruben runs his bayonet into the next Yankee in line. The blade sticks in the ribs of the dying soldier, and he can't pull it out.

By this time, the rest of the squad is up on the wall, firing into the Yankees and using their bayonets. In short order the Yankee soldiers are either killed or they retreat to another line of trench-es, just behind the first line.

"We made it! We whuped 'em!" yells Ruben, as he puts both feet on the dead Yankee, to pull his rifle free. The squad is now down in the captured trench loading their weapons, thinking the enemy may counterattack at any time.

Once Ruben has his piece reloaded, he jumps up on the rear of the trench and fires at a fleeing Yankee, hitting him in the back. Yelling like a wild man, Ruben screams, "I got you!" Then he pulls his pistol and starts firing at other targets who are trying to get to the rear.

"Get down Ruben!" yells Neal. "Get down!"

At this time Thompson starts toward Ruben, while Melton reaches up with both hands and grabs Ruben's belt with his right hand. This action leaves his left hand exposed, and a Yankee six pound gun, which was hidden in the smoke, fires grape shot at the Confederate line. Unscratched, but having his belt and hat shot to pieces, Ruben turns to see Melton's left hand explode, and the top of Thompson's head come off, from the heavy lead shot.

Neal, seeing his two brothers go down, runs to their aid and Ruben jumps back in the trench as the other men in the squad put up fire at the now charging Yankees.

Taking what is left of his belt off, Ruben makes a tourniquet out of it and puts it on the bloody stump of Melton's wrist. As he moves over toward Thompson, Neal grabs his younger brother by his shoulders and tells him, "Ruben! Thompson is gone."

"No! He can't be! I won't let it happen!" screams the sob-bing Ruben unable to accept the fact that Thompson has just been killed.

Neal slaps Ruben, who is struggling to get to where Thompson's body lies in the trench; hoping to bring him back to his senses. He then yells, "Grow Up! Now get Melton to the rear, there ain't nothing we can do for Thompson." With tears stream-ing from his eyes, he remains the lieutenant in charge, disre-garding the pain of losing a brother, he continues to do what is best for the men of the squad who have just lost their sergeant, and comrade.

NEAL'S HOMECOMING

Ruben, with streaks made by the tears that stream down his smoke blackened cheeks, gets himself in hand and takes Thompson's watch, a little money, and some other things out of his pockets, to keep for their mother.

"Here, take my pistol, and get Melton out of here," orders Neal.

"But—"

"Don't but me Ruben. That's an order!" yells Neal.

Ruben then picks the weakened Melton up, throws him over his shoulder and climbs out of the trench with Melton helping as much as he can.

As they disappear into the smoke, Neal takes charge of Thompson's squad. He picks up his dead brother's rifle, checks to see if it's ready to be fired, and orders the squad to prepare for another charge.

Dan and Norris move closer to Neal, so as to close the void left in the line now that Melton and Ruben are retreating and Thompson is dead.

Chris and Luke look on in shock and disbelief over the death of Thompson, their sergeant and friend. He has been the 'old mother hen' to all the squad: now he is gone the two boys start to cry.

"You two, cut that crying out." orders Neal. "Ya'll think you're just gonna set there crying while some Yankees come pouring in here and kills you? You both gotta take care of the business at hand or we all may wind up like Thompson. Do ya' understand?"

"Yes Sir," answer the two Tyler boys.

"Now get them rifles pointed at them Yankees and maybe we'll live through this thing."

"Yes Sir!" comes the now steadier voices of the two young kids who have been thrown into a war, and are now following the leadership of a man they know they can trust.

Neal looks over at Dan and Norris, who have been with the company from the beginning. "Ya' know what's a-coming, don't cha' boys?" asks Neal, counting on the men he knows he can rely on for loyalty and support.

"Yeah Neal, we do," answers Norris.

"We'll be ready for them," adds Dan.

"Well I don't think it'll be very long coming, so let's everybody keep our eyes open," orders Neal, with the sounds of battle going on all around them.

Royce moves in closer to the Tyler boys, and winks at them saying, "You two just do what ole Neal says and we'll make it out of here, you'll see."

"I sure hope you're right," Luke says, as he looks down the barrel of his rifle for any sign of the Yankees.

"Be ready Men!" yells Neal. "They'll be coming anytime now."

Just after Neal has spoken, the flash of the six pound gun can be seen before any sound or lead hits the 8th's position. The men duck down in a blink of the eye as the heavy lead balls cut the earth all around them.

With the sound of the gun's blast rolling over their heads, the Rebs jump back to their positions on the north wall. Their getting back in positions is none too soon, as this is the beginning of the attack they were expecting.

"Fire at will!" Neal yells to the squad. The immediate blast of the rebel guns is loud and deadly. Many Yankee boys are seen dropping before they can get their attack started. The rest of the Yankees keep coming and the squad braces for close-in fighting. A shell comes in from nowhere, landing in the attacking Yankee's line. It explodes with terrific force twenty yards in front of Neal's line of men. The Union charge is broken off and the boys in blue fall back to regroup.

"Where did that come from Neal?" yells Dan.

Norris hollows, "Mus'ta been God-sent, huh Neal!"

"Yeah, I guess it must've been, but most likely it was a short Yankee round," answers Neal. "Get your weapons reloaded, and keep your eyes open, they'll be back."

Time is short before the Yankee six pounder starts firing shells into the Confederate line. After a few minutes of shells flying just over their heads and exploding close by, the firing stops. Men move to their assigned positions, knowing what is coming next. The charging blue line is already moving toward Neal and his men. Firing orders are not needed because the Yankees are that close. The squad starts firing at the closest targets. To a man, Neal's men fire and move out with bayonets, to meet their enemies.

As they move up out of the trench, the Yankee line fires, and both Royce and Chris go down, hit in the lower part of their bodies. As Royce falls to the ground, he pulls his pistol which he has gotten in an earlier battle, and starts firing at close range.

Chris is up on his knees using his bayonet, with Luke close by clubbing the Yankees with his rifle butt. Neal is using his saber while Dan and Norris are closing in tight with their bayonets. The squad works close to their two wounded comrades, protecting them as much as possible.

Royce's pistol keeps the Yankees guessing. Neal wishes he had kept his pistol with him, but remembers that Melton and Ruben might have needed it. After a hard fight, the Yankees start a withdrawal, leaving several of their men dead on the ground around McNair's Squad.

Neal moves to help Luke carry Chris back to the trench when a rifle ball hits him in the left chest, right under his breast. He is thrown backward to the ground. Dan and Norris drag him back into the trench, while Royce keeps firing at the retreating Yankees.

Luke pulls Chris back into the ditch while Dan and Norris rush out to move Royce back to the safety of the ditch.

"Dan, you and Norris get those two kids and Royce, and get out of here," says Neal in a low voice, gasping for air, while blood gushes out of the hole in his chest.

"Neal, if any of us leave, we are all going to leave," answers Norris matter-of-factly.

"That's right Neal," agrees Dan.

"Look boys, I ain't got to tell ya'll I'm a-dying, but I'm still in charge here. I'm ordering you two to get the rest of the squad out of here before the Yankees come back. Now git!" Neal speaks firmly as the good officer that he is, but his pain and weakening condition makes talking difficult for him. While his order for them to leave him is a hard command to obey, they have no choice but to follow orders.

Reluctantly, Norris and Dan move over to the other two wounded men. Royce has his hip all busted up, and Chris has a hole through his thigh, barely missing the bone. Norris and Dan pick up Royce and their weapons, then start for the rear. Luke gets his weapon and helps Chris walk, as they leave with the others.

As they are leaving, Dan and Norris stop to look at Neal, their fallen comrade, who has been their leader and friend through all of the war years. Before they can say anything to him, he speaks to them again in a voice that is weak but leaves no doubt about what he expects them to do.

"You two know I'm right, now git if you don't want to wind up like me!"

"Yes Sir!" answers Dan sadly, as they start their march to the rear. Without a word being spoken, they all feel that leaving Neal is the toughest command they have ever had to obey.

When the five men have cleared the trench and disappeared into the smoke, Neal is left all alone, knowing the Yankees are about to attack. "Well I'm about to see what it's like to be dead," Neal says to himself. "I only hope those boys can get out of harm's way before them Blue Bellies come back."

The Union Army fires one round from the six pounder, and is on its way back. Royce, Chris, Luke, Dan, and Norris are lucky to be gone as the Yankees pour into the trench. Men in new uniforms, well equipped, jump into the trench. Neal thinks, "These troops must have just arrived, new equipment, clean and all, Green Troops." Then he smiles.

"Well lookie' here George," says one of the Union soldiers to another. We have ourselves a dying Reb."

"Yeah, we have," answers the other, as they look down at the smiling Neal.

A sense of peace comes over Neal, as he prepares to die and thoughts of home race through his mind.

"We might as well go on and put him out of his misery, don't ya think George?" the first soldier asks.

"Might as well," answers George. Then the two green troopers turn their backs on the front, ready to finish Neal off.

Looking between the two Union Soldiers, Neal sees Ruben jump up on the south wall with pistols in hand. Neal starts waving one hand in the air, speaking as loudly as he can, to his little brother, "Go back! Go back!"

The Yankees must have thought he was talking to them. As they raise their guns to shoot, both of them are cut down by the pistols in Ruben's hands. He continues to fire until his guns are empty, and several other Union troops are either dead or wounded. At this time, he starts to jump into the ditch to rescue Neal, but is stopped by other Yankee soldiers jumping in the trench from the north side.

Neal is still yelling for Ruben to go back, as he passes out. Then Ruben turns and runs back to catch up with what is left of the retreating Squad. The Union soldiers, who have come into the trench, did not see Ruben, due to all the smoke, which lies heavy over this area.

"Look here Sergeant," says one of the Union men. "We got ourselves a dying Reb Officer."

"Well so we do, let's get him back to the hospital, he may live long enough to tell us something that will help," orders the sergeant.

HOSPITAL IN NASHVILLE

• • • • • • • • • • • • • • • • •

December - 1864

Neal is recovering from surgery in a Yankee Hospital in Nashville, Tennessee. He has not regained consciousness, from his ordeal on the battlefield and the trauma of surgery.

Then on the 4ᵗʰ **of December**:

"Go back! Go back!" yells Neal, as he starts coming around in a clean hospital bed.

"Lieutenant! Lieutenant!" calls the forty odd year old Union doctor, trying to break through the haze of medication and pain to get to Neal.

"Go back! Go back!" Neal repeats the last order he had spoken, before losing consciousness, back in the trench.

"Lieutenant, wake up you're in a hospital, and the war for you is over," says the doctor in a gentle voice. He tries again to bring Neal away from the battle scene, which he is remembering so painfully.

"Go! — Huh?— What?—- Where am I?" Neal asks in a weak voice.

"Lieutenant, you are in a Union hospital, in Nashville. You have been wounded very badly and you need to save your strength," explains the concerned doctor.

"Yes Sir."

"Now can you tell me your name Lieutenant?" asks the doctor.

"Name?" responds the dazed Neal.

"Yes Lieutenant, your name," smiles the doctor. "Like mine is Colonel D.W. Voge, United States Medical Core. Now, what is yours?"

"Name, huh? I can't."

"You can't remember? Well, who are you telling to go back?"

"Sir, uh--- I don't know, all I can see is this young kid up over me shooting pistols all around and it's so smoky you can hardly see."

"Who is this kid you are telling to go back Son?" asks the doctor with a look of concern on his face.

"Doctor, I just don't know. I can't remember nothing!" Neal exclaims as tears of pain and confusion gather in his eyes.

"Now just calm down Son, it will come back to you. Just rest and I'll get the nurses to get you something to eat and drink. They will be here in just a little while. You just try to rest until then. After you have eaten, I'll come back," instructs Doctor Voge as he turns to go give orders for food and drink to be brought to Neal.

With the doctor walking away through the ward filled with other wounded men, Neal feels so alone, not being able to remember his family, his friends or any part of his past. He can remember the events and problems of his country, but can't remember anything about himself. As he lies there trying to remember, a feeling of fear comes over him, almost like the fear one has when he gets turned around and is lost in the woods.

Doctor Voge walks down where the nurses are located and orders some broth and bread for Neal. He also tells the nurse to get him some water to drink, and to see to it that he is comfortable. He tells her not to ask Neal any questions because of his weakened physical condition and the mental confusion that is so painful for him to deal with at this time. Then Doctor Voge goes to his office to look through his medical library where he hopes to find some information that will help solve this wounded soldier's problem of memory loss.

As Neal lies in his bed confused about his situation, a tall, older woman, with graying black hair and blue eyes, brings his meal to him. "Here you go Young Man," says the nurse as she fixes the tray of food for Neal to eat.

"Thank you, Ma'am," answers Neal, as he positions his body so he can reach the food and water. The nurse then turns and goes back to her desk, leaving Neal alone with his meal and his thoughts, like the doctor ordered.

Neal had not realized that he was so hungry and thirsty until he started eating. Neal sees Doctor Voge walk back into the ward about the time he is finishing the food and water on his tray. He notices the doctor stop and visit with each soldier in the ward, as he makes his way back to his bed.

When Doctor Voge gets back to Neal, he is lying a little higher on his pillow, "How was the broth Son?" he asks as he pulls up a chair next to Neal's bed.

"It was fine Doc, I didn't realize I was that hungry and dry," answers Neal, looking straight at Doctor Voge.

"I know what must be rushing through your mind Lieutenant," states the doctor, in a gentle yet positive manner.

"Yes Sir, I would like to know who I am and where I'm from," answers Neal with tears in his eyes and a quiver in his voice.

"I've started looking through all my medical books and I'll be talking to other doctors about you Lieutenant, but right now, I have no answers for you," informs doctor Voge with the sound of sincerity and regret unmistakable in his voice.

"Doctor, you keep calling me Lieutenant, well how do you know that I am one?"

"You see Son, when they brought you in, you had the bars of a Lieutenant on your shoulders."

"What army, Doctor Voge? I can't even remember what army I was in."

"Son, you are in the Confederate Army."

"That's just about as bad for me as it can be huh Doc?"

"How do you mean Son?"

"Heck Doc, not only can I not remember who I am or anything about me, but I'm also a prisoner of war."

"No Son, you are my patient, until I say different."

"But Doc, why would you, a Union officer, care two hoots about me?"

"I'm a doctor Son, and my job is to save lines and repair broken bodies. You came in here almost dead with a rifle ball that had just barely missed your heart. It was bulging up under the skin on your back. I removed it and repaired where the ball had broken your ribs, just about two inches under your heart. You bled a lot which helped cleanse the wound. I did not think at first you would make it but you have proven me wrong, I think you are going to be just fine now."

"Oh yeah, I'm gonna be just fine, a man with no memory and no past."

"I'm still working on that, and I feel that nature has it's own way of working things out."

"Doc, I wasn't shot in the head, so why am I this way?"

"The brain is a funny thing Son. When we see and do things, or have things done to us, that are so terrible, our mind can just block it out to protect us from reality with all of its pain."

"How do you know how terrible the war is Doc? You are here in the rear, just seeing the results of it."

"You really don't know. You see, when I was about your age, I was in the Mexican War, and that war, like this war, was not pretty."

Neal stares off in a frozen stare, seeing something from the past, but only a single glimpse.

"Son you remembered something, didn't you?" Doctor Voge asks.

"Yes sir, I saw this big man at a fence on a horse saying he was in the Mexican War. He said that it shore wasn't prutty and that this one was not going to be prutty either," answers Neal.

"Good! You see it will take time, but your memory will come back."

"Why do you care, you're a Union doctor and I'm a Confederate soldier?"

"Well as I was saying, I was in the Mexican War and I was in it with boys from all over, both the north and the south. When this war started I had been a doctor for several years and being from Tennessee, it was hard for me to see my country split. See, I wanted to help both sides as best I could. I felt that being a doctor for the north, I could save lives on both sides better than I could by working for the south. I had my share of fighting and killing in the Mexican War, now I just fight to save lives."

"I'm sorry I back-talked you Doctor Voge."

"You really didn't Son, you are just trying to get answers to the many questions you have in your mind. They will come, and I'm going to help you find those answers. Right now, you need your rest so try to sleep while I check the other wards."

"Yes Sir, I am feeling tired."

As Neal drops off to sleep, Doctor Voge begins his rounds to see all of his patients and he plans to get as much help as he can from doctors on this hospital staff along with others he may contact, who might have information on this type illness.

Tired and weak, Neal sleeps through the night, but for Doctor Voge, sleep is postponed as he digs deep in research among the medical books in his library. Along about eleven o'clock, the light from his lamp still shows under the door of his office and when a colleague of his comes walking down the hall after making his night rounds, he notices both the light and the time.

Doctor Lawrence Daniel opens the door and sticks his head inside doctor Voge's office. "Dennis what are you doing studying at this hour?" he asks.

"Come in Lawrence, I'm having a problem with one of my patients and I could sure use your help."

"Very well, how may I help you?" asks Daniel as he walks into doctor Voge's office.

"I haven't had time to confront any of the other doctors here about this Confederate Lieutenant who's in my charge. He was wounded very badly in the chest, but is recovering remarkably well from the wound."

"If he's recovering, then what's the problem with him?"

"I'm coming to that. When he regained consciousness I was there and began to talk to him. Everything seemed normal until I asked for his name. He could not remember his name or anything about his past."

"Aw- Dennis, this Rebel is just playing sick, he doesn't want the regular army to come and question him."

"No Lawrence, I feel that he is genuine, in this loss of his memory. He looked like a whipped child, scared and alone. Those were real tears in his eyes, and when I couldn't give him any answers, he was sincerely interested in finding out about himself. He didn't even know what army he was in. There was one brief memory that came to his mind of a man on a horse, talking about the Mexican War. Also, he could remember this young boy shooting pistols in the smoke, but he could not remember any names. I am confident he has truly lost his memory and wants it back more than anything else at this time. I really need your help in this case Lawrence."

"Well Dennis, if he really has lost his memory, he will be asking more and more questions."

"I agree with you. We had some studies of the mind in school, but I can't find my notes on the subject of memory."

"I remember from my studies, that when a person of a younger age lost their memory, it was usually from a head injury. Also memory loss could result from a terrible scene or event which produced intense mental anguish, or physical pain."

"Yeah, and with the head injury, the person usually would not regain their memory," agrees Dennis.

"Yet if the memory loss was from fright, pain, or emotional distress, it would usually come back with rest, in time," adds Lawrence.

"That's what I was thinking too Lawrence, but I can't find my notes to back it up. I'm mighty glad you stopped by tonight."

"Think nothing of it Dennis, I'll help you anyway I can, but now I'm going to go get some sleep and I suggest that you do the same."

"Let me put these notes up and I'll be right with you." Doctor Voge carefully puts his papers back in place, while Doctor Daniel moves over to wait for him by the door. When the lamp has been blown out, Dennis walks over to the door, joins his friend and the two of them walk together to their quarters, where they hope to get some much needed sleep.

December 5th, 1864

"Good morning Lieutenant!" greets the older nurse, cheerfully, as she brings Neal his breakfast.

Waking up with a start, Neal jumps to the side of the bed and tries to get up.

"Easy son," she speaks softly. "Remember where you are now."

Realizing where he is, Neal relaxes back in the bed. "Ma'am, what is your name, if I may ask?"

"Ruth Walters," answers the woman, looking at Neal with kindness showing in her blue eyes. "Son, Dr. Voge told me about your problem."

"He did!"

"Yes Son, and I want you to know, I think he is the best and most caring doctor in this hospital. If there is anyway you can be cured, he'll figure it out."

"Thank you, Miss Ruth."

"Mrs. Ruth Son. I've got a husband and two boys about your age, all off in this war."

"I'm sorry Ma'am. I hope everything works out well for them, and you," replies Neal. "Were you a nurse before the war, Mrs. Ruth?"

"No, but with my men gone from home, I had to do something, or go crazy, so I just became a nurse, to try to help out."

"Oh, I see, and you get to work on the men your men have been fighting. Somehow that just don't seem right, does it?"

"Son, the men on both sides are the same, you know the ones doing the fighting did not start the war. They go out there and foolhardily fight each other, when the rich, or the politicians, should be out there in battle, instead of you boys."

"Yes Ma'am, I feel you are right, but I guess it's too late now, ain't it?"

"Yes it is," answers Mrs. Walters. "Well, I hope you enjoy your breakfast."

"Thank you, Ma'am."

"I have a bunch of hungry boys to feed, so I best be going. Oh, by the way, we will be getting another young man in the vacant bed, here next to you, in a little while. The doctors told us to have it ready for him when they finish operating."

"That will be nice to have someone close by to talk with, Mrs. Ruth," answers Neal as Mrs. Walters turns and leaves.

Ruth goes back and forth to the kitchen until there is a tray with breakfast on it at each man's bed in the ward. While she is doing this work of kindness, Neal, being the last man in the line of beds, watches. He sees that all of the twelve beds in the room are occupied, except the one which is ready for the soldier who is still in surgery. He wonders if the other men in this room know that he is a Confederate soldier.

By the time Ruth has finished getting all the men's breakfast to them, Neal has finished with his tray of eggs, ham, hash brown potatoes, coffee, and a small glass of milk.

When she has served all of the other men, she looks back to see that Neal has eaten all of the food on his tray. She walks back to him and picks up the empty tray. "My, you were hungry Lieutenant!"

"Yes Ma'am, and it surely was good," compliments Neal, as Ruth takes the tray and goes on with her work.

Neal lies there in his bed and wonders about himself, what kind of family he has, if he even has a family, and where his home is located. Then he looks at the other men in the ward and wonders about them. Could he have fought these men? Could one of them have been the soldier who shot him?

As he is lying there with his many unanswered questions, Doctor Voge leads two stretcher bearers into the ward. They are carrying a young soldier, who is covered with a sheet. Neal notices that the doctor looks tired and the strain of his work shows on his face. His heavy eye brows give his eyes a squinting look, as the two men bearing the stretcher, step up along side the vacant bed and stop. Doctor Voge stoops his six foot frame over and as gently as possible, he slides the sleeping soldier over onto the bed, from the stretcher, and then adjusts the sheet back straight on the patient.

"Lieutenant, I'm counting on you to help with this young boy when he wakes up. He's going to be in for a shock and you will be the first person to see and talk to him," informs Doctor Voge, knowing that giving Neal some type of assignment will be good for him

"Yes Sir, I will, but what's the matter with him Doctor Voge?"

"He was hit in his hand and it got infected. We were hoping we could save it, but we couldn't, had to take it off."

"I understand Doc, I'll help as much as I can," answers Neal, thinking that it could have been his bullet that caused the boy all of his grief.

Doctor Voge turns and leaves, knowing with the war so close at hand, there will be a lot more work to be done. Everyone knows that Hood's Army of Tennessee has been fortifying Franklin ever since he has taken it from the Yankees. Voge knows that his army will be taking it back in a matter of time. Because Franklin is just a short distance southeast of Nashville, the hospital needs to be prepared for the hordes of wounded that will be pouring in to be treated.

Only a short while after Doctor Voge has gone, the young soldier in the bed next to Neal starts coming around. Neal watches his every move and by sitting up on the side of his own bed, can see him clearly as he tries to wake from the heavy drugs he was given for the surgery. He notices his eyes open and then close for a while, then he opens them again.

"How you feeling Soldier?" asks Neal, in a soft voice.

"Huh?" the still sleepy boy responds to Neal's question. "Okay I guess, but I'm afraid to look under this sheet at my hand," answers the frightened boy.

"Well it's as bad as you may expect, but at least you are alive," encourages Neal.

Mrs. Walters is busy with her duties but she sees Neal up on the side of his bed, talking to the new patient, and she walks back to them.

"Lieutenant, you know that you are not to be up yet, now lie back down before you hurt yourself," orders the nurse.

"Yes Ma'am," answers Neal as he gets back into his bed.

"Now you two can talk, but I don't want to catch you up until Doctor Voge gives you permission, is that understood?"

"Yes Mrs. Ruth, it is," smiles Neal. Ruth then goes on with her work as the two men get back into their conversation.

"Lieutenant, huh?"

"Yeah, that is what they call me," replies Neal. "What is your name?"

"Henry Cheek, Sir," answers Henry, as he brings his bandaged stump out from under the sheet.

When Neal sees the bloody bandage, there is a shock, as battle scenes race through his mind, then they stop in the trench with the young soldier who he has seen before. He sees him with the pistols and he can see the smoke all around, but he does not have a name for him. Now he sees him tying off a bloody stump of a hand, with part of a belt. He sees the rear of a soldier who is missing the hand, and then remembers looking down on a body with part of the head missing.

"Sir my hand is gone!" exclaims Henry, but Neal is frozen in a distant scene from his past. "Sir!" Henry speaks again a bit louder. "Yeah, what is?" questions Neal as he is jerked back to the present.

"My hand is gone Lieutenant."

"I'm sorry, but it is best this way Henry, I talked to Doctor Voge, and he said that you would die if the hand was not removed."

"Yes Sir, I know, but I still don't know what I'm gonna do without it."

"It will take time, but you'll learn to make do," states Neal not knowing anything else to say.

"It's going to be hard to dig coal back home with just one hand," states Henry sarcastically.

"You're a coal miner, huh?"

"Yes Sir, from West Virginia Sir." answers Henry, as if he were standing in formation.

"Look Henry, you don't have to Sir me," explains Neal.

"Yes Sir I do, that is what privates do to officers, Sir."

"You don't understand Henry, I'm in, or I was in, the Confederate army."

"You are a Reb Sir?" questions a dumbfounded Henry.

"Yeah, I guess I am, or was, at least that is what they tell me."

"Gosh! I ain't never talked to a Reb Officer before and very few Rebs otherwise."

Smiling, Neal says, "Well there ain't much difference in Rebs and Yankees Henry, specially the ones fightin' this war."

"Well Sir, what's your name?"

"Henry, you don't have to call me Sir," grins Neal, "And my name is lost with my memory. I don't know who I am, where I'm from, or anything about my past."

"You shot in the head Sir?"

"Henry, no I'm not shot in the head, now don't Sir me."

"Well then Sir, I mean whatever, what do I call you?"

"I guess you just call me Lieutenant, that is what everybody else, or the ones who've talked to me, call me."

"Well okay Lieutenant, that is what I'll call you, but I won't Sir you," grins the puzzled Henry.

"That's good Henry," Neal says as he lies on his bed, staring at the ceiling.

"I lost a hand, and you lost your mind, I guess I'm the lucky one, huh Lieutenant?" Henry asks as he turns on his side to look at Neal.

"I guess you are Henry, I got shot in the chest and lived, but I lost my whole life, or my past life anyway."

"At least I got a home and family to go back to when I'm out of this here hospital, Lieutenant. When the war is over, what are you going to do?"

"I don't know. I guess the outcome of the war will have some bearing on that, but for now I don't have a past to go back to."

"What do the doctors say?" questions Henry, really puzzled by Neal's unusual ailment.

"They say it will take time, and Doctor Voge is working as hard as he can for me."

"I hope it will be okay Lieutenant, after talking to you I don't feel so bad about myself," says Henry, rolling over on his back and looking at the ceiling like Neal.

After an hour or so, Doctor Voge comes into the ward and starts with the first patients near the door, working back one man at the time. Neal and Henry are watching as he talks with each man. Some of the men are missing arms while others are missing legs, so it appears that Henry and Neal's wounds are not as serious as the others in this ward. The doctor takes his time with each man and gets in no hurry when it comes to his patients.

Finally, Doctor Voge gets back to Henry's bed. "How you feeling Henry?" the concerned doctor inquires.

"Oh, I'll be okay Doc," answers Henry. "The lieutenant there has lost his mind, or something like that. He can't remember beans, Doc. Ya' don't suppose he's a Reb lunatic, do you? Anyhow, I just lost a hand, and he said I'd find a way to work the mines again, and I believe him, even though he is a crazy Reb."

Neal hears every word Henry is saying and he laughs to himself. "Well maybe I am a crazy Reb, but I got a-lotta crazy Yankees for company and that Henry takes the cake."

"Henry, you shouldn't talk so loud; the lieutenant may hear what you are saying," smiles the doctor knowing there's nothing wrong with Neal's hearing and he could not have missed Henry's loud talk from his bed right next to him.

"Aw Doc, he don't care, he knows he's lost his mind, even told me so hisself. He even said I didn't have to 'Sir' him, now what do you think about that?"

"Henry, he's in, or was in, a different army from the one you and I are in, so maybe he's just trying to be nice to you."

"Oh he is real nice Doctor, a little crazy, but real nice."

"I'm glad you think so Henry, because I'm going to let you and him start moving around and you are to be his guard."

"Really, you really mean it, I'm going to get to guard the lieutenant?"

Smiling real big, Doctor Voge answers, "Yes Henry, you really are." Then he moves on to Neal's bed.

"Did you hear that conversation, Lieutenant?"

"Yes Sir, I did."

"What do you think about Henry being your guard?"

"Suits me fine Sir, I am ready to get out of bed and move around a bit."

"Son you've been good help with Henry, and he will stay with you, so you can move about the hospital at will. I don't want you thinking about escaping though."

"I don't believe you'll have to worry about that Sir. If I did get out of here, I wouldn't know where to go."

"I was hoping you would say that. You see Son, the South can't hold out much longer. Grant will be getting the attacks started against Hood before long and drive him back. Hood had to be the commander of the forces you were with. In your weakened condition, you could never catch up with them once they are forced to retreat. I feel that the best thing for you to do is stay in this hospital as long as I can keep you here. When you do leave, if the war is not over, it will be a prison camp."

"I'll do whatever you say Doctor, I surely do want to get my memory back."

"You will, and you can start by trying to get your strength back. You will need to start walking and exercising, but always take Henry along with you as your guard," instructs Doctor Voge, with a wink.

"I will Sir," answers Neal as Doctor Voge gets up to leave.

After the doctor has gone, Neal sits up on the side of his bed and tells Henry that he is going for a walk to the door and back. "Now you keep your eye on me, so I won't run off," and smiles.

"That sounds fine with me Lieutenant, and while you are walking, I'm gonna catch up on my sleep, just see to it that you don't run off Sir, uh- I mean Lieutenant."

Neal gets up slowly and starts walking, feeling light headed, at first. He walks to the door of the ward, turns and walks back to his bed. He finds Henry sound asleep when he gets back. "That boy is something else, he needs his sleep after the operation he had this morning and the shock of losing his hand, all in one day. I'll just walk around here in the ward until he is able to go with me," thinks Neal as he sits down on his bed.

Henry sleeps off and on the rest of the day, and as the shadows grow long on the wall, from the evening sun. Neal is gaining his strength and feeling much better.

December 6, 1864

General Grant is tired of waiting on General Thomas, the commander of the Union force in Nashville. Grant now sends him a direct order to attack Hood's Army at once. Many of Thomas's cavalrymen are still without horses. He is delaying while trying to gather up enough, so his horse soldiers will have sufficient mounts to be effective. Thomas warns Grant that an attack without cavalry, will be risky.

After the breakfast that Mrs. Walters has brought them, Henry and Neal are sitting on the edge of their beds, waiting for Doctor Voge to make his rounds. They see that he is working his way back to their area, as he stops to talk with each patient on his list. The weather outside is turning colder, and they speak of the change while waiting for the doctor to get to their beds.

"You know Lieutenant, I sure am glad to be in this here warm hospital and not out there living in a tent on that cold ground."

"Yeah, I bet it was bad out there, specially when the weather takes a turn for the worse."

"It sure was, but you ought to know how it was. Oh, I forgot Lieutenant, I'm sorry."

While the two men sit facing each other, Doctor Voge walks up, having finished with all of his patients, except them. "I see you two are feeling better," greets the doctor with a smile.

"Yeah Doc we sure do," answers Henry. "But the breakfast they brought us wasn't enough, we're still hungry."

"Yes you are getting better Henry, and how about you Lieutenant?" asks the caring doctor.

"Oh I'm a whole lot stronger than I was yesterday. After you left I walked the floor and got my blood flowing good," answers Neal.

"And he didn't try to run off one time," adds Henry.

"Well now that's good that you didn't try to run off, and that you are stronger," laughs Voge.

"It would be kinda hard for him to run off in these hospital gowns, Doc. Do you suppose you could get us some real clothes to wear if'n we're gonna be walking about, like you said yesterday?" asks Henry.

"You got a point Henry, I'll see what I can do," answers Doctor Voge.

"That would help if you can Doctor, see, it will be kinda air'ish in these gowns out in the halls." Neal says, pointing to the hospital gown he's wearing.

"I will boys, until I get you some clothes, the two of you just walk around here in the ward," orders the doctor.

"Yes Sir." answer the two soldiers together, as Voge gets up and moves toward the door.

"Hey Reb!" comes a call from the man in the bed next to Henry.

"Yeah, what do you need?" asks Neal as he gets up and walks to the soldier's bed. It's obvious what this patient's problem is, with the hump of only one leg showing under the bed covers.

"I'm about to freeze. Do you think you could build up the fire in the stove a little bit?"

"Yes Sir," answers Neal. "I believe I can do that." Then he turns and walks to the wood stove, which heats the room, located in the front of the long ward, down next to the door. As Neal walks down the ward, it dawns on him that this Union soldier called him Reb and asked a favor, just like they were friends or something.

Neal gets over to the stove, picks up a couple pieces of stove wood, and puts them on the fire in the belly of the iron heater. While he has the door open he stokes the fire, hoping more warmth will reach the soldier who has lost one of his legs, and is cold. He walks back to his own bed, takes a quilt off the top of his covers and returns to the soldier who asked for more heat.

"Here, you can have my quilt." Neal says as he spreads it gently over the man's shivering body. "Since I'm up and moving about, I won't be needing it."

"Thank you Boy," says the man of about thirty or thirty-five years of age.

Neal asks, "Can I help you any more?"

"No Reb, I'll be fine now, I'm much obliged to ye, I was just having a chill, I guess."

"Well you just call out, if you need me," states Neal, and he goes back to his bed.

Doctor Voge returns with some clothing for Henry and Neal. He has a blue Union uniform for Henry, and a pair of gray pants with a pair of red long-johns for Neal.

"I can't give you a uniform, Lieutenant. These were your pants, but the pockets had been picked when you were brought in. I've had them cleaned, and the long-johns are issue. These should keep you two warm enough and you don't need to be going outside," explains the doctor as he gives the clothing to the two men.

"Thank you Doc," answers Neal for Henry and himself.

"Oh yeah Lieutenant, I have wired New York about your case. I'm hoping to hear back from up there any day now," adds Voge, as he prepares to leave again

"That's good Doctor Voge, but do you think it will do any good?" questions Neal.

"Yeah Doc, or is the lieutenant's mind going to just stay hid, like it is now?" asks Henry.

"Well boys, it can't do any harm, and who knows, maybe somebody up there will know more about what to do, than I do."

"I sure hope so," adds Neal, as the doctor continues on his way.

"Come on Lieutenant, let's get out of these women's clothes and walk around," suggests Henry as he starts taking his gown off.

"Fine by me Henry," answers Neal, and he too, takes his gown off. As he is getting out of it, he glances at the soldier he gave his quilt to and sees that he has gone to sleep. Having gotten warm and comfortable, he seems to have relaxed into a restful sleep.

"Henry, do you know that soldier's name, the one there next to you?" Neal asks as he nods in the direction of the sleeping soldier.

"No Lieutenant, I don't. I don't know any of these here boys. I was with a bunch of volunteers from West Virginia. We were put with a group of boys from Ohio when we got to Franklin, on the day you Rebs attacked. We didn't have time to learn nobody, and so many were wounded, then we got pushed back and all. It was purtty bad. I was cut across the back of my hand on the first day of battle, but I didn't think it was too bad. The second day, we got pushed back and my hand started bothering me, so they sent me back to have it looked at and I wound up here, with this," Henry explains, as he holds his arm up, in sight.

Neal stops in the process of taking his hospital clothes off, and stares at Henry's bandaged stump. "What's a'matter Lieutenant?" asks Henry.

"Aw' Henry, I keep seeing this boy in my mind, tying off another boy's hand that's a bloody mess, but I don't know who they are..."

"It will come Sir, ah, I mean Lieutenant," answers Henry as he stands up and removes the last of the hospital clothes. He is standing there stark naked, when Mrs. Walters walks in the door of the ward, to check on her charges.

"Mrs. Walters!" screams Henry. "Can't you see I'm naked as a jay bird?"

"Why Henry, I would never have guessed," laughing, Mrs. Walters turns and leaves.

The whole ward of men laugh at Henry's scream of embarrassment, waking up the sleeping soldier next to Henry's bed. The sleepy soldier, not knowing anything about what's going on, tells Henry to quieten down so he can get some sleep.

After a little bit, when Neal and Henry have finished dressing, Mrs. Walters comes back into the ward. As she comes in Neal is walking toward the door, with the gray pants and red shirt showing off the long-johns. Henry is right behind him, in a new Union uniform.

"Who has been fooling with this fire?" she asks as she checks the wood stove.

"I did Mrs. Ruth. One of the men was cold, so I just put a couple of sticks of wood in there and poked it up. I hope that was okay," answers Neal.

"Oh that's fine Lieutenant, that's what I was coming in here to do," she explains.

"Well Mrs. Ruth, it sounds to me like you need some help. Now, me and Henry here are able to move around the hospital, so maybe we can help you with your work."

"Yeah, we can help you Mrs. Ruth, and while we are doing it, I'll be a-guardin' the Lieutenant," adds Henry, proud of his assignment to guard Neal.

"That's mighty nice of you boys, but before I can give you any work to do, I'll have to get Doctor Voge to say that it's okay, then I'll find the two of you some jobs to do."

"That will be good, Mrs. Ruth, you just let us know when," answers Neal. "For now, we're just going to walk out and about in the halls of the hospital. That way we can learn our way around, and be able to do a better job for you, when you tell us what to do."

"Yeah, that's what we are a-doin' now. Get moving Reb," grins Henry, as he and Neal begin their exploring of the hospital.

"I'll see you boys later, now don't overdo your walking and hurt yourselves," warns Mrs. Walters as they start walking down the hall.

The hospital is the largest building either of the two boys have ever been in. Neal just doesn't remember, and Henry won't shut up about how long the halls are, as they walk up and down them.

When they get a few steps from their own ward, Henry exclaims in an astonished tone of voice, "Gosh Lieutenant, I ain't never seen a hall this long before!"

"Yeah, it's a long hall, Henry." Neal agrees, as they walk slowly past door after door, all with wards behind them filled with wounded soldiers. Neal is wondering if he has ever seen a hall this long before in some other place.

After a little while, the two come to an intersection of halls. "Which way Lieutenant?" Henry asks, since they have to make up their minds on which hall to take.

"Left Henry," answers Neal, as he leads down another hall as long as the one they just came down.

Coal oil lamps line the walls in each hall to give light, even in the daytime hours. The smell of oil from the burning lamps fills the air in the halls. After going down the left hall for a while, a different smell permeates the air, and they both pick up the strong odor at the same time.

"Lieutenant, this is as far as I'm a-going," states Henry.

"Why, Henry, what's the matter?" questions Neal

"You see that door down yonder at the end?"

"Yeah I do, but what about it?"

"You smell what I smell?"

"Yeah."

"Well behind that door yonder, is where they cut my hand off. That smell is chloroform, and if we don't go on back right quick, it's gonna make me sick," explains Henry, looking paler with each step that takes them closer to the door.

"OK, Henry, we'll go on back."

Then the two turn and retrace their route back to their ward. By the time they get there they are kinda tired, and they walk on back to their beds to rest.

While they are resting, Dr. Voge comes by their ward again, to check on his boys as he always does. After checking with the other men, he walks on back to Neal and Henry.

"I talked to Mrs. Walters, down the hall about you two, and she tells me that both of you want to help her with the work to be done around here," states Voge.

"Yes Sir we do," answers Neal.

"That's a good idea, but I don't want you boys to overdo it. Just work here in your ward for now, then as you get stronger, maybe you can branch out," orders Dr. Voge.

"You don't have to worry about that Doc. Shoot, we just walked down the hall a-ways, I'm tuckered out," assures Henry, to the danger of overdoing it.

"Lieutenant, Mrs. Walters found your quilt on Sergeant Beech's bed. She heard about the way you helped him, and it was a good thing you did. You see, after losing a leg, the body is very weak so if his chill hadn't been stopped, he could have easily gotten pneumonia, which would have killed him," explains Dr. Voge.

"I'll help anybody that's cold Sir, and I feel that the sergeant would too," answers Neal.

"You're right about that, he is a good man and if you would keep an eye on him for me, it would help."

"Oh I will do that," answers Neal.

"Me too!" adds Henry.

"Thank you both. Oh by the way Lieutenant, Mrs. Walters is bringing you another quilt so the sergeant can keep yours."

"That's fine sir."

"Keep the fire going in here, it's really turning cold outside," adds Voge as he gets up and starts out of the ward.

"Oh Doctor," calls Neal.

"Yes, what is it Lieutenant?" responds Voge, turning to face Neal.

"Have you heard anything about me from New York sir?" Neal asks in an almost pleading tone of voice.

"No son, I have not. When I do, I'll come straight here and tell you."

"Thank you Sir," replies Neal, as the doctor goes on his way.

"Well Lieutenant, what do you want to do now?" questions Henry.

"I guess we can just sit here and wait on Mrs. Ruth. It won't be long before it'll be time to eat, and we can help her get the trays out to the men," answers Neal, as he kicks back on his bed to rest.

In a little while, Mrs. Walters brings the first tray of food into the ward. Neal and Henry both get up, walk to the front and offer their help in handling the trays for her. While Neal and Henry walk to and fro, between kitchen and ward with the hot food, Henry asks why the doctor did not get Neal a new Union uniform.

"It's like this Henry, if I were to go outside this hospital and a Union soldier, who knows I'm a Reb, should stop me, he could say I was trying to escape. If I had a Union uniform on, they could shoot me as a spy," explains Neal.

"Oh, so Doc Voge is really watching out for you still, huh Lieutenant?"

"Yeah, he is Henry," smiles Neal

As Dr. Voge has said, the weather really turns bad. The rain that moves in with the cold weather, soon turns to ice, and then the rain turns to sleet.

Neal and Henry are kept busy, just keeping the fire going and keeping the other ten men warm, who are in their ward. Sergeant Beech, is gaining his strength, as are all the other amputees in this ward. They all take a shine to Neal and Henry, so in good humor, they call Neal their pet Reb. They learn that Neal has no recollection of his past, or of his personal life.

He and Henry are given the job of keeping the fires in the other wards on their wing of the hospital burning, to provide as much warmth for the patients as possible. Along with keeping the fires going, they continue serving the food trays to those in the ward with them. These chores are good for Neal and Henry and Mrs. Ruth is happy to have the extra help on her wing.

December 12, 1864

General Thomas sends a message to Grant, telling him that he is going to attack as soon as the ice on the ground melts enough to allow troop movements. Grant is pleased with the message and hopes it won't be long before the attack begins.

Dr. Voge is making his rounds and comes into Neal's ward. Neal and Henry are busy taking breakfast trays back to the kitchen when Dr. Voge gets to sergeant Beech's bed. Neal has just picked up the sergeant's tray and is turning to go back to the kitchen.

"Dr. Voge, do you think that you could get all of us amputees, a pet Reb, to take home with us when we're mustered out?" Beech asks with a grin on his face.

"I don't know Sergeant, why do you ask?" laughs Voge.

"Well Doc, it's like this, that Reb there is a mighty fine boy, house broke and all, he works hard and never complains. It would be a shame for him to go to a prison camp, and I shore could use him on my farm back in Ohio."

"You are serious, aren't you Sergeant?" Dr. Voge asks.

"I shore am Doc, that boy don't need to be in no prison camp."

Neal is shocked to learn that the men he has been fighting, feel the way they do about him.

"I don't think the army would go along with your idea Sergeant, but we'll try to keep him here, because he is such good help for everyone," smiles Dr. Voge.

Neal goes on with the tray and comes back to find Dr. Voge waiting for him, at his bed.

"Lieutenant, I've heard back from New York," announces Voge, as he rubs his chin, as if he's in deep thought."

"What did they have to say Doc?" questions Neal, in an anxious voice.

"It seems that you are suffering from what they call amnesia Son."

"Am—, amnesia?" stammers Neal, puzzled by this new word.

"Yes, it's an illness where a person suffers a partial or complete loss of memory, due to an injury to the brain, or it can be caused by shock," answers the doctor.

"But Doctor Voge, I didn't have an injury to my head," protests Neal.

"I know that Son, but we don't know what traumatic circumstance you were in when you were shot in the chest, or the things you witnessed, right before it happened," explains Doctor Voge.

"I wish I did Sir, then maybe I would be able to remember about myself."

"That's the problem Son, it must have been very hard on you, because your brain is blotting your past out, and won't let you remember it."

"But, what can I do about it Doc?"

"I'll have you come into my office after I've finished my rounds and then I'll tell you what the people I wired in New York said to do."

"That's fine Sir, I'll be waiting." Neal gets on his bed, when Dr. Voge leaves to finish his rounds.

NEAL'S HOMECOMING

Henry comes back from the kitchen and gets on his bed. He saw Doctor Voge talking to Neal, and he knows that something may have been discussed concerning Neal's problem of remembering his past. As he is getting into his bed, he asks, "Well Lieutenant, you gonna tell me what the doctor said?"

"Oh Henry, he didn't say much, but he did say he heard back from New York, and that I'm suffering from something called amnesia."

"Ab- ? What?"

"Amnesia Henry, and he's going to tell me more when he's through making the rounds."

"Amnesia huh, sounds like a prutty name for as bad-a thing as losing your mind."

"I guess so, Henry."

"Now don't you worry none Lieutenant, this amnesia thing ain't so bad, shoot, you'll lick it, you won't stay mindless forever."

"Henry, why don't you leave the Reb alone for a while now, cause he's gonna have to go with the doctor in a little while," butts in Sergeant Beech. He had been listening to the two talk, and feels that Neal needs some time to think before Dr. Voge comes back.

"O. K. Sergeant, I guess you're right, he does need to gather up as much of his wit as he can before the doctor starts a-doctoring on him," answers Henry.

"That's a fact," thinks Neal. "I really need to try harder to remember, but I don't know where or how to start."

After a while Dr. Voge returns for Neal, and they walk down the long halls to his office. When they get into the office, Dr. Voge lights two lamps, and tells Neal to have a seat. When the two of them are settled, the doctor begins the conversation by telling Neal what his instructions are, for treating him. "First, they tell me to treat your physical wounds. That we have done, and you're coming along nicely."

"But Doc, I don't have the wind I should have."

"No you don't right now, because you lost the bottom of your left lung. The wind will return though in time, this I do know. Now, about the amnesia, they tell me that you should rest until you are able to get up and about. This you have done. Third, they say that we should have a talking session every day."

"Talking session?"

"That's right Lieutenant, but the way we are to do it is; I'll ask you a question, and you will answer it. We will do this until you see a glimpse of your past. Then you will tell me of the glimpse that you see."

Doctor Voge continues, "We already have the picture of the young boy and the pistols. We see the same boy tying off the stub of another man's hand, but we can't see the man's face. Then there is the man down in the ditch with part of his head missing."

"I've already told you that Sir, and I can't remember any names or anything about those men," interrupts Neal.

"We'll work on that Son, you will remember, but it's going to take time."

"How long Doc?"

"I don't know Son, but the doctors up in New York said that getting away from the cause of the problem, and into a restful place would help."

"Where is a wounded prisoner of war going to find that place of rest Sir?"

"I don't know Lieutenant, but it may be after the war, when you can leave, that you find that place of rest."

"I hope you are right when you say the war won't last much longer, Sir."

"Me too Son, and I hope I can keep you from going to a real prison camp."

"That's mighty nice of you Sir."

"We best get busy now Lieutenant."

"Yes Sir."

"Remember what we are doing here, I'll ask a question and you will answer as best you can. When something comes to mind from the past, then you will tell me as much as you can about it. Now, what is your name?"

"I don't know."

"Where are you from?"

"I don't know."

"Are you married?"

"I don't know."

"Where are you now?"

"In a Union hospital in Nashville, Tennessee."

"Have you ever been to Tennessee before?"

"I," a scene from the past is seen just at this moment by Neal. He sees a train in Selmer, Tennessee, with sick Confederate soldiers getting off. They are not sick with an illness, because the smell of whiskey is very strong in the rail car they've been riding in. After a few moments Neal's stare shows that he's coming back to the present.

Doctor Voge asks, "Did you see something Lieutenant?"

"I've been to Tennessee before Sir, I've been to Selmer."

"Tell me about it Son."

"I ride a train into Selmer early in the morning. I'm walking back by this one rail car, when all these boys start coming off of it, and they're all sick from too much whisky. I see the young boy I've seen before, the one I've told you about, and several others, but their faces don't stay with me," answers Neal. "I just can't remember."

"That's fine Son, it will come, look at the progress we've made already. Now, you just go on and rest, we'll try again tomorrow," orders Doctor Voge, in a soft tone of voice.

"Yes sir, thank you Sir," answers Neal in a tired way, as he gets up and leaves the doctor's office.

On the 14th, General Thomas lets Grant know that he plans to attack Hood's army on the 15th.

December 15th, 1864

Union troops at Nashville attack Hood's army of Tennessee.

Outnumbered two to one, the Confederate army contracts it's lines.

General Thomas, at the end of the day feels that the Confederate army will withdraw under cover of darkness.

Doctor Voge, and all the other medical staff at the hospital, start receiving wounded soldiers about 3 o'clock in the afternoon, on the 15th.

Neal has become more open and relaxed, and Voge feels that with more probing sessions, much good can be accomplished toward restoring his memory. Now the sessions will have to be postponed due to the flow of wounded coming into the hospital.

Henry and Neal help with taking the wounded out of the wagons and carrying them into the hospital. Neal helps with the stretcher cases, while Henry helps with the walking wounded.

December 16, 1864

To Thomas's dismay, morning finds the Confederate army still in position to fight, south of Nashville, at Franklin. The battle continues the same as the day before. Union soldiers finally succeed in turning the Confederate's left flank, and in doing so causes the center of the Rebel defense to collapse.

At this point Hood's army retreats in a disorganized manner. The right flank fights off the Federals in a desperate rearguard action, as the Southern army retreats through Franklin.

The army of Tennessee is finished, as an effective fighting force, and during the next several days will retreat all the way back to Corinth, Mississippi.

The horde of wounded that is brought back to Nashville, stops the normal routine which Neal had grown accustomed to keeping. He is working hard, helping with the wounded, when on the afternoon of the 16th, a load of wounded soldiers is brought in to the hospital.

Neal is there to help, along with Henry, and as they begin helping the wounded men down out of the wagon, a Union sergeant comes from the front of the wagon. When he sees Neal's gray pants, he rushes up behind him, grabs his shoulders and throws him to the cold muddy ground.

He yells angrily at Neal, "You Reb dog, keep your filthy hands off our boys!"

Seeing this take place, Henry runs to Neal's aid and lifts him up with his one hand. "Sergeant, I'm in charge of this here Confederate lieutenant, and I'd advise you to keep yore hands off him," states Henry, as he stares into the sergeant's anger filled eyes

"If you are in charge of him, then get him away from our boys, or better yet, get him out of this hospital!" yells the red faced sergeant.

As the argument gets louder, a Union major hears the commotion and walks over to investigate. "What's going on here Sergeant?" questions the Union officer as he comes up to them.

"Sir, I don't want a Reb around our men, and this soldier is in charge of him," answers the sergeant.

"I see," replies the major. "Soldier, if you are in charge of this Reb prisoner, I suggest that you take him back to his quarters."

"Yes Sir," answers Henry, then he and Neal turn and head back to their ward. As they leave, they hear the sergeant speak to the major.

"Major, this ain't no place for a Reb. I don't want him around our boys."

"I think you're right Sergeant. I'll see what I can do about getting rid of him."

Nothing is said between Henry and Neal until they are both back in their ward, sitting on their beds.

"Henry, why would you stand up to that sergeant for me?"

"Lieutenant, that man had no right to throw you down the way he did."

"Maybe he did Henry. You see, I don't know how I was or anything else before I woke up here."

"Aw, Sir, I mean Lieutenant, you couldn't have been any different than anybody else in this fool war."

"What do you mean by that Henry?"

"Oh, you know, just do what you are told and don't ask questions, and maybe you'll come out alive at the end."

"Oh, I see what you mean."

"Lieutenant, do you suppose those two at the wagon are going to cause trouble for you? You did hear what they were saying when we were walking off, didn't you?"

"Yeah, I heard, but I don't really know if they will cause me trouble or not. They had just come from the battlefield, and seeing a Rebel at their hospital was not a welcoming sight to them."

"I sure hope they don't Sir, and don't say I can't call you sir, if I want to, you see, I have grown real fond of you, and I hope we're friends."

"Henry, you are my friend, I just hope that I'm a person who is worthy of your friendship, cause I really don't know."

"You are Sir, I can tell."

As these two continue in their conversation, the angry sergeant and major are busy filing a protest to their commander about the Reb who is walking around in the hospital.

The administrator of the hospital, is soon visited by the combat branch of the Federal Army. He is questioned about the Reb soldier who is being allowed to roam at will among patients from the battle front, where he was actively their enemy. Doctor Sams, the administrator, finds out that the Rebel soldier in question, is under Dr. D. W. Voge's care.

Doctor Lawrence Daniel hears of the complaints and ill rumors concerning the prisoner who is allowed to move about the hospital freely. Realizing that his friend, D.W., may not have heard, he goes to him and forewarns him of the coming investigation.

"Thank you for letting me in on the ill feelings that our fellow officers are having about my patient, Lawrence. I'm going to the chief and explain to him this situation," states Voge to Lawrence in the hall outside his office. Then he goes into his office and changes his blouse. After changing, he heads up to the administrator's office. As he enters the office, he stops at the clerk's desk and asks to see Dr. Louis Sams.

Dr. Voge has never liked the little tyrant of a doctor, who the Federal Government sent down here from up north, to be the head of Nashville's hospital. He respects Dr. Sams as a physician, but not as a humanitarian.

"Dr. Sams will see you now Dr. Voge," announces the clerk, as he returns from Sam's office.

Voge enters the office and is greeted by Dr. Sam's cheerful greeting, "Dennis my boy, do come in."

"Thank you Doctor Sams."

"Be seated Dennis, be seated!" invites Sams. "What brings you here to see me Doctor?"

"Doctor Sams, you know good and well what my purpose is for being here."

"I'm sure I do Dennis, it's that Reb patient of yours."

"Yes sir, it is, and I've checked out the whole incident in question. The Confederate lieutenant was just trying to help with the wounded, when the sergeant started the whole matter."

"Doctor Voge, it makes no difference as to what happened at the wagons. The problem, as the army see it, is that we have a Rebel prisoner of war, roaming at will, in our hospital."

"That's not a valid account of the situation Sir. I have assigned private Henry Cheek to be in charge of the lieutenant."

"That simple minded boy is in charge! Come now Dennis, who are we trying to mislead? I've done my checking into this matter also, just as you have."

"Doctor Sams, the Confederate officer in question, is suffering from amnesia, the loss of one's memory."

"Enough Doctor, amnesia is an illness that could be easily faked, and if the Confederate in question were to escape, he could leave with valuable information that would aid the enemy."

"But he is not a—"

"No butts Doctor, you have one week to get him out of the hospital, and in transit to a prison camp, is that clear, Colonel?"

"Yes sir."

"That is final then, dismissed."

Disgusted, Voge stands and leaves Sam's office, then he goes to Neal's ward, and gives him the discouraging news.

The wounded keep coming in, and Neal is confined to his ward. Dr. Voge is too busy to have the conference time with him that he needs.

The other men in the ward learn of Neal's departure which is soon to take place, and they let him know they are all sorry he is to be transferred to a prison camp. Everyone knows that prison camps are very hard. With Neal's condition of mind, and missing part of his lung besides, it is going to be especially hard for him, just to stay alive.

December 18, 1864

Hood's army is in full retreat and wounded are still coming into the hospital.

Neal and Henry are in their beds, having already stoked the fire and carried the other wounded men their breakfast trays, when in walks the Yankee sergeant, who threw Neal to the ground back at the wagons.

"Where is that sorry Reb?" demands the sergeant, in a loud voice, as he comes into the ward.

Jumping to the edge of his bed, Neal is spotted by the angry sergeant, who keeps marching toward him. Henry moves up on the edge of his bed and stands up.

"Get up Reb, or I'm gonna whip you where you set," orders the sergeant, as he walks up to Neal's bed.

"Leave him alone Sergeant," orders Henry, as he moves between Neal and the sergeant.

"Yeah Sergeant, leave him be," agrees Sergeant Beech, as he turns his one foot to the cold floor and stands up on his crutches. "This ward is for fighting men and not company clerks like you."

"I'm here to get that Reb!" barks the sergeant.

"He don't leave for five more days, and you ain't a-gettin him Sergeant," announces a visibly disturbed Henry, speaking through clenched teeth.

Neal is up on his feet by now, and standing behind Henry.

"What's a'matter yeller belly, you going to hide behind this simple boy?" yells the sergeant, while reaching over Henry's shoulder to grab Neal by the red collar on his long-johns. With this sudden movement, Henry brings his one good hand into play, landing a hard punch, square on the sergeant's chin, knocking him back toward Sergeant Beech.

Sergeant Beech, quickly puts out one of his crutches and trips the bully of a soldier, causing him to fall flat on his back. Neal and Henry are surprised at this move, but not at all unhappy about it, considering the unnecessary violence the Union soldier had in mind for Neal.

When the angry sergeant hits the floor with a loud thud, Sergeant Beech, balancing on one leg, hits him across the bridge of his nose with the foot of his crutch. The hard lick causes blood to explode forth from his nose as the cartilage breaks.

The furious sergeant is dazed for a moment, and starts to get up, but before he can get on his feet, all the men in the ward have gathered over him. Some of these men have arms missing, some are missing legs, all of them have disabilities, yet they are ready to support and defend Neal. As the sergeant continues to struggle to his feet, Sergeant Beech says, "I don't think I would be getting up with the same intentions that you hit the floor with Sergeant, if I were you. See, this here Reb lieutenant has become our friend over the past weeks, and we don't take kindly to you picking on him. Anyway, the war is over for all of us, so if you want a fight, there is plenty of it still going on up on the front, but not here in the hospital. Now, if you got guts enough to fight when you get up, you can fight us all, or get out there where the war is. Do you understand?"

"Yeah, I believe I do," answers the sergeant from the floor, where he is still lying in pain, holding his bleeding nose.

"Well you'd better!" orders Beech as he taps the sergeant gently with his crutch, on the side of his head. "Now get up and leave."

The angry Union soldier gets up, still holding his nose, which continues to bleed, and starts walking out of the ward. As he leaves, Doctor Voge meets him, as he is coming in to make his morning rounds. Without saying a word to each other, the two men pass just inside the door. Doctor Voge sees his bloody face and the group of men standing in the rear of the ward, and walks on back to join them.

"What's going on here Sergeant Beech?" questions Voge, as he walks up to the quiet group, who still stand together, looking at the door leading into the hall.

"Extra training sir. The sergeant and I were demonstrating how a crutch can be used as a weapon sir," answers Beech.

"That so? I've never thought of that, it's amazing what the army comes up with these days," smiles Voge.

"It sure is, ain't it," laughs Henry.

The whole group of men have a good laugh with Doctor Voge's encouragement, and for most of them this is the last fight they will ever be in.

December 21, 1864

Federal Troops occupy the city of Savannah, and the news is uplifting to the men in the hospital. They know that the south is split in two, and that the war will not last much longer. The ones in Neal's ward are preparing to go home and Neal is preparing to go to a prison camp.

Dr. Voge comes in to check on his boys before they leave the hospital. After seeing and checking them over, he walks on back to Neal's bed and talks to him.

"Lieutenant, you'll be leaving day after tomorrow. You'll be going by train to a prison camp at Rock Island, Illinois. This is a new camp so maybe it won't be too bad for you."

"Thank you Sir, I appreciate everything you have done for me," answers Neal.

"I only wish that I could have done more."

"I know that Doctor Voge, but I remember everything you have told me and I'll find that place of peace and when I do, I'll find my memory too."

"I'm sure you will Son. They'll be coming to get you tomorrow and move you to a holding pen, then transport you to your new destination. I may not see you again before you leave, so after this war is over, get in touch with me and we'll continue to work on your amnesia.

"Yes Sir, I will. Thank you Sir, and I hope I'll see you again."

Doctor Voge turns and leaves with a very solemn expression on his face. When he leaves, Neal goes back to helping his friends pack for their trip home.

December 22, 1864

After Neal and Henry have served breakfast, they take the trays back to the kitchen. They then go back to sit on their beds to talk for the last time before the others are transported to their homes. "Lieutenant, if you're ever up my way, you've got an invite to stop and stay as long as you like in my home," states Henry, as the other men gather around their beds.

"The same goes for all of us," agrees Sergeant Beech. "This war won't last much longer, and if you don't get your memory back before it's over, look me up and I'll do all I can to help you." The other men agree with Beech, in unison.

"Ya'll have been very kind to me, even though I've been your enemy at some time or another. I appreciate everyone of ya'll," declares Neal, as tears come in his eyes and he swallows over the lump in his throat. He looks at the men circled around the two beds and thinks, "These are the only friends I know and now I'm about to leave them for who knows what."

"Ah Lieutenant, the reason we were on opposite sides in this war is because we were born on opposite sides of the country," reasons Henry, trying in his simple way to explain why friendship has developed between men who fought each other just a short time ago.

"Yeah, and it's us pore' boys fighting the rich people's war that caused us to be at war in the first place. It's over, so let's forget it," adds Sergeant Beech, showing strong feelings of being weary of the war and all the pain it's brought to all of them.

The whole group gives Neal their best wishes with good luck as they leave him in the ward all alone. When all of them have gone he feels a real loss. Without his friends around, his spirit is at a low ebb.

He's sitting on his bed waiting for the escorts to come for him when he hears footsteps. Looking up, he see his old enemy, the sergeant from the wagons, walking into the ward.

As the angry man walks in and continues toward Neal, he says, "Well Reb, you ain't got nobody to hide behind now."

"I might'a known it'd be you coming to get me," sighs Neal, shaking his head as the sergeant walks up to his bed.

"Get up!" orders the sergeant.

"Yes Sergeant," answers Neal, starting to get up from the bed. At this point of obedience to the command, the sergeant hits Neal on his left cheek knocking him across the bed. Neal is on his feet in a snap.

"O.K. Sergeant, you've had your fun now let's drop this whole thing and get going to wherever it is I'm to be going," says Neal in a cold discouraged tone.

"Reb, I ain't got to have you any place until I take you to the train at six o'clock tomorrow morning," answers the sergeant as he comes around the bed.

Knowing that this man is about to hurt him, Neal strikes out with a strong lick of his own landing on the still broken nose, from the crutch of Sergeant Beech. The nose is reopened and blood begins to pour, as the fat sergeant staggers backward. Before he can regain his balance Neal strikes him again in the same place, sending him to the floor moaning with pain.

"I'll get you for this Reb," growls the bleeding sergeant, as he rolls up on his feet.

"Hold on there!" comes a loud voice from the door of the ward. It's Doctor Voge, speaking as he walks toward the two men. "What's going on here Sergeant?"

"This Reb struck me Sir," yells the Yankee sergeant, with blood still pouring down his face while he holds his hand over the bleeding nose.

"That so Lieutenant?" questions Doctor Voge.

"Yes Sir. After he struck me Sir," answers Neal.

"That's a lie Sir! He hit me first," barks the Union sergeant.

"Well Sergeant, if that's the case, I'd better take over here. You are relieved of this prisoner, and I'll see to him, Sergeant," informs Doctor Voge.

"But Sir!"

"You heard me Sergeant. Now go take care of yourself," orders the doctor.

"Yes Sir," answers the sergeant as he picks up his cap and marches out of the ward.

"Doctor Voge, I didn't hit first.

"I know Lieutenant," butts in Voge. "I heard the whole thing outside the door. If he was supposed to keep you until six o'clock tomorrow morning, I don't see why I can't do the same. He won't tell anybody any different because he knows that he's lying to me and that I probably know he's lying. Now, I'm going to take the rest of the day off and take you home with me so maybe we can work on your amnesia."

"Yes Sir, that sure sounds good to me," agrees Neal, with a big smile on his face.

While Neal is getting the few belongings he has together, Mrs. Ruth comes into the ward. "Lieutenant you are leaving us I see," she says with a smile.

"Yes Ma-am, I'm leaving," answers Neal, turning his head to face this woman who has been so kind to him from the time he first came into this hospital.

When he turns toward her, she sees his left cheek which is beginning to swell from the sergeant's punch. She asks, "What's happened to you Lieutenant? Looks like you've been in a fight."

"Yes Ma'am, but don't fret yourself none, I'm leaving with Doctor Voge here, and you know he'll take good care of me," assures Neal.

"Well what happened?" she questions, sincerely interested in Neal's welfare.

"I'll fill you in later Ruth," promises Voge. "The lieutenant and I need to be leaving just in case somebody else is looking for him."

"Okay, but you two be careful. Do you understand?" orders Mrs. Ruth.

"Yes Ma'am," answer the two men as they start to leave, stopping just long enough for Neal to give Mrs. Ruth a farewell hug.

Doctor Voge checks out and the two of them walk to his home which is only five blocks from the hospital. The weather is still cold, but the doctor has gotten Neal warm clothes to wear before leaving the hospital.

As they go into his home, which is a large, comfortable house, Doctor Voge calls out to his wife, "Karol, we will have a guest for lunch and supper."

Hearing her husband's voice at the front door, Mrs. Voge walks into the parlor in time to see the two men removing their heavy coats. "You said we're having a guest for lunch and supper?" questions Karol.

"That's correct Dear. This is one of my patients who has lost his memory so we don't know his name," informs Doctor Voge.

"This is a Confederate soldier Dennis!" exclaims Karol in a polite but startled manner.

"Yes Ma'am, that's the one thing we know for sure," laughs Neal.

"It will be okay Karol," assures Dennis, understanding her concern, and knowing there must be questions she would like to ask about this unexpected visitor he has brought into their home.

"Well alright, if you two say so, it's fine by me. Now what would you like for lunch?" asks Karol, with a big smile on her face.

"Anything will be fine Mrs. Voge," answers Neal.

"Yeah, anything, because the lieutenant and I have lots of work to do," adds the doctor.

Karol turns to leave the men in the front room and Neal says, "Doctor Voge, you didn't say you had such a pretty wife," while both of them watch the middle age blond go toward the kitchen to prepare their meal.

"You didn't ask Lieutenant," laughs Doctor Voge, pleased with the compliment Neal has paid his wife. "Now we need to start our session and Karol will call us when dinner is ready."

"Yes Sir."

"Let's get comfortably seated before we start this," suggests Voge, as he turns to find a seat for himself and Neal. When they are seated, he asks, "Are you ready to begin?"

"Yes Sir."

"Now Lieutenant, when did you go into the Confederate Army?"

"I don't know."

"Do you know how many battles you've been in? Now think Lieutenant."

"I'm trying Sir, but for the life of me, I can't recall anything."

After several hours of hard continuous questions have gone by, Karol comes back into the parlor where they are talking. She announces, "Lunch is ready Dennis, you two can come back to this after you've eaten."

"You hungry Lieutenant?"

"Yes Sir. I surely am."

"Then time's a-wasting. Let's go eat."

Turning, Karol leads the men back to the dining room. She is truly pleased to have them, she thinks to herself, while they're following her to the table. She has really put on the dog, going all out in preparing this meal. Feeling now that her efforts will be appreciated by the two hungry men, she looks forward to seeing them enjoy the food.

When they step into the dining room, both men are surprised to see the table loaded with fried chicken, rice, peas, cornbread, and apple pie.

"Karol, you have really gone all out haven't you Girl?" compliments Dennis, with a big smile.

"With the war Darling, we haven't had a guest in our home in over a year," answers Mrs. Voge.

"The war has really messed a lotta things up Mrs. Voge, I apologize for my inconveniencing you," says Neal, in a very sincere tone of voice, with an expression of concern on his face.

"Think nothing of it Son, I'm really glad you are here to give me a reason to do something special," replies Karol. "Now you two have a seat while I go get the coffee."

Neal and Doctor Voge find their places at the table and Karol returns with a steaming cup of coffee for each of them. She places Neal's cup next to his plate then walks around the large table to place Doctor Voge's cup beside his plate. He thanks her with a hug around her waist.

This action, causes Neal to see a blond woman of middle age, handing a cup of hot coffee to a man in a modest kitchen, and he sees three other boys standing in the room. He recognizes the youngest of the three boys as the one he keeps seeing in battle.

"Son, son!" startles Neal back to the present, as Mrs. Voge's voice breaks through his dazed lapse into a scene from his past.

He answers, "Ma'am?"

"What would you like for me to pass you?" asks Mrs. Voge, while Doctor Voge is watching Neal's strained expression and every move he makes.

"Anything Mother will be fine," answers Neal, still a bit confused between the past and present.

"Lieutenant, it's nice of you to call me mother," begins Mrs. Voge in a soft voice.

Then Doctor Voge's quiet "Shh-hh," stops her in mid-sentence.

"I'm sorry Mrs. Voge, I must'a been day dreaming or something," explains Neal, embarrassed that he has called this woman, who he has only just met, mother.

"Lieutenant, you saw something, don't be embarrassed, I think you may have seen your mother in something Karol did, so after we have eaten, we can get back to work on your problem," explains Doctor Voge

After the lovely meal, the men go back to the parlor to continue their question and answer session.

"What did you see at the table Lieutenant?" asks Voge, anxious to get back to work while the glimpse of the past is fresh in Neal's mind.

After Neal has told the doctor who, and what he has seen, Doctor Voge thinks quietly for a short time, then begins with a probable explanation. "Son, I feel that you have just looked into the past, or should I say remembered a certain moment of your past? The blond woman you saw was your mother, the man is your father, and the three boys must be your brothers. Now don't forget their faces, and this will help you remember all that you have forgotten. I think now that I've been wrong in the way I've been conducting these sessions. I've been asking questions concerning the war, or events occurring in the war, when it was the war that blocked out your memory and caused the amnesia. From now on, don't even think about the war, it is over and it never happened as far as you're concerned. We are going to concentrate on your life as a young boy before the war. Now let's see where we can begin."

"Did you ever go to school?"

Neal has another glimpse from the past and after a moment says, "Yes Sir, I did."

"Can you tell me about it?"

"Yes Sir, but very little. I'm in a classroom and the blond headed woman is teaching the class."

"The same one you saw in the kitchen?"

"Yes Sir."

"Your mother was a teacher, huh? Can't you remember anything else?"

"I'm sorry Sir. I can't, but I still see their faces."

"Good, then let's continue."

"Yes Sir."

"Were you reared on a farm?"

"Yes Sir."

"How do you know this Lieutenant?"

"I've told you about the big man on the horse at the fence, well I'm working in fresh plowed dirt and the boys I've told you about are there along with the older man."

"Good Lieutenant, I think we may be getting some place." answers Doctor Voge. "Now, can you tell me what you were doing in the fresh dirt."

"No sir."

Doctor Voge turns the page of his tablet and continues writing each question and answer down, as he asks and Neal answers each question.

"Are you married Lieutenant?"

"No sir, I don't think so."

"Why is that Son?"

"Well if the people that I see in these glimpses are my family, I believe I would see some woman in there with them, if I were married."

"Good, now did your family have any slaves?"

This question causes a moment of silence, as Neal sees a young black girl walking with the man who he believes to be his father. "I don't rightly know for sure," comes his hesitant answer, after a few moments have passed.

"Can you explain what you mean by that Son?"

"Yes Sir. I see the man that I believe is my father, with a young colored girl coming toward the steps of a porch. I'm standing on this porch with the three other boys, as they are walking our way. She's been beaten in the face really bad, but she's not afraid of the older man, or of walking toward us. There's some words said when they reach us, but I don't remember what they were. Then after a little bit, the blond woman comes out past us and sits on the steps next to this young girl and gives her something to eat."

"Is that all you can make out of what you see here?"

"Yes Sir, but if we were slave owners and had beaten this girl up like this, why would she not be afraid of us? Also, why would the blond woman be so kind to her?"

"You may have a point Son. Your family may not have done this atrocious thing to the girl. They may have just been helping her because she had been hurt by other people."

"I sure hope we would help others, rather than hurt them, no matter what color they are Sir."

"I have a feeling that you were not hurting anyone Son. Now can you tell me anything more about this colored girl?"

After a moment, Neal answers, "No Sir."

"Let's talk about your mother."

"Okay, Doctor, I'll tell you all that I can remember."

"Now we think that she may have taught school, and that she has blond hair, correct?"

"Yes sir, I believe that is correct."

"We know that she is a caring person by the way she was caring for the young colored girl."

"Yes Sir."

"Can you tell me her name?"

"No Sir. I can't."

"Do you want to keep trying?"

"Oh yes Sir, I do."

"O.K., let's work on your mother's name, shall we?"

"Yes Sir, that's fine with me."

Doctor Voge calls out a ladies name and Neal thinks about it and responds. This goes on for a while, with none of the names the doctor calls, sounding familiar to Neal. While they are working this way, Mrs. Voge walks through the room, headed toward the front door.

"Dennis, I'm going to walk over to Milly's house for a while, you two don't need me here and I'll be back shortly."

"That's fine, enjoy your visit," answers Dennis, with a smile.

As she closes the door behind her, Neal with a really big smile on his face says, "That's it! That's it! My mother's name."

"What Son, what is your mother's name?" questions Voge, anxious to hear the name Neal remembers.

"Milly Sir, that's my mother's name."

"Milly? How can you be sure?"

"That is, or that's what I believe, the older man calls her when he's standing out from the steps, with the colored girl."

"That's good. Now you know that we may be altogether wrong in what we are calling your mother, and the identities we have given the people, in these glimpses of your past."

"Yes Sir, I realize that I could have just dreamed all of this up, but it seems right to me: I just can't get the whole picture in my mind."

"Knowing this, we are going to have to work with what we believe to be right, then grow from that. You understand don't you Son?"

"Yes Sir I do, but I'm feeling better about myself already."

"Good, let's take a break and get a cup of coffee."

"Yes Sir, anything you say," agrees Neal, with a feeling that he has made some progress in establishing his identity.

The two men get up and walk back to the kitchen where Karol has left a pot of coffee on the stove. After pouring two cups, they sit down at the kitchen table to enjoy the brew.

"Doctor Voge, you said that you were in the Mexican War."

"Yes Lieutenant, I was, what about it?"

"Was that war much different than this one?"

"The actual fighting bears a strong resemblance, but over all it was very different. It was much smaller and had less men, and less destruction. But war is war and human beings are destroyed in every one of them. Why do you ask?"

"Are there parts of it that you wish you couldn't remember?"

"Yes Son, several parts, but there are good parts also. The friends I made and the good times we had, I would not take a thousand dollars for those memories."

"Well, maybe some day I'll just remember the good parts of this war and not the bad ones," smiles Neal, as he takes a good sip of his coffee.

"That's a boy, try and remember the good and it will help in restoring your memory."

After the coffee, the two go back to their session of questions and answers, for the remainder of the afternoon. Karol comes home about 4:00 p.m. to warm up the leftovers for supper. She calls the men when she has the meal on the table and the three of them gather to eat about five o'clock in the Voge's dining room.

"Mrs. Voge, this meal is as good now as it was at dinner," comments Neal, as he bites into a piece of fried chicken.

"You are mighty kind Lieutenant, I'm glad that you are enjoying the food, and we are happy to have you as a guest in our home," replies Mrs. Voge, showing her pretty white teeth with a warm smile.

After supper, Neal starts back to the parlor, but Doctor Voge stops him and says they have worked hard enough for today.

"Son, when you leave tomorrow, I'm going to give you your medical records to take with you to the camp. When you get there, give them to the doctor that is stationed there and let him take up where I've left off," instructs Dennis.

"Yes Sir, I will," answers Neal.

"Now, after the dishes are put away, maybe Karol will be so kind as to entertain us with some of her musical talent."

"Oh, I'd love to play for you two, but first, you'll have to help me with the dishes," laughs Karol.

"It's a deal Mrs. Voge," grins Neal, "Let's get to it."

When the dishes are done the three go back to the parlor, where Neal and Doctor Voge, take the chairs they have been using in the question and answer sessions. Karol goes to the piano, pulls the bench out and opens it to choose some sheets of music. When she has made her selections, she closes the top of the bench and sits down, places her music above the keyboard, smiles at the two men, then turns her attention to the piano and starts playing. The melodious notes of music fill the room with a sound that is soothing to the nerves. Before long, the tired doctor is sound asleep, and Neal appears to be in a trance, as he hangs on to each note, as Mrs. Voge plays one tune after another. She senses the calming effect the music has on Neal and continues to play for almost an hour. She finishes her concert with the gospel tune, "Shall We Gather At The River." When the music stops, Dennis wakes up immediately and yawns real big. Karol puts her music away, smiles at the men and stands by the piano for a few moments, as if she is waiting for their applause.

"I told you she was good didn't I, Lieutenant?" boasts Doctor Voge.

"Yes Sir, you did and she certainly is that and more. She is very good," compliments Neal, now more relaxed and comfortable.

"Well Son, it's almost seven o'clock, we had better go to bed, if you are to get up and going early in the morning," states Dennis.

"Dennis, you can show the Lieutenant his bedroom," suggests Karol.

"The music was really lovely, and ya'll have been overly kind," says Neal, as he gets up to follow the doctor to the guest bedroom.

Doctor Voge shows Neal a large comfortable room, with space to spare. Once Doctor Voge leaves him alone, he wonders what kind of room he had in the home he can't remember. When he's in bed he tries to remember more of his past, but falls asleep wondering what the morrow will bring.

December 23, 1864

The morrow comes all to soon for Neal. This has been the first peaceful night's rest he has had in two years. Consciously, he knows that he has rested well but can only guess at the reasons. Mrs. Voge comes in to awaken him at 4:30, to eat the breakfast she and Doctor Voge have prepared, while they let him sleep. The hardy breakfast is well received by all, and then it is time to leave for the train station so they can be there before 6:00 o'clock.

When Neal says good-bye and expresses his gratitude to Mrs. Voge, he hugs her, then he and Doctor Voge walk to the train station. Along the way there, they hear news of the war from soldiers who are going about their duties.

Federal Troops continue to pursue hood's Army south. Yesterday skirmishing occurred between the two sides, around Columbia, Tennessee.

After hearing the news, Neal is disturbed, and it shows on his face. "Lieutenant, you look troubled," comments Doctor Voge.

"I am Sir," replies Neal.

"How's that Son?"

"Well Sir, it's like this: after hearing about the fighting that's going on south of here with General Hood's Army, I know I should be concerned about some of those men I served with, but I'm not, because I can't remember them."

"Don't blame yourself Son, if you were well it would be different and if you were with them you would be doing your duty just as good as any soldier."

"Thank you Sir, I'm glad you feel that way about me."

"I do Son, and because you are a person with the character that you have, you are going to overcome your illness."

"You really think so Sir?"

"Yes, Son, I do and if you continue to work on your question and answer sessions, when you can find a place to have them, you will overcome this amnesia and recall your past. Just remember, this amnesia can be whipped."

"If you say it can be whipped Sir, I'll do my best to whip it."

"I know you will, and can, Son."

The two of them continue walking toward the train station. "Well here we are Lieutenant," says Doctor Voge as he leads Neal over to a group of southern prisoners. "Now here are your medical records, you give them to the doctor of the camp when you get there."

"Sir, yes, thank you for everything Doctor Voge." Neal speaks with sincerity as he struggles to keep his voice from breaking and he blinks back the tears that threaten to overflow. He is feeling love and appreciation for this man who has proven himself to be a real friend, at a time when Neal felt so alone and friendless. Leaving his friend with little assurance that he will ever see him again, not knowing what his future in a prison camp will be, unable to remember his past, all stir his emotions and he feels a deep sense of loss in leaving Doctor Voge.

"You're welcome Son." Doctor Voge speaks quietly, but with an expression of real concern on his face as he takes Neal's right hand in both of his, then puts his arm around Neal's shoulder and turns him toward the group he is to leave with. "Now you'd better go Son, keep in touch and good luck to you."

"All you prisoners fall in!" shouts an army sergeant as he comes out of the depot.

"Thanks again, Sir, and I'll try to keep in touch," says Neal again as he picks up his belongings and joins the other prisoners and they fall into formation.

Once formed they are marched down the side of the train until they come to an open rail car and are ordered to climb aboard. When they are inside the door is slammed shut and locked. Neal stands in the middle of the car while the other men start choosing spots and talking freely to each other.

"Soldier, my name is Gregory Bailey, what is yours?" questions a tall dark headed, dark eyed Confederate lieutenant, as he walks over to Neal.

"Lieutenant, I don't remember my name or any of my past. The Yankee doctors tell me I'm suffering from amnesia," answers Neal as he turns to face the Confederate Officer.

"Amnesia, sounds like something you ought to eat, doesn't sound like a sickness. How do we know that you aren't a spy?"

"Well, if I were a spy I would most certainly have myself a name now wouldn't I Lieutenant Bailey? I sure wouldn't call attention to myself by not having a name," Neal answers matter-of-factly.

"Yes, I guess you may be right, but where did the heavy coat come from?"

"The doctor who was helping me back at the hospital gave it to me. Do you have any more questions?"

"Yes, what rank are you?"

"The people at the hospital call me Lieutenant. If I have to give an answer to your question, I'll have to say, I don't know."

"Come on let's you and me go over here and find us a place to sit," suggests Gregory, as he leads the way to the side of the rail car. Just as the two of them sit down and get comfortable, the jerk of the engine is felt, and the rail car begins to roll.

"It'll be about twenty-four hours before we get to where we're going, so we can spend time getting to know each other," explains Gregory.

"I wish you did know me; it might make it easier for me to recall my past."

"Sorry, I forgot. What have you got in the folder?"

"Oh, these are my medical records that Dr. Voge kept on me. He told me to give them to the doctor in charge in the prison where we are headed."

"Can I look at them?"

"I guess so, but be careful, these papers are all I have linking me with my past."

Gregory takes the papers and using the light that comes in through the cracks in the wall of their rail car, begins to read them. After a while, when he has read all the notes Doctor Voge has recorded on Neal, he looks up and says, "You were right Lieutenant. Your records say you were brought in off the battlefield at Franklin. You were shot in the chest and wearing the bars of a Confederate lieutenant. You got a scar to prove the wound?"

Neal pulls his coat and shirt open, then unbuttons the long-johns, and shows Gregory the scar on his chest, which is still pink and new.

"I had to be sure that you are what you say you are Lieutenant."

"That's okay Lieutenant Bailey, you had to do just what you did."

"It's good that you understand Lieutenant, because I'm going to take it on myself to do the question and answer sessions with you like Dr. Voge wanted."

"That will be fine by me Gregory," smiles Neal, knowing he has just made a new friend.

"We have a long day in front of us Lieutenant, so why don't we do some of the questions and answers the way Doctor Voge has explained in your records?"

"That will be fine Gregory," answers Neal as the train begins to pick up speed.

"He said to think of only the good things and not the war, so here we go," begins Gregory as he gets out a pencil to record their questions and answers. "Who is your favorite girl?"

"I don't know but I sure would like too." answers Neal with a smile.

"Now come on Lieutenant, be serious with this!" snaps Gregory.

"Yes Sir, I will," grins Neal.

"Do you like to go fishing?"

"I can't recall if I do or not."

"Do you like to go hunting?"

Neal is silent for a few moments as he gets a glimpse of something from the past. When he starts to stir, as if waking up, Gregory observes his actions and speaks.

"You remembered something didn't you Lieutenant? Tell me what you remembered or saw.

"You read Dr. Voge's notes, and the part about the boy I keep seeing in the smoke with the pistols."

"Yes, I did read his notes and I remember about the boy, who you're talking about."

"Well I just saw the same boy on the back porch of the house dressing game. This is the same porch where we were standing when this man brought a colored girl up to the boys, as I have recorded in the notes."

"You can't call his name, or any of the others?"

"No, I can't."

"These people must have been very close to you."

"I feel that they were. I think they are my family and that my mother's name is Milly."

Gregory writes down all that is being said, adding his notes to the record Dr. Voge has kept on past sessions with Neal.

Neal asks, "Gregory, why are you so interested in me? Do you still feel that I am a spy?"

Laughing, Gregory replies, "No Lieutenant, you see before the war, I was an apprentice to a lawyer and when this war is over, I'm going back to Union City, Tennessee to become one."

"You going to be a lawyer?"

"Yeah, that's what I want to be and if I can help you win your case and you recover, I'd say I've got a good start toward being a trial lawyer."

"If you can do that, I surely will vouch for you," smiles Neal. "Now let's get busy with some more questions."

"No, let's quit for a while. Dr. Voge states in his records, that you are not to make the sessions last too long at one time. He also states that everything you may remember, both in the question and answer sessions, or the glimpses that come at other times, all should be recorded."

"Okay, you are the doctor, or should I say the lawyer?" laughs Neal, feeling very relaxed with his new-found friend.

The train rolls on through the day, stopping only for wood and water. The men move around talking to each other, except for Neal, who stays in his place, feeling uneasy about himself. Gregory informs the other prisoners about Neal's condition, and tells them he is convinced Neal is on the level with his memory disorder. There are about twenty prisoners in the rail car, who are cavalry officers, with a captain being the highest rank in the group.

The captain walks over to Neal and starts a conversation. "Lieutenant, Lieutenant Bailey has just told me about your problem. He says that it's called uh, am-knees."

"Amnesia, Sir," answers Near.

"Yeah, that's what he said. He also said that he had checked you out as close as he can and he feels that you are not a spy. He believes that this illness is genuine."

"I'll have to thank him for that Sir," answers Neal.

"He is one of the best officers I've ever known and if he says you are what you say you are, then I'll go along with his judgment."

"Thank you, Sir."

"Oh I didn't tell you my name, it's Richard Watson."

"Thank you, Captain Watson," replies Neal.

"Gregory says you were wounded at Franklin."

"That's what Doctor Voge figures, Captain."

"We were at Franklin and I didn't see you, but there were a lotta' men at Franklin."

"I suppose so Sir, I really don't remember."

"Oh, I was not putting you under the question Lieutenant: guess I was jes' thinking out loud. Yeah, you see, you must have been an infantry officer."

"That would explain why I keep seeing this boy on the side of a trench firing pistols, wouldn't it Sir? You see, I'm in the bottom of the trench and the Yankees are all around and this boy is just shooting away: There are no horses, so I must have been infantry."

"I think you are right Lieutenant, and it explains why our paths never crossed," explains Watson as he gets up to move around. "Come on and meet the men with me."

"Yes Sir, I will," agrees Neal, getting to his feet to move around with Captain Watson. He begins to feel better about himself, as the men seem to accept him and no longer look at him as a suspected spy or doubt that he has no memory of his past. He follows the captain around to meet the other prisoners in the rail car. When he has been introduced to all of them, they ease back to where they started from and Neal asks, "Sir, everybody here is an officer, don't that seem odd to you?"

"No Lieutenant, you see where they're sending us is a prison for officers only," answers Watson.

"Oh, I understand now Sir," states Neal as he leans back and closes his eyes.

The temperature is in the low forties and the cold wind blowing in through the cracks in the rail car feels refreshing to Neal's face. The time-keeping thumps of the car crossing joints in the rails and the rocking of the car, soon put him to sleep. During his restful slumber, he starts dreaming but the dream is not of a peaceful time, nor place.

Neal sees himself running in line all out, toward a wall of men in blue who are putting volley after volley of rifle fire, seemingly, right at him. The two lines converge and the blue line falls back. Then he is in the bottom of the trench they were fighting over, and the Yankees are pouring back into it. There is a sharp burning pain in Neal's chest: then out of nowhere this young Confederate soldier is on the side of the trench firing two pistols.

"Go back Ruben! Go back!" screams Neal as he jumps into a sitting position. Sweat forms in beads on his face, even though the cold wind is blowing through the cracks of the rail car. Rubbing his face and eyes with both hands to clear them, he realizes Gregory is sitting close by.

"Who is Ruben, Lieutenant?" questions Gregory hoping that this amnesia patient can remember.

"Ruben? Ruben, is the boy on the wall of the trench who's firing the pistols," answers Neal. "I think he's my brother."

"What happens to him?"

"I don't know, I go blank when he is up there shooting. All I can remember is yelling, Go back!" Neal answers with tears beginning to form in his eyes.

"That's good Lieutenant, now we know who this young soldier is. Ruben, most likely is your brother. When we talk in the future, we will address him as Ruben and we'll add his name to our notes. If we use his name, we may jog your memory even more. You rest now and I'll put together an outline of questions, using Ruben's name and Milly's to aid us in helping you remember your family and your home."

"Aw right Gregory, whatever you say," replies Neal as he lies back down.

Gregory goes about writing more notes and he outlines his approach for questioning Neal at the next session. The train rolls on through the day and the shadows of the setting sun soon turn to darkness. At this point, Neal is still sleeping and Gregory puts his notes away feeling confident that the outline and questions he has worked out will aid him in breaking into Neal's frozen past.

The train continues on through the night stopping for water and wood only. The men have been sleeping and talking all day, but now hunger pains are being felt by all of them. They know they will reach their destination a little after sunrise; and hopefully the Yankees will give them something to eat, when they get to the prison.

PRISON AT ROCK ISLAND, ILLINOIS

• • • • • • • • • • • • • • • • •

December 24, 1864

Christmas Eve and the cold, hungry, Confederate prisoners are glad to see the light of day beginning to show in the east. The train they are riding keeps its steady pace toward the prison camp at Rock Island, Illinois.

"Merry Christmas, Lieutenant!" says Gregory with a smile.

Stretching to get the kinks out, Neal answers, "It is Christmas Eve, isn't it? I guess it will be merry for some, but I don't remember any Christmas so I don't know how to have one."

"Well to start Lieutenant, you can count your blessings." states Gregory.

"Count my blessings? How?"

"Number one, you are alive and chances are this Christmas will be a lot safer for you than last Christmas. I know it will be for me because we are out of the war. Number two, although you have amnesia, you are getting some of your memory back and the doctor said it would take time for you to heal. Time is all we're going to have where we're going, so we can work a lot on your problem. Number three, I don't think this war can last much longer. The South can't take much more of the beatings the North is putting on it."

"Is that all Gregory?"

"No, but I'll stop there if you want me to."

"Just as well, you have made me feel kinda foolish, feeling sorry for myself. Heck, it could be a whole lot worse, I could be dead and you don't recover from that do you?" smiles Neal.

"No, you sure don't," grins Gregory, happy to be alive and with his new friend.

The train starts slowing down as it prepares to stop at the station. After reducing speed for about one mile, it stops at a depot that has several Union guards around it. A line of wagons are waiting for the prisoners as they disembark from the rail car.

"You Rebels get off that train!" yells an angry Union sergeant. "It's Christmas Eve and I don't want to spend the whole day with the likes of you. I want'a go home to my family, so you'd better not give me any trouble. Now get on those wagons, set on the floor with your backs together. Move! Move!"

The Confederate men leave the rail car running to the wagons, boarding them as quickly as possible. Gregory and Neal are sitting in the back of the second wagon, in a line of four. Their feet are pushed up against the sides, and their knees are bent up into their chests, with their backs touching each other.

When all the wagons are loaded, a guard gets up in the seat next to the driver of each wagon. The sergeant in charge mounts a horse, along with three other soldiers. The sergeant and one of the mounted guards go to the front of the wagon train, while the other two guards stay at the rear. The sergeant gives a command and the chains rattle, as the mules of each wagon respond to the pop of leather across their rumps and jerk forward.

"Here we go Lieutenant," says Gregory in a low voice.

"Shut your mouth back there!" yells the guard next to the driver.

The distance to the Rock Island Prison is only seven or eight miles from the depot, which takes about one hour and twenty minutes to travel by wagon. Although the ride is a short one, the men have plenty of time to think of the fate awaiting them in prison. As they look at the surrounding countryside, from the confines of the prison wagon, they wish for happier times, home and families. These thoughts are in the minds of all of them, with one exception. Neal is deep in a world of confusion. With no past memories to recall, he's lost in a world at war, with only a small bit of it that he can recollect.

When the wagons stop at the edge of the Mississippi River, the prisoners are ordered out of them. On wobbly legs, the men get out of the wagons and fall in beside the one which they've been riding in to this point. Soldiers in large row boats come to the wooden dock at the river's edge, the boats are tied off, and the men aboard each boat bring leg-irons out of the bottom of their boat, and walk up to the prisoners who are waiting by the wagons. When the leg-irons are locked on each of the Confederate soldiers, they are ordered to follow the sergeant to the boats. As they get down to the waters edge, the cold wind which comes down the Mississippi cuts through the clothing they're wearing, and reminds the southern boys just how far north they've come. Then they are loaded in the same order they were in on the wagons, and the Union soldiers man the oars. The boats are turned toward a new brick structure built on a peninsula on the south side of the river. In just a few minutes the boats are up against another dock, tied off, and are unloading their cargo of Confederate soldiers. The chained men are herded into line, and driven through a gate where each man is accounted for by name and number

"Gregory Bailey, Lieutenant, Confederate Army," states Gregory to the officer behind the table, as he steps to the front of it, taking his turn in the line.

"Lieutenant Bailey your number is P.W. 43," informs the officer, as he glances up at Gregory in recognition of his presence.

"Name unknown Sir," says Neal when he steps to the spot where Gregory stood.

"Name Unknown?" questions the Union captain.

"Yes Sir, here are my medical records," answers Neal as he hands his voucher to the Union officer.

When he looks through the letter of introduction, the officer understands some of Neal's problems. "Lieutenant, your number is P.W. 44, and you will need to see our doctor on the day after tomorrow," instructs the captain.

"Thank you Sir," answers Neal. "Merry Christmas to you," continues Neal as he gathers his papers and turns to join Gregory.

"Next," yells the captain.

Neal joins Gregory as they follow the other men down a stone hall that leads into a guarded courtyard. There they are lead by Union soldiers to a block house that overlooks the river and has bars on the windows. At the door which is also barred, a lieutenant leads the men into the cell block and assigns the cells to two men at a time.

"PW-43 and PW-44, this is your cell," announces the Union officer, as he turns and points to the open door that leads to a six foot by ten foot room with iron bars over the opening for a window. The cell has two bunks, a small table, and a bucket in it.

Neal and Gregory walk in, dragging their leg-irons, and the door is slammed behind them. After the rattle of keys, as the door is locked, Gregory says, "This is our new home Lieutenant."

"Yeah, I guess it is, but this ain't no island at all, so why do you suppose they call it Rock Island?" asks Neal.

"I don't know, but if I had my guess, I'd say this area may get cut off in high water," answers Gregory.

"Well maybe we won't be here long enough to find out if it turns to an island when the spring rains come."

"That's a thought, but right now all I can think about is food," gripes Gregory with one hand on his empty stomach.

"Now that you mention it, I'm hungry too," agrees Neal.

Ignoring their hunger pains, the two men lie down on their bunks and are surprised to find that the beds are comfortable. After the long train ride, the uncomfortable wagon ride, and then the boat ride, Neal and Gregory realize they are tired. Now being able to stretch their bodies on the bunk, they relax, and soon fall asleep, even without the food they need to quieten their stomachs, which are now growling from hunger.

Around 9:00 o'clock, on the morning of Christmas Eve, 1864, after an hour or so of good sleep, Gregory and Neal are awakened by the rattling of keys at the door of their cell. Quickly the two swing their chained feet to the floor and sit up on the side of their bunks. The door swings open and a heavy set, older man, who is a Yankee sergeant, steps into the cell.

"If you two boys want to eat, follow me," he invites with a kindly smile. He steps back out of the cell and continues down the hall opening doors and getting the other prisoners out of their cells, as he gets to them.

The Confederate prisoners follow the Union soldier out into the court-yard, where a large pot is steaming over a fire. Plates and spoons are stacked to one side of the pot and the men are lined up beside the plates. A Union private dips into the pot of stew, which smells good to the hungry men. As the prisoners come through, plate in hand, he fills each plate with the stew, which is made of meat and potatoes, in a thick gravy.

"Gregory this is good ain't it? It sure beats mule don't it?" comments Neal, without realizing what he has said.

"It sure does beat mule I guess, but then I don't really know since I've never had mule: tell me about it," answers Gregory picking up on what Neal has said, unknowingly.

"Oh you know when we got them mules back in Georgia," explains Neal as he takes a big spoonful of stew, then he stops, realizing what he was saying.

"Don't stop now Lieutenant," encourages Gregory.

"I can't —-"

"Well don't stop eating, this is good and you are getting more of your memory back."

"I don't know if I am are not."

"Ah yeah, you are, now eat and we will work on the session later," smiles Gregory.

"Alright," answers Neal as he goes back to eating the tasty, thick stew.

After the meal is finished, the prisoners are shown a water barrel where they are to wash their plates and spoons. When the dishes have been washed, they are stacked back in the place they were picked up from before the meal.

About 12:00 o'clock, the sun is shining and the high walls surrounding the court yard are lined with armed guards. The walls also keep some of the cold north wind off the boys from the south, while they are allowed to walk in the sunshine for a couple of hours, before being ordered back to their cell block.

When they go inside another group of prisoners are brought out into the yard for food and exercise. When Gregory and Neal are back in their cell, Gregory begins the questioning session.

"Have you ever eaten mule?" Gregory asks.

"Yes, I have."

"Do you want to talk about it?"

"Yes, but I don't really remember that much about it."

"Go on."

"We are up on the side, or top, of these big hills and I can see the Yankees coming into the hollow below. They have wagons that are pulled by mules. When we start firing they are trapped and the ones that can, retreat. Afterwards, we take the captured wagons and their contents for our own use. We also skin the mules and cut up the meat to be eaten. I don't really remember eating the animals or what it tastes like. That's all I can remember."

"Your bunch must have really been low on food! The doctor says in his notes to work on remembering the good things: getting the mules must have been a good thing, to a bunch of hungry men."

"Yeah Gregory, I guess it was, but it just don't come back to me."

"Don't worry it will, you'll see, and we have all the time we need to work on unlocking your memory."

"It must be somethin' real bad I did that causes me not to want to remember."

"Don't think that way Lieutenant. I can tell from the kind of person that I think you are, it was not something you did that caused you to get amnesia."

"I'm glad you think so Gregory, that really helps my feelings," smiles Neal.

"We've had enough work for now Lieutenant. I'm going to put together my notes and study the doctor's notes, to see if I can find some parallel to go on."

"Good, I'm going to go back to sleep," grins Neal as he gets comfortable on his bed.

December 25, 1864

Unknown to Neal, or anyone of the prisoners, Hood's Army of Tennessee, finally reaches the Tennessee River. From this point it will cross the river by the 27th, but will be ineffective as a fighting force, for the remainder of the war.

"Merry Christmas Gregory!" says Neal cheerfully, as he gets out of bed and steps to the window.

"Merry Christmas Lieutenant," yawns Gregory, as he rolls over in his bunk.

"It's really a prutty morning out there. I only hope that whoever the friends and relatives I've been separated from are lucky enough to see the beauty of this Christmas morning."

"I'll bet they will wherever they are Lieutenant," answers Gregory, as he sits up on the side of his bunk.

The day in prison is spent much as the day before. Two meals are served and exercise periods are given at alternate times, for the two different groups of prisoners. This will be the routine for the next few weeks, until the weather warms up. Gregory does give Neal a memory session, but he remembers nothing new at this time.

December 26th, 1864

When the Union sergeant comes to open the cells for the men to go eat, Neal tells him that he is supposed to meet with the prison doctor.

"You supposed to meet with old Doc Everett, are you?" questions the sergeant.

"Yes Sir, and here are my medical records," answers Neal, as he extends the medical file to the sergeant.

"Don't hand those papers to me Boy, I can't read. You'll just have to tell me your problem," smiles the sergeant.

"Well it's a long story Sergeant, but to make a short one out of it; I have amnesia."

"What?"

"Amnesia, it's the loss of one's memory. See, I can't even remember my own name."

"Well Boy, that's hard to believe."

"It's true Sergeant," Gregory speaks up after listening to the conversation between Neal and the sergeant.

"Well my name is Farrell Monroe, and I hope I don't ever forget it."

"I sure hope not too Sir," smiles Neal showing sincerity in his expression.

"Well thank you Boy. You and I will go and see the Doc after your group eats," answers the overweight soldier.

After the routine of the meal, the men are ordered back to their cell-block. Sergeant Monroe then takes Neal out of the line.

"Wait a minute Sergeant Monroe," protests Neal, "I don't have my records with me and I'm supposed to give them to the doctor."

"Time's a-wasting boy and if he's sober enough to see us, I'll come back to get your records for ya'."

"Yes Sir," answers Neal as the two step off in the direction of Dr. Everett's office.

Once they get there, Sergeant Monroe knocks on the door of the office.

"Come in!" comes a loud slurred voice from inside the room.

Sergeant Monroe opens the door and leads the way, with Neal right behind him. The two of them come to a stop and stand at attention in front of the doctor's desk.

"Well Sergeant, you are wasting my time," growls Everett. "What is it?"

"Sir, this prisoner has uh-uh- he has a sickness, where he's lost his memory. He can't even remember nothing, and the hospital doctor where he come from, said he was to report to the prison doctor here."

"Report to the doctor here!" yells Everett. "Don't anybody know how busy I am?"

"Yes Sir," snaps Monroe.

"Talk to me Reb, what's the problem?" orders the doctor impatiently, looking directly at Neal.

"I just can't remember my past Sir," answers Neal.

"Sounds to me like you're healthy. You look healthy enough, and besides, you are probably better off not remembering this war and your past," slurs Everett.

"But Sir, I don't want to stay this way. I want to remember my family---"

"Hush!" interrupts Everett. "You're not going to get any special consideration here; I can't treat all the people I have to treat, and give you special treatment," continues the doctor, in an unconcerned manner.

"But Sir," injects Sergeant Monroe.

"That's final Sergeant," snaps Everett. "Now you two are dismissed."

"Yes Sir," answer the two men as they turn about face and leave the doctor's office.

Once they are in the hall, they hear the cork of a liquor bottle pop, as the doctor gets back to his demanding schedule.

"I'm sorry Son, I had a feeling it would be this way," states Monroe, as they walk down the hall together. "He has done very little doctoring for anyone here, so I didn't expect he would just up and start on you today."

"That's jes' the way it is Sergeant. I'm mighty glad I still have my records, and that my cellmate is Gregory. He's acting jes' like Dr. Voge, writing down everything he asks me and everything I say; it will be better to keep working with him I guess," answers Neal, with a touch of disappointment in his voice.

"I'd say you're real lucky to have that boy working with you, but I guess I don't really know. I will help you anyway I can, jus' remember that."

"Thank you Sir, that's mighty nice of you," smiles Neal. "But why would you help me, a Reb?"

"Let's just say this here war has been bad on us all in one way or another. I'm too old to be a true fightin' soldier, but my son ain't. The bad thing for me is, my son is wearing the gray and I'm wearing the blue."

"You mean you have a son that is fightin' for the south?" questions a puzzled Neal, as he stops abruptly in the hall and waits for the answer to his question.

"Yes Son, I do," answers Monroe, and they begin to walk on down the hall to Neal's cell.

"But how?"

"It don't really matter now, it jus' happened, but if he was in your shape, I hope somebody, somewhere, would be willing to help him."

"I'm sure there would be Sergeant."

"I don't think so Son. You see, not all prisons are as easy as this one. You being an officer helps too. He is not an officer, that I know about anyway, but I can't tell you anymore about him. I haven't heard from him in over two years now."

"That's an awful long time, but I don't even know how long it's been since I heard from my folks."

While the other group is still eating, Neal and Sergeant Monroe walk across the courtyard, to Neal's block house. Once he is back in his cell and the sergeant has gone, he tells Gregory about Sergeant Monroe's son being in the Confederate army.

"That's hard on Sergeant Monroe," states Gregory, "But what about the doctor, what did he say?"

"Oh, I forgot. He ain't gonna do nothing for me; said he was too busy to give me special treatment."

"That so, huh? Well, I guess the two of us will just have to work it out then," Gregory answers Neal, who now seems to be in deep concentration.

After a few minutes, Gregory gets up from his bed and says, "Lieutenant, stretch out on your bed and make yourself comfortable."

"Do what?"

"Yeah, Doctor Voge said in his notes, for you to rest and relax, now just do it, and I'll give you some questions."

"Okay, you're the doctor Gregory," says Neal as he reclines on his bunk.

Gregory begins pacing back and forth in the small room, dragging the leg-iron chains on the floor with every step. "Now Lieutenant, these are the things we know, or think we know. You are a lieutenant, in the Confederate Army. Is this correct?"

"Yes, I believe so."

"Your mother's name is Milly?"

"I think so."

"You have a brother named Ruben?"

"Yeah, I think so."

"You were in the infantry?"

"Yes, I believe that's true."

"You were a farm boy?"

"Yes, I think so, but how did you come up with that?" asks Neal, puzzled by this question.

"I've studied your records over and over, and it's in Doctor Voge's notes about you seeing a man on a horse, talking with three other boys and a man, in a freshly plowed field."

"That's right! You have really studied, haven't you?"

"Don't question me, I'll do the questioning," instructs Gregory.

"Yes Sir," grins Neal.

"Now think on this question. Is Ruben one of the boys who is in the field with you?"

After a few moments, Neal answers, "Yes he is. He's been dropping seed: I can see the seed bucket in his arms."

"Good, now we are getting somewhere. You just continue with that thought for now and see if anything more comes back to you," says Gregory. He then gets back on his bed, to make the room quiet, so Neal can relax and concentrate.

HARDSHIPS OF PRISON LIFE

• • • • • • • • • • • • • • • •

January 1, 1865

Word is heard in the prison that Union Soldiers are trying to clear Arkansas of its troublesome and ubiquitous guerrilla bands. The new year brings hope among many, that the war will be over soon. The food in the prison is getting worse. The reason for this is, the Federals think men in prison don't work, therefore they don't need as many calories to live on. The effects of this decision will be felt by the men in prison, all over the north. The enlisted men will feel it more than others. Neal has made little progress in recapturing his memory.

"Happy New Year Lieutenant," says Gregory as he stands staring out through the barred window, at the riverboats passing.

"Maybe it will be Gregory, but the beginning of it don't look too bright, does it?"

"Lieutenant, you got to look for something good in everything."

"How is that?"

"Well for one thing, this year has got to be better than the last one," smiles Gregory.

"Yeah, I suppose you are right. I guess I was feeling a little sorry for myself."

Their conversation is interrupted by the sound of doors being opened down the way. "I wonder what's going on," comments Neal.

"Whatever it is Lieutenant, I'm sure we are going to find out."

"Oh, you are always so smart, don't guess I'd ever have figured that out." Grinning, Neal throws his shoe at Gregory.

"That's one way to get me to hush: I can't talk for the smell."

"Smell! I don't guess you smell huh?"

"I'm just kiddin' Lieutenant. I do wish they would let us get a bath, or at least just wash off."

"Me too," agrees Neal, as the sound of keys are heard at their door.

"Good news boys," smiles Sergeant Monroe, as he opens the door.

"What's that Sergeant?" questions Neal, as the big man steps into the cell.

"Get your feet up. We're going to take them leg-irons off."

"That is good news Sergeant," grins Gregory as he sits on the bed and picks his feet up, while Neal, is on his bed doing the same thing.

After Sergeant Monroe has taken Gregory's irons off, he turns to Neal who has his bare feet still up in the air. "Boy your feet stink so bad I don't know if I can stand it long enough to get the irons off," laughs Monroe.

"Come on Sergeant, it can't be that bad once you get used to it," laughs Neal.

"Yeah Sergeant, we are pretty ripe. When do you suppose we can get washed up?" questions Gregory.

"Well boys it's going to be a while. The weather has to warm up first, and maybe we can let you boys get in the river then."

"Shoot Sergeant, that's months off," gripes Gregory.

"Yeah I know boys, but there ain't nothing I can do about it," answer's Monroe, with a look of understanding on his face. After he takes the leg-irons off he leaves, locking the door behind him.

"Dirty and stinking, I surely feel better with them irons off," states Neal, holding his legs straight up in the air, waving them freely.

"Me too," answers Gregory, "See I told you that this year had to be better than the last."

"Oh, you are truly smart, ain't you?" laughs Neal.

January 5, 1865

Neal is in much better spirits.

Gregory has learned in studying Doctor Voge's notes, that when a person is happy and feeling good with himself, his mind will reflect on happier times and pleasant events.

Neal and Gregory are being returned to their cell, after their morning meal and exercise period. As they enter the cell, the door is being closed and locked behind them, when Neal asks Sergeant Monroe if he has had any news from his boy who is fighting for the South.

"No Son, I have not received any news from him, and the way the war is going, I won't most likely, because the South has had all communications cut for some time now."

"I'm sorry that you are still in the dark on knowing how your son is Sergeant," replies Neal.

"Me to Son, oh, before I go, thought I'd tell you boys that we are getting some more p.w.'s in a few days."

"Where are ya'll going to put them Sergeant?" questions Gregory.

"I don't know boy, but I guess we'll have to find a place," answers Monroe, as he turns and leaves, locking the door behind him.

"More p.w.'s, gosh Gregory, they're starving us now! That soup, if you want to call it that, was no more than greasy water, just now."

"Yeah Lieutenant, it has gotten much worse since we first got here, and I see your point. If they have more mouths to feed, they'll just add more water to the pot."

"Just think about it Gregory: if they put one or two more men in these little bitty cells, we won't have room to turn around."

Sensing that Neal is getting depressed and worried, Gregory changes the subject saying, "Well let's not worry about that now, we'll cross that bridge when we get to it."

"I guess we'll have to, don't look like we're gonna have much of a choice," answers Neal.

"Ain't you the smart one today?" Gregory grins and says, "I wouldn't ever have figured that out without your help."

"Aw hush, Smart Eleck," laughs Neal.

"Have you got any horses Lieutenant," asks Gregory, knowing that Neal's mind is clear and relaxed now, after the moment of laughter.

"No, I don't, but my pa has two mules, why?" answers Neal, without thinking.

"Really, what are their names?"

"Hum-m-m, I can't remember," replies Neal, realizing that his family did have two big Missouri mules. "I can see them, but I can't put a name on them."

"That's great Lieutenant! We can work from this. We know that ya'll had two mules and that's more than we knew a few minutes ago."

"Yeah it is ain't it?" agrees Neal.

"Sure is, and I want you to just lay there and think about those mules," orders Gregory, while getting out his note pad to record the question and answer.

"I'll try Gregory, but I don't know how long I will be able to do it, my belly is starting to cramp something awful. Must be that soup we ate."

"There's the bucket, if you gotta go, but try and remember those mule's names," states Gregory, hoping that his stomach won't start hurting like Neal's.

As the day wears on Neal's condition worsens. He is not able to concentrate on anything but his sad physical condition. With no water in the cell to drink, Neal grows weaker from the continual loss of body fluids.

"Lieutenant, do you need to go to the bucket again?" asks Gregory, knowing that Neal may be seriously ill, and that there is no help available in this place.

"Not now. How much longer before Sergeant Monroe will be coming around?"

"Not long," answers Gregory, wishing that the sergeant would hurry up, and come get the block of men for their second meal.

A few minutes later, the opening of doors and rattle of keys out in the hall is heard. When Sergeant Monroe gets to Neal and Gregory's cell, he knows of the problem as he opens their door. The smell of the sick Neal, greets him even before the door is unlocked.

"Which one of you is sick?" questions the sergeant, as he opens the door and lingers in the hall.

"It's the lieutenant, Sergeant," answers Gregory.

"Well Gregory, you'd better come on out of there, if you don't want to catch what he's got. We're putting all the sick ones in cells together, to try and keep the whole lot of you from coming down with whatever it is," states Sergeant Monroe.

"No Sergeant I'm not leaving the lieutenant."

"Boy, you are asking for trouble, if you don't get sick, that ole Doc Everett will be all over us all."

"Well you can just tell him I'm sick too, and from the way he does his doctoring, he won't know the difference. He hasn't even been around to check on any of us since we've been here. I don't even know what he looks like."

"Suit yourself Boy. If that's the way you want to do it, I'll go along with you."

"It is Sergeant."

"Fine, you just stay here in the cell and after the others are moved, and the healthy ones have been fed their meal, I'll be coming around with water and stew for the sick."

Neal has been lying in his bed, hearing the two men talk.

"Lieutenant, I told you that you were lucky to have a friend like Gregory here, but now I know that he's truly a friend, and a caring person, to stay here in this cell with you. Boy I don't want to scare you or anything like that, but what you got has already killed some boys in the other cell block. Now if you are not at peace with your God, it ain't a bad idea to get it made. Gregory don't you want to change your mind about what you are doing?"

"No," answers Gregory, in a tone of voice that is sure and final.

"But why, you may be just making yourself sick, and not helping the lieutenant a'tall."

"Well Sergeant, I guess we just hob/knob good together," smiles Gregory, looking at Neal, who is now very pale and weak.

"I'll be back in a little while boys," says Monroe, as he closes the door.

Still looking at Neal, Gregory sees a faint smile coming on his face, and says, "Don't you think for one minute I'm going to let you die, without ever knowing who you are."

In a weakened voice Neal answers, "Oh you are so smart, you won't even let a man die in peace, but you did give me the names of my pa's two mules."

"I did!"

"Yeah, but I may die before I tell you what they are," grins Neal.

"No you're not, now what are the names of the mules?"

"You said it to the sergeant, Hob and Nob."

"That's good. Now listen to me, you're not going to die. I'm going to see to that: and you are going to get your memory back."

"Yeah," answers Neal, in a sleepy voice, as he closes his eyes. Gregory takes out his papers and records this new bit of information from Neal's past, hopeful that more memories will soon come to his mind.

When Sergeant Monroe comes back with the stew and water, Gregory begins nursing his very sick friend. He only eats half of his stew and gives the other half to Neal. He drinks only a small amount of his own water, so Neal will have something to drink later on. This continues for the next several days and Neal is lucky indeed to have a friend such as Gregory there to take care of his needs. The extra food and water help him and he begins recovering in a week or ten days.

The unselfish sacrifices Gregory makes to help Neal have taken their toll on his own body, and by the fifteenth of January, he is down to skin and bones.

January 16th, 1865

A detailed report is given to President Lincoln, by Francis P. Blair. In the report, there is an account of Blair's recent conversation with Jefferson Davis, over possibilities for peace between the North and South.

"Gregory, you ain't nothing but skin and bones," says Neal as he rolls over on his bed, which he has not done for several days.

"Yeah I know, but it was either me lose a few pounds or you lose your life," answers Gregory, noticing that Neal seems to be getting stronger.

"You're right. I don't guess I would have made it, had it not been for the extra food and water I got cause you went without."

"Like I said, you can't die before you tell me your name," smiles Gregory.

"You can count on that Gregory, but let's not kill you just to keep me alive."

"We aren't, now you rest assured of that, you understand?"

"Yeah."

"Do you feel up to some questions?"

"No, not really, I'm uh- just tuckered out, I guess,"

"That's fine, we can do it tomorrow, but if you had a wish, what would you wish for?"

"If I had a wish what would I wish for? Let me see," answers Neal, rolling over onto his back, and closing his eyes, in thought. After a minute or two has passed, he answers, "I'd wish for two dozen oranges."

"What?"

"I'd wish for two dozen oranges," replies Neal.

"Oranges, what in the world are oranges?"

"It's a fruit I got in Florida. My brother and me carried them home to the family," answers Neal, not realizing what he is remembering.

"Go on, tell me more about these oranges."

"Well it's kind of a sweet, watery fruit, with a thick, smooth peel around it. My little brother, Ruben, wanted to eat anybody's that didn't want theirs."

"Really? What did your mother, Milly, have to say about that?"

"Milly? My mother's name is Lilly, and she said, uh-uh- I can't remember," answers Neal, just realizing what was going on.

"Lilly, Ruben, and oranges," smiles Gregory. "Lieutenant, we're getting someplace!"

"Really?"

"Yeah, we are, and you just rest while I update my notes, then I'll explain to you," answers Gregory.

"Fine," answers Neal, as he drops his head back on the bed to rest.

When Neal has rested for a while, Gregory explains that they know for a fact that his little brother's name is Ruben, and that his mother's name is Lilly. Also, he figures that his home state must border on Florida, or may be Florida, because the oranges would have spoiled if he had to travel very far with them.

"You are jes' too smart Gregory," grins Neal. "You are going to make a real good lawyer."

"I hope to, but now I only want to help you," answers Gregory.

NEAL'S HOMECOMING

"Maybe you ought to become a doctor and then you could help people get well," states Neal seriously.

"It's a thought, but don't fret about what I ought to be, let's fret about you for now."

"You're the doctor," smiles Neal, as Gregory hands him a drink of water.

January 20th, 1865

"There's fighting in Kansas between Federal troops and Indians, Boys," informs Sergeant Monroe, as he brings the morning stew and water to Neal and Gregory.

"That a fact Sergeant? Why don't ya'll let us out of this here prison, and we'll go out there and whoop them Indians for ya'll?" grins Neal.

"Yeah Lieutenant, I believe you are better," laughs Monroe.

"He sure is, wanting to go help the Yankees fight the Indians," laughs Gregory.

"I'd do anything almost to get out of this prison," gripes Neal.

"Well Son, I don't think it will be over two or three months before this war is over and then you can go home," states Monroe.

"Yeah, if I only knew where home is," answers Neal.

"I'm sorry Son," apologizes Monroe for forgetting Neal's problem.

"No problem Sergeant, we're going to have the lieutenant straightened out in a few days now that he's better physically and all," states Gregory, not wanting Neal to revert back into depression.

After the sergeant leaves, Gregory insists on doing a questioning session. "Do you have any sisters?"

"No."

"Why do you say no?"

"I've never seen any females but my mother, in any of my recollections."

"Lieutenant you are forgetting the colored girl."

"Well she ain't my sister!" snaps Neal.

Smiling, Gregory asks, "Do ya'll have any slaves?"

"Yes and no," answers Neal.

"Now what kinda answer is that?"

NEAL'S HOMECOMING

"I don't know what kind of answer it is, but if we had slaves, would I have been working in the fields? Would Ruben have been putting in the seed?"

"I see what you mean," answers Gregory. "But what about the colored girl?"

"I suppose she was ours, but I don't feel right saying we owned anybody."

"Why?"

"Uh- uh, my pa said so, I think it was when us boys were on the porch with him."

"I see." answers Gregory while taking down every word. "Did you ever ride Hob and Nob?"

"Sure we did."

"Where did you ride them to?"

"Well the last time we rode them, was when Thompson and me rode them up to Raleigh."

"Who?"

"Thompson, uh, I think."

"Who is Thompson?"

"I don't know for sure, but I think he's my brother," answers Neal, appearing tired and strained at something about this situation.

"That's good Lieutenant," says Gregory, not wanting to push Neal too hard. "That's enough for today."

January 28th, 1865

Sergeant Monroe tells of an upcoming peace talk between President Lincoln and Vice President Alexander Stephens of the Confederate States of America.

After the sergeant has gone to carry water and stew to the other prisoners, Neal says, "Gosh Gregory, I didn't even know who the Vice President of the South was, did you?"

"No, so that is one thing you can say you have learned, and not remembered," laughs Gregory.

"No, I'm being serious. It is kinda sad for us to be fightin', or we was fightin' a war, and don't know who our vice president is. We don't even know who or what Jefferson Davis is all about."

"Yeah, I guess you are right to some degree. Maybe we, or the South, jumped into this war too quick," answers Gregory.

"I've always heard that the rich politicians start wars, and the poor young'uns fight them," explains Neal.

"I suppose to some extent, that is true, Lieutenant."

"What do you mean by some extent?" questions Neal.

"Well in the beginning it was mostly so, that is, what you say. But the war has lasted so long that it has drawn all the people in the South into it," explains Gregory.

"Oh I see what you are saying," agrees Neal.

"I'm so afraid that the whole South, as we know it, will be destroyed by the North when the war is finally over," warns Gregory.

"Maybe I'll be the lucky one after all Gregory."

"How's that Lieutenant?"

"I can't remember how my home really was, and if my memory don't come back, I may be the lucky one that don't know what he's lost."

"Don't talk like that. A man has got to have roots so he can grow. Now we've got to keep working on getting your memory back, so you can work better on your future," explains Gregory.

"Whatever you say Doc."

February 4th, 1865

President Lincoln returns to the White House after his unsuccessful peace mission with Vice President Stephens in Hampton Roads, Virginia.

After the afternoon meal, Gregory asks Neal if he thinks he can start exercising again, and eating outside tomorrow.

"I do feel much better and I think it would do us both some good just to get out of this cell," answers Neal.

"Good, I'm mighty glad you feel up to it. We haven't been out of this cell since we took them ole leg irons off."

"You are right. I'd forgot about that. We probably won't be able to walk right once we get out in the court yard," grins Neal.

February 5th, 1865

President Lincoln presents a plan to his cabinet, pledging that the Federal Government will pay $400,000,000.00 to the slave states, if they will lay down their arms before April 1st. The cabinet is opposed to the scheme, and the matter is dropped.

"Gregory, I didn't realize just how bad the air was back in our cell, until we got out here in the open."

"Yeah, it has been a while since we had some good fresh air," answers Gregory, as he takes a deep breath.

"With this good air and warm sunshine, I should be fully recovered in a couple of days," smiles Neal.

"I'm glad to hear that Lieutenant. Maybe in a month they'll let us wash in the river too."

"I think a good washing will help everybody. I know it will help the smell, if nothing else," agrees Neal.

"It sure won't hurt," smiles Gregory, scratching his uncared for beard. "Can you swim?"

"Yeah, I can swim, but now that you mention it, I remember a boy named Chris that couldn't, and we were crossing a river in Alabama. The boys were giving him down the country. He was afraid the boats would sink and all," laughs Neal.

Gregory hears every word that Neal has said but makes no mention of it and Neal doesn't notice that he is remembering a moment in his past out loud.

When their time is up, the men are moved back to their cells and Neal gets in bed to rest, while Gregory records the experience that Neal was talking about when they were in the court yard.

February 12th, 1865

The electoral college meets and by a vote of 212 to 21, Lincoln is elected President of the United States of America, for a second term. Although Louisiana and Tennessee had voted in the November election, Vice President Hamlin, who presides over the college, does not present the votes of these two states.

February 13th, 1865

During the afternoon meal, Captain Watson, Neal, and Gregory, have finished eating and are walking around the court yard together when Sergeant Monroe walks up and joins them.

"I guess you boys have heard already, but if you haven't, Lincoln has been confirmed for a second term as president. Andrew Johnson, the Tennessee war-governor, has been confirmed also, as vice president," informs Sergeant Monroe.

"Andrew Johnson, I'll be! I thought Tennessee was a part of the Confederacy," complains Gregory.

"Now Boy, we've got to get used to it. A lot of the people back home were Unionist and when the war is over we are going to have to get along with them," explains Watson.

"The captain is right Gregory, with the way things are going, the South won't last over two more months at the most," agrees Monroe. "Also, it won't be as hard for you to go back to Tennessee, as it will be for my son to come back to Illinois."

"I guess you are right Sergeant," replies Gregory.

"Heck Gregory you know he is right," agrees Watson. "Ain't that so Lieutenant?"

"I think the sergeant is right. When this war does get over, we all have got to learn to get along again. It will be hard on the boys that go back south, to split states. It is going to be even harder on the boys coming back north who fought for the South," explains Neal.

The conversation goes on in this manner until the prisoners are ordered back to their cells. When Neal and Gregory are back in the cell, Gregory continues to think and comment on the subject.

"Lieutenant you spoke some good advice out there in the yard about learning to get along after this war. Where did you ever learn to think with such logic?"

"Guess I ain't as dumb as you may think I am, even though I can't remember all my past," grins Neal.

"That's not what I mean at all, I wonder if you are from a split state or split family, that's all."

"Oh, I see. Well I don't think I'm from a split family, or state. Besides, you said I'd have to be from the Deep South to have taken oranges home with me."

"That is correct," answers Gregory.

"Are we going to do any questions and answers?" asks Neal, as he gets back on his bed.

NEAL'S HOMECOMING

"No, not now. I think I'm going to study my notes while the light is still good. Maybe I can come up with something."

When the sun starts going down and the light through the bars begins to dim, Gregory stops looking at his notes. He writes down a few things and folds up his papers.

"Did you figure out anything Gregory?"

"Well, I don't really know. The oranges say you came from the Deep South. Therefore, you are from Florida, South Carolina, Georgia, or Alabama."

"That may be so, but it don't feel right," answers Neal.

"Now that's just a guess, you may even be from Mississippi it ain't that far across the bottom of Alabama," explains Gregory. "We'll start working on what state you are from tomorrow."

February 14th, 1865

"You awake Lieutenant?" asks Gregory, as he rolls over in his bed.

"Yeah, I'm awake," answers Neal, as the early morning light comes in the window of their cell.

"I've been thinking, and according to Doctor Voge, we should not push too hard in trying to recover your memory. He says that you should be rested and relaxed."

"Yeah, I know that, so what's your point?"

"When are we more rested and relaxed than when we first wake up?"

"Oh, you are so smart, aren't you? Supposing I still wanted to sleep?"

"I'd just pull rank on you," laughs Gregory. "Yeah? Well I'll have you know that I'm a lieutenant too."

"Really, but how long have you been one?"

"I don't know."

"I know how long I've been one and I'll say that I have more time in grade than you, so I'm in charge," grins Gregory.

"Oh, aw-right, you're in charge," agrees Neal, with a smile on his face. "We officers have to keep a certain air about us, don't we Lieutenant?"

"Yeah, I reckon so."

"So when we become officers, we also become officers and gentlemen."

"Huh?"

"Yeah, you know when you come into the service and are commissioned, you have to act the part."

"Oh," wonders Neal.

"Aw, now for instance, when I went in and got my uniform, all the young ladies were impressed," explains Gregory.

"Young ladies? When I went in there were no young ladies."

"Really?"

"Yeah, you see there ain't that many people in Raleigh, and the young men were all in the army. The young girls were not allowed around the soldiers that were training, so there were no young ladies to be impressed."

"You did go in as an officer, didn't you?"

"No, I went in as a sergeant, then I was promoted to help Captain Ward."

"You went in at Raleigh?"

"Yes," answers Neal, his words becoming slower.

"Raleigh what?" asks Gregory.

"I, uh, I can't remember," groans Neal.

"That's fine, Lieutenant. We know two more things now, than we did," smiles Gregory.

"Raleigh and what?" Asks Neal.

"Captain Ward must have been your C.O., and you were promoted to help him."

"Yeah, that's right!" says Neal, showing some excitement in his voice.

"Now, let me record this and we may continue after Sergeant Monroe lets us out, and brings us back here."

Gregory gets busy recording all the details of the conversation and Neal rolls over on his side, to watch through the bars, as the light of day grows brighter and brighter. Traffic on the river starts picking up as the new day begins.

"Gregory, did we ever get those other prisoners Sergeant Monroe told us about?"

"Yeah, they came in, but since we were in the sick block, they put them in the other blocks."

"We lucked out again didn't we? We could be stuck here with three or four to the cell."

"Yeah, that's right. See I told you things were going to get better. We've just got to keep our minds on the good things, and in the end everything will work out fine."

"I believe you are right Gregory, at least I sure hope so."

It's not long until Sergeant Monroe comes through opening cells and getting the men out for their morning meal and exercise. Gregory realizes that the more Neal relaxes, the more he tells of his past. The Captain Ward that he mentioned, may have been acquainted with some of the other officers in the prison. On the way out Gregory lags back and tells Sergeant Monroe that he wants him to stay and talk to the lieutenant, while he makes inquiries among the other prisoners about a Captain Ward.

When Sergeant Monroe understands what Gregory is doing and why, he readily agrees to keep the lieutenant company during the court yard walking period.

Once the meal is eaten and the dishes are done, Sergeant Monroe comes to Neal and begins a conversation with him, which allows Gregory to mingle with the other men.

Gregory goes to men that he knows, and men that he doesn't know, asking them if they ever knew a Captain Ward in the infantry. After many negative replies he finally asks one officer who did remember meeting a Captain Ward who was in the infantry.

"Like you Lieutenant, I was in the cavalry. I was serving under Forrest at Franklin and we were chasing these Yankee horse soldiers as they headed back to their place to forge the river. Our infantry had scouted the river, found their crossing spot and laid a trap for the Yankees. When we pushed them back, they ran into the trap set by the infantry and were captured. When we rode in my captain wanted to shoot all the prisoners. The reason he wanted to do this was that half of them were Negroes and the other half were foreigners who did not speak English. I rode up with another junior officer and was listening to our captain arguing with the infantry captain. The infantry captain made it clear, the Yankees were his prisoners and that nobody was going to shoot them. About that time, two infantry privates walked up, and one of them offered his captain some assistance, if he needed it. This private looked like he meant it. That was the first time I ever knew of my captain backing down. We turned and rode off, but before we were clear of the foot soldiers, I asked one of them who that captain of theirs was and I was told that he was a Captain Ward."

"That's all you know?"

"Yeah, that Captain Ward will be a general some day. He is tough!"

"So you did not really know him?"

"No, just met him the one time."

"Well thank you, aw- aw-"

"Forty Jones."

"Well thank you Forty, I really appreciate the help," answers Gregory.

"Glad to help, uh -"

"Gregory Bailey," smiles Gregory. "Oh, I almost forgot. What outfit was Captain Ward with?"

"Best I can remember the northwest of Franklin was defended by the Third and Fourth Louisiana and the 8th Mississippi," answers Jones.

"Thank you! You really have been a big help," grins Gregory.

"The way you are grinning, I'd say I have, but I really don't know how I did it," states the puzzled Jones.

"You just told me where the lieutenant I was telling you about is from."

"Really? Where from?"

"Mississippi!" answers Gregory as he thanks Jones again, and leaves.

Walking up to Monroe and Neal, Gregory tells the two of them he has some good news and will tell them in the cell, when they get back there.

Once back in the block, Monroe and Neal stand ready for Gregory to give them the good news.

"Well come on out with it," grins Neal. "What have you got that is so good?"

"For one thing, what state you are from," answers Gregory with a smirk.

"You better tell me or Sergeant Monroe will go get his gun and shoot you for keeping it to yourself," laughs Neal.

"Aw-right, just to keep you from getting me shot, I'll tell you. Mississippi!" yells Gregory, with a big smile on his face.

"Mississippi now how did you find that out?"

"I talked to this Lieutenant Jones who has met a Captain Ward that was in the infantry at Franklin. The captain was in charge of some men at the river. These men were either the Third or Fourth Louisiana, or the 8th Mississippi. Since you had fresh oranges at home, I'd say you were in the 8th Mississippi and that you are from Mississippi."

"Gregory, I believe you are right. How can I ever repay you?"

"I have my fee, and I'll send you a bill," laughs Gregory.

"You're going to be a great lawyer, if you ever get out of this jail," laughs Neal.

"That's for sure," agrees Monroe, joining in their laughter, happy to see these men feeling better about something good, after the sickness and discouragement they've suffered.

"Also, I'd say you joined up at Raleigh, Mississippi. When we get out of here, all you have to do is go back down to Raleigh and find somebody who knows you, and then you'll get home," explains Gregory.

"Boys this is mighty fine, now you can rest easy Lieutenant, knowing that you will get home after this war is over," states Sergeant Monroe.

"That shouldn't be too hard to do, now should it?" asks Neal.

"Naw, it will be easy compared to what you have been through. The fighting at Franklin, going to the hospital in Nashville, and now the prison here; going home will be easy for you," explains Gregory.

"Yeah, it will be Lieutenant and I'm mighty proud for you," adds Monroe. "I've got to be going to the other cell block now, but I'll be back this afternoon."

"Thanks Sergeant for helping," says Neal sincerely, as the big sergeant goes out the door and locks it behind him

"Yeah, everything is getting better," smiles Gregory.

"It sure is, now if we could do something about the smell and filth, it would really be looking up," adds Neal as he scratches his long matted hair.

Throughout the rest of February, a few new prisoners continue to come into the Rock Island Prison. These new men bring news of the war, as they arrive from different battlefronts. Sherman's troops in unofficial acts of vengeance, destroy private homes and businesses. The word of the destruction that is going on in the South, and the fact that the Confederate Army can do little to stop it, makes the p.w.'s more anxious to get home. Their reasoning is, that with a real man at home to defend the place, the cowardly soldiers would move on, rather than get into a real fight.

March 2nd, 1865

Neal continues to get small glimpses of the past, which he cannot really put a time or a name to; which is somewhat confusing for him. Gregory encourages him to see the glimpses as progress in getting his memory restored. Maybe a little bit now and then, is nature's way of healing.

At Petersburg, General Lee sends a message through the lines to General Grant, suggesting that the two of them hold a military convention, to try and reach a satisfactory adjustment of the difficulties at hand.

The weather at Rock Island warms up a bit, and as Sergeant Monroe opens the door to Neal and Gregory's cell he makes a welcome announcement. He tells them that this morning after they eat, they can go through the gate of the yard, to the river where they can wash off the accumulation of filth, they have been complaining about.

This is great news to both men since they have been here since Christmas and have not washed in this length of time.

"Gosh Sergeant, we have grown used to the smell now, and if we get rid of it, we'll have to get used to no smell," smiles Gregory.

"Gregory, you were the one complaining the most about wanting to take a bath," laughs Monroe.

"He sure was Sergeant. Guess that's cause he's the one who stinks the most," adds Neal with a sly grin.

"Augh, you two hush, you know I really do want to wash and can hardly wait to do it," grins Gregory.

"A word of warning Boys, don't go out too far from the bank, cause there will be armed guards with orders to shoot anyone who tries to escape."

After the meal, the men wash the dishes in a hurry and line up at the gate with Monroe at the head of the line.

"Follow me out Men. When you get within twenty feet of the water, drop your clothes. I have some soap here in a bucket and I'll give each pair of you one piece of soap. The two of you will stay together so as not to lose the soap. After you've washed your bodies, both of you come out and wash your clothes. When you have washed your clothes, carry them in your hands back to your cell to dry."

"Sergeant, you mean we've got to walk back neck'ed as jay birds?" questions Neal, shocked at this idea.

"There ain't no women around here, and we all know what a man looks like, now let's go get cleaned up," orders the sergeant.

Neal and Gregory are paired up, and when everyone reaches the spot where they are to undress, the clothes start hitting the dirt. They are kept in small piles so every man can find his own things.

"Heck Gregory, it's still cold out here with no clothes on!" complains Neal.

"Aw hush your griping, at least we're gonna' get clean," replies Gregory, as he leads the way out into the water.

Neal follows him in, and the cold water has a breath taking effect on both of them. As they are washing, they see the guards on either side of their group and up on the wall. All of them have rifles ready and anybody who tries to escape will surely be a fool.

After about five minutes, the men began coming out and getting their clothing to carry them back to the water's edge for washing. Some hard scrubbing takes place with the lye soap, before the rags come clean . After the months of use, without laundering or being changed, their clothes are tattered and filthy. When they have been washed, the men turn the soap bars back over to Monroe who in turn, puts them back into his bucket.

With wet clothing in their arms, the men are marched to the gate which leads back to the court yard. As they are walking across the court yard, the other cell block's barred windows are open. The men in that block start yelling and chanting from their windows, at the naked men, all in fun, because this procedure is something all of them will be doing in the very same manner today.

Once they are back in their cell, Neal and Gregory hang their wet clothes out to dry, and both of them get on their beds. They stretch out and enjoy the freshness of their clean bodies, even though the beds are in bad need of sunning and airing.

"Lieutenant, I don't remember feeling this clean ever before," comments Gregory, enjoying the moment.

"I'd say the same, if I could remember all my past," laughs Neal. "But I'd say you ain't never needed a bath that bad before."

"You are probably right," laughs Gregory, in complete agreement with Neal's comment.

March 3rd, 1865

Grant receives instructions from Lincoln, concerning Lee's peace overtures. The President orders Grant not to have any conferences with Lee unless it's to accept the surrender of his troops, or it is purely a military matter. Grant passes this word to General Lee. Lee will have to bargain with Lincoln on political matters personally.

"Good morning Boys!" Greets Sergeant Monroe, to Neal and Gregory, as he unlocks their cell."

"My, don't it smell a mite better in here this morning?"

"Sergeant Monroe, you know that ain't so. We may smell a little better, but this cell could use some airing out," complains Neal.

"Right you are Lieutenant, and so it will be. As you two come out for your morning meal, bring your bedding with you. We'll let it air in the sun until your afternoon meal: then you can pick it up and bring it back here."

"See, I told you things had to get better, and they really are," smiles Gregory.

"Also, bring your bucket and wash it out. Then you can get fresh water in it, so you can wash down your cell, between meals."

"Yes sir Sergeant!" Reply the two cell-mates.

Once they are outside with their bedding airing and soaking up the sunlight, the men find that life in the P.W. camp is getting a little better with the coming of warmer weather. The food is the same watered down stew, but at least they are cleaner than what they were day before yesterday.

"Why do you suppose they are letting us clean up our cells and so on, Captain?" Asks Gregory to Captain Watson, as he and Neal walk with him around the court-yard.

"The only thing I can figure Gregory is that they know this war ain't going to last much longer. They want us in as good'a physical health as they can get us under the circumstances, before they turn us out for our walk home."

"What you mean is, they don't want any sick Reb officers holding them back when the war is over. They went'a go home too, ain't that right Captain?" asks Neal.

"I guess it can work both ways, but I am glad for the consideration we are getting, and I'm proud to be half-way clean. Aren't you?"

"Yes sir!" smiles Neal.

The three men continue walking around the court-yard, as they have done every day, all the weeks they have been in this prison. They know the looks on all the guard's faces, and they know where each puddle of water will stand when it rains. They even know where the odd joints are, in the way the bricks are laid, where two different brick layers have brought the walls to join together.

"Yeah, it won't be long now Lieutenant, and we'll be getting out of here. They are treating us so good, they may even give us some bay rum, to splash on before they turn us out," states Gregory.

"Some what?"

"Some what, what?" inquires Gregory, not understanding Neal's question.

"Some what you said to splash on?" questions Neal.

"Oh, some bay rum. It's a good smelling perfume that gentlemen of leisure put on for the ladies," answers Gregory.

"Oh, I see," replies Neal.

"But you being a farm boy from Mississippi you wouldn't know the finer things that gentlemen do for their ladies," smirks Gregory, feeling good in the warm sunlight.

"Well of all the gall, you have gotta be a Yankee spy stuck here in the middle of all us Confederate officers," snaps Neal.

"Now, now Lieutenant, I was only kidd'n," laughs Gregory.

"Kidd'n my foot," growls Neal, as he starts for Gregory.

Gregory begins to run away laughing, and Neal stops his pursuit to laugh with him.

Laughing, Captain Watson says, "It's good to see you boys coming around so good. I hope everybody else is doing as well."

"We do too captain. I just wish they would improve on the food," states Neal.

"Well when the gardens start coming in, maybe they will," answers Watson.

"Sir, I don't think we'll be in here when the gardens start coming in," comments Neal.

"I hope you are right son. I believe I could walk home as skinny as I am, knowing that when I stopped walking, I'd be home," states Watson, wistfully.

"If they do let us out soon Lieutenant, you and I only have to make it to Union City, Tennessee. Then we can fatten you up for your trip on down to Raleigh, Mississippi," explains Gregory, "and I may even let us use some bay rum."

"Aw, ain't you so smart?" smiles Neal.

March 4th, 1865

President Lincoln is given the oath for a second term by the newly appointed Chief Justice, Salmon P. Chase. In his inaugural speech, Lincoln gives hope, and prays that the horrors of war will quickly pass away. He also vows to fight it to the end, however long it takes. With an eye to the future, the president gives the crowd his view of a proper peace.

"With malice toward none, with charity toward all, with firmness in the right; as God gives us wisdom to see the right, let us strive on to finish the work we are in; to bind up the nation's wounds and achieve a lasting peace among ourselves and with all nations."

March 6th, 1865

"Gregory, you awake?" asks Neal, as the early morning light begins to show across the sky, as seen through the bars of their window.

"Yeah Lieutenant, I'm awake."

"Good, I was feeling kinda, uh- alone."

"How's that?"

"Well when we get out of here, and from what Lincoln said, it won't be long, we'll be headed home."

"Yeah, but you're going home with me."

"Yeah, I know, but after a'while, I'll still have to go on back home and try to put my past together," sighs Neal.

"So?"

"I'm afraid of what I may find out."

"Why is that?"

"I don't know how to explain it, but I guess what I'm trying to say is, I'm afraid of finding out what I was."

"Don't be afraid, I can tell—"

"Let me finish Gregory. What if I was a coward in battle and ran, or what, what if—"

"Now that's enough of that kind of talk. I know that you were not a coward."

"How can you say that? You don't know for sure."

"Let's just say that I've studied all the facts that are available. From those that I read in Doctor Voge's notes, and what you have told me, the things you've remembered, it all lets me know that you are no coward."

"Tell me how you can be so sure."

"Let's see now, for one thing they don't promote men in ranks to officers, who are cowards. You keep ordering Ruben to go back, in your sleep, and most important, you were shot in the chest facing the Yankees, not in the back running from them. Now get this nonsense out of your head about being a coward or anything less than an honorable officer of the Confederate Army."

"Gregory, you'll never know just how much you've helped my feelings about myself. Thank you for standing by me, and most of all, for being my friend."

NEAL'S HOMECOMING

"Aw Lieutenant, it's just part of my job. Remember, I am your lawyer."

"Yeah, but—"

"Now stop your worrying and get some sleep. We may need our rest any day now, so it's best that we get as much of it as we can."

"Thanks again Gregory, I think I can rest now."

Neal closes his eyes in an attempt to get some more sleep. Gregory turns his back to his friend, and tries to figure out some way to open up the rest of his blocked memory. It has been some time now since any glimpse of the past has come to the lieutenant. Gregory knows he has got to keep his spirits up and not let the lieutenant get down and out. As he starts drifting back into restful sleep, his thoughts are of what horrible thing could have locked the mind of a man like this.

March 10th, 1865

General Bragg withdraws his troops back to Kinston, North Carolina. His forces are too weak to defeat or turn back the Federal Troops who are advancing westward from New Berne. The war is dragging on and the fighting is still severe. Men on both sides continue to die in a war that has already been decided.

March 13th, 1865

"Good morning Boys," greets Sergeant Monroe, as he unlocks the door and steps into Neal and Gregory's cell.

"Good morning Sergeant!" returns the two, as one.

"You boys know that I'm going to miss seeing the pair of you each morning when the war is over and they turn you out."

"I'll bet you will," laughs Gregory.

"Yeah, you'll be high-tailing it out of here, just like us won't you Sergeant?" asks Neal.

"Yes and no Lieutenant, you see I don't live far from here, and if there's fightin' in the West, they could send us out there."

"Aw Sergeant, they ain't gonna send a prison garrison into battle," grins Neal.

"I hope you are right Lieutenant, but with that General Bragg of yours grouping up with Johnston, that bunch could hold a large group of troops fightin' in the Carolinas for some time. I heard Lee is about whipped, and there is trouble west of the river here.

"Bragg? That name seems odd. Yeah, that's what Ruben said when we were assigned to him in Tennessee," laughs Neal. "I served under him!"

"He's causing trouble still Lieutenant," states the sergeant, as he leaves to open the other cells in the block.

"You were under Bragg?" questions Gregory.

"Yeah, I can remember being at Chattanooga with him I think that's where Ruben said that his name was odd, you know, Braxton Bragg."

"Lieutenant if you were with him at Chattanooga, you were at Chickamauga and on back to Atlanta. Boy, you have really seen some fightin!"

"Yeah, I guess so Gregory, but all I remember is Ruben being tickled by the name."

"That's aw'right. Remember the good and forget the bad," states Gregory, remembering what Doctor Voge warned about in his notes.

"Fine, let's go eat before it's all gone," replies Neal, getting up to lead the way.

With the warming of the weather and regular bathing twice each week, the men in the cells are beginning to feel like human beings again.

The month of March draws to a close with the Appomattox Campaign starting on March 29, 1865.

NEAL'S HOMECOMING

ROBERT E. LEE SURRENDERS

• • • • • • • • • • • • • • • • • •

April, 1865

The fighting around Appomattox is severe. Things move rapidly, and Lee's Army is trapped. To the person who was not in the fighting, the 9th of April, 1865, comes quickly and suddenly. General Robert E. Lee realizes that further resistance is futile. He orders a white flag of truce to be carried through the Union lines, with a request for a cease fire until he can work out terms of surrender with Grant.

After Lee and Grant have worked out the terms of surrender and Lee has signed it, Lee returns to his men on his faithful old horse, Traveller. Once he is back among his soldiers, he tells them, "Go to your homes and resume your occupations. Obey the laws and become as good a citizen as you were soldiers."

The news of Lee's surrender travels fast across both the North and the South. A lot a people think that the war is over, but this is a misconception. Johnston's Army and Taylor's Army have not yet surrendered. There is still some fighting in what is to become America's worst war.

April 10th, 1865

"Good morning Boys!" greets Sergeant Monroe, as he opens the door to Neal and Gregory's cell.

"Good morning Sergeant," reply the two.

"Great news this morning Boys! Lee has surrendered," announces Monroe.

The shock of surrender is sudden, though not unexpected by Neal and Gregory. The sober expressions on their faces as they look at each other, then back at the sergeant, register their mixed emotions.

"Come on Boys, it ain't that bad. We all knew it was a-comin' and now you two can go home," smiles Monroe.

"Yeah, you are right Sergeant, but it is still a disappointment to know that we lost," answers Gregory.

"It sure is Gregory, but at least now we can get on with our lives, or with finding our lives," replies Neal.

"Atta' boy Lieutenant," smiles Monroe, as he leaves to open the other cells.

"What now Gregory?"

"Let's go eat now, and when they let us out, we'll go home," smiles Gregory.

After the meal and kitchenry duty, Captain Watson, Gregory and Neal start walking in the courtyard, as they think over the news they've just received this morning.

"We'll be getting out soon boys and getting back to our lives and homes," states Captain Watson.

"Yeah, and the lieutenant will get all of his memory back, once he gets back to his home and family," says Gregory, hoping that it will happen this way.

"I suppose so, but don't this whole thing make you wonder if it was worth it?" asks Neal.

"What do you mean, Lieutenant?" questions Watson.

"The war Sir. Was it worth it?"

"Son, that will be the question that will be asked for the next hundred and fifty years. To try and answer the question for you, I'd have to say it was according to which side one fought on. The North will always say yes, and the South will always be looking for the answer," explains Watson.

"In other words we'll never have a satisfying answer," agrees Gregory.

When the men are gathered to march back to their cells, those who fought with Lee are ordered to stand fast, while the others are marched back to the cells. As Neal enters his cell alone, he wonders what the separation is all about.

It's not long before Gregory comes walking in through the open door of their cell, with Sergeant Monroe not far behind. The sergeant is pulling the doors of the cells shut, and locking them, as he goes on down the block.

"Just what was that all about Gregory? Why did they keep the ones that fought with Lee outside, and send us in?"

"Lieutenant, they feel that the ones who served with Lee, have also surrendered with him. Therefore, they are allowing us to be paroled tomorrow."

"That's good Gregory! You can be home in less than a week, can't you?"

"Yeah," answers Gregory, dropping his head.

"What's the matter? Don't you want out'a here, and to get to go home?"

"Yeah, but since we're friends, I'm gonna tell 'em to keep me here with you, then I'll leave when you leave."

"Gregory, I like what you're saying about us being friends, but you will do no such thing as to tell 'em you're staying until I'm paroled."

"And just why not? It won't be long till the rest of 'em surrender."

"I thought you was my lawyer! Think now, we'll be getting out soon enough anyway, and if ya'll go on now; there will be more food for the rest of us. Besides, I always wanted a room all by myself anyway," laughs Neal.

"You probably do at that," agrees Gregory.

"All you have to do is tell me how to get to Union City, and when I get out, I'll come on down there. You and your folks will have reunited, and had a chance to catch up on your visiting, and you can be expecting me."

"And you call me the smart one. Look who is so smart now," grins Gregory.

"Not smart, just hungry," laughs Neal, knowing that Gregory really does want to get out of prison, and that he really needs to go on home.

April 11th, 1865

The day begins the same as all the rest, with Sergeant Monroe opening the doors for the morning meal.

"Lieutenant, we are going to be leaving after breakfast, is there anything of mine that you want to keep?"

"No Gregory, I'm fine."

"Well here are the notes that I've kept on your condition and the progress we've made while we've been together. Also, Doctor Voge's notes are all here."

"Gregory, you keep all of those, since I wouldn't know what to do with them anyway."

"If you say so. We can renew them when you get to my house in Tennessee," answers Gregory, as he finishes packing his things. He puts the notes back into the bundle of clothing he is tying up to carry with him.

"Now let's go eat. This will be our last time to leave this cell together. After we eat breakfast, Lee's bunch is being paroled."

"Let's go then," agrees Neal.

The men go out to the court-yard and line up for the stew. Then after the meal, when the dishes are washed, Lee's officers are pulled away from the rest of the group. They are carried through the gate which they came in a few months ago. As they leave, they sign papers at a desk, and take folded copies with them. Then they march out the gate, and they're on their way home.

Neal watches as Gregory goes up the line of men until it's his turn to fill in the papers. When he finishes his papers, he stands straight and looks for Neal. When he sees him, he waves real big and yells, "You remember how to get to my house?"

Waving in return, Neal nods his head, "Yes." Gregory then goes out the gate.

Neal turns and starts walking the court-yard by himself. Even though there are other men in the yard, Neal misses the company of his friend. He feels so alone, now that Gregory has gone and is out of his sight. This feeling of loneliness is compounded when he returns to the cell which he has shared with Gregory since they were brought to this place.

"Boy quit acting like a scared child. You are a grown man now, and you'll be getting out of this cell before long," says Neal out loud to himself. With that thought, he smiles and thinks, "Oh ain't you the smart one?"

NEAL'S HOMECOMING

April 12th, 1864

A formal surrender ceremony takes place at Appomattox Court House. General Lee and Grant do not attend. Formalities are not necessary, when so much pain has been endured. "Good morning Lieutenant," greets Sergeant Monroe cheerfully, as he opens the door to Neal's cell.

"Good morning," answers Neal, rolling over on his bunk and stretching. "What's for breakfast?"

"If you don't know by now son, I ain't gonna' tell you," laughs Monroe. "Yeah, I got a purtty good guess as to what it is. Have you heard any more news about the war?"

"Yeah. Johnston's army is still fighting."

"I guess that it'll take a while longer then."

"I suppose so Son. This war shor'ley is dying hard."

"It's gonna get better, let's go eat," smiles Neal.

"What's gonna get better, the war?"

"No Sergeant," laughs Neal. "The food."

April 13th, 1865

The draft is halted and the requisitions of war supplies are reduced by the President of the United States. The order is received and carried out by a nation that is ready and eager to put the war behind it and go on with life. Sherman occupies Raleigh, the capitol of North Carolina, on his way to Greensboro.

Neal is walking in the yard after his afternoon meal when Sergeant Monroe comes up to him. "Lieutenant, there is so much going on since Lee's surrendered."

"Really, what's going on now?"

"For one thing, Lincoln has stopped the draft."

"The draft?"

"You know, taking men into the army."

"Oh."

"You don't seem too excited."

"He's not gonna conscript me anyway Sergeant," smiles Neal.

"Son, I'm serious. This means that the president thinks that there are enough men in the army. Therefore, he must think the war is over, or that the rest of the South will give up soon."

"I see what you mean Sergeant, so when do I get out of here?"

"Oh, that I don't really know, but probably when Johnston gives up," answers Monroe.

"Yeah, that's about what I figured."

"Now, don't be so down. It's got better ain't it? Even the stew has got thicker ain't it?" grins Monroe.

"You're right, the stew is better and this warm weather helps make the body feel real good," grins Neal. "Have you heard any news from your son?"

"No, we ain't heard nothing. I shore hope he'll come back home when it's all over."

"He will, you'll see. It's gonna take some time for this war to get it's wounds healed and forgotten."

"I hope you are right Lieutenant, but it may be that all the wounds don't get healed, and I'm mighty afraid they won't ever all be forgotten."

April 14th, 1865

The men who are still being held in cells at Rock Island, have high hopes of going home soon.

President Lincoln confers with his cabinet, and then with General Grant. After the busy day, Lincoln attends the play, "Our American Cousin," at Ford's Theater. He is accompanied by his wife and a senator's daughter, Clara Harris, and her fiancee, Major Henry Rathbone.

About 10:00 in the evening, an actor by the name of John Wilkes Booth, makes his way up to the president's box. After entering through the door in the rear of the box, Booth walks up behind the president and shoots him behind the left ear. He then stabs Major Rathbone, and jumps from the box to the stage floor, yelling, according to some witnesses, "Sic semper tyrannus!" (Thus be it ever to tyrants.) Booth then exits from the stage and rides off on a horse.

The news of the president being shot travels like the wind to all parts of the country. The president dies nine and one-half hours later in a house across the street from the theater.

April 15th, 1865

Robert Lincoln, son of the president, Senator Charles Sumner, Secretary Stanton, and many others are at the president's side at his death.

Andrew Johnson takes the oath at 11:00 a.m. that morning, and takes over the office, as president.

Sergeant Monroe opens the door to Neal's cell at one-thirty in the afternoon.

"Sergeant, you are a little early for the afternoon meal aren't you? Are the powers up high going to let us poor Rebel rabble, out and bid us a fond farewell journey home?" grins Neal, picking at his friend.

"No," answers Monroe, as he walks into the cell and sits on the vacant bunk across from Neal.

Sensing something to be wrong, Neal asks, "Sergeant, what's the matter? What's wrong?"

Knowing that Neal is sincere in his questions, he begins to answer him with tears forming in his eyes. "It's the president. He's been killed."

"President? Which one?"

"President Lincoln was shot in the back last night at a play, and he died this morning."

"Now who would have done a cowardly thing like that?"

"A sorry man called John Wilkes Booth, or so the witnesses report."

"Heck Sergeant, I'm sorry. My so called country is dying and won't need a president much longer. Lincoln has seen his dream come true, and now with an opportunity to pull the country back together in his second term, a sorry coward does this from his backside. I'd even bet you the man wouldn't take up arms on either side, north or south, like men do."

"I don't know about that Son, but he did take up arms against us all."

"He surely did that. Lincoln wanted to heal the nation, we don't know what's in store now."

"You're right Son, and I'm mighty afraid that it will be even worse on the South, now after this."

NEAL'S HOMECOMING

"You are probably right Sergeant, and after this they'll never let us out of jail."

"Yeah, you'll get out, but it may be longer in coming."

April 17th, 1865

General Sherman and General Johnston meet at Durham Station, North Carolina to discuss peace. The two men look beyond the surrender of Johnston's army to lasting peace between the North and the South.

April 18th, 1865

Sherman and Johnston meet again to discuss peace, and an agreement is reached and signed by the two generals. It not only calls for the end of fighting, but promises a general amnesty for all Southerners. Also it pledges the Federal Government to recognize all the State Governments of the South, as soon as their officers take an oath of allegiance to the United States. Both men realize that the agreement will have to be approved by the two governments.

The Federal Government is very critical of Sherman and rejects the terms of the agreement. Some in the South want to keep fighting a partisan war or guerrilla war. General Lee writes Jefferson Davis opposing such a war, and asks that an end to all fighting be brought about. General Johnston is in agreement with General Lee. One may wonder how the Federal Government would have received Sherman's plan, had President Lincoln not been assassinated.

April 26th, 1865

Federal troops that have been following Booth for eleven days have surrounded him and a companion at the Garrett barn. The troopers call out to the two fugitives to surrender and come out in the open. Booth refuses, but his companion does come out, to be taken into custody by the troopers. After this, the soldiers set fire to the barn, and as it begins to burn, a shot is heard. Booth is dragged from the burning barn, mortally wounded. He dies a short time later. Whether the shot was fired by one of the soldiers, or by Booth himself, will never be completely settled. The body of Booth, is carried back to Washington for an autopsy and burial at Arsenal Penitentiary.

On the same day that the capture of Booth takes place, General Johnston surrenders his army of nearly thirty thousand men to General Sherman, under virtually the same terms that General Lee surrendered to Grant.

NEAL HEADS SOUTH

. . . .

April 27th, 1865

"Good morning Lieutenant," says Sergeant Monroe, as he opens the door to Neal's cell.

"Good morning Sergeant," answers Neal, as he does his usual roll and stretch before getting out of his bunk.

"You better get your things in order today Boy."

"You mean we're finally getting out Sergeant?"

"Yeah Son, you are. Johnston gave up yesterday and they want us to empty the cells, as fast as we can."

"Do tell!" answers Neal as he jumps up and starts putting his things together.

Sergeant Monroe goes on down the hall opening doors and giving the good news to the other prisoners.

After breakfast, the men wash the dishes and are sent back to their cells. They are to clean the cells out, and gather their belongings. Once this is completed, they are mustered in the all too familiar court-yard. There a line is formed headed toward the gate that they came in, what seems so long ago. Neal falls to the rear of the line and drops out, to go over where Sergeant Monroe is standing.

"Sergeant Monroe, I want to thank you for all the help you have given me."

"Aw' Lieutenant, I tried to help all you boys."

"I know that Sergeant, and I just want to say thank you and I hope your son gets home aw'right."

"Well thank you Lieutenant," answers the big sergeant with a tear coming to his eyes, "I do too. Now you better get in line, if you want to get out of this place."

"Yes Sir Sergeant," smiles Neal, "But I'll come back here some day, to see you again."

"That's a deal Boy, I live ten miles south of here, on the river. I'll be looking for you. Now git!"

When Neal has said his farewell to Sergeant Monroe, he goes back to the line of men and follows it up to the table.

"Name?" Comes the question from a Union Officer, behind the table.

"P.W. 44, Lieutenant Confederate Infantry," answers Neal.

"What's your name?"

"I don't know."

Sergeant Monroe hears the discussion, walks up to the table and gives the officer an explanation about Neal.

"Well P.W. 44, sign here and be off with you," orders the officer.

"Yes Sir," answers Neal as he signs the papers, P.W. 44, and turns to Sergeant Monroe, with a smile, saying, "Thanks again Sergeant, I'll see you again some day."

"Be careful Son," adds Monroe, as Neal turns and walks out into a new world, a free man with only parts of his past as a reminder as to who he is.

The weather is perfect. It's in the low seventies, the sky is a clear blue, and spring is showing new life all over. The flowers and dogwoods are in full bloom, as Neal heads away from the prison. Starting south to Union City, his thoughts are of regaining his past, and going on with the future. After a little while, he overtakes a group of men from the prison and as they walk on together, the people along the wayside yell obscenities at them. Some of them are yelling for them to get back south, where they belong, while others are blaming them for the death of Lincoln.

When they leave the city of Rock Island, and get into the countryside, the wrath of the farm people is just as harsh. It is decided among the group, that if they broke up, it would not call too much attention to themselves. This they do about mid-day, with each soldier picking and choosing his way home by himself.

Once Neal is by himself, he figures that walking south has got to be a fool-hardy way to get there, with the father of waters just a mile or so to his right. When everyone else is out of sight, Neal heads toward the Mississippi River. His plan is to get to the first boat landing that he can find, and try to get a ride south on a boat of some sort.

NEAL'S HOMECOMING

Neal is not the only one who feels that a boat will be the easiest and fastest way to get home. A river boat by the name of the Sultana, is working it's way north, with some two thousand Union soldiers on board, who have just been released from prison camps in the South. The boat catches fire after one of it's boilers explodes, claiming at least twelve hundred and thirty-eight lives of men who were anxious to get home.

Neal makes it to Andalusia, about mid-afternoon. He finds his way to the docks, in hopes of catching a ride south. As he walks up to the dock, he sees two young boys with a small boat. "Hey Boys, where ya'll headed?" asks Neal with a smile.

"South, but it ain't none of your business Reb," answers the youngest boy of about eleven or twelve.

"You got me all wrong Boy. I ain't no reb anymore. Ya'll done whupped the daylights out of us and all I want to do is go back home," explains Neal.

"That so?" questions the youngest.

"Aw hush Tom, can't you see, this man must have just got out of jail up at Rock Island."

"So what if he did Pete?"

"We got'ta get this boat back home before dark," explains Pete, the oldest of the two boys, about thirteen or fourteen, "And if he wants to ride and paddle for us, we'll let him."

"That's a good i'dey Pete, why not? Get in Mister, you get to paddle."

"Much oblige Boys," answers Neal, as he gets into the middle of the boat and takes up both oars, "Where we headed Boys?"

"South Mister, the same way you want to go," answers Pete.

Neal pushes the boat out from the bank and pulls on the oars. When the boat gets out in the main stream, the current picks it up, and Neal is able to keep it moving at a good clip of about five miles an hour.

"You boys never did say how far we're going," states Neal, as he pulls on the oars.

"New Boston Mister. If you can keep this pace, we should get their about dark or a little after," answers Pete.

"I'll do my best Son," answers Neal.

After about seven hours and that many blisters, Neal pulls the boat up to the dock at New Boston. As Pete and Tom tie the boat up, Neal gets out and thanks the two boys, then starts to move on.

"Hey Mister, thank your for the help," yells Tom "Where you headed now?'

"Oh, I'll find a place to sleep and try to catch another ride tomorrow."

"What'cha gonna do for supper?" asks Pete.

"Go without I guess."

"Well here, take this, we don't want it no way," offers Pete, as he tosses a sack of food to Neal.

"Thanks again Son," says Neal as he moves off into the dark.

Once Neal finds a place to stretch out under a shed close to the docks, he puts his hand into the bag. He is surprised when he pulls out three cold biscuits and two baked sweet potatoes. After chewing his first food in quite awhile, he curls up and goes to sleep.

April 28th, 1865

The special train, carrying Lincoln's corpse, reaches Cleveland, Ohio. While it rests in Cleveland, fifty some odd thousand people, view the dead president's body.

As the sun comes up on Neal's second day of freedom, the work on the river starts early. New Boston is no different than any other river town on the Mississippi.

"Hey you! Wake up! What the dickens are you doing sleeping in my shed for any how?" asks an elderly man of about sixty, in the early morning light."

Jumping to his feet, Neal answers, "Huh? Sir I got in here after dark last night! I got a ride down river with two boys, so I 'jes stretched out here for the night. I'll be on my way now."

"Hold up just a minute there Boy! You one of them Rebs they turned out of prison up at Rock Island, ain't 'cha?"

"Yes Sir, I am."

"What's yor' name Boy?"

"Uh, P.W. Uh, Paul Wood Sir."

"Paul Wood, huh? Where you from Boy?"

"Uh, Raleigh, Mississippi Sir." answers a scared Neal.

"Well don't be so nervous Boy, I ain't a-gonna hurt ya'cha none."

"Thank you Sir, that's mighty kind of you."

"My name is Dan Ponder," smiles the older man.

"Mighty glad to make your acquaintance Mr. Ponder."

"What's yor' intentions on gettin' home Boy?"

"I thought I'd work my way down this here river until I can get off in Mississippi, Mr. Ponder," answers Neal, with a smile.

"Sounds like a good idea Boy, I wish I was a-goin with ya. I've been all over Boy. You been many places?"

"No Sir."

"Well, I've been out in Indian Territory in Oklahoma and Arkansas. I've even been in Texas."

"Don't say!"

"Yeah, I wish I was a-goin' with you, but that's no never mind. Let's go get the wife to fix ya' some breakfast, then I'll help you catch a boat south."

"Yes Sir, thank you Sir," grins a happier Neal, as the two of them start for the Ponder's home.

Once they are in the house, Neal is shown kind hospitality, and is served a good meal by the older couple. After the meal, Dan takes Neal back to his shop and tells him that a steamer will be coming through sometime today. This boat will be headed south to St. Louis to get some captured cotton, and he should be able to get a ride on it, if he's willing to work.

"Yes Sir, I'm willing to work."

"I figured you might be willing Paul," smiles the old man, with a twinkle in his eye.

Dan sees the boat easing down the river and carries Neal out to meet it in a row boat. When they get out to the boat, he introduces Neal (Paul Wood), to the boat's captain and explains Neal's predicament. The captain takes him on, just to cook and keep the boat clean.

"Thank you Mr. Ponder, and you thank your wife for that good breakfast she fixed for me," yells Neal, as Mr. Ponder pushes off, going back to his shop.

Neal finds that cooking for the crew, and keeping the galley clean, is not that hard a job for him. His biscuits and hoe-cakes are well received by the men, and the captain tries to talk him into staying on the boat.

"Thank you Captain, for the offer. You see, I just want to get back home," explains Neal, when he's talking to the captain in the wheel house, as the old steamer pushes on down the river.

"The men really like your cooking you know, and we'll be making this trip ever two weeks."

"Sounds good Sir, but the men have just had one meal of my cooking, and that's about all I can cook," laughs Neal. He looks off to the side of the big river at the beautiful countryside and wonders about many things, as the afternoon wears on.

"Well we'll see, it won't be long before you'll have to cook supper. We'll tie up in Burlington for a short stay and check the river on south of here."

About 4:00, in the afternoon, the old Cordova pulls into Burlington. Once the boat is tied up, the captain goes to the dock office and telegraphs for news on the river, checking the movement of sandbars and other conditions that can affect navigation.

After about forty-five minutes in the office marking charts and telegrams, he returns to his boat. He finds that Neal is still waiting in the wheel house for his return. Also, a few of the other men and officers have gathered there to find out what he has learned, when he gets back from the dock office.

"Men, there has been an awful tragedy down stream. The Sultana was coming up river, with a load of soldiers on board when one of it's boilers blowed up and killed a whole lot of people."

"Gosh Captain, I used to be on the Sultana!" exclaims the first mate.

"Yeah Jake, I knew you were, but she's gone now, and a lott'a men with her," answers the captain. He continues, "They said all the soldiers had just gotten out of Confederate prisons and were going home."

"Like me, huh Captain?" questions Neal.

"Yeah Paul, like you. Well there ain't nothing we can do about it now. The sand bars have not shifted any since our last trip, so untie the boat men, we're gonna push off," orders the captain.

The men jump to the business of loosening the lines and shoving off.

Neal goes back to the galley to start cooking supper, and the Cordova starts stirring up mud in the shallow water, as it heads for mid-stream. Once they are in mid-stream, the men can relax and take it easy.

Neal has supper well under way in a short time, cooking salt pork, biscuits and gravy for the hungry crew. Just before he's ready to call supper time, the captain has his first mate take the wheel, and he goes to the galley door.

"Hey Paul, how you doing?" he questions Neal.

"Tolerable well Captain, tell the men to come 'n' get it."

The crew comes in for their supper, and make short order of the meal Neal has prepared for them.

As the darkness of night comes on the river, lamps are lit and markers are posted to yell instructions to the wheel house. Lines with weights are thrown to mark depth of water, and shouts of "Mark" and "Twain," are heard throughout the night.

AIDED BY TWO WOMEN

• • • • • • • • • • • • • • • • •

May 3rd, 1865

Lincoln's special train reaches Springfield, Illinois on the same day that the Cordova pulls into St. Louis.

"Paul, I really wish you would stay on board as our cook," states the Cordova's captain.

"I'm much obliged to you Sir, for helping me get this far south, but I gotta be goin' home, so I can't stay on and work," replies a thoughtful Neal.

"Well, it didn't hurt to try one more time to get you to stay," smiles the captain. "Now if you'll wait a bit, I'll help you find passage on another boat going further south."

"You will?"

"Yeah, it's the least I can do for you."

"Well thanks again, Sir," smiles Neal, pleased at this offer of help from the captain.

The Cordova's captain helps Neal find work on another boat which is headed to Cape Girardeau. After two days of doing the same thing he had been doing on the Cordova, Neal arrives at Cape Girardeau, on the 5th of May. Here he learns that the traffic south has been slowed, because of the boat that blew up just north of Memphis, and killed so many soldiers.

With the holding up of boats, Neal finds out that it is only sixty or seventy miles to Union City, Tennessee across land. Thus, he decides to head out southeast on foot. He makes his way to Thebes by dark on the 5th, and lies down by the road to rest for the night.

May 6th, 1865

Neal is up early, walking toward Olive Branch, as the sun is coming up on the horizon. About 8:30 or 9:00, he passes through

Olive Branch. Unknown to him, he catches the eye of a few young roughens who realize that Neal is an ex-confederate soldier passing through their town. Since this is southern Illinois, sentiments can run high one way or the other. These boys just happen to be pro Union and they are angry about Lincoln's death, so they decide to take it out on Neal.

Neal is making good time southeast of Olive Branch, when he hears the footsteps and voices of a number of people behind him. He turns and sees four half-grown boys of about fourteen or fifteen, walking his way. Neal keeps walking but since he would like to have some company, he slows down a bit to let the boys overtake him. He listens to their footsteps and voices as they grow closer. When they are about twenty yards behind him, he stops and turns to greet the four boys.

"Hey boys," starts Neal, as he turns to face them. To his surprise, the four boys begin a full charge, running at him, with no sign of friendliness on their faces. Neal manages to sidestep the first boy, but the other three take him to the ground.

"You dirty Reb!" shouts one of the boys, as he hits Neal in the face. The other three join hitting and kicking Neal from the top of his head to the groin area. After several minutes of repeated blows by the four boys, using both fists and feet in their attack on Neal, they hear a wagon coming on the road from the northwest.

"Come on boys, I hear a wagon and team headed this way," snaps one of the young hoodlums.

"Yeah, let's get out of here before we get caught. We might have killed this here Reb," says another one of the boys, as all four of them jump up and run off into the woods.

Neal passes out from the beating he has taken, as the boys disappear into the wooded area along the roadside.

The wagon pulled by a pair of gray mules, with a woman and her daughter in it, rolls up where Neal is lying.

"Mickey! Look at that poor man!" says Rebecca Wilson, a thirty four year old blond, blue eyed, fair complected woman, as she slows the team down. "What do you think we should do?"

"You know what we should do mother," answers her daughter Mickey, a tall brown eyed, brunette. "The bible tells us of the good Samaritan, and even though he is a Rebel, we should help him."

Rebecca stops the team and the two women get down off the wagon and go to Neal. Once they reach him, they turn him over and look into the face of the badly beaten man.

"Mickey, help me get him into the wagon. We'll get him home and dress these wounds," orders Rebecca.

"Yes Ma'am!"

Once the struggle of loading the unconscious man is over, Rebecca challenges the pair of mules and the wagon begins to roll. What had started out as a beautiful day, has been ruined by hate and anger.

The wagon rolls on down the road with Neal drifting in and out of consciousness. He feels the movement of the wagon, and the pain that shoots over most of his body, in the moments he is awake, as they jolt along on the rough country road. After four or five miles are covered, Rebecca turns the team down a road to the left, which leads into what is called, Canny Community.

About forty-five minutes, and four miles further down the road, she pulls the team to a stop at the Wilson Farm. She and Mickey go into the house and bring medical supplies and two quilts out to the wagon. Then Mickey goes into the barn and makes a pallet on the soft hay in the first stable, with the two quilts from the wagon. When she finishes, she returns to the wagon and helps her mother pick the unconscious man up, and they carry him into the barn. There they lay him on the bed Mickey has prepared for him.

Once Neal is on the pallet, Rebecca goes back to the wagon and gets the bandages and ointments. When she comes back into the barn, she sees Neal moving, as he begins to regain consciousness. When she starts cleaning and closing the open wounds and washing his face, he flinches with pain.

"Ouch!"

"That hurt young man?" asks Rebecca, a look of concern showing on her face.

"Yes Ma'am."

"Well, we just got to get you cleaned up, so these cuts and bruises can heal. I'm sorry it hurts, but it's gotta be done, can you understand that?" Rebecca asks, pausing for a moment, in her doctoring, as she waits for Neal's response.

"Yes Ma'am, it don't hurt that bad."

"Well you just hush now while I doctor on you," orders Rebecca, looking into Neal's eyes and seeing the pain he is trying to hide. "Now, when we get you all fixed up, you can tell us about what happened to you, and who you are."

"Yes Ma'am," answers Neal, looking into the face of a woman, that he feels he has known some place before.

While Rebecca continues to work, taking care of Neal's wounds, he looks at the young girl standing at his feet. She is a natural beauty with big brown eyes. Then she notices that Neal is looking at her, and smiles, showing her pretty white teeth. Blushing ever so slightly, she looks away, turning her attention back to his wounds, and her mother's progress in caring for them.

"Turn your head son, so I can get to the other side," instructs Rebecca, as she rinses out the bloody cloth she has been using for cleaning the wounds. A few minutes later, Neal's face is bandaged up and the cuts pulled back together.

"Roll over on your stomach now, and let me see to the cuts on the back of your head," explains Rebecca.

"Ouch! This is going to be harder than I thought," exclaims Neal, as he holds the left side of his chest.

"You may have some broken ribs boy. Let's pull your shirt off, so I can examine you," says Rebecca, while she starts unbuttoning Neal's shirt. As she opens the blouse, the scars of the bullet he took at Franklin shows still fresh and pink on his chest.

"My gosh son, what has happened to you?" asks Rebecca, shocked by what she sees.

Hearing the question, Mickey steps up, so she can see why her mother is asking this question and sounding as if she's surprised by something she has just uncovered.

"I was shot at the battle of Franklin Ma'am."

"You are one lucky boy!" state's Rebecca, as she starts checking his ribs on the left side. She brings her hand slowly down the ribs one at a time, looking into Neal's eyes for any sign of pain. When her hand reaches the fourth rib, he flinches with pain. "That one's broken," explains Rebecca. As she continues on down the rib cage, she finds three more that show signs of being broken.

After wrapping Neal up tightly, to hold the ribs in tact, Rebecca backs up a bit and Neal lies back down on the pallet.

"Now Son, what's your name?" asks Rebecca, as she puts away her medical supplies.

"My name, uh, uh, well Ma'am, I really don't know."

"You don't know?" questions Mickey, puzzled at Neal's answer.

"That's right. You see, I have amnesia."

"Amnesia? What is that?" Asks Rebecca, never having heard this word before.

"It's an illness where a'body loses their memory," answers Neal.

"You wouldn't put me on, now would you Boy?" questions Rebecca, showing a hint of sternness in her voice.

"No Ma'am. All I can tell you is the facts that a Doctor Voge, and a friend of mine, Gregory Bailey, come up with, from what they could find out about me. They say that I was a Lieutenant in the Confederate Infantry, and that I was wounded and captured at Franklin, Tennessee. I woke up in a Union Hospital in Nashville, and after I stayed a few weeks there, I was moved to Rock Island, Illinois. I met Gregory on the train to the prison. Doctor Voge had been keeping notes on me at the hospital, so when Gregory read the notes on the train, he started keeping notes on me from there on. He's going to become a lawyer, and said it would be good practice for him to fig'er out who I was. I'm from Mississippi. Raleigh, I think. I've got a brother named Ruben, and my mother's name is Lilly and she looks a-lot like you. We've got two mules, named Hob and Nob. My number at prison was P.W. 44, but everybody called me Lieutenant. When I left the prison camp and met up with people in passing, I told them my name was Paul Wood. I got that from the P.W. No Ma'am, I would not put you and your daughter on a-tall," declares Neal, with all seriousness.

"Well now that's interesting," smiles Rebecca, "And you are headed home now?"

"Well, no ma'am, I'm a'headed to Union City, Tennessee. I want to get back with Gregory, on a'count of that's where he lives, and he has all the notes that he and Doctor Voge made on me."

"Why weren't you two traveling together?" questions a bright Mickey.

"Gregory got out of jail about three weeks before me, on a'count of he was under Lee, and Lee surrendered, so they turned all the ones that were under him out. I was under Johnston, and when he gave up, they let the rest of us go."

"Oh, I understand now," smiles Mickey.

"Lieutenant, I know you're hungry, so you just rest while Mickey and me go an' fix us some victuals."

"I surely will Mrs. uh-"

"Wilson," smiles Rebecca.

"If it ain't prying Ma'am, may I ask where your man is?" questions Neal, as the two women prepare to leave.

"He has been over in the Carolinas in the Union army. Now that your General Johnston has surrendered, I feel sure he and some of the other men from this area are on their way home," smiles Rebecca, with relief at the war being over for her husband, Clyde.

"That's good to know Ma'am," states Neal, as the women leave the stable of hay, to fix some food.

As the women are walking back to the house, "Mother, what do you think the lieutenant will look like when all of them cuts, scrapes and bruises heal up?" asks Mickey, with a strange grin on her lips.

"Oh, he'll be fine girl, why?"

"Because he's got the nicest eyes I've ever seen," answers Mickey, shyly.

"Aw girl, there's a lot more men in the world than him," instructs Rebecca.

Back in the barn, Neal is thinking "Ole Gregory said that this was gonna be a better year than last year. A-side from getting out of jail, and the war ending, I've just met the best looking girl I've ever seen. Now why did I go sayin' that to myself? For all I know I may be married, but Gregory didn't seem to think so. Anyhow, the folks back home think I'm dead anyway, so I could jes' stay up here and they wouldn't ever know any different. Now there I go thinking crazy, acting like this girl would take a-liking to me, she may not, so it must be the devil making me think these things."

After a little bit, Mickey brings a plate of food to Neal for supper. The plate has peas, cornbread, potatoes and some ham on it, and there's a cup of fresh milk to drink. Neal digs in with a hearty appetite. Very little is said while Neal eats, but some looking takes place between this couple and both of them wonder what the other is thinking.

After Neal has finished his meal, he says, "That was mighty fittin' Ma'am."

"Well thank you kindly Lieutenant, but you don't have to call me ma'am, my name is Mickey."

"I wish I could tell you mine, and maybe some day I can," smiles Neal, under all the bandages.

"I surely hope you will, I mean I hope that you can regain your memory.

"Thank you Mickey! If I can get back to Gregory, he'll help me to remember all of my past."

"Oh, I sure hope so."

"If he does, you'll be the first person I'll tell my name too."

"You mean it?" grins Mickey, sounding excited with the idea of being the first to hear this man's name.

"I surely do Mickey."

"Mickey! What's keeping you so long?" yells Rebecca, from the porch of the house.

"Coming Mother!" replies Mickey. 'Now Lieutenant, you remember what you promised."

"I will Mickey," smiles Neal, as Mickey takes the plate back to the house.

Once Mickey has gone, Neal lets his mind wander about this girl who he has just met. He wonders if she could possibly feel about him, the way he feels about her. As he lies there thinking about her, his pain and discomfort from he beating he suffered is almost forgotten.

It's not long before the chores are done, the sun is set, and Neal drifts off to sleep with Mickey still on his mind.

May 7th, 1865

Mickey is up early helping her mother get breakfast started. Once she has built the fire in the stove, Mickey gets her milk bucket and heads to the barn.

"You seem to be in a hurry to get out to the barn this morning," states her mother, with a smile as Mickey goes out the door.

"Could be Mother, could be," answers the young woman as she continues on toward the barn and the chore that is awaiting her.

Mickey eases into the barn and gets the feed for the cow as quietly as she can so as not to awaken Neal. Once the feed is in the trough, she opens the gate to let the cow into the hall of the barn. As quiet as she has been, the opening of the creaking door in the hall woke Neal, but he lies still on his pallet, as if he is asleep. Once Mickey starts milking the cow, she begins to sing softly, out of the habit of singing as she goes about her daily chores. The song she sings is "Amazing Grace" and when she has sung it through two times, her milking job is finished for the morning. Then she lets the cow out in the pasture and starts back down the hall, to go back to the house, thinking Neal is still sleeping.

"That was some pretty singing Mickey," says Neal, from his bed in the stable, as she passes by the door on her way down the hall.

"Oh, I'm sorry Lieutenant, I didn't mean to wake you. It's just a habit of mine, to sing while I'm milking. It seems to make the time pass faster, and the cow to give more milk."

"You didn't wake me, and I truly enjoyed the song," smiles Neal, looking up at Mickey as she stands in the door of the stable.

"I'm glad you did enjoy it, it's my very favorite hymn. Now you just rest easy and I'll be back in ah' little while with your breakfast."

"I'll just get up and come to the house."

"No you won't, now just stay put till I get back, understand?"

"Yes Ma'am," smiles Neal as Mickey starts for the house.

Once Mickey is back in the kitchen with the fresh milk, her mother asks, "What took you so long with the milking this morning Girl?"

"Aw Mother, I didn't take any longer than usual."

After the two women have eaten their meal, Mickey fixes Neal a plate of hash browns, eggs, streak-of-lean meat, biscuits and coffee, and puts it all on a platter to carry it out to him.

"Do you want me to take that food out to the lieutenant, Mickey?" asks Rebecca, in a kidding manner, as she smiles at her daughter.

"Oh, no Ma'am, I'll carry it out, if you have no objections," answers Mickey quickly, as she picks up the breakfast platter.

"No Darlin', I have no objections."

Mickey heads back to the barn at a fast walk and the creaking of the door announces her return to Neal. She steps into the stable and places the platter of food on the quilt beside him. She picks the cup of hot coffee up and holds it for him.

"I'll hold your coffee while you eat, so you won't turn it over," explains Mickey as she sits down on the edge of Neal's quilt.

"Thank you kindly Mickey, but you don't have to do that."

"I know I don't, but I want to."

"That's fine then," answers Neal smiling his approval to Mickey.

Neal eats some of his breakfast and reaches for the coffee. As he takes the cup, his fingers touch Mickey's hand and their eyes meet at the same time. Without a word being spoken, each one knows the thoughts that are racing through the other's mind. Both hearts are pounding and each one is aware that the same thing is happening within the heart of the other. Neal eats as slowly as he can, to make the moment last. He takes small sips of coffee so their hands will touch often, and the touching is equally pleasing to both parties as they sit together there on the quilt.

The contented silence is broken when Neal asks, "When do ya'll start planting around here?"

"What?"

"You know, when do ya'll plant your crops?"

"Oh, it's almost too late now. It needs to be going on right now, if anything is to be harvested, and that's why Papa is coming on home, so he can plant the crops. If he gets home real soon, maybe he can get the planting done and we'll be able to get them in, before fall kills them.

"Who do you mean we, you and your mother?"

"Yeah, Papa will still be in the army when he gets here and he may have to go back."

"Oh, I understand."

"Mickey what's keeping you?" yells Rebecca from the door of the house.

"Coming mother," answers Mickey in a loud voice. In a hushed voice, she speaks to Neal, "We'll talk more when I bring your dinner to you."

"I surely hope so," smiles Neal as he hands the cup back and holds her hand for a moment. Mickey takes the cup, picks up the platter, gets up from the pallet, and starts to leave the barn.

"I'm mighty glad that you feel that way," she smiles at Neal, with a blush tinting her face a rosy shade of pink.

"Mickey!"

"Coming Mother," answers Mickey, hurrying out of the stable, down the hall and back to the house.

The time drags on slowly for Neal, lying on his pallets in the barn, while the women do the chores around the house. "This has got to be the longest morning of my life," he says to himself. "I wish dinner would hurry up and get here. Aw hush boy, it's coming as fast as it can and you can't hurry it up none by wishing. Besides, that girl you've taken a fancy to, may not fancy you. Yes she does too. I just know it. How do you know it. I just do." Neal thinks on, asking and answering his own doubts and questions. "Oh, cause you are so smart or something? No! Well how? I don't really know. I guess I'll just have to ask her how she feels about me when she comes back out here at dinner."

Mickey and Rebecca are going about their chores when Mickey asks her mother if she thinks she should go out to the barn and check on the lieutenant.

"Well Girl, I don't rightly know if you should bother him or not."

"Mother, I won't bother him. If he's resting, I'll just come back here to the house."

"You must be taking a shine to that boy, and you don't know anything about him."

"I guess you're right Mother."

"You know I'm right, it's written all over your face."

"It is?"

"Yes Girl," smiles Rebecca. "You remind me of myself when I first saw your papa."

"I do?"

"Yes, and the only warning I can give you is, you'd better know all there is to know about this boy, or any other boy, before you go and give him your heart."

"Oh I will Mother," smiles Mickey.

NEAL'S HOMECOMING

"You can wait until you take his dinner out to him, and you two can talk more then," suggests Rebecca.

"Yes Ma'am, dinnertime will be here in a just a little while anyway," answers Mickey.

Neal is resting in the barn still very sore from the beating he took yesterday, when he sees Mickey coming off the porch with a platter in her hands.

Mickey walks at a quickened pace toward the barn, not knowing that Neal is watching her through the cracks in the front wall of the stable. When the door of the barn lets out its familiar creak, Neal says, "Come in, Mickey!"

"How did you know it was me?" questions Mickey as she brings the dinner she has prepared for him into the stable.

"Lucky guess," laughs Neal.

"You're feeling better, aren't you?"

"Yeah, I sure am, and it's all because of you and your mother, but mostly because of you."

"Now just what do you mean by that?" smiles Mickey.

"You know what I mean don't you?"

"No," grins Mickey. "You'll just have to tell me."

"Well I don't rightly know how to put it, but I find myself thinking about you all the time. I can't get you out of my mind."

"Oh Lieutenant, do you really?"

"Yes Mickey, I do."

"I do too, Lieutenant, think of you all the time that is, but you've got that memory loss problem."

"Yeah I know."

"Mother says I shouldn't give my heart to anybody that I don't know all about."

"How old are you Mickey?"

"Seventeen, why, what's that got to do with giving my heart to somebody?" asks Mickey, puzzled by Neal's question.

"Your mother is right," sighs Neal, laying back on the pallet, looking at the ceiling, with a very discouraged look on his face.

"How's that?" questions Mickey, sensing a change in Neal's mood.

"You're seventeen and a grown woman. I don't even know how old I am, or who I am."

Neal speaks as if these words, stating his mental condition, are very painful, especially now when it may stand between him and the girl he is beginning to care for, in a very special way.

"You said that, that Gregory whoever, was going to help you find your memory," reminds Mickey, hopefully.

"Yeah, I know, but what if I don't."

"I don't know, but it's awful scary."

"Doctor Voge told me that something real bad had to have happened, to make my brain forget the past. He also said that I would have to find something to make me truly want to remember."

"Well, have you found that something?"

"Yeah, you know I have, but it ain't fair to you."

"I'll be the judge as to what's fair and what ain't fair to me," smiles Mickey.

"I really got a reason to remember now," says Neal, as he reaches out his hand and takes Mickey's.

"I'll help you anyway I can," answers Mickey in a soft voice. Her hand, still in Neal's, is held just a bit tighter and they look deeply into one another's eyes.

The silent moment is shattered by Rebecca's voice calling from the porch, "Mickey! What's keeping you?"

"I'll be there directly Mother, he ain't finished eating yet."

Neal sits up quickly, disregarding the pain sudden movement causes, and starts eating the bread, dried peas and ham, as quickly as he can. Once he has finished the food, he downs the milk which has been kept cool in the well till mealtime.

"I'll try and slip back out to see you about mid-afternoon," whispers Mickey, as she gets up and leaves reluctantly.

When Mickey has gone back to the house, Neal begins thinking and talking to himself, while watching the house through the cracks in the wall of the stable. "Come on brain, start working. You've really got some good reason to call up the past now. I just hope my past ain't bad, when it comes back."

Mickey slips back out to see Neal about mid-afternoon, like she said she would. Rebecca sees her slipping out quietly and remembers happier days, when Clyde was home. She takes this quiet moment to bow her head and pray that he will get home safely.

Mickey stays with Neal for about forty-five minutes, and in these brief minutes spent gazing into each others eyes and holding hands, a mutual love is confirmed. There is also an understanding that Neal's past could halt any hopes for a future together. Neal makes plans to leave the next day, to move on south to Union City, where he hopes Gregory can help him more in regaining his memory.

"Mickey!" yells Rebecca, "What're you doing out there?"

"Moving hay for the animals Mother," answers Mickey as she gets up and reaches for the pitchfork. When her mother gets to the barn, Mickey is busy throwing hay out of Neal's stable, into the feed troughs.

"Come on Girl, I need you to help me fix supper," orders Rebecca.

Mickey leans the pitch-fork up in the corner and starts to the house with her mother.

"She'll be back in a little while to milk Lieutenant," says Rebecca, giving Neal an understanding smile, as they leave the barn.

"Thank you Ma'am." answers Neal, with a grin.

He leans back against the wall of the stable, feeling his whole well being much improved by the visit with Mickey. His ribs are still painfully sore, the scrapes and cuts have scabbed over and the groin area is turning black and blue, from the vicious kicks. He struggles to get up on his feet, and finds that when standing, the rush of blood downward, causes more pain in the lower parts of his body. He then eases back down on the quilts and focuses his attention to the cracks in the wall where he watches for Mickey's return. Time moves slowly for the love struck lieutenant, but it does move. After what seems like an eternity, Mickey appears on the porch with her bucket in hand and walking his way.

As she crosses the yard, she looks at the wall Neal rests behind and smiles. After taking a few more steps, she says in a voice loud enough for him to hear, "I sure feel as though some eyes are peering out of that wall at me."

When Mickey opens the door to the hall and starts in, Neal answers her with, "And what if there were no eyes peering at you?"

"There better have been some eyes looking for me, that is if the one who owns them wants to win my heart."

"Rest assured Girl that there were two eyes watching you all the way from the house," laughs Neal as he rolls back, flat on his back.

"Well now that's good, then I can go on with my chores and you can just rest for a while."

Mickey gets feed for the cow and lets her into the barn. As usual with the first streams of milk, she begins to sing. "Amazing grace how sweet the sound that-"

As she sings, Neal rolls his head toward the front wall and gazes through the cracks at the sun going down in the west. He thinks how sweet the sound of Mickey's voice is, and he prays to God that their future can be with one another.

As Neal enjoys the moment of peaceful thoughts, and the beauty of the sunset, he sees about a dozen mounted men armed to the teeth, walking their horses very slowly, into the Wilson's yard. The mounted men are wearing a mixture of Union and Confederate uniforms, as they quietly ease into the yard. The leader who is out in front of the men, motions for the last man in the group to go in to the barn, where the singing is coming from, while the other men continue to walk their horses toward the house.

Mickey is singing and does not hear the muffled steps of the horses as they approach the house, nor does she hear the one horse walk up to the door of the barn. Neal's heart begins to race because of who he thinks these men are, and what is about to happen.

Rebecca is alone in the house when she hears the soft sounds of horses walking in the yard. Looking out of her bedroom window, she sees the men and reacts by getting Clyde's old Greener from the corner of their bedroom. She rushes to the side of the kitchen door on the rear of the house. From here she can hear Mickey singing in the barn, and she sees a man starting to go in the hall door, where Mickey is milking the cow.

Neal struggles to his feet ignoring the terrible pain this effort causes, he goes for the pitchfork which is still in the corner of the stable where Mickey left it earlier. Just as he gets the pitchfork in his hand, he hears the hall door open slightly and Mickey still singing. He steps to the front side of the stable door as the renegade guerrilla starts down the hall, walking softly, as he attempts to ease up behind Mickey. He passes the door where Neal is standing without looking in, because his eyes are glued on the beautiful young girl who is singing and milking at the other end of the hall. He walks up to her back so as not to be noticed. When he has passed the front stable door Neal steps in behind him, stalking quietly, he holds the pitchfork ready to lunge into the man if it's necessary.

"What do you men want?" questions Rebecca in a loud voice, as she steps out on the porch to face the group with the old double barrel ready.

Hearing her mother's raised voice, Mickey stands and turns into the face of the intruder. In a flash, she is struck with the fist of the man's right hand and knocked up against the cow, then she crumples to the ground.

Neal is about eight feet behind the outlaw. He takes one big step and thrusts the prongs of the pitchfork up through the base of the man's skull and into his brain. The man flinches up on his toes as if he is hung in the air by the pitchfork, then falls to the ground kicking a few times, then he's still, dead all the time. Neal bends over and removes the two Confederate Colt-44's, that are carried in reverse holsters on the dead man's belt. The guns feel strangely familiar in his hands, as he rushes back down the hall to the door.

"I said what do you want Mister?" repeating her question, Rebecca draws the hammers back on her shotgun.

As Neal goes toward the door, the cow Mickey was milking, rushes out the opening and into the yard behind the horsemen. The men turn, distracted by the racket the scared cow makes, but once they see the cow, they burst into laughter.

"Mickey!" screams Rebecca.

"Shut up woman! That there cow should tell you what we're after," yells the leader, with a crude sort of laugh. "Now that ole double-barrel ain't gonna reach us at thirty steps, so why don't you just be obliging and give in?"

"That ole cow ought to be telling ya'll a different story," yells Neal as he brings the Colt-44 up in his right hand.

The startled men on horses swing around to see who is behind them, knowing that their comrade has come to no good in the barn. The man nearest Neal, tries to cross draw his pistol with his right hand, but as the gun comes out of the holster, the sound of Neal's pistol breaks the silence of dusk. The heavy lead ball from the 44 strikes the man under his right shoulder blade, going through his body and out the left side of his chest, exploding his heart on the way. Blood gushes from the dead man as he tumbles forward over the horse's head.

Rebecca joins in with the right barrel of the old Greener, throwing buck shot into the whole group. The horses are scared and begin rearing and bucking from the sting of the lead balls.

Neal works the hammer of the pistol in his right hand and fires again, striking a charging guerrilla in the chest, knocking him backwards off his horse. The horsemen who have weapons drawn, return fire at Neal, but their shots fly wildly because of the startled horses.

Rebecca fires the left barrel of the old shotgun into the group, hitting men and horses. Neal starts firing the gun in his right hand at any target, be it man or horse, as the guerrilla band hightails it out of the Wilson's yard. Neal saves the gun in his left hand, in case they decide to come back to finish what they started out to do. Rebecca drops the shotgun on the porch as she starts running to the barn.

Neal stands for a moment looking at the two dead men on the ground, not thirty feet from him, then he says out loud, "Oh Ruben, I hope you got back home safe."

Rebecca rushes past Neal into the barn not knowing what she may find there. First, she sees the dead man on the ground with the pitchfork in the back of his head. Then she sees Mickey lying not far away and it's too much for her. She drops to her knees in uncontrollable weeping, fearing the worst.

Neal hobbles past the crying Rebecca, saying, "She's awright Mrs. Wilson, she'll be just fine!" When he gets to Mickey he drops to his knees beside her, picks her up and wipes the hay off her face along with the blood that is coming from a cut lip. Mickey opens her eyes, hears her mother crying and starts to scream.

"It's fine, we are safe for now Mickey," states Neal, showing the control of a soldier who has been in many battles.

"Yeah, we're fine now, but what if they come back?" questions Rebecca, as she walks up to the couple, having regained her composure, and realizing that Mickey appears to be all right.

"We gotta be ready. Let's get the guns off them two dead ones outside, and we'll reload the ones we fired. Then if they come back, we'll be ready," orders Neal, taking command of the situation as he's done many times before.

Mickey gets up on her feet and dusts off her dress, then Rebecca walks toward the door which opens to the outside. When Mickey starts following her mother, Neal says, "Mickey, my name is Neal McNair."

"What did you say?" questions a shocked Mickey as she stops in mid-step and turns back toward Neal.

"I said, my name is Neal McNair."

"Oh Darlin!" exclaims Mickey as she rushes to Neal, throws her arms around him and kisses him on the lips.

Rebecca stops and looks back at the embracing couple. When they have moved apart enough to look into each others eyes for a brief moment, Mickey then turns to look at her mother and says, "Did you hear what the lieutenant just said?"

"No Girl, but I think we should take his advice and start preparing ourselves, just in case that gang comes back."

"Mother! He told me his name. He's got his memory back."

"My name is Neal McNair, Mrs. Wilson, and I'll tell the two of you all about myself later. Right now we do need to get ready for a counter attack, I mean, if that gang of outlaws wuz to turn and come back here."

The three of them walk out into the yard and Mickey gets the cow back into the barn. Neal and Rebecca drag the two dead men into the hall of the barn, and catch their horses that are standing up next to the house.

Neal takes all three of the dead men's pistols, belts, and cartridge boxes, and the one Springfield Rifle which is on the saddle ring of one of the horses. Once he has the guns, he reloads all the empty cylinders and checks the rifle to be sure it's ready to use. While he's doing this Rebecca gets the shotgun and reloads it. Mickey gets together some food and the three of them eat their supper quickly and their plans are made. The two women are to block the doors of the house, and Neal is going to stay outside in the barn. Mickey and Rebecca each have a pistol, the shotgun, and the rifle. Neal instructs them on how to load them, and then goes out to the barn with a pair of pistols on his hips.

Once he is in the barn, Neal pulls the door shut, and latches it. Then he goes to the front stable and stretches out on his pallet. There he watches through the cracks in the stable wall, as the last rays of the sun slip from sight. Looking at the house, Neal thinks how dark it is, and he realizes just how lucky they all are to be alive.

After about ten minutes have passed, Neal hears a team of horses pulling a wagon, coming hard toward the farm. Knowing that this can't be the outlaws returning, Neal gets his bruised and battered body up, and on his feet again. He moves out the door of the barn just as a wagon pulled by a pair of horses rushes into the Wilson's yard.

"Rebecca! Mickey! You two in the house?" yells a man, as he draws the team to a stop. Once the wagon stops rolling, he drops the lines and stands up, picking up a long gun which was lying beside him.

Rebecca and Mickey both answer the man, and come quickly out on the porch so their neighbor can see they are both there, and all right.

Neal moves up behind the wagon, and the man hearing his footsteps, turns with his gun ready.

"It's aw'right, Mr. Taylor, this is Neal McNair, and he's staying in our barn," explains Rebecca.

"Well what in thunder was all that shooting about?" questions Mr. Taylor. "I heard all that gunfire and before I got the team hitched up, a band of men come galloping by my place headed east. That's when I really knew something was wrong."

"Yes sir, you're surely right about something a-being wrong Mr. Taylor," explains Neal. As he tells Mr. Taylor what's happened here, Taylor gets down from his wagon, and it's obvious that he has a stiff leg. The two men move up on the porch where

Rebecca and Mickey are still standing, as they continue their conversation.

"You say they kept going east?" asks Neal.

"Yeah Son they did, and the way they wuz a-moving, I don't think they'll be coming back anytime soon," answers Taylor.

Mickey and Rebecca bring chairs out on the porch for the men, so they can all sit together and talk for a while. Neal tells them about himself and his war experience, and how he and the older boys were to care for Ruben. He feels this may be part of the reason he lost his memory. He also tells them that Mickey had made him want to remember so badly. When the shooting started, and he held the familiar weapons in his hands pulling the trigger, everything came back to him. He remembered the grave danger his baby brother was facing, when he came back to him in the trench. He knew also, that he was supposed to care for Ruben, and now his brother was facing almost sure death from the Yankee guns, while he lay helpless in the ditch. His mind just closed down at that time from an overload of pain, both physical and mental. Until just a few minutes ago, he was unable to recall more than an occasional glimpse into his past. Now he is Neal McNair, and he remembers everything. When he remembered the scene on the battlefield at Franklin, his first concern was for Ruben. He could only hope that he made it home, safely.

"So you are a Reb, huh Boy?" asks Taylor.

"Yes Sir."

"Boy you don't have to sir me, just call me Red," smiles Mr. Taylor.

"Well thank you Sir, I mean Red," answers Neal.

"Yeah Boy, that war was fought over a whole lotta nothing," comments Taylor.

"Were you a part of it Red?" questions a sincere Neal, with the ladies listening intently.

"Yeah Son I was. I was one of the lucky ones at Chickamauga, under Rosecrans. I got to come home with only a bum leg," explains Red Taylor.

"May be that both of us got lucky Red, I don't know if my brothers survived Franklin or not," adds Neal, very thoughtfully, as Taylor gets up and starts to his wagon.

NEAL'S HOMECOMING

"Those men won't be back tonight Boy," encourages Taylor.

"Well that's good to know," answers Neal. "Who do you think they were anyway?"

"My guess is they were the Quantrill guerrillas."

"Sorry bunch of men."

"Yeah, well good night all," bids Taylor, as he turns his team toward his farm two miles away.

"That's a good man," comments Neal, as the wagon rolls away.

"He surely is," agrees Rebecca.

The three of them visit for a little while and make plans for tomorrow, then Neal goes back to the barn for the night. He hopes to rest and heal in the night time hours. This day has been so eventful, giving him memories to reflect on, and a future to think about, he knows sleep will not come quickly.

Neal does have a hard time falling asleep. Now that he knows who he is, and remembers his past, he is worried about Milton and Ruben. Then later on into the night, he remembers that he is not married and that the future for him and Mickey can be very bright.

May 8th, 1865

The war is still going on and the Federals clash with the enemy near Readsville, Missouri. This may cause one to think with the larger portion of the Confederacy defeated, and already given up, that these clashes are with guerrilla bands like Quantrill.

Clyde Wilson is in charge of a platoon of men who are headed home on furlough. They have been released to go home and farm until the crops come in, and then they are to report back. At that time they will either be discharged, or continue with other duties in the Union Army.

Clyde is anxious to get home to his wife Rebecca, and daughter, Mickey. The men were loaned horses to travel home on, and to use until their crops are gathered. Then they are to report back with all their equipment, which includes the horses.

Neal is up early and meets Mickey on the porch, as she starts out of the house with his breakfast. He sits down to eat and she goes on to the barn to do her chores. Neal has covered the three dead outlaws with hay, so they are not exposed to Mickey when she goes inside the barn.

Once Mickey leaves the house, Rebecca comes out on the porch to sit with Neal, and they talk. She tells him that he had better be who he says that he is, and not be trying to pull some kind of trick on them. Neal assures Rebecca that he is telling the truth in every way, and that he plans to get on home to check on the well being of his family. While they are talking, the mail rider comes through on his horse, and gives Rebecca a letter from Clyde.

Mickey comes back from the barn with the fresh milk, and while Neal finishes his breakfast Rebecca reads the letter she just received, to them. Clyde writes that he will be home on the 15th of this month.

"Daddy will be home on the fifteenth," laughs Mickey, happy with the thought of her father being home again in just a few days.

"That's what the letter says Girl," smiles Rebecca.

"Neal you'll get to meet my father. Won't that be aw'right with you?" asks Mickey.

"Sure, but I think since I'm cured of my amnesia, and know that I have a family, I need to get on home and check on them," states Neal.

"Aw Neal, once you leave, you won't ever come back," complains Mickey, while Rebecca just watches, listens, and smiles.

"Oh that's one thing you can count on. I'll be back!" promises Neal.

"You could stay till the fifteen, just to meet my daddy and then go home," pleads Mickey.

"You sure could, and besides, if them outlaws come back, we really could use you," adds Rebecca.

"Aw'right, I'll stay till your pa gets here, and then I'll get on home. I'm still pretty stove up and could use the rest anyway," smiles Neal, not really anxious to leave Mickey.

"Wonderful!" exclaims Mickey, with a sigh of relief.

When Neal finishes his breakfast, he goes back to the barn, gets a pick and shovel, then goes about the job of burying the three dead men. He takes everything from them that the family may be able to use, before he drops them in the grave he has dug. He checks the horses out, and finds them to be a good pair, and they are outfitted with good harness. The walk home just got a little easier.

May 9th, 1865

Jefferson Davis is considered a fugitive and northern forces are beginning to close in on him. Davis and his small band join forces with his wife at Dublin, Georgia.

One of the most feared of all Southern Generals, Nathan B. Forrest, disbands his troops. With true soldiers disbanding and going home, what's left are the outlaws who have been taking advantage of the war, for their own personal gain. Now since the war is at an end, they can no longer hide under the pretext of the flag, or the cause, and they are considered outlaws by both the North and the South.

Clyde's troop is making good time headed west through Kentucky and the men he is traveling with, are all from the same area.

"Sergeant Wilson," calls one of the younger boys in his troop.

"Yeah Taylor, what do you want?" answers Clyde, "And if it's how much further we gotta go, I'm gonna stop this here horse and wear you out just for being bothersome."

"Uh- nothing Sergeant," answers the young Glenn Taylor, son of Red Taylor, of Olive Branch, Illinois.

William Clarke Quantrill's group is heading east through Kentucky. They have been recently engaged, and two of his group of nine men, have their arms in slings from wounds they received just a couple of days ago.

At the Wilson farm, Neal is going about getting the equipment ready for plowing and planting. The women are glad to have him there for their protection, and Mickey is just glad to have him there and plans to make it a permanent thing, if she has her way in the matter.

May 10th, 1865

President Johnson tells the country that the war can be considered virtually over.

The Confederate President, along with his wife and a few followers, are captured by the 4th Michigan Cavalry near Irwinville, Georgia. The prisoners are ordered to be escorted to Nashville, under heavy guard.

General Samuel Jones surrenders his command at Tallahassee, Florida.

Neal and the two Wilson women continue preparations for the spring plowing and planting of the crops. Neal does not have to be told what to do in this task because as he puts it, "Farming is farming. Makes no difference if it's in the North or in the South."

Clyde is leading his troop west from Taylorsville, Kentucky.

"Sergeant Wilson!" yells Glenn Taylor.

"What is it this time Private Taylor?" replies Clyde with a grin.

"Sergeant ain't we infantry?"

"That's right Glenn, we sure are."

"So why don't we stop these here horses and walk? My tail-end is about to kill me," complains Taylor.

"Cause if we get down and walk, we'll cover the distance between here and home much slower," answers Wilson, "So just hang in there, it won't be but three or so more days and we'll be home."

"Yes Sergeant," answers a reluctant Taylor, as Clyde keeps the troop moving at a steady gait.

William Quantrill is leading his men east on the same road that Clyde Wilson is bringing his troop on, headed west. Quantrill has picked up a few in numbers, and now his band is up to fifteen or sixteen men. Three of the new men he's added are Frank and Jesse James, and Cole Younger, who have raided with Quantrill before, and they plan to pick up more men. The war will never be over to these men who use the gun as a tool for profit.

"Sergeant Wilson!" yells Private Taylor.

"What is it this time Glenn?" questions Clyde getting a little annoyed because his backside is hurting also, and Private Taylor just keeps on asking him questions.

"Sergeant Wilson, why did we bring these long rifles on these here horses, with us? If we're going to ride horses like cowboys, why don't they give us all a pistol like yours, and a carbine."

"Cause they just loaned us these horses, but we're still infantry, so why change our weapons?"

"Shoot, I don't know Sergeant, I wuz a-asking you."

"Jus' hush Taylor. Everybody's tired and saddle-sore, and we ain't in no mood to listen to you complain'n," orders Wilson, as the two groups of men continue to close on each other, at a steady pace.

Up about mid-morning, both groups call a halt to their march, to rest and to feed their horses. While the horses feed, the men use this time to feed themselves. Quantrill's men being horsemen, lie around and rest, while they have the chance. Wilson's men being infantry, and not accustomed to riding, walk about rubbing their backsides and the insides of their legs. Sergeant Wilson is not spared the pain and discomfort his men are experiencing, and he is doing as much walking, stretching and rubbing as anyone else in the troop.

Quantrill is approached by one of his men who has ridden with him for some time, and reminded that they are pushing through enemy country.

"You are right Jesse, we do need to put out a point man," answers Quantrill, "I should have already done it."

When the two groups of men on horses, start to move again, Quantrill sends one of his troopers on ahead, as his point scout. This man leads on down the road for about amile in front of the main body, his job being to spot any danger and report back to Quantrill, before the whole group runs into a trap.

Not being cavalry, Wilson is bringing his men west in one group, with no scouts out in front. He's accustomed to keeping his men all together and fighting in strength. The two groups are closing the distance between them at about fifteen miles per hour.

It's a warm sunny day with wild wood flowers showing their presence all along the way, and the furthermost thing from the minds of Wilson and his men is the war. Their thoughts tend to be of home, family, and getting off these horses.

On the contrary, Quantrill is on the prowl as usual, looking for trouble with unsuspecting people, who have anything of value. The one thing he doesn't want, is to have an encounter with the Union Army.

Over in the afternoon as Quantrill's scout, who is leading the way, rounds a sharp curve in the road and comes out in front of the mounted Union soldiers.

"Whoa!" Yells the scout, who is both surprised and excited. His horse drops his hind quarters, sliding to a stop; but with a nudge of the spurs, it spins and is galloping away from Clyde's mounted infantry.

"Hey Sergeant!" yells Private Taylor, "That was a Reb."

"Yeah we all know that Taylor," answers Wilson.

"Let's run him down Sergeant!" continues Taylor.

"Just hush!" orders a worried Sergeant Wilson, realizing they have just bumped into a lead scout for some Confederate cavalry group. Knowing that his position will be given away in just a matter of time, Clyde tries to figure out a plan of action, for safe guarding his troop.

The scout covers the distance back to Quantrill in just a few minutes. "I just run head-on into a platoon of Yankee cavalry!" yells the scout, as he gallops into hearing distance of Quantrill's men.

Quick to respond, Quantrill sees that the Union cavalry is not close behind his scout, and asks, "Where is this cavalry group? They didn't even give chase?"

"I don't know Sir, but I did run right into them."

"If they're not giving chase, they must be retiring to their main body. We'll go forward past where you run into them, and lay in wait to ambush 'em when they come back," orders Quantrill, as he moves his men up.

Clyde, on the other hand, has never fought a battle on a horse, nor have any of his fellow men. "Follow me!" orders Clyde, when it's clear in his mind what he's going to do. He then kicks his horse and starts to the middle of the curve in front of him. After running his horse a short ways, he halts the men behind him. "Dismount and hide the horses," he orders. "Taylor, you stay behind us with the horses so they won't get away."

Clyde sends Taylor about a hundred and fifty yards up in the woods, and positions the other eight men and himself, on the outside of the curve in the road. The infantry men have their long Springfields ready for action quickly, and they use the trees for cover.

Quantrill brings his men down the road at a trot, thinking that the Yankee cavalry will be coming along shortly. His men are ready for a cavalry engagement, with pistols drawn. As Quantrill leads his men on down the road; in the woods, Clyde cautions his men to be sure of their shots.

It's not long before the Union squad hears the beat of trotting horse's hooves. "Steady boys, fire when I fire," orders Clyde, taking command of the platoon, like he has done many times in the year's past.

As the outlaws enter the curve, the Union soldiers lie in wait, rifles ready. Clyde pulls the hammer back on his Remington 44, and the metallic click lets the men around him know that a battle is about to begin.

Quantrill is leading his men as they reach the middle of the curve, and Clyde tightens up on the trigger of his pistol. Once the slack of the trigger is taken up the sear skips on the catch of the hammer releasing the spring forward. With the blast of Clyde's 44, a heavy lead ball races through the air and strikes Quantrill under his right rib cage, tearing a hole through the bottom of his lung and the top of his stomach.

William Clarke Quantrill, the most notorious of all Confederate guerrillas is knocked from his saddle, mortally wounded. Clyde's shot is followed closely by the reports of the eight Springfields, and more of the Quantrill men are thrown from their horses by speeding lead.

As the Union soldiers pour powder and push more lead down the muzzles of their weapons, Clyde works the hammer of his pistol, firing shot after shot at the confused Rebels.

The Rebels respond with shots aimed at the smoke of Clyde's pistol. After two or three quick shots by the remaining eleven or twelve Rebels, they spin their horses and gallop back down the road around the curve from the direction they came.

Once the Union rifles are reloaded and ready, the men wait. These soldiers know better than to get up and give their positions away so soon after a battle. After a few minutes pass, the moans from the dying men in the road start. The Union soldiers are feeling lucky, that they're not one of those in pain, until a moan is heard from the end of their own line. John White, one of Clyde's men hears the moan, and crawls to the sound.

"Clyde what's the matter? Where did they hit you?" asks White, as he crawls up beside Clyde, who is sitting on the ground with his back up against a big oak tree.

"I got a ball in the leg John," answers Clyde as he tries to stuff a bandage into the hole in his right thigh to stop the bleeding. John then takes over on doctoring the wound.

"What do we do now Clyde?" asks John as he puts pressure on the leg to slow the bleeding before tying a bandage around it.

"We wait here. Go back to where Glenn is with the horses and tie them up. Then send Glenn back to Taylorsville to get help and a doctor," orders Clyde.

John leaves, and in a short while, the sound of a horse galloping on the eight or so mile stretch of road leading back to Taylorsville, Kentucky, is heard. The young Taylor, forgetting his saddle soreness, heads all out back to the town for help and a doctor.

The remaining men in Quantrill's gang don't let up for several miles; then when they do, they turn south off the road and head for cover. This is the end of Quantrill's guerrillas. The men who are left make their way back across the Mississippi River. Jesse James, comes up as a new leader from this group, but it won't be long before his name will become well known.

It takes Glenn Taylor about two hours to get to town, gather up some men and a doctor, then get back to the platoon with it's wounded leader.

With the added men, guards are put down the road, and Clyde is brought back up on the road and placed in the back of a wagon, so the doctor can work on his leg. While this is going on the sheriff looks over the dead bodies from the Rebel group and when he turns Quantrill's body over, he recognizes him from posters he has received in his office.

"By golly, this one here is William Quantrill!" exclaims the older man, as the others gather around to get a look at the outlaw.

"Sergeant your leg is broken and the ball is on the back side of it, right under the skin," states the doctor, after examining

Clyde's wound. "I can get the lead out aw'right, but it's gonna be some time before this bone will work right again."

"Well get the lead out and splint the leg up so I can ride a horse," orders Clyde. "I'm going home if it's the last thing I do."

"But Sergeant!"

"Don't argue with him Doctor," recommends John White. "We're all going home and if we have to tote him, we'll do it."

"Suit yourselves," answers the doctor as he removes the bullet and splints the leg. "You were very lucky Sergeant. That bullet didn't cut your artery, or you would've bled to death."

"I know that. We were all lucky," answers Clyde, as the sun is setting and his men set up camp for a long night.

May 11th, 1865

General M. J. Thompson, the commander of the Confederate Forces, in the Missouri-Arkansas region, surrenders the remnant of his command at Chalk Bluffs, Arkansas. Thompson is given the same terms that Grant gave Lee at Appomattox.

Clyde's platoon of men are up early, fixing breakfast and coffee. Clyde has had a hard night, filled with pain from his gunshot leg.

"Clyde, we can stay here a day or two till you feel better, before we travel," states John, as he brings a plate and coffee to his sergeant.

"That wouldn't be right for me to keep you boys from going on home," answers Clyde, as he takes a sip of the hot coffee.

"We'll get home soon enough Clyde, and besides that leg of yours has got to be paining you something awful."

"John, I'm still in charge, and I say we ride. We may not cover as much ground as I would like, but at least we'll be headed home. Besides, my leg is gonna hurt anyway, so I might as well let it hurt headed home," smiles Clyde. As Clyde finishes telling John how it's gonna be, Glenn walks up to them.

"We're staying here for a while ain't we Sergeant?" questions Glenn.

"Why foot naw Boy? We're headed home," states Clyde.

"Aw Sergeant, my backside ain't ever gonna make it," complains Glenn.

"Well, just leave your backside here then, but the rest of you is a-headed home Boy," laughs John White. "The sergeant here, has done made up his mind."

After breakfast the men saddle the horses and pack up the camp. John and Glenn help Clyde up into the saddle and observe the pain that this movement brings, even though he tries to hide it from them. He has a hint of a smile on his face, but they note the gritting of his teeth, and the large drops of perspiration that pop out on his forehead, and course down his face. They can see both the pain and his determination to stay mounted, regardless of the pain he feels. Once in the saddle Clyde's splinted right leg sticks out to the side, but with his left leg in the stirrup, he is able to raise himself up a little, allowing the stiff leg to hang a bit more comfortably. When the pain is too much to bear, he does this to ease it.

All morning long Clyde is up and down on his left leg. They take an hour break for dinner and then the same painful ordeal begins again, and continues until it's time to stop for the night. All through the day Clyde did not complain to his men. After the camp is set and supper is cooking, Glenn walks over to where Clyde is stretched out on a bed roll.

"Sergeant, I know ya' were in a-lotta pain a-ridin' and all—" starts Glenn.

Cutting Glenn off in mid-sentence, Clyde answers, "Yeah, I was, and still am, so get to the point!"

"Well Sergeant, I was a-wondering if'n I was to make a travois to drag behind your horse, you know, like the Indians do, would it make it any easier on you to travel?"

"I'm sorry about being short with you Glenn, but if you could make me a travois, I would be much obliged to ya," answers Clyde kindly, surprised at Glenn's thoughtful suggestion.

"Think no never mind, I know that you are hurting real bad, so I'll get started making the travois for you right now," promises Glenn, as he gets up and starts out to cut the two straight poles he will need.

At the Wilson farm, Neal has started breaking up the ground so Mr. Wilson will have a head start on planting when he gets home. Mickey carries water out to him in a bucket, about mid-morning. When Neal is thirstily drinking the water from a gourd dipper, Mickey asks him, "Are you trying to make a good impression on my father by doing all of this work before he gets home?"

"I surely am," answers Neal.

"Now why would you want to do that?" giggles Mickey.

"Well Girl, if you want me to look like some lazy Rebel, when he gets here, I can surely oblige," grins Neal as he continues drinking the cool water.

"You'd better not," snaps Mickey with a smile.

"Aw'right then, I've got to get this field broke up before he gets here and jes look at you out here a-hindering me," laughs Neal.

"Oh, aw'right then," says Mickey as she takes the dipper back out of Neal's hand pausing long enough to hold his fingers on the handle for a moment. "I'll leave you to your work."

"I'll see you at dinner," smiles Neal as she turns and prisses back across the fresh plowed ground, headed toward the house. "That is if I can wait that long."

"Oh, you can Lieutenant," laughs Mickey as she continues walking a bit more lady-like.

May 12th, 1865

President Johnson appoints General Oliver Howard to head the Bureau of Refugees, Freedmen, and Abandoned Land. The bureau will be in charge of helping newly freed Negroes adjust to their freedom. Land confiscated by the Federal government during the war is also under the bureau's direction. The eight defendants charged in the plot of assassinating Lincoln, plead not guilty. Federal troops under the command of Colonel Theodore Barrett, attack and capture the Southern Camp at Palmitto Ranch, on the Rio Grande River.

Mickey brings Neal's breakfast out to the barn but she is not greeted with any smart words from him as she crosses the yard. As she opens the barn door, the creaking sound awakens him and she calls out, "Are you al'right?" She then carries the platter of food into the front stable.

"Oh, I'm fine, just a little sore," answers Neal, as he rolls over and stretches, "Why?"

"I was worried when I didn't hear a 'good mornin' from you, as I came across the yard."

"I guess that plowing yesterday must'a done me in."

"Well it's your own fault. You didn't haf'ta do the whole field in one day," scolds Mickey.

"Now the way I see it is, I don't have to work in that field today, cause it's done."

"Yeah, but there's another one to be done, and another."

"So, as I said, I don't haf' to work that field today," grins Neal as he begins to eat his breakfast.

"Oh, what's the use? You'll probably go and work yourself to death before daddy even gets here."

"No, I'll still be here and his work load will be greatly reduced," smiles Neal with a wink at Mickey.

"What was that for?" grins Mickey, showing that she loved it for whatever reason.

"I'll tell you someday," laughs Neal, as he takes a drink of his coffee.

In Kentucky, Clyde's group is on the road early. The travois Glenn has made, consists of two long straight poles harnessed at one end to Clyde's horse, leaving the other ends to trail along on the ground. Smaller crossbars connect the poles and a bed is made on these crossbars. Clyde's horse is being lead by Glenn and the traveling is made much easier for Clyde because he is resting on his back. This is far better than being astride the horse with his wounded leg in an uncomfortable hanging position.

"Hey Glenn!"

"Yes Sergeant," answers Glenn.

"I surely appreciate this here drag," says Clyde as he looks up at the sky.

"It's all that I could think of that might help you," explains Glenn, as John rides up next to the two talking men.

"You traveling better now Clyde?"

"Yeah John I am, thanks to this boy."

"You make it sound so good Sergeant, think I'm gonna make myself one cause my back side is still killin' me."

"Aw hush your complaining Glenn," laughs John. "We'll be home in another three or so days."

NEAL'S HOMECOMING

"You said that two days ago!" reminds Glenn, rubbing the seat of his pants.

"We'll make it Glenn, and if you don't, we'll tell all the folks back home you died from a saddle sore bottom," laughs John, moving away to talk to some of the other men.

"I'm dead serious and I'm being truthful Sergeant," explains Glenn.

"Yeah, I know Glenn, we're both in a bad way ain't we Boy?"

"That's the truth for sure," agrees Glenn rubbing his back side again as the troop keeps moving steadily on the way home.

May 13, 1865

The South is crumbling and the Confederate governors of Arkansas, Mississippi and Louisiana meet with Edmund K. Smith, the commander in the Trans-Mississippi area. The purpose for the meeting is to advise him to surrender under the terms which they have outlined for him. Others in the western parts of the Confederacy, including Jo Shelly, threaten to arrest Smith if he surrenders.

In what will be the last significant land battle of the war, Union troops return to the Palmitto Ranch in Texas, and drive away the Confederate forces. Later in the day the Confederates counter attack, under Colonel John S. Ford, and the Northern force is forced to withdraw.

Clyde's troop is still making headway toward home. It is obvious that the group won't make it home by the fifteenth as they'd planned and Clyde knows that he's the reason for their slow progress. With these men who have been together for so long it's only a minor delay and they've accepted the fact that they're all going home, and they're all going together.

At the Wilson farm, Neal is still getting the fields ready to plant. As he brings the team into the lot at dinner time, Mickey meets him at the gate. He shuts the gate and starts to the house for the meal which the women have prepared. For the past few days they have been serving meals to him on the front porch where it is cool and they can sit together and talk with him

"I still say you are working too hard," states Mickey.

"Yeah, well I'm enjoying it. It gives me time to think and my body is getting stronger ever day," answers Neal.

"That's good, and just what do you think about?" grins Mickey, hoping she is some where in those thoughts.

"Well for one thing, this war is over and we can let the politicians argue 'bout what is to be done in government. We shouldn't have fought this war for them to begin with. Now they'll be fussing about it for years, but the outcome will always be the same. What takes place in government will affect a-lotta people, but it's going to affect the man who farms his own land the least. I destroyed things during my time in the war and now I can help make things grow and live. Wars are for the dying and people who want war jes' don't want to live. So I've decided to live the rest of my life for the living, and to build up and help make things grow."

"And?" questions Mickey, though impressed by Neal's ideas, she is just a little disappointed.

"And what?" grins Neal.

"You know what I mean!" snaps Mickey.

"Oh yeah, I almost forgot. I got to get me some land and two mules."

"Oh, you're hopeless! All you think about is work, work, or some ole farm," snaps Mickey showing a little anger.

"No Darlin' I didn't forget. I was just kiddin' you," says Neal in a soft voice.

"You were?"

"Yeah, you know what I said yesterday when I winked at you?"

"Yeah, you said that you would tell me something later, when I asked you what it was for," answers Mickey, stopping on the steps of the porch.

"Well - uh- uh, I love you, and I'm gonna ask Mr. Wilson if I can marry you," explains Neal, a little embarrassed with these words. Though they came straight from his heart, they were not easy to speak out loud.

"Well, before you ask him, I think you'd better ask me first," snaps Mickey, hiding her happiness at Neal's declaration of love for her.

"Uh, uh- oh sure. Uh, Mickey I do love you and will you marry me?" asks Neal quickly, answering Mickey while he still has the nerve.

"Oh yes Darling," responds Mickey as she runs into his arms and kisses him all over his sweaty face. Just at this time Rebecca steps out the door with Neal's lunch in her hands.

"See here Girl, you know better than to be acting like that. This is the second time I've seen you two kissing now. The first time was in the barn after that shooting, but this is uncalled for," snaps Rebecca, trying to hide her approval of their obvious love for one another.

"But Mother, Neal and I are going to be married if you and Papa will let us, that is."

"Well Girl, you're just seventeen!" answers her mother.

"Mother you were seventeen when you and papa had me. You two got married when you were jes' sixteen and I'll be eighteen on the 22nd of November, but I'm grown right now," argues Mickey.

"Well you two will jus' haf' to wait till your papa gets home," instructs Rebecca, setting the platter of food down for Neal, she turns back into the house, hiding the smile that appears on her face.

May 16th, 1865

Neal finishes the breaking up of the ground and the fields are now ready for planting. When he brings the mules to the barn about mid-afternoon, Mickey meets him there.

"I'm worried about Papa. He said in his letter the other day he would be home by the fifteenth. Now the sixteenth is on the short side and he ain't here yet," explains Mickey.

"Oh I wouldn't worry too much. You forget he's still in the army, and he has to do what they tell him to. He may not have been able to leave when he thought he was going to, there could be delays in leaving or on the road," answers Neal as he unharnesses the mules. When they are free of their burden, they each trot into the middle of the lot and roll in the dust.

"Yeah, but mother says it ain't like him to be late for anything and she is really worried about him," reports Mickey, with her own concern showing on her face.

"Still, you two ought not to fret, because he most likely just had to stay a little longer than he had planned at the time he sent the letter."

"Oh I hope you are right Neal," states Mickey as she watches the mules rolling in the dust. "Tell me something, why do those two roll in the dust every time after they've been pulling the plow?"

"Well it's probably b'cause of the harness. Their backs are wet from sweat and the harness must make it itch, so rolling on their backs in the dust dries it out and scratches the itch at the same time."

"You've got it all figured out don't you?"

"It's as good'a guess as any, I reckon," answers Neal.

"Yeah, I reckon it is," smiles Mickey as she turns and starts back to the house, obviously still concerned about her father.

May 17, 1865

General Philip Sheridan is appointed commander of the district west of the Mississippi River and south of the Arkansas River. Sheridan's reputation of wholesale destruction during his campaign in the Shenandoah Valley, causes concern in the South. For this reason considerable resistance rises to his appointment from the South.

Neal is eating breakfast on the front porch of the Wilson's house with Mickey, when Rebecca comes out and joins the couple.

"What is it you two young people are talking about?" She questions, as she drags a chair over to the steps where they are seated.

"Oh nothin' of any importance," answers Mickey.

Rebecca knows very well that they are making plans for their future, but she is too worried about Clyde to stay in the house alone. She needs somebody to talk with, so she comes out to join Neal and Mickey.

"Mickey tells me that you're not too worried about her papa," states Rebecca, looking at Neal for any reassurance he has to offer as to the well-being of her husband.

"Shoot Mrs. Wilson, if that Yankee army is anything like the one I was in, it still may be weeks before he gets to come home."

"Don't say that Boy. I do hope he'll be home soon, and that he will be well when he gets here."

"Yes Ma'am, I do too. How long has it been since he was home?" questions Neal. He eats his breakfast and gives

Rebecca a chance to talk about the object of her concern. He hopes talking will help relieve some of the anxiety that is evident in the faces of both women.

"Year ago last Christmas. It's been hard on me, and also on Mickey. You've been a big help in breaking up the fields for us. I jes' couldn't a-done it another year," answers Rebecca, tears showing in her eyes and determination not to let them flow, written on her face.

"How long has it been since you were at home Neal?" asks Mickey, turning to look at him for his answer.

"Let me see now. It was Christmas too, yeah, that's right, Christmas of sixty-one," answers Neal thoughtfully, as he reaches for the cup of hot coffee.

"Sixty-one!" exclaims Rebecca. "Boy, your folks have gotta be powerful worried about you."

"Yes Ma'am, I 'specs so; but in my family, no news is good news."

"You two kids keep a-talkin. You've made me feel better already," states Rebecca, as she gets up and goes back in the house.

"You ain't been home in three and a-half years Neal?"

"That's right and I'm anxious to get there, but I don't want to leave you Mickey Darlin."

"All you got to do is take me with you," smiles a radiant Mickey.

"It wouldn't be right if we weren't married."

"Well?"

"We've got to get your pa's permission."

"He'll be home soon and then we can."

"Mickey, I might need to go back home first. I may need to tell my folks about this Yankee girl I've fallen in love with, you know, kinda feel them out."

"You mean you don't think they'll take a-liking to me."

"Well, it's been a long time since I've been home, and the last one I remember seeing of my family was Ruben, you know my little brother."

"Yeah." agrees Mickey, not pleased with the idea of Neal going home without her.

"Well I don't even know if he lived through the war. Thompson didn't. If Melton did, he is missin' one hand. So you see, it would

be best if I went back first and prepared everybody for you."
Neal speaks slowly, as if he's thinking of each member of his
family and how they may feel about this girl who is not from the
South.

"I reckon you're right, but when are you going?"

"Jes as soon as I can, after your pa gets home."

"How long will you be gone?"

"Oh, four or five months I guess, but I'll be back as soon as I
can, and you remember that."

"How long will it take you to get there?"

"I figure two and a-half or three weeks, with those captured
horses we've got."

"Are you scared to go home?"

"Yeah in a way, but I got to get there and find out what has
happened to my folks and the place. In all this time there must'a
been lots of things that happened, specially in these war years,
and I don't know about any of it. Darlin, you do understand that I
really need to go home, at least long enough to check on my
family and let them know I'm alive. Then I can tell them about you
and your family."

"What if they don't like me?"

"Well I really think they will, but if they don't I'll just leave
home, move somewhere else, and take you with me."

"You will?"

"I surely will if'n they object to you being my wife and taking
your place in our family."

"Oh Neal, I love you so much and I wish we were married
right now," declares Mickey as she slides over closer to Neal.

"Not so close Sweetheart, your mother may come back out
and then what?" says Neals, as he reluctantly moves a little bit
away from Mickey.

"Neal, how old are you?"

"Twenty-four, why?"

"You are a grown man, now act like it," grins Mickey, sliding
close again.

"Yeah, I'm a grown man and I've got work to do," says Neal,
getting up, now that he's finished breakfast, he heads toward
the barn.

NEAL'S HOMECOMING

"Aren't you even going to kiss me good morning Neal McNair?" questions Mickey, a little peeved that she had to ask.

"Well, aw'right," as he turns to give her a peck on the cheek but before he can stop her she puts her arms around his neck and kisses him on the lips, a sweet lingering kiss. When the kiss is over, he backs up and Mickey says, "Now, that's the way I want to be kissed ever morning, when we're married."

"Yes Ma'am," grins Neal, as he turns and heads to the barn.

Five hours later at noon, Neal has gotten all the plows sharpened and ready for planting, when he hears the sound of horses moving slowly down the road. This sound brings back the memory of the outlaw gang's visit and he's quick to strap on the brace of Confederate Colts, just in case. Not knowing what to expect, Neal tries to prepare for whatever may come as best he can. When he heads to the door of the barn, he hears one of the horsemen ride ahead of the other men in the group and his heart pounds a little faster. Opening the barn door, he sees the man stop in front of the Wilson house. Also, he can see this is a mounted Union soldier. Then he knows that the group he hears is a Union army group, and he has no doubt Mr. Wilson is with it. Neal ducks back in the barn and drops the pistols without anyone seeing him. He walks out, just as the lead man calls out to someone inside.

"Mrs. Wilson, are you in the house? Mrs. Wilson, this is John White, come on outside."

"Yes John, what is it?" responds Rebecca as she comes out the front door and Neal starts across the yard, behind the Union soldiers.

John hears the footsteps behind him and not being too far removed from the war, swings his horse around to investigate. Seeing a strange man in what is left of a Confederate uniform, out of instinct he starts unslinging his rifle.

"Easy John," snaps Rebecca, "He's our friend."

Relaxing, John tightens the strap on the rifle as Neal, having stopped with the threat, begins to walk again on toward the horse and rider in front of the house.

"Where's Clyde John?" questions Rebecca, anxiously looking at the road.

"He's with the rest of the squad Rebecca, he'll be here direct-ly," answers John as Neal walks up next to his horse.

"What's the matter John?" asks Rebecca, sensing something is not right.

"Clyde's been shot in the leg and it's broken. He'll be laid up for some time."

"I knew it! I 'jes knew that something was wrong or he'd have been here when he said he would," cries Rebecca. Just then the rest of the Wilson squad ride into the yard, pulling the travois, with Clyde on it. Mickey has joined her mother on the porch and at first sight of Clyde both of them run out to him. They take his hands and with one on either side of the travois, they walk with him to the edge of the porch both blinded by tears of joy at his being home, and tears of sorrow at the painful condition he is in upon arrival.

The thrill of having Clyde in their home again, is somewhat overshadowed by the wound he has sustained, and their sadness over his not being able to get up and fully enjoy his homecoming. They are also worried about the extent of the injury and Rebecca wanting to see for herself, starts by taking the bandage off his leg. The squad has kept it bandaged and changed regularly since the doctor removed the bullet, and the ride home started.

"Honey I'm going to be fine, it's gonna take some time to heal, but I'll be aw'right now that I'm home and have you to take care of me," assures Clyde as he hugs his wife first, then reach-es for Mickey who is still standing on the other side of him.

Neal keeps to himself and out of the way of these men who are just returning from the war. He doesn't want his presence to cause any bad feelings, or take anything away from the family's reunion.

After Clyde has been moved into the house and on to his bed, the squad says good-bye to his family, who in turn thank them for bringing Clyde home and wish them Godspeed as they leave for their respective homes.

"Rebecca, I saw a strange man out there in our yard when the boys were bringing me in the house. He looked like a Reb," states Clyde obviously expecting an explanation from Rebecca.

"Yeah honey that's Neal McNair, and he was a Reb lieutenant," answers Rebecca trying to gather her thoughts as to how to explain this man being here at their home. Not only is Neal a strange man, but he's a Reb, the very ones her husband has been fighting for so long.

"Neal McNair's a Reb, and he's here at my farm! Heck Honey, we've been fightin them Rebs for four years and you go and let one stay here in my home! Honey how could you?"

"Jes, simmer down Clyde and I'll tell you all about him," pleads Rebecca.

"Aw'right dear, I'm a-waitin'."

"You see it all started back a week or so ago when Mickey and me were coming home from town, after we had bought the seed for this year's planting. We came upon this Rebel boy who was lying unconscious in the road. Now I started to pass him by, but Mickey reminded me of the good Samaritan in the bible and how we are to help anyone who needs our help, so we stopped. Together we loaded him into the wagon and brought him home. He was hurt bad plus, he had a illness where he couldn't remember much of anything. Clyde, the boy didn't even know his own name."

"I saw that happen to some of our boys after a bad fight," explains Clyde, beginning to understand why they had helped this boy.

"Well anyhow, we brought him home and put him up in the barn, and doctored on his cuts and bruises as best we could. He had broken ribs and was jes' bruised up in a bad way. The scar on his breast, from his battle wound was still red and tender so he was weak from that, even before the beating he'd taken. Well it's a good thing we helped him too, cause jes' a day or so later, a guerrilla band came a-ridin' in and one of them attacked Mickey in the barn while she was milkin'. Neal put the pitch fork up through the base of the man's skull and he was dead before he could harm her anymore. After killing that one, he took the man's guns, and he come out the barn door real fast when the rest of 'em were about to do me harm. Neal called their hand on that, and the shooting started with him killing two more of the rascals before they rode off."

NEAL'S HOMECOMING

"Didn't you have my shotgun?"

"Yes, and I shot too, but they must'a been out of range to do any real harm, kinda peppered 'em I guess cause the horses sure got out'a hand. Anyhow, Neal got all the guns and two horses that belonged to the dead men. He showed us how to load the guns and we prepared for their return. That's when Red Taylor rode in and said he'd seen them pass his place headed east. He said he thought that this bunch must'a been Quantrill's band. He said they wouldn't be likely to come back, but I was real glad to have Neal staying in the barn jest in case."

"That's the group we had the fight with coming home. Quantrill was identified by the sheriff, and the other dead men had wounds bandaged up as if they had been in battle recently, it could'a been the same bunch, and probably was," explains Clyde.

"Now let me finish."

"Aw'right Hun' you go right on and tell me everything you got on your mind."

"Neal's worked hard ever day after he got well enough to stay on his feet. He's broke up all the fields and has them ready for plantin'."

"He has?"

"Yes, and he has all the plows and harness ready to begin planting, and said he was leaving when you got home."

"Well I'm much obliged for what he has done but—"

"Don't talk now, you jes' rest a-while and you can talk some more at sundown," says Rebecca. She kisses Clyde, straightens up the sheets, fluffs up his pillow and tries to make him comfortable so he can rest easy after the long trip home.

"This will be jes' fine," states Clyde as he closes his eyes and relaxes on his own bed, and Rebecca eases out of the room.

Once out of the room she gathers Mickey and Neal up and tells them that she's told the whole story to Clyde. Course that is, all but about Mickey and Neal wanting to get married. "That's something you two will have to do for yourselves, but I think it would be best to wait until Neal has won Clyde's trust, and he gets to know him a little better.

"Neal and me have been talking too Mother, and that's about what we decided to do," agrees Mickey.

NEAL'S HOMECOMING

Neal explains that he is going to stay and plant the fields. After the planting is done, he will head on home. By the time crops are ready to harvest Mr. Wilson should be well enough to do that for himself.

Both women are thrilled that Neal is staying and doing the planting for them. Mickey says she is going to help Neal in the fields and that will make the job go faster. Later in the day as the sun's going down, Neal's eating his supper on the porch and Mickey is keeping him company there when Rebecca comes out to join them in the cool of the late evening.

"How's Mr. Wilson doing now Ma'am?" questions Neal as she sits down in a chair close by the spot on the porch steps where he and Mickey are sitting.

"Neal, he was going to visit with you this evening, but he jes' don't feel up to it today. He's decided to stay in bed and try to get rested up from the trip and maybe he'll feel stronger tomorrow."

"A good nights rest will do him good. I know he's still in lots of pain," states Neal in complete understanding of pain and weariness.

"Yes he is," agrees Rebecca.

"Well after a good night's rest in his own bed maybe a'lotta the pain will leave him. Also, I plan to make him some crutches tomorrow like the ones I saw in the hospital in Nashville," declares Neal. "They will help him to get around better."

"Oh would you?" asks Mickey. "That would be so helpful, who but you would think of doing that?"

"I said I would and I will, but right now it's almost bed time," answers Neal, getting up and walking toward the barn in the darkness. He turns and calls back, "Good night ladies."

"Good night Neal," replies the two ladies together.

"Oh mother he's impossible."

"How's that Girl?"

"He won't talk much around you. He must be scared of you," speculates Mickey.

"It will come when he gets to know me better," laughs Rebecca as she gets up and says, "Good night Mickey".

"Good night Mother," answers Mickey and they both head for bed.

As Rebecca crawls into the bed next to Clyde, a feeling she has not felt for a year and a-half comes over her, now she feels secure and loved. When he reaches over and draws her close into his arms there in the darkness, they kiss lovingly as if to make up for the long months they have been apart.

"I thought you were feeling poorly," whispers Rebecca.

"No Darling, jes' saving my strength," answers Clyde in a soft voice as their lips come together in another lingering kiss.

May 18th, 1865

When Mickey brings Neal's breakfast out on the porch, she is surprised to find he has one of the mules harnessed and hooked to the plow, out next to the door of the barn and now he is walking her way.

"You're planning on getting a early start this morning, aren't 'cha?" asks Mickey as she sits down on the top step with the food.

"Yeah, I need to get as much done each day as I can," answers Neal, walking on up to the steps.

"After I help mother clean up after breakfast, I'll be out to help you."

"That will be good. I can surely use your company anytime," smiles Neal.

"Well now, I'm mighty glad to hear that!"

"Now let me see if I have the planting straight in my mind. Ya'll want corn in the big field to the West, the taters in the two fields to the South, then the peas and beans in the small field on the East."

"That's right."

"Well jes' as soon as I get breakfast down, I'll be working in the corn field when you decide to come out."

"Don't eat so fast, the field work will wait on you," smiles Mickey, touching Neal's arm as he starts to put another bite of egg and biscuit in his mouth.

"Yeah, I guess it will at that."

When Neal has finished his breakfast, he is off to the field, where Mickey joins him shortly after she has helped Rebecca in the house work. She walks along the rows he is making, dropping the corn, out of the bucket she carries the seed in.

NEAL'S HOMECOMING

Rebecca brings them some cool water out, about mid-morning. Mickey drinks first from the dipper, refills it and hands it to Neal.

"You two working out here in this field reminds me of how it was before the war, when I would help Clyde do the planting," comments Rebecca, looking at the young couple standing close together. Neal leans up against the plow handles and Mickey stands beside him.

"Do we really Mother?"

"Yes Girl, you sure do. Maybe it won't be long till your papa will be up and about again," says Rebecca, with a worried look on her face, as she looks out across the field, remembering the better days.

"Well Mrs. Wilson, don't you worry none now, I can take care of this here farming. You just take care of Mr. Wilson and everything will be aw'right," smiles Neal, giving Rebecca a reassuring pat on her shoulder. He then turns back to the plow, rolls the lines across the mule's backside and says, "Get up boy."

The mule pulls forward with the plow rowing up a bed for Mickey to drop the corn in, as she falls in behind Neal, with her bucket of seed corn, and Rebecca returns to the house, and her husband.

At noon, Neal changes the mules, tying the fresh one up in the shade, and taking feed and water to the one he's been working all morning. While the animal is eating, Neal heads to the crib and soon the sound of a hand saw can be heard, then the banging of a hammer.

"Where is Neal?" questions Rebecca, while she and Mickey are preparing the noon meal.

"Oh he's working out in the barn," answers Mickey.

"In the barn working?"

"Yes Ma'am, soon as he'd taken care of the mule, he went straight to the barn and while I was gettin' out'a my field clothes I could hear him a-sawin' and hammerin' on something."

"That's all that boy does."

"What's that Mother?"

"Work."

"Oh."

"Well you'd better go call him to dinner."

"Yes Ma'am," answers Mickey as she heads to the porch to call Neal. When she gets out on the porch, she sees Neal walking toward the house and he's carrying a pair of crutches, which he's just finished making.

"I should have remembered that you said you were going to make those for papa," smiles Mickey.

"Well, I hope they'll work for him. Here, you take them in and see if they will," says Neal holding the crutches out to Mickey.

"I'll do no such thing. You can come in and give them to him yourself," smiles Mickey.

"You better ask your mother about this first," states Neal, not wanting to do something that will upset Mr. Wilson.

"Oh alright," answers Mickey, going back into the house to get her mother.

After a few minutes have passed, the two women come back out where Neal is waiting on the porch. "Mickey tells me that you've made Clyde some crutches. I agree with her that you should bring them in, and give them to him yourself," informs Rebecca.

"Yes ma'am," answers Neal as he steps into the Wilson's home for the first time.

The women go into Clyde's room first, and announce that Neal has made something for him and would like to bring it in to him.

"Sure, tell him to come on in!" answers Clyde.

Neal steps into the bedroom with the crutches held out in front of him. "Mr. Wilson Sir, I thought these crutches might help until you are on your own two feet again," says Neal, speaking in a soft voice and his kind manner showing in his eyes.

"They surely will Son," smiles Clyde realizing this is a good boy, even though he was a Reb. "Rebecca tells me you've started the planting today."

"Yes Sir."

"She also said that you've already broke up all the fields."

"Yes Sir."

"Son, you've been in a army just the same as me, and you ought to know that I ain't got no money to pay you for all you've done," explains Clyde, with Rebecca and Mickey listening to every word.

"Yes Sir, uh- I mean no Sir. I don't want no money, I'm jes' trying to pay back a debt of kindness that your wife and daughter showed me when I was hurt on the road," states Neal, wanting Clyde to fully understand how much he appreciates all this family did for him, and that he's done the field work out of gratitude, and never has thought of receiving money in return.

"All I can say then is, that I'm mighty obliged for the help. With this war and all, every man who is home on leave has got to care for his own."

"Oh I understand, and when the planting is done, I need to get on home to check on my folks and things there. You should be well enough by fall to work and then you won't need help."

"I surely hope so Son," answers Clyde reaching down to rub his wounded leg.

"You two fellers can go on talking while us women set the table for dinner," suggests Rebecca as she leads the way out of the bedroom.

After a little while, the table is set and they call the men to come eat. Clyde is cautious as he walks on his new crutches into the kitchen where the four of them take their places round the table for the meal.

Clyde gives thanks for the food, and toward the end of his prayer, he thanks God for sending Neal their way to care for his family and their needs, as a good shepherd careth for his flock. The sincere words and obvious gratitude included in the prayer, bring tears to the eyes of the four people who are following the words and thinking thoughts of their own. Rebecca and Mickey are both proud of this man who is head of their home, and happy that he's here to lead this prayer of thanksgiving. Neal is thankful that he's been accepted by the Wilson family, and that he remembers the good home he grew up in, where prayers like this were prayed daily

After they've eaten, they all ease out on the porch to enjoy the cool breeze and visit for a while, before Neal and Mickey go back to the field.

When the young folks are back in the field working again, Clyde and Rebecca continue sitting on the porch, just watching them. As they go about the work at hand, they appear to be working together in perfect harmony.

"You know Honey, they remind me of us before the war," says Clyde, never taking his eyes off the two people who are working the soil.

"You know, I said the same thing this morning to them," agrees Rebecca.

"You remember when you and Mickey left us alone in the bedroom, while ya'll set the table?"

"Yes."

"Neal and I talked a little and he's from a farm down in Mississippi."

"Yeah, that's what he has told me."

"We talked about the war some, and found out we were facing each other in battle a few times."

"Really?"

"Yeah, but he said it made him feel kind'a bad to talk about it."

"I guess he told you he lost one brother for sure, and he don't know yet about the other two."

"Wars are terrible, and the ones where you're fighting your own kind, shouldn't ever be fought," explains Clyde, getting a little restless.

"That's true Dear, but this one is over and you're home, now let's talk about something else," suggests Rebecca, sensing that Clyde is getting uneasy.

"Yes Luv let's do, and since we're changing the subject, let me choose it."

"Aw'right, then what do you want'a talk about?"

"That boy. It's not right to let him eat on the porch so from now on, let him eat with the family at the table."

"Sure, the only reason he was eating outside was because you weren't at home yet, and we didn't want the neighbors talking."

"Let them talk. He's a fine boy, and let him have some of my clothes. Those ole Reb rags were worn out years ago."

"Yes dear," smiles Rebecca.

NEAL'S HOMECOMING

When Neal has put the mules up in the lot at the end of the day, and cleaned up in the watering trough, he goes to his stable to get a different shirt, to change from the sweat soaked one he's worked in all day. When he gets there he's surprised to find two pair of pants and three shirts that Rebecca has left there for him. He quickly changes into a shirt and pair of pants, from the stack he's just found in his stable. Surprisingly the clothes fit him nicely, and he's pleased to be wearing something clean and in good condition, as he heads to the porch for supper. Once he gets there he finds Mickey waiting for him.

"You do look good in those clothes!"

"Yeah, you'd never know I was a Reb," grins Neal, pleased with the compliment from Mickey.

"Oh, from now on you'll be eating your meals in the house with our family," smiles Mickey, really pleased with this arrangement. "I think my papa's taking a likin' to you."

May 20th, 1865

Neal is up as Mickey comes into the barn to milk. "Good morning Neal," she calls out, when she's walking down the hall.

"Good morning to you Mickey."

"You going to church with us this morning?"

"Church? Uh- I don't know."

"What'a you mean you don't know?"

"Well, what will all your neighbors think about ya'll bringing a Reb to church with you?"

"Oh don't be silly! If they're going to church for the right reason, they'll be glad to have you. If they ain't there for the right thing, it won't make no difference no how," states Mickey in a no nonsense tone of voice.

"Well since you put it that way, think I'll jes' go."

"Good Darlin'. I knew you would," smiles a happy Mickey as she goes on about her chores.

After breakfast Neal hitches the team up to the wagon and helps Clyde to get up in the rear. Once Clyde is placed on a pallet in the back, Neal climbs in with him, trying to help keep his leg steady. Rebecca takes the lines as she climbs up on the board seat at the front part of the wagon, with Mickey sitting beside her. She gives just a snap of the wrist, and the mules lunge forward with a jerk and they're on their way.

After they've been on the road for a little while, they pass Red Taylor's place and see that he and his son have already left for church. About a mile farther along they arrive at a large wood frame church house and Rebecca pulls the team in to a shaded area and stops. Neal helps Clyde out of the wagon and hands him his crutches. The four of them walk in the building together, with the ladies just in front of Clyde and Neal. As they enter, the congregation starts singing "The Old Rugged Cross."

The Wilson's and Neal find their seats in the back right hand corner just behind Red Taylor and his son, Glenn. As they are easing into their seats, Red nods at them and Glenn smiles. Clyde's family returns the friendly greeting with smiles and nods as they blend their voices in song.

After the hymn, the preacher steps up into the pulpit to deliver the message of the hour. Neal and Mickey are sitting next to each other, and it's all they can do to keep from holding hands, as they share spiritual unity in the spoken word, and the thoughts of their hearts.

The preacher sees all the soldiers from the community are home, and gives them a hearty welcome back. He looks at Neal and points him out as a guest of the Wilson's, and he too is welcomed to this worship service, with a cordial invitation to come again.

The message is a reminder of the many blessings we receive on a daily basis from a God who loves us. Often he blesses us in strange ways, and we don't always understand, or even recognize these blessings, at the time. We take so much for granted, we forget that every good and every perfect gift cometh from above, and we don't take time out to thank Him, as we should. This is a perfect message for all the returning soldiers, because each one has been blessed just to have survived the war. Being able to come home to their families, to be here today in a service like this with friends and neighbors, these too should be considered blessings from a loving Heavenly Father.

When the sermon is over, the preacher stands at the door while the people pass on their way outside. He speaks to each one as they go by and welcomes them back. When the Wilson family is outside in the church yard, Red Taylor overtakes them.

"Clyde, I heard about your wounded leg, sure hope it heals better than mine did," states Red.

"Thank you Red," answers Clyde.

"You got this boy helping with the farming, I hear."

"Yeah Red, I do and the sermon today really touched me, cause without him, I don't know what we would've done."

"I know what you mean Clyde, if it weren't for Glenn my fields would not be worked cause I ain't able to do it."

"Yeah you and me both have been blessed, ain't we Red?" states Clyde, asking his neighbor to agree with his statement.

"Sure are, and so are a bunch of other folks who had loved ones that come home with you."

Once the group breaks up and everybody's headed home, Neal to himself, wonders why no one mentioned anything about him being a Reb. Then he remembers they were in God's House, where there is peace, forgiveness and understanding. He understands now, and he's glad that he came, cause he feels he has been blessed in doing so.

-May 22nd, 1865

Neal and Mickey are back in the fields planting the crops which the family will need to make it through the winter.

"Mickey you know if your papa lets us get married, we'll need a place of our own, cause once he's well he can take care of this one by himself," comments Neal, continuing to row up the rows so Mickey, still walking behind him, can drop in the seed.

"You may be right about that, but I'm sure he'll let us stay here until we can find us a place of our own."

"If he lets us get married, he may do just that, but we still need our own place."

"I'm not disagreeing with you Darling, but it may take some time to find a place and come up with the money to buy it."

"Yeah, the Confederate army did not pay at all, at the end," agrees Neal showing his concern because there's a need for money, which he does not have, nor does he see any way of earning it, at this time.

"Don't worry none about it now, we'll make it just you wait and see," smiles Mickey as she follows along behind Neal dropping seed into the hills he has rowed up for the corn.

"Well when we get through plantin' these fields, I'm headed home to find us a place."

"Whatever you say Dear is fine by me," answers a happy Mickey.

On this same day, President Johnson makes the 1st of July, the deadline to open all southern ports to trade, except the four in Texas.

President Jefferson Davis arrives at Fort Monroe, Virginia. The people of the North have very bad feelings toward him, after the assassination of Lincoln.

May 23rd, 1865

The U. S. Capitol holds a grand review for the Army of the Potomac. When the army marches past the viewing stand, the American flags of the city fly at full mast for the first time in four years.

The family at the Wilson farm is having dinner at 12:00 o'clock. Neal is eating with the family and he tells them that he should have the fields all planted, with Mickey's help, by the 29th. Clyde says he should not work so hard, there is plenty of time to get the seed in the soil. Neal reminds the family that he has got to get home, both to check on his family and for other personal reasons.

Mickey understands what his personal reasons are, and Clyde and Rebecca are not curious to the point of asking what reasons he has, other than seeing his family, after his long absence from home. The date for his departure is set, at whatever time he finishes with the crop planting. When the meal is over, Mickey and Neal go back to the field and Clyde calls Rebecca out on the porch where he's sitting, watching the two working in the field.

"In the morning, when them two get out to the field, I want you to go fetch the doctor for me."

"What's the matter Clyde, do you think your leg has infection set up in it?"

"No, I don't think it's infected, but I don't think it's healing as it should."

"Why do you think that?"

"It's still loose or something, like the bone's not healing back together. We just need the doctor to look at it and tell us if something more needs be done."

"Aw'right Honey, I'll get him first thing in the mornin' for you," promises Rebecca, with a look of concern on her face.

May 24th, 1865

After the death of Quantrill near Taylorsville, Kentucky, his gang has escaped capture and a new leader has taken over command. Jesse James with his brother Frank's support, is in the process of turning this guerrilla band into the most famous of all outlaw gangs.

Clyde explains to Mickey and Neal, at the breakfast table, that Rebecca is going into town to fetch the doctor to come check his leg, because he's not sure it's healing as it should.

Neal offers, "I'll ride into town and get the doctor for you."

"No," Clyde replies. "If you go problems could arise over you being there. The risk of a Confederate soldier going into a Union town, this soon after the war could cause trouble. Also, the doctor would be more likely to come for a woman he knows, rather than someone he doesn't know."

"You're probably right, hadn't thought about that," agrees Neal.

After breakfast, Neal hitches a pair of the horses to the wagon for Rebecca. By the time Mickey has finished milking, Neal has hitched one of the mules to the plow, and they are off to the field.

"You'd better keep up with me today Girl, I don't want you laggin' back none, ya' hear?" grins Neal, when the sun is just beginning to burn the dew off the grass.

"Did you say laggin' back? Well of all the nerve! I'll have you know I've been pushing you for the past two days," laughs Mickey.

"Well Luv, if you push me like you been doing, we'll finish the corn field today. Then we'll get the 'tater fields in two days and the peas and beans in a day or two for shore."

"You sound like you want to get it done in a'hurry."

"Yeah, some what."

"What's the matter? Don't you like being with me?"

"Oh yeah, I do—lots."

"Well I'd never thought working in the fields could be fun, but since you come along, I jes' love doing whatever, as long as you're with me."

"Well now since you put it that way, I'll have to say the same's true with me, Darling," smiles Neal, turning to look at Mickey with a wink.

"Good! Now don't you forget it," orders Mickey, smugly.

"I won't, you can count on that," answers Neal as he sets his plow. "Get up Boy!"

The days work has begun and Mickey falls in behind Neal with the bucket of seed corn, while Rebecca is already well on her way toward town. When she gets there, she finds the elderly Dr. Kellum, and tells him the problem with Clyde's leg.

"Tell you what Rebecca, you go on back home, and after I see ole lady Greer, I'll be headed out to your place. I should get there about noon," explains the gray-headed old doctor.

"I'll be looking for you and will have a meal fixed for you, when you get there Doctor Kellum," answers Rebecca as she leaves to go back to her wagon.

Mickey and Neal walk in to change mules at noon, and to eat their dinner. When they are putting the harness on the second animal, Dr. Kellum rides up in the yard in his old buggy.

"Hi Doctor Kellum! It's been a while since I saw you," greets Mickey with a smile.

"Yeah Girl, it's been some time since I was out this way."

"Doc, I want you to meet Neal McNair. He's been helping us out here with the farm, for a while now."

"I've already heard a-lot about this boy. The town is talking about the Reb that you two women took in, and how he stood up to that Quantrill bunch."

"Is the town really talking about Neal?" questions Mickey surprised to hear this news.

"Yeah Girl, he's quite a hero, back in town."

Blushing, Neal joins in the conversation, "It wasn't me that backed them down Sir, I came out of the barn behind them, and Mrs. Wilson was confronting them with a shotgun."

"Neal you know—"

"Now you jes' hush Mickey, you know it weren't nothing."

"Well whatever Boy, the town people are glad that you were here to give a hand when you were needed," adds Doctor Kellum.

"We are too," smiles Mickey.

"What's keeping the three of you out there? Come on into dinner," orders Rebecca from the porch.

The three of them walk on up to the house and Doctor Kellum says, "Let's get the work done before we eat then afterwards, we can visit."

"Fine Doc, let me take you on into Clyde's room," suggests Rebecca.

After the doctor has been in the room a short while, Rebecca steps out and calls Mickey and Neal to the door.

"The doctor says that Clyde's leg is not set. The bullet that hit him, knocked out a piece of the bone, and if it's going to get well, he'll have to set the leg again. That means he'll have to shove the bones together, so they'll grow back right. He says Clyde's leg will be a inch or two shorter than what it used to be, but it should work alright. Neal, he's gonna need your help to set it now," explains Rebecca.

"Yes Ma'am," answers Neal as he steps into the bedroom, ready to help the doctor.

"Come over here Boy. I want you to hold him down because this is gonna hurt like thunder."

"Yes Sir."

"You ready Clyde?" asks Dr. Kellum.

"Anytime Doc," answers Clyde. Then Neal taking hold of his shoulders, presses them down on the bed and holds them steady.

With the go-ahead from Clyde, the old doctor gives the straightened leg a hard push, from the heel upward. The pain this action brings, is too much for Clyde to be quiet about, and he lets out a yell of torment. Dr. Kellum feels the bones as they touch together and says, "That ought to do it."

While Neal is still holding his shoulders down on the bed, Clyde says, with relief, "Well I'm glad of that." His shortness of breath and the perspiration rolling off his face, is evidence of the pain caused by this procedure on his broken leg. He lies without protest, waiting for the doctor to finish the job. He hopes that he can relax enough to rest then, until the tormenting pain subsides.

"Now let me put the splints back on to support and hold the bone in place, and you remember to stay in bed for the next thirty days," instructs the doctor.

"Whatever you say Doc, I shore don't want to do this again," answers Clyde, gritting his teeth and trying not to complain even though the pain is almost unbearable.

The two women come back in with cool rags to rub his face and chest, trying to comfort him in the only way they can think of at this time.

When Dr. Kellum has finished, Clyde closes his eyes and tries to rest. The women go to the kitchen and set the table for the four of them, while they hope Clyde is napping.

"Now the three of you see to it that he don't let that leg hang down, for thirty days," instructs the doctor while he is eating his lunch. "Cause if he lets it drop down, it will pull the bones apart again, and we'll have to start all over."

"We won't let that happen Doc," assures Rebecca as she passes the corn bread to Neal.

"Watch those wounds, and if there's any sign of infection, get me back out here as soon as you can.

"We understand Dr. Kellum," answers Mickey.

"Those wounds look good for now, but after I aggravated the leg today, you can't ever tell how it will go."

"We'll watch them closely, and we'll be extra careful to keep them clean and dry," assures Rebecca.

"That's the best thing you can do," advises the doctor.

After all the discussion about Clyde's care and instructions from Dr. Kellum, the subject changes to other things of common interest to the Wilson's and the elderly doctor. Neal enters the conversation and makes informative comments about his home and farm life in Mississippi. He tells those around the table, that doctors who make house calls to folks living in the country, are very special people. He states further, that they should be awarded medals for the service they render. This pleases Doctor Kellum, who cares about his patients, many of which are his friends.

The good meal Rebecca prepared is enjoyed by one and all. After the meal and a short visit, the doctor is on his way back to town and Mickey and Neal head back to the corn field. Rebecca cleans up the kitchen, then tiptoes to the bedroom door, to keep a watchful eye on her husband, who now appears to be sleeping comfortably.

May 25th, 1865

Union troops have some running battles with guerrilla bands in the West, near Rockport, Missouri. In Mobile there is an explosion of some twenty tons of captured Confederate gunpowder, with the blast causing three hundred casualties.

At the breakfast table in the Wilson home, Neal tells the two women that he'll stay with them until Mr. Wilson is up and about again.

"No son, I feel that you've done enough," answers Rebecca. "And we should not keep you from going on home, at least long enough to check on your family."

"Well, if ya'll are sure, I'll leave after I finish the planting, but I'll be back as soon as I can and when I come back, I'm gonna approach Mr. Wilson about Mickey."

"That will be fine Neal," smiles Rebecca, taking a sip of coffee she watches Mickey, who is blushing with excitement as she sits beside Neal at the table.

May 29th, 1865

Neal and Mickey walk slowly in from the field to the East, "Well Darling, I'm glad this job is finished. You know tomorrow I'll be headed south, but I hate to go and leave you here. I'm kinda in a predicament. I don't know what I want to do, go home, or stay here with you."

"Don't be silly, you know you want to go see your family and find out how they all are now that the war is over. Besides, you know I'll be waiting for you right here when you get back. Neal Darling, you do know that I'll wait for you, don't cha?" questions Mickey, seeing indecision and concern in the expression on Neal's face.

"That's the reason I'll be headed back up here before you know it," smiles Neal, stopping to unlatch the lot gate.

"I sure hope so," sighs Mickey as she stands on tip toe to kiss Neal on the cheek.

"What was that for?"

"Jes' because I love you," answers Mickey softly, as she turns and heads to the house.

May 30th, 1865

Neal is up early and picks the best of the two horses that belonged to the dead outlaws. Once he has the animal saddled, he leads him over to the house and ties him to a post. Breakfast is quiet, since everyone is sad, because Neal is leaving for a few months, and they have begun to feel more secure with him being there. Since Clyde has to remain in bed for the next twenty-five days, Rebecca and Mickey have all the responsibility on their shoulders for maintaining the farm, the housework, and taking care of Clyde. Too, they have come to love Neal, and appreciate him not only for his help around the place, but because he's a warm and caring person who's always ready with a helping hand, for everyone in the family. He has become special indeed to Mickey, and she's not looking forward to the months ahead without him. Only the hope of his coming back, and their future life together, keeps her from begging him not to leave this morning.

When they've finished breakfast, Neal goes in to tell Mr. Wilson farewell, and promises that he will be back in just a few months.

"You're coming back here?" questions Clyde from his bed.

"Oh yes Sir, and when I do, you and me Sir, are going to have to talk."

"Oh! About what?" smiles Clyde, with a pretty good idea of his own, about this future talk, Neal is planning to have with him.

"It will keep till I get back Sir," answers Neal, as he leaves the bedroom.

"Well, if that's the way you want it, but you take care of yourself; and I surely hope you find your family well. Enjoy your visit, and we'll see you when you get back. May God go with you on the road back home, and keep you safe all the way."

"Thank you Mr. Wilson, and don't you forget what Doctor Kellum said you gotta do, so that leg will heal and you can get around again."

As Neal goes out to his horse, he reaches up and takes the two holstered pistols off the horn of his saddle and straps them around his waist. Mickey and Rebecca have followed him out to see him off on his journey back to Mississippi. When they see him put the guns on, they are reminded that they still live in a world that is unsafe, and one must be prepared for the dangers that may come at any time.

"You be careful, you hear?" Mickey says as she walks up to Neal, hugs and kisses him, right there in front of Rebecca. When the embrace is broken between the young couple, Rebecca just steps in and hugs Neal herself.

"Yeah, you listen to Mickey and be careful, I don't want anything to happen to my future son-in-law," smiles Rebecca. She steps back then and Neal pulls himself up into the saddle.

He takes one last look back at the two women who have become very important to him in just a short period of time. He notes that they are smiling through tear filled eyes while standing side by side there in the front yard, waving good-bye to him.

"You two don't fret none, I'll be fine," he says as he turns his horse and starts out. "I'll be back!"

They watch him until he is out of sight, then they go back inside. Very quietly with thoughtful expressions on both faces, they start doing their chores.

The day is sunny and bright as Neal heads toward Union City, Tennessee. He figures he can make it by mid-to-late afternoon, and he is anxious to get there and see his old friend from Rock Island, Gregory Bailey. He knows Gregory will be somewhat taken back to see him coming in, and he's really going to be surprised to learn that he's got his memory back. "It's going to be such a pleasure to tell him my name," thinks Neal, as the horse saddles (a particular gait) down the road.

Neal turns his attention to the horse and is very pleased by the way it handles, rides, and so forth, which makes the long ride ahead look much easier, than it might have been on a rough or untrained animal.

"Now what should I name you?" asks Neal out loud to the well tempered horse. "Let me see. Outlaw, now that's a suitin' name for you," he smiles as he leans over and rubs the big horse on his neck, to show the animal he likes him.

Outlaw covers the distance down to Mound City, Illinois in a little over an hour and a-half, leaving another fifty or sixty miles to go on to Union City. At the rate he is traveling Neal figures this horse will get him to Gregory's about four o'clock, that is if Outlaw can keep this gait for that distance.

The big roan colored horse with four white stockings, black mane and tail, never falters his gait. Twenty more miles after crossing the Ohio River at Cairo, Neal stops Outlaw just outside of Columbus, Kentucky on the bank of the Mississippi River. He gets some grain out of the sack he brought, and puts it in his hat for Outlaw. While the big animal eats, Neal pulls some bread out for himself from the sack the Wilson women sacked up for him this morning back at the farm. After a few minutes the horse raises his head, now finished with the grain he steps down to the water's edge to get a drink. Neal finishes his bread quickly and joins Outlaw at the edge of the river, to enjoy a drink of the cool water himself.

Their thirst quenched, Neal leads Outlaw back up to the road and mounts him. "You ready Boy?" asks Neal as he positions himself in the saddle and pats the horse on his neck. As if to say yes, the big roan bobs his head in an up and down motion. "Aw'right then, let's get going," laughs Neal at the horse's response to his question. Admiring his prize, and pleased with the ready obedience to each command he's given, he nudges Outlaw with his heel and they're off again with the smooth saddling gait, headed south into Columbus.

On through Columbus and down to Clinton, Kentucky, takes about an hour as Neal pushes for Union City. It's near one o'clock, as horse and rider leave Clinton with fifteen or twenty miles yet to go to reach their goal. Neal smiles to himself at the way this horse works and feels real proud to have him.

Outlaw never misses a step and at 3:15 p.m. he carries his new master into Union City, Tennessee. As Neal rides down the main street, he sees a man crossing the street and rides up to him. "Say Mister, can you tell me where bouts Gregory Bailey might be?" questions Neal in a polite manner.

"Yeah Son, he just opened a law office down yonder on the right. If you just keep on goin' you can't miss it."

"Thank you kindly Sir," replies Neal as he heads Outlaw on down the street. When he comes to Gregory's new office, he pulls the horse to a stop at the hitching rail in front of the porch. After tying the reins, he looks at the sign on the outside of the law office more closely.

Private Gregory Bailey
Attorney at Law

After laughing a little bit, Neal goes through the front door.

"May I help you sir?" Greets a tall, blond headed, brown-eyed, woman about twenty years old.

"Yes Ma'am, I would like to see Gregory Bailey."

"Can I tell him who's calling?" politely questions the young women, with a curious look on her face.

"Yeah, tell him the Lieutenant is calling," answers Neal, knowing that his gray pants, red shirt, and the pair of pistols he's wearing, must present a fearful sight to this woman.

"Yes sir," she replies as she goes through another door, to report to Gregory about the mysterious stranger who's asking to see him.

"The Lieutenant!" yells Gregory from the other office. Then his hurrying footsteps are heard as he runs to the outer office, to see for himself if this really is his old friend.

"Lieutenant, boy I'm glad to see you!" laughs Gregory as he puts out his hand to shake, but before he can, Neal reaches out with both arms and hugs him like a long lost brother.

"I'm mighty glad to see you too, Gregory," answers Neal, as each of them look at the other for a brief, thought filled, moment, deep emotion showing on their faces.

"You almost scared the wits out of Teresa. She said a man who had to be Jesse James was here to see me. When I asked her what his name was, all she could tell me was, the Lieutenant. I knew it had to be you, and I sure am glad it is," smiles Gregory, patting Neal on the back. "You're trying to get home aren't you."

"Yeah, I am," answers Neal with a smile, enjoying Gregory's excitement over seeing him again.

"Where did you get that pair of pistols?"

"That's a long story, I'll have to tell you about later."

"Good, then you'll stay for a few days with us."

"A few."

"Wonderful! Teresa, come here, I want you to meet my friend. This is the one I told you about from up at Rock Island. Teresa, this is the Lieutenant. Lieutenant, this is Teresa Shaw."

"Ma'am, you'll have to excuse my friend here. My name is Neal McNair," smiles Neal, pleased with the quick look of surprise that comes over Gregory's face.

"What, what did you say?" questions Gregory.

"I said, my name is Neal McNair."

"Neal McNair, well I'll be, you've got your memory back. How did that come about?"

"That too, is a long story and has to do with these here pistols and my horse outside," grins Neal, loving the suspense he's creating in Gregory's mind.

"Well, before I forget with all this excitement, Teresa and me are going to be married on July 20th," smiles Gregory as he puts his arm around Teresa and they look briefly into each other's eyes.

"Do tell! Well I'm fixin' to be getting married when I come back up this way."

"You are, to who?"

"Mickey Wilson, up at Olive Branch, Illinois."

"That's good Neal! You're going to have to tell me all about it after supper tonight."

"I'll do that, but first you can tell me about yourself."

The two friends go back into Gregory's office where they can talk more privately.

"Where do you want me to start?" questions Gregory as he puts his feet up on his desk.

"Well first, why's that sign out there, got you being a private? You were a lieutenant like myself; and you know it."

Laughing, Gregory answers, "Yeah, you're right, but I look at it this way. First, there were more privates than there were officers."

"Yeah, so go on."

"You see since there were more privates, they'll come to a private over an officer. So if they need a lawyer, they are bound to come to me over an uppity officer."

"Oh you are so smart aren't you?" laughs Neal, thoroughly enjoying this reunion with his good friend.

"After I get married, it had better work or I'll starve to death."

"I don't think that will happen. You most likely will do al'right for yourself and Teresa."

"Why thank you Lieutenant, I mean Neal, for having that much confidence in me."

"That's the one thing I do have in you. If it had not been for you, I'd most likely have gone real crazy, or maybe killed myself."

"Well that's what friends are for." There's a knock on the door and Teresa walks in. "A Mr. Mullins is here to see you Gregory."

"Oh I forgot about seeing him."

"That's al'right Gregory, I need to go and wash up if I only knew where to go."

"I'll show you," offers Teresa. "While Gregory meets with Mr. Mullins."

"That will be fine, Neal you get your horse and Teresa will walk you down to my folks place," agrees Gregory.

"Good, I'll see you at supper," promises Neal, as he gets up and follows Teresa out of the office.

"Mr. Bailey will see you now Mr. Mullins," says Teresa as she shows the man into Gregory's office and then follows Neal out to the hitching post where Outlaw is tied up.

Neal unties his horse and says, "Come on Outlaw," and the big horse falls in behind him and Teresa, and follows them along.

"Outlaw? What an odd name," states Teresa.

"Yeah, I guess it is, but there's some meaning behind it."

"How is that?" questions Teresa as they start down a long hill.

"Are you going to be eating at the Bailey's place tonight?"

"Yeah, I've been invited to eat there tonight. Well, it's really a standing invitation."

"Good, I'll tell you and Gregory the whole story then."

"All right, sounds fine to me."

"Now tell me more about you and Gregory," smiles Neal. He looks into Teresa eyes and adds, "You know that you're getting one of the best men I know, as well as my best friend, for your husband."

"Yes Neal, I surely do, and I love him very much," smiles Teresa with a blush.

It's just a short time until the Bailey home is in sight and Teresa points it out to Neal. It's a big Yankee Farm House style painted white with a tin roof, and it has a gray porch on the front.

"Here we are!" announces Teresa, as she leads Neal into the lane by the house.

"Ole Gregory comes from a well-to-do family doesn't he?" asks Neal, as he stops in the lane and looks at the house.

"Mr. Bailey is the president of the bank here, and I agree with you, they aren't hurting for anything."

"I hope that the war ending, and the shake-up in government doesn't put them under."

"Maybe it won't, but we can't worry about that. Gregory says we have got to conform to the new ways, and by doing so, we'll make it," states Teresa, confidant that what Gregory says is just the way it will be.

"He's always thinking ahead."

Teresa shows Neal where to stable Outlaw, and then takes him in the house to meet Mrs. Bailey. Supper is being prepared, and in the meantime Neal is shown to a room where he will sleep, and he can get cleaned up before the meal.

It's not long before the sound of the front door being opened is heard as Gregory and his father come in from work. Neal is introduced to Mr. Bailey, who extends him a cordial welcome to their home. Neal feels pleased since he now has met all

Gregory's family and his wife to be, and without exception each one has seemed happy to meet him, and to have him here in their home.

The meal is served with all who are seated round the table enjoying the good food and the relaxed feeling of visiting with friends over a pleasurable meal. Thoughts, ideas, and future plans are exchanged and discussed among these people, who sincerely care about others, since there's not one selfish or self-centered person in the group. After apple pie and coffee, the dishes are put away and the family with their new friend, move into the parlor to continue their conversation.

"Aw'right Neal" states Gregory, "Tell us what has happened in your life since I was paroled ahead of you."

"Aw Gregory, your family wouldn't want to hear all that, let's talk about something else," answers Neal.

"Boy if you only knew how much Gregory talked about you and your amnesia when he got home, you'd understand that we're all interested in hearing about you and all that's been happening since Gregory came home," states Mr. Bailey, while he's lighting his pipe.

"Ya'll asked for it, so here goes," answers Neal with a grin. "Gregory, when they let ya'll go before us because ya'll had served under Lee, I felt lost, specially when I got back to our cell. Sergeant Monroe did everything he could to cheer me and make things better for me. You know we kept thinking we could be getting out ever day, but it was three weeks or so after ya'll were paroled before they let us go. I was never so glad to get out of a place in my life. Anyhow, I started walking South, I didn't know my name or much of anything. After a while I figured that if I could get a boat going South, it would be faster than walking. The people we passed on our way, were not overly kind to all us Rebs, and I wanted to get South as fast as I could. I went West to the river and caught a ride with two young boys. Then after that, I got a ride on a steamboat. I used the name Paul Wood for my own name."

"How did you come up with that name?" questions Gregory.

"From our prison numbers, mine was P.W. 44, so I jes' used Paul Wood, from P.W."

"Oh, I see."

"Anyway, I worked as a cook on a paddle wheeler down to Cape Girardeau and got off there, and started walking here. After I passed through Olive Branch, I was jumped by a bunch of young ruffians. These two women came by, found me, and took me in. They nursed me a day or so, took real good care of me. Their names were Rebecca Wilson and her daughter Mickey. Mr. Wilson was off in the Yankee army, and can you believe it, they took a Reb in? As I said, a day or so later, I was still bad off, when a guerrilla band rode in to cause harm to these women, who were caring for me. I was able to get this pair of pistols off one of them and run the others off. When they left, I was two horses better off, and had my memory back because of the shock, I guess. Anyway when the shooting started, I remembered everything to do, and even remembered my past. So Teresa, that jus' seemed like a suitin' name for my horse."

"What did you name him Neal?" questions Gregory.

"Outlaw," answers Neal with a smile.

"Oh you are so smart," grins Gregory.

"Now as I was saying, the outlaw band rode off, so there we were. I needed the Wilson's, until I gained my strength and was more able to travel. They needed me for whatever help I could give in case the outlaws returned, or another gang was out looking for women, who's husbands were off in the war. Mickey and I became fond of each other right off, and I decided to stay with them until Mr. Wilson got home. When he did get home, he had been shot in the leg. I had already begun plowing his fields for him, hoping to give him a head start on planting the crops. Since he came home hurt from being in a shoot out with Quantrill's bunch, I decided to plant his crops for him. When we talked about the outlaws that came to the farm, and the gang his group ran into, we decided it was the same men, who his wife and I had run off from his farm. Quantrill was killed in the fight he had with Mr. Wilson and his men, so I guess that ended the gang. As time passed, I asked Mickey to marry me and she said yeah, so after my visit back home, I'm coming back up here to get her pa's permission."

"I'd say that you've been real busy since you got out of jail," laughs Gregory.

NEAL'S HOMECOMING

"That was some story Neal, you ought to put it in a book," comments Teresa.

"Nobody but my friends and family would read it, and I can tell them the whole story," laughs Neal.

"That was very interesting, Neal, thanks for bringing us up to date on what's happened to you, cause we sure have wondered ever since Gregory came home," yawns Mrs. Bailey. "Excuse me, I must be getting sleepy."

"Yes it's about that time," agrees Mr. Bailey. "I believe I'll head on up to bed."

"I'll join you dear," says Mrs. Bailey. The two of them get up and excuse themselves, as they leave the group in the parlor.

The young folks talk on into the night, then Gregory takes Teresa home and Neal gets in bed around 11:00 p.m.

May 31st, 1865

Neal awakens to the smell of breakfast being prepared. He has slept soundly in the nice comfortable bed and feels more rested. He remembers that this is the first bed he's slept in since Rock Island, if one wants to call those cots a bed. If not, he has not slept in a real bed since Doctor Voge's back in Nashville. He gets up and dresses then goes down stairs, where he finds the Bailey family waiting, with breakfast on the table.

After breakfast Gregory tells Neal to come on down to his office around 9:30, and they'll go to the hotel across the street for coffee and they can talk some more.

While Neal is waiting for the time to go meet with Gregory, he goes out to the stable and feeds Outlaw. When he's finished eating the grain, Neal leads him to the water trough. He lets him drink, walks him around the barn, and rubs him down good, then Neal starts to leave the lot. Outlaw loves all the attention that he's gotten and doesn't want to give up on getting more, so every time Neal starts to leave, Outlaw runs up behind him and nuzzles him on the back. Neal thinks, "This is really some horse, and I believe he likes having me around." Time has passed and it's time to meet Gregory, so he pats his horse on the neck, scratches his mane then hurries through the lot-gate, leaving Outlaw nickering at the fence.

Neal goes to Gregory's office at 9:00 a.m., and they continue talking about things they did not cover in last night's visit. Neal tells of his home and family, now that he remembers everything. They smile at how close Gregory came to figuring out all these things about him, back at Rock Island.

At 9:30, they cross the street for coffee and as they go into the cafe, Gregory picks up a newspaper. The waiter comes to their table and takes their order for black coffee, while they talk a little bit more. Then Gregory opens up the paper and starts reading.

Suddenly, he says, still looking at the paper, "Oh my Goodness!"

"What's that all about?" questions Neal, as he takes another sip of coffee, but he notices the look of shock on Gregory's face.

"That Jesse James gang has hit again," answers Gregory with a look of disgust on his face, as he lays the paper down on the table.

"Really and that's who I was dressed like yesterday?" questions Neal, with a smile.

"Yeah, you really looked rough with those guns on," laughs Gregory.

"Jesse James huh? Where did they hit?"

"Up at Thebes, Illinois," answers Gregory.

"Thebes! That ain't but eight or ten miles from Olive Branch," exclaims Neal, showing a growing concern on his face. "Who is this Jesse James?"

"Some say he rode with Quantrill and now he has taken over the gang, since Quantrill is dead."

"I thought the gang was broke up when Quantrill was killed and the ones left run off," states Neal.

"Yeah, I remember you saying that and I didn't want to dispute your word."

"Gregory, I killed three of those men, they just didn't give me their guns and horses."

"Yeah, I'd figured that out last night. Men just don't give up their gun or horse, without being dead."

"If they were at the Wilson farm before, they may be headed back for revenge.

"I wouldn't think so," answers Gregory.

NEAL'S HOMECOMING

"Yeah, but you know they would like to get me, and then they would take the women. Gregory, Mr. Wilson can't even get out of the bed. I'm going back, today! That James gang is jes' too close to some people I love," declares Neal, disturbed at the thought of what could happen to the Wilson's.

"You want me to go with you?" offers Gregory, seeing the depth of emotion that is obvious on the face of his friend.

"No, not now, but if I need you, I'll send for you some how. Besides you may be needed here by your pa and his bank," states Neal as he stands up to leave.

Gregory pays for the coffee and joins Neal outside the hotel. "Neal, I'll go with you if you want me too, just say the word and I'll saddle my horse," offers Gregory again.

"No Gregory, you need to stay here, chances are nothing will happen, but if it does, I wanta be there."

"I don't blame you," says Gregory, understanding Neal's need to leave.

"Thanks for everything you've done for me, and I'll be back for your wedding."

"That will be great, you can be my best man."

"Deal, now I gotta go," states Neal, as he shakes Gregory's hand, puts his arm around his shoulder and says, "Thanks for understanding." Then he turns and starts walking hurriedly back to the Bailey's home.

"What's got you in such'a all-fired hurry boy?" asks Mrs. Bailey, seeing Neal almost running up into the yard, where she's pruning her rose bushes in front of the house.

"Mrs. Bailey, I can't take time to explain it all, but I've got to get back up to Olive Branch. The James Gang's in that area and I feel I may be needed there," Neal says as he continues on into the house to gather up his things.

He's only inside for a few minutes then he's headed toward the stables to saddle Outlaw. Mrs. Bailey tries to keep step with him as he walks rapidly up to the lot gate, strapping his pistols on as he goes.

"Surely you don't think you'll be using those things again!" exclaims Mrs. Bailey, watching Neal as he gets his saddle and blanket out of the barn.

NEAL'S HOMECOMING

"I hope not Mrs. Bailey, but you can never tell," answers Neal as he throws the blanket and saddle on Outlaw's back. The horse had trotted up to him when he started to open the lot gate, just as if he's been waiting for Neal to come back for him.

As he swings up into the saddle he says, "Gregory knows the whole story about why I'm headed back North. He can tell you more, but I must be on my way. Thanks for the good food and bed. I did really enjoy meeting and visiting with ya'll, and hope to see you at the wedding."

Neal is half-way down the drive when Mrs. Bailey waves and calls out, "Then go on boy, I know you must, but be careful."

"Yes ma'am," answers Neal as he gives Outlaw his head and they're on their way back to the Wilson Farm.

The big horse seems to sense Neal's need to get back North, and his saddle (gait) is quicker than the day before. They stop at the same spot on the river for grain and water, but the need to be pushing onward, is greater than the need to rest and refresh themselves.

It's an hour after dark when Neal and Outlaw make it to the Wilson farm. As they come into the yard no lights are seen in the house. Neal stops Outlaw at the front steps, runs up them, and knocks on the door. To his relief, he hears Rebecca's voice call out from inside. "Who is it?"

"It's me, Neal, Mrs. Wilson, I'm back and I'll be staying in the barn, if you need me."

With the sound of Neal's voice, the front door swings open and Mickey bursts out of the house and right into Neal's arms. "I'm so glad you're back Darling!" she says as she hugs and kisses him freely.

"Me too, my love," answers Neal, glad to find that the family is alright, and that the James Gang has not been there. It's also good to hold Mickey in his arms again, and be assured that she has come to no harm while he was away.

"But why are you back Neal?" questions Rebecca, curious to know why he has returned so soon.

"I learned from the newspaper in Union City, that the James gang is in the area and the thought that they might come here, drove me crazy to get back. I had to come to be sure ya'll were alright, or to be here if something should happen."

"I'm mighty glad you're back. I was jes' lost without you Darlin," sighs Mickey while still hanging on to Neal's arm.

"Well, if I can help it, I won't ever be away from you, if it means leaving you unprotected again," states Neal very sincerely.

"Oh Neal I do love you," declares Mickey as she looks into Neal's eyes, and sees the love he feels for her reflected there.

"Now Kids, Mr. Wilson is still awake in there, and he may be able to hear you, jes' remember that," informs Rebecca.

"Mrs. Wilson, that will be alright, for tomorrow I'm gonna ask him for Mickey's hand in marriage, because I love her so much. I think he should know how I feel, and besides, I can't wait no longer to know if he will consider me for a son-in-law. Now it's late and I'm tired, so I'm going to the barn to put Outlaw up. That's my horse's name, then I'm going to bed. Don't ya'll worry, cause I'm a light sleeper, and I'm close by," assures Neal.

"That's wonderful that you are going to talk with Clyde tomorrow, and I was concerned about those outlaws being in the area, but now that you're back, I'll sleep much better tonight," smiles Rebecca.

"Good-night Ladies."

"Good-night Neal, we all love you," declares Mickey, as Neal leads Outlaw to the barn. Mickey adds, "I'll leave some food out here for you."

Once he's inside the barn, Neal feeds, waters, and then rubs Outlaw down good before leaving him. When his horse has been taken care of, Neal goes back to the porch of the house and gets the platter of food which Mickey has left out for him. When he picks it up, he hears Mickey's voice coming out of the darkness, as she says softly, "I hope you enjoy the supper My Love."

"I'm sure I will Sweetheart," answers a tired Neal, as he makes his way back to the barn.

Back in his stable at the barn, Neal eats his supper by the light of the coal oil lamp, removes his dusty clothing and lies down on his pallet. He is confidant that he has made the right decision about talking to Mr. Wilson tomorrow concerning Mickey and the desire he has to marry her. As he falls asleep, he thinks that the one thing he is completely sure of is his love for Mickey. Though the world is in a state of chaos, he feels that this is most important, of all that matters to him. He figures once they are married and the needs of the family have been taken care of, he'll go back home and let his family, or what's left of it, meet his wife. If his marrying a northern woman should be a problem, it will not be his problem, but theirs. With this settled in his mind, sleep comes quickly with pleasant thoughts of being married to Mickey, and their future together.

YANKEE SERGEANT ACCEPTS REB

. . . .

June 1st, 1865

Neal wakes up feeling rested after a good night's sleep, just when the sun is showing on the horizon in the East, and the old rooster begins to crow. With nature's alarm clock sounding off, Neal gets up and dresses for the day. It's not long before Mickey comes out of the house, walking toward the barn with her milk bucket in her hand. Once she is on the path to the barn, Neal opens the door and walks out to meet her.

She says, "Good morning Neal," with a big happy smile on her face.

"Good morning Mickey," responds Neal, but he keeps walking toward the house.

When he's about to pass her on the path walking like a man with a serious mission, she questions, "Neal wait, where are you going in such a hurry?"

"To have that talk with your pa, like I told you I would."

"Oh, well good luck Darlin'," smiles Mickey as Neal keeps right on going.

Mickey goes on to the barn and begins milking, while Neal goes into the house and finds Mrs. Wilson in the kitchen.

"Mrs. Wilson."

"Yes Neal."

"Would you go into Mr. Wilson's room and announce me please?"

"Sure Neal," answers Rebecca and she turns immediately to go into her bedroom.

Neal can hear Rebecca telling Clyde that he is out in the kitchen, and wants to talk with him.

"I know he is here. I heard him ride in last night. Can't it keep, whatever it is he wants to talk to me about?" asks Clyde, pretty sure he knows that Neal is going to ask for his only daughter's hand.

"No Darlin' it won't keep, now you be nice," suggests Rebecca, confidant that he will be kind to Neal, as she leaves the bedroom. Going back into the kitchen, where Neal is waiting restlessly, she pats him on the shoulder, smiles and tells him to go on in, that Clyde is expecting him.

Neal steps into the bedroom and immediately develops a good case of cold feet, so he just stands there, trying to sum up the courage he had before he crossed the threshold of this room.

"Well Boy, you wanted to talk to me I believe," states Clyde, amazed at Neal's shyness, which has never been evident before when he's visited in this room.

"Uh, good morning Mr. Wilson!"

"Good morning Neal," answers Clyde from his bed. "Now what is it you want to talk about?"

"Uh, uh, how are the crops Sir?"

"Neal the crops are fine I guess, I've not been out of bed to check on them," smiles Clyde.

"Well, uh, I guess I should go check on them, don't you?"

"Yeah Son, you should, but now what else?"

"Uh—uh- Mr. Wilson," stammers Neal, walking closer to Clyde's bedside. "I —augh, I mean uh—"

"Yes Neal?"

"It's uh- Mickey, Sir, uh-"

"Something the matter with Mickey?" grins Clyde, remembering the day he asked for the hand of Rebecca.

"Uh, uh, no Sir, I mean yes Sir, uh- I think she needs to be married, I mean, I want to marry her, uh- Sir, with your agreein' to it, of course, Sir."

"You do want to marry her?"

"Oh, yes Sir."

"Well, do you love her?"

"Oh yes Sir, very much," smiles Neal, the tension now broken.

"Do you like her?" asks Clyde.

"Huh? Yes Sir, I love her."

"But do you like her?"

"Yes Sir, very much Sir."

"Good, because if you like her, you and her will find out what love is, just like her mother and me have done."

"Does this mean you approve of us getting married?"

"Yeah Boy it does, but let me add one thing. Mickey is my only little girl and she always will be. Now you can be my son, but you had better be good to her, cause my leg won't be broke forever. You do understand what I'm asking of you, don't you Neal?"

"Oh yes Sir, I sure do Sir. Can I go now?" asks Neal.

"Yeah Boy, go tell Mickey the good news," smiles Clyde as Neal turns and almost runs out of the room.

After Neal rushes from the room, Rebecca goes in and looks at Clyde. He holds his arms out to her so she goes to his bedside and leans into them. He holds her close for some time while they reflect on how their lives began, and the way their love has grown and deepened through the years. They share one heartfelt request in their silent prayer for the marriage of their daughter. "May it equal or exceed the happiness they've found in their own marriage, through mutual love, respect, and sharing of each day together, whether it be good or bad. They've been blessed and strengthened by their love for God and each other."

As the embrace is broken, the eyes of both are moist, and their hearts are tender but they smile lovingly at each other and Clyde asks, "You got breakfast ready yet?" He winks at her and grins.

"Oh Clyde that ain't what you are supposed to be thinking about now."

"Darlin' we've had our serious thoughts, and now I'm hungry so I ask again, have you got breakfast ready, huh?"

"Oh, alright. Men! You gotta love 'em and feed 'em," laughs Rebecca on her way to the kitchen for Clyde's breakfast.

Meanwhile, Neal has run to the barn and as he runs in, he finds Mickey waiting just inside the door. He picks her up and kisses her, holding her close, he says, "He said yes!"

"Oh Darlin," smiles Mickey as tears fill her eyes. They look at each other lovingly, still finding it hard to believe this last hurdle has been vaulted, and their marriage plans can be made. Neal kisses Mickey again, and they continue holding each other close, while they cherish this precious moment in their lives. Then Mickey pulls back, and looking at Neal she asks, "Well, when are we going to get married?"

"I guess we should wait a little while, don't you?"

"Wait! Why?"

"I don't want the neighbors to think this is a shot-gun wedding," answers Neal.

"Oh Neal, be serious."

"I am serious, and I've already got a date in mind, if it's alright with you."

"Well, this could be risky, but I'll ask. When?"

"Alright, last night I was thinking. Now don't get mad."

"I won't, silly."

"Well, I was thinking you see, you Yankees won the war and still celebrate the fourth of July. We Rebs don't celebrate the fourth, and so if we get married on that date, it will give me a reason for celebrating."

"Oh! I think that's a good idea Darlin'," agrees Mickey with a big smile.

"You do?"

"Yeah, and another reason for making our wedding on that day, is because it's my papa's birthday."

"Really, I didn't know that."

"I know that, and I think the fourth will be great."

"Well then, it's set. The fourth it will be."

"Good," agrees Mickey, again sealing their agreement with a kiss.

"Boy I'm hungry. I didn't know getting permission to get married could be so much work. It surely does work up one's appetite," states Neal after the lingering kiss, and the close embrace is broken. He really is hungry, but he also feels that they've been in the barn long enough, and Mickey's parents are probably looking for them to get back to the house.

"Oh aw'right, mother has got breakfast ready by now, so let's go join her," says Mickey.

At breakfast Mickey and Rebecca make plans for the wedding. They will announce the engagement at church Sunday, and give the date for the wedding. They plan a yard wedding, and while they are deep in plans and conversation, Neal gets up unnoticed and goes out to the barn. He saddles Outlaw to ride over the fields and check the crops so he can give Mr. Wilson a run down on how they're coming along.

The military phase of the Civil War is coming to an end. In June of 1865, the last large group of Confederate soldiers surrender in Oklahoma Territory. The Confederate leader is Brigadier General Watie, a Cherokee, and his battalion is made up of Indians. An end to the Federal blockade to the Southern States comes. President Johnson names provisional governors to six Southern states. He also restores the State of Tennessee to the Union, saying it is because Tennessee has reorganized it's own government. One must remember that President Johnson comes from Tennessee.

The word of Mickey's upcoming wedding spreads all over Canny Community. The news of this event is something bright and happy in a community that has been split asunder by war. One must remember that this is southern Illinois, and not all the people's feelings were for the North, in this area. A war that has spread dark clouds, which rained pain and destruction over all the country, has been felt in a special way by this community, due to the division in the state. All of the folks look at this happy occasion with hope. It seems to be a reminder that good things can still happen, and love is the beginning of them all. Young love and weddings have always been looked upon as special and joyous events, which all ages look forward to attending. Mickey and Neal's has come at a time when people of communities all over the nation need to see a happy beginning.

Neal writes a letter to Union City, telling Gregory that he needs him to come to the Wilson farm on July 4th, at noon. He wants his friend to share his happiness, be his best man, and to meet his bride and her family. Since he has told Gregory he will send for him if he needs him, he feels sure he will come in reply to this brief note, without any further explanation.

NEAL'S HOMECOMING

WEDDING WITH HOPE FOR FUTURE

• • • • • • • • • • • • • • • • • • •

July 1, 1865

Clyde receives a letter telling him that he is to report to the county seat, on July 15th.

"Honey, I wonder what the army is going to do now," says Rebecca.

"I don't know, but this is an order, and I need to be there when my name is called."

"Yeah, but you've got a broken leg and just been out'a bed a couple of days."

"Sweetheart, the army don't know I've been hurt," answers Clyde. "When the squad and I get there, we'll tell them what happened to us on our way home."

"You don't think they'll take you back with one leg shorter than the other, do you?"

"My guess is that they'll muster us all out, when they get their weapons and horses back, but I won't know until I get there just what the army has in mind for us."

"Oh I really hope they don't send you away from home again," says Rebecca as she leaves the porch, and goes inside to help Mickey with her wedding dress.

Neal comes in from the fields, after checking on the crops. Clyde asks, "How're they doing," as he gets up on the crutches Neal made for him

"Oh, they are coming along just fine Mr. Wilson," he replies.

"Well now, it won't be long Boy, till you'll be an old married man," comments Clyde, taking his pipe out and filling it with tobacco.

"That's right, and Mickey and me was thinking that maybe you would let us fix that stable I'm staying in, into a room until we can find a place of our own," says Neal.

"I know how you feel Neal. We all want a place of our own and the privacy it gives us when we get married and start our new life together."

"Yes Sir, that's the way we feel."

"That will be jus' fine, you go ahead and make a room for yourselves out of that stable."

"Thank you Sir."

"Where do you want to find a place Neal?"

"Well, if things are like I figure they are back home, it would be best for us to find a place up here."

"How's that Son?"

"I figure it's gonna be hard for years to come, because of the war, and the fact that the South put everything it had into it."

"Oh, I see."

"Also, I know my brother Melton, lost a hand, and if he made it home, he'll be there with my mother and pa until he can find a trade for himself. My brother Thompson, was killed, and then there's Ruben, my youngest brother, I don't even know if he made it home. But, if I had to guess, that little knot head did make it, if anybody did, and that will be another mouth for the farm to feed. Then there's Ivory and Alice, who're jes' like family, so if Mickey and me go back there to settle, the farm will have that much more of a burden to carry. Even if we had a place to buy there, I don't have anything to put into it."

"You can help farm this place. Besides, it will belong to the two of you one day anyway."

"I know that Sir, but we really want a place of our own. You are going to be able to work this place yourself next year."

"I don't know about that. I've yet to walk on this leg, so I'll just have to wait and see how it turns out," explains Clyde.

"That makes two of us. We'll find a place some where, some day, but we're jes' gonna have to wait and see what the future brings, like you."

Neal leaves the porch and heads to the barn. When he gets there he starts clearing out the stable so he can make a room out of it. Where it has been just a stable with a pallet, he plans to put a floor in it, then seal it up and add a window. Where he's been looking through a crack in the wall, he wants a real window, before he and Mickey move into it.

Mickey and Rebecca are busy in the kitchen, cooking tea cakes and pies for the wedding. Between the cooking and baking, they pin up and sew on Mickey's wedding dress. As the sweets begin baking, the air is filled with a mouth watering aroma. Between the cooking and sewing, they discuss details to be taken care of before the wedding day. It's a busy day, but excitement keeps them happily chattering about the day of July 4th.

When the dress is finished, Mickey takes some of the freshly baked tea cakes out to Neal, where he's working on their room in the barn.

"I brought you some sweets," announces Mickey, as she steps upon the new floor now covering the area, where the stable has been.

"That's mighty nice of you," answers Neal, while nailing the last board in the floor of their new room.

"You've done a whole lotta' work today, why don't you and me go for a walk?"

"I'd love to sweetheart, but I need to have this room finished day after tomorrow, so I better stick with it," smiles Neal as he takes one of the tea cakes out of Mickey's hand.

"Think I know what you mean," smiles Mickey. "Can I help?"

"Yeah I guess you can, if you're sure you want to. We don't have any paint, but I know how to make a paint, if the color will suit you."

"What color will it be?"

"Well I don't know, but when I was in Tennessee, I saw people take red dirt out of caves and mix it with buttermilk, to make a red paint. If we had some white chalk that was dry and dusty, I bet we could get a white colored paint that would look better than these plain boards, I'm fixin' to put up."

"Neal, I know where we can get some powdery chalk dirt!"

"Where is that?" questions Neal.

"Down yonder where the Canny Road tee's into the main road," explains Mickey.

"And the wagons and horses have beat it into a dust," interrupts Neal.

"Yeah."

"Let's me and you ride down there and get it, when I get this room boarded up."

"Fine, and I'll make three or four gallons of buttermilk up, so we'll have that ready when we need it."

"We don't have long, so I'll push hard to be through by dinner on the third. We'll go after the chalk, and paint it that afternoon."

"Good!" Answers Mickey, as she stands on tiptoe to kiss Neal, then turns and goes back to the house.

Neal says, "See you at dinner Honey," picks up his hammer, a board, and some nails, and he turns back to work on their room.

July 3rd, 1865

As the Wilson's and Neal are eating dinner, Clyde asks, "Did you get finished with the room Neal?" He continues to crumble his corn bread up in the peas already on his plate.

"Yes Sir. All I lack now is painting the walls," answers Neal.

"That's good Neal," states Rebecca, "But where are you going to get any paint?"

"Oh Neal has that all figured out, Mother. That's why I made up so much buttermilk," explains Mickey.

Then Neal tells of his idea on how to make the paint, and he sure hopes it will be white, he can't be sure until it's mixed and on the walls.

"It's worth a try Son. You and Mickey need to leave right after dinner, so you will have time to spread the paint this afternoon," instructs Clyde.

After the meal, Neal saddles Outlaw, while Mickey puts a pair of her fathers pants on under her dress, and in this way she'll be able to ride double behind Neal. On their way to the tee of the road, Neal stops by Red Taylor's place so Mickey can be assured that Red will play his fiddle at the wedding tomorrow.

When the couple rides into the Taylor place, they find Red sitting on his front porch. He says, "Well look who has come to visit," as he struggles to stand up, with his cripple leg making it difficult as usual.

"Howdy Mr. Red," greets Mickey, dropping her arms from around Neal's waist.

"What brings you two by here Girl?" Red questions, now on his feet and stretching out his arms to flex his body.

"We're doing a chore and I asked Neal to stop by jus' to make sure you remember to come play your fiddle at our wedding tomorrow. It will be at two o'clock," answers Mickey.

"Oh you can count on it. I wouldn't miss it for the world," affirms Red, with a big smile. "It's been a long time since we've had a weddin' in this community and I'm looking forward to yours. I ain't forgot the date either, but I'm glad you two stopped by."

Glenn steps out on the porch, from the front room of the house. "I thought I heard some talking going on out here," he smiles.

"Yeah, you sure did, you know Mickey here, and this is her husband to be, Neal McNair," says Red as he introduces the two young men.

"Good to meet you Neal," states Glenn and adds, "Pa, I'm a-goin to town this afternoon. Got to see if anybody knows what the army has in mind doin' with us."

"I wish you wouldn't boy, but go ahead on, if you've got to," answers Red as Glenn heads out toward the barn to saddle a horse.

"That boy hasn't been the same since his mama died and he went into the army. All he wants to do is stay in the army," states Red to Mickey and Neal.

"He wasn't in the places I was in, or he would get as far out of the army as he could," declares Neal.

"Yeah, me too," agrees Red.

Glenn leads the horse out of the barn, mounts up and heads toward town, giving a brief wave to his father on the porch, and the couple still sitting on their horse, out in the front yard.

"If he stays in the army I don't know what I'll do with this place. I can't farm it with this here bad leg," says Red with a look of hopelessness on his face.

"I'll help you as much as I can, if Glenn does go back to the army Mr. Taylor," promises Neal, as he watches Glenn go around a curve in the road, and out of their sight.

"Well I'm much obliged Neal but you're going to have your hands full with Clyde's place. If that boy stays in the army, I'll have to find me a trade that I can handle, and sell this place," says Red, having made up his mind that he can't continue to struggle with farming.

Hearing this, Mickey and Neal both perk up, their minds in tune and their ears open. "Mr. Taylor, if you do sell this place, I'd like first crack at it," states Neal.

"We surely would Mr. Red," agrees Mickey enthusiastically.

"Well Kids if I sell it, I'll surely give you two a chance to get it. That Glenn got in on the tail end of the war, and he's rolling in glory I guess. If he stays in the army, I'll find something else to do and talk to you two about buying the place," promises Red.

"We'd sure appreciate it, and we'd best be going now Mr. Taylor," states Neal.

"See you tomorrow Mr. Red," says Mickey as Neal turns Outlaw and they head out of the yard.

"You two can count on seeing me, I wouldn't miss it," laughs Red as the young couple ride out with Mickey putting her arms up over Neal's pistols, and wrapping them around him to hold on.

After about thirty minutes, the two are at the tee of the road and they find that the chalky white dirt is as fine as dust, due to all the travel on it by horses and wagons. After filling two flour sacks and tying them on Outlaw, they head back to the Wilson farm. As they pass the Taylor place, Neal says, "I've not wished so hard for someone to be in the army, since I wished to be in it myself, four years ago. Am I wrong to be thinking like this?"

"No Darlin', if Glenn wants to make the army his way of life, then that's his choice," says Mickey.

"I sure do hope he does."

"Yeah, me too," agrees Mickey.

As they continue on home, they talk about tomorrow and make plans for the rest of their lives together.

In a few minutes they are back at the barn where they quickly mix-up the solution of white chalk and buttermilk. To their dismay, it makes a thick paste which is much too thick to use on the walls as they had planned. Neal and Mickey are just sitting next to the bucket of paste, feeling discouraged because they have no alternate plan for painting the walls when Rebecca walks up to see what progress has been made on the room.

She takes one look at their faces and asks, "What's the matter with you two?"

"Oh mother, this stuff is too thick to brush on the walls," replies Mickey with a sigh of disgust.

"Oh you two, all you have to do is add water to thin it the way you want it," laughs Rebecca.

"Why didn't I think of that?" asks Neal as he gets up and starts out of the barn for a bucket of water.

"Because you are not as smart as you think you are," laughs Mickey.

Once the water is added and the texture is thin enough, Neal and Mickey spread the white wash on the inside walls of their new room, with corn shuck brushes. They have finished the job in about an hour and to their amazement, the walls are now a dirty white.

"It looks better than what it did," says Mickey as they look at their handiwork, not really unhappy with the way it looks.

"Yeah, it does for now, but I don't know how long it will stay on the walls," laughs Neal.

"Maybe long enough for us to get to buy the Taylor place," smiles Mickey. "Oh I do love you Neal McNair!" The two embrace and share a lingering kiss, for the first time in their finished, white, room.

July 4th, 1865

The Wilson farm is up early. Rebecca and Mickey sweep the yard, while Neal places a few new benches, he has just built, out in front of the porch. A table is set up on saw horses, for the sweets that will be served after the ceremony. The chairs are removed from the porch, except for one, which is reserved for Red Taylor and his fiddle.

It is eleven o'clock before everything is in place, according to the way Mickey and Rebecca have planned. Rebecca then serves a lunch of cornbread and milk, saying that they don't need anything heavy, since the wedding will take place soon, and there will be sweets later. It's twelve o'clock when the family members go to their rooms to get cleaned up for the occasion.

Neal is dressing in the new room in the barn, and people are gathering outside, when he hears a horse come into the yard, traveling at a fast gait. Not knowing who this may be, Neal quickly gets one of his pistols and goes to the new window to look out. To his surprise it's Gregory on a big Tennessee walking mare.

A few people have already walked up to Gregory, to answer his questions, and to find out who he may be, when Neal runs out of the room, and to the barn door, where he drops his gun. He rushes outside, bare footed and buttoning his shirt as he hurries out to welcome his old friend.

"Gregory!" yells Neal, "Come on over here."

Gregory turns the mare and she trots to the lot gate, where Neal is standing on the inside. Gregory leans over and the two friends shake hands, then Neal opens the gate and the mare trots right through. The few people who have gathered early, observe this meeting and look at Gregory curiously, knowing he is not someone from Canny community.

Once he's inside the lot, Gregory swings down out of the saddle and buttons his coat, attempting to cover the pair of pistols he wears on the belt under it. Then he takes the saddle and bridle off his horse and she trots over to the water trough.

"I'm mighty glad to see you Gregory. I didn't know if you got my letter or not," says Neal as he greets his special guest with a warm smile and a pat on the back.

"I got your letter all right, but you failed to tell me why you needed me here on the Fourth, and I didn't know what to expect. I remembered you saying you were getting married, but I didn't know when, so I put my coat and pants on about three this morning, along with my pistols and here I am. I'd say from the way everything is fixed up, you're getting married today."

"Yeah, and you are gonna be my best man, Ole Friend!"

"Good!" smiles Gregory, pleased to see Neal happily excited, having seen him existing in a painful world of confusion not too long ago.

"Pistols. Can't get away from them the way the world is today, with the outlaws and all that may show up anywhere at anytime," comments Neal as he leads Gregory back to the barn.

"You are so right about that," agrees Gregory.

When the two men go in the barn door, Neal bends over and picks his pistol up where he dropped it on the straw when he went outside, to call to Gregory. Blowing the dust off of it, he says, "You never can tell when you may need one of these," and grins, as they walk on back toward the new room.

"You're right, just keep it handy. Ya'll heard any more out of the James gang?" asks Gregory as he follows Neal into the new room.

"No, not here. They're still hittin' north and west of here though," replies Neal.

"Well you'd better stay prepared," advises Gregory in a serious tone of voice.

"You can count on it," assures Neal, as Gregory takes his brace of pistols off and hangs them on a nail in the wall. Neal holsters his pistol back with it's mate on the head of his newly built bed.

They hear a whinny from Gregory's mare in the lot, and when Neal looks out the window, he sees Outlaw with his head over the fence from the pasture side and he too, is making soft nickering sounds in the mare's direction. "Gregory, I believe Outlaw is taking a shine to your mare."

Smiling, Gregory answers, "I was kinda hoping he would, that mare is just about ready to come in and I sure hope that Outlaw does the service for her."

"I'm sure he will, why don't you go out and let her in the pasture with him," suggests Neal.

"Believe I will," says Gregory, getting up and going out of the barn and into the lot. After a little bit, when he gets to the pasture gate, he notices that Outlaw is monitoring every move he makes. "Come on Tally," says Gregory, opening the gate, "Get out there and make friends with Outlaw."

The tall mare runs through the gate, the minute the opening is wide enough for her to squeeze through. The two horses inspect each other for a moment, then they gallop over the hill as if to find some privacy.

Gregory goes back to Neal's room, and Neal says, "That didn't take long," when Gregory steps up through the door.

"No it didn't. Those two have already gone to the back side of the pasture."

Neal finishes dressing, looks out the window and sees that Red Taylor has already taken his chair on the porch. Glenn is sitting on the first bench in the yard next to John White and his family. Other people are there who Neal has seen in the community, but he can't call them by name.

"It won't be long now," says Neal, just a bit nervous, but happy that this is his wedding day. He thinks of his parents and the good life they've shared together, wishing they could be here to share this day with him and Mickey. He looks forward to taking her to his home, having some minor reservations, because she is from the Northern part of the country. He knows that when they have a chance to know her, they too, will love her and treat her as a daughter.

"Here, while I'm thinking about it, this is the ring you are to hand me when it's time for me to put it on Mickey's hand," says Neal as he takes out a silver wedding band and hands it to Gregory.

"Neal where did you get this ring?" asks Gregory, "With times being so hard, this is a perfect silver band, and it must have cost you some money."

"I made it out of a four-bit piece, and the one Mickey has for me, I made out of a dollar," answers Neal.

"How?"

"I took a spoon and held the coins, then beat the edges. When I had the outside of the ring shaped, I measured the inside. When it was down to the size I needed, I just bored the middle out and had the two rings," answers Neal with a big grin.

"Oh aren't you so smart," laughs Gregory.

About that time, Red starts playing the fiddle and Neal says, "Here we go!" He leads Gregory out of the barn and across the yard.

When the two of them reach the porch steps and step up them, Red stops playing and the preacher comes out the front door of the house to join them. Then Red starts playing the wedding march and Rebecca comes out on the porch in her blue Sunday dress, goes down the steps and seats herself with the White family and Glenn Taylor. When she is seated, Mickey comes out, escorted by her father who is on the crutches Neal made for him.

The ceremony is short and the preacher soon asks "Who gives this woman in marriage?"

Clyde answers, "Her mother and I do." Then he turns and hobbles to the steps where Glenn and John stand up, step forward, and help him down to his seat beside Rebecca.

Mickey is dressed in an ankle length white cotton dress with tatting around the hem, waist and neck line. Neal is wearing a pair of Clyde's black Sunday pants, white shirt and a black string tie. They both wear radiant expressions on their faces, which leaves no room for anyone to doubt that this is a happy couple, who are very much in love. Their smiles have an infectious effect on the friends who are present, and they all start smiling with them. Even the ladies who shed happy tears, as ladies always seem to do at weddings, are now rejoicing with Mickey and Neal on this very special occasion in their lives.

When the preacher calls for the rings, Gregory hands Neal Mickey's ring, and Mickey takes Neal's ring from under the cuff on her left wrist. The preacher then tells the meaning of the ring, and it's symbol of unbroken, unending love. Neal and Mickey exchange rings and the vows that are so meaningful, and a commitment for life to one another. The preacher pauses and then says, "By the authority of God and the State of Illinois, I now pronounce you man and wife. Neal, you may kiss your bride."

With these words being spoken, Red Taylor begins playing a lively tune, while Neal and Mickey embrace, and share their first kiss as man and wife.

With Neal and his bride still clinging to one another, seemingly unaware that they are not the only people in the world, Gregory steps back up to them. He says, "You two've got the rest of your lives for this, and some of us have got to be going home soon. I guess I should kiss the bride now, before all the other men out there, get up here on the porch."

"Well I won't kiss you, if you're gonna be leaving this soon," protests Mickey. "Here I've just met you and from what Neal's told me about you, I owe you a'lot, so make up your mind to stay awhile, then I'll kiss you," promises Mickey, smiling her irresistible smile.

"Oh, al'right," laughs Gregory. "I'll find some place to stay."

Mickey then gives him a kiss and tells him, "Thanks for everything you did for Neal while you two were in that ole prison. Also for being a friend to him when he didn't even know who he was. Now I especially, thank you for coming to our wedding, cause it means so much to both of us."

Neal is still standing next to Mickey with his arm holding her close to his side, while, she and Gregory are talking and he just puts his other arm around Gregory's shoulder and says, "Thanks for all of that, and for being my friend, I won't ever forget you."

Red Taylor steps up and says, "I heard all of that, now this boy can stay over at my place with me and Glenn so don't look no further. Now, where's my kiss?"

Neal and Gregory step over to the side as all the men line up to get a kiss from Mickey, and Rebecca and Mrs. White go into the house to bring out the sweets and sassafras tea for everyone to enjoy.

As the party begins and Red is playing his fiddle, Neal tells Gregory that he owes him a'lot, and again he tries to express to him just how much he appreciates him and his friendship.

"Oh you're gonna get to pay me back on the twentieth, remember?" asks Gregory.

"I sure do, and Mickey and I will most defiantly be there," grins Neal.

"I really wish you and Mickey all the happiness in the world," adds Gregory.

"We know you do Gregory, and I certainly am glad to call you my friend," replies Neal as he reaches out to Gregory and hugs him, just like he's one of his own brothers. "Now let's go get some of the food before it's all gone."

The party goes on until four o'clock, then the friends and neighbors give them their congratulations and best wishes, before leaving to go home and do their evening chores. As the Taylor's load up into their wagon, Gregory gets in with them to go to their home for the night.

"I sure am glad that ya'll got married on the Fourth of July," says Gregory, smiling at Neal. "It will make it easier now, to start recognizing it again."

"I was thinking the same thing," grins Neal. "After the whuppin' the Yankees gave us, we need something to celebrate."

"Well that better not be the only reason you married me, Neal McNair," snaps Mickey with a wink.

"You boys had better hush 'fore you get into a lot worse trouble than you got in during the war," laughs Red, as he pops the lines and his team starts toward home.

"Honey you know I was only funnin' don't you?" asks Neal.

"Get him Mickey!" yells Glenn laughing as the wagon leaves the yard.

"Oh, I know it, you Silly Bee," answers Mickey, throwing her arms around her new husband, kissing him lovingly, with passion and possessiveness. Now that they belong to one another, this is her joyful privilege and she fully intends to exercise it from this day forward.

Gregory stays with the Taylor's for three more days to make sure Outlaw has serviced Tally, before he leaves for Union City. While he is with Neal they talk about plans for the future. Neal in one of their conversations, tells Gregory that he and Mickey hope to get the Taylor place for their home. When Gregory hears this, he is just as anxious as Neal about getting the place because it will mean they'll live close enough to visit back and forth in the years ahead.

July 15th, 1865

Neal and Clyde are up early, headed to the County Seat. Neal has hitched up the mules to the wagon and loaded up all of Clyde's army equipment in the back, along with the army saddle. He tied the army's gelding to the rear of the wagon, so it will follow along. Clyde plans to turn all of this in since he does not feel that he will be fit for military service, even when he gets off the crutches.

It's nine o'clock when Neal gets Clyde to the court house and pulls the wagon under the shade of a tree. He helps Clyde down out of it, then he stays with the team, while Clyde goes inside. While he waits, John White goes by on his horse, leading the saddled army horse behind. John speaks to him, and Neal asks, "You're planning on turning your stuff in too, aren't you Mr. White?"

"Yeah Neal I am. I've had enough of the army and war," answers John as he swings down from his horse.

"I'd say we all have, Mr. White," agrees Neal.

"Not all of us Son, look a-comin' yonder," says John, nodding his head in the direction, where a horseman is riding up from the South. "That will be Glenn Taylor, I passed him on the road and he's planning on staying in the army."

Neal's heart jumps to a quick beat of joyful anticipation, knowing what this can mean to Mickey and himself. As Glenn gets closer, he can see that he has a clean uniform on and is dressed for inspection.

When Glenn rides close by, he recognizes John and Neal, nods his head to them, and continues on up to the court house.

"That boy really likes the army," states John, shaking his head as if he can't understand why anyone would want to stay in military service.

"Well Mr. White, it takes all kinds to make up the world, and to keep the world safe we need people like Glenn who are willing to protect us at all times," says Neal, keeping his hope of getting the Taylor place to himself, at least for right now.

"I suppose you're right and I best be getting on inside," agrees John, leading the horses over in front of the court house. When he has tied the animals up, he goes on inside while other men are riding or walking in to join their comrades for the scheduled meeting.

After about an hour and thirty minutes, the first few men start coming out of the building indicating to Neal that the meeting is over. He notices that the men who were carrying rifles when they went in, are leaving without them. This is a sign to Neal that Clyde's squad has been mustered out of service.

After a little while, Glenn comes out with a Union officer and they gather up the horses that have U.S. brands on them, including the one tied to the back of Clyde's wagon. They also take the saddle and U. S. rifle out of the back of his wagon, taking it along with the horses they have rounded up to turn-in.

"Ya'll get mustered out?" questions Neal, when Glenn picks up the saddle.

"Yeah, the one's who wanted out, got papers, but me, I'm staying in and taking the equipment and horses back to Nashville to be stored or re-issued," explains Glenn.

"Well good luck to you," wishes Neal, not letting Glenn know how happy he is that Glenn is staying in the service.

"Thanks Neal, I jes' wish pa was in better shape."

"Oh, I'll look in on him ever once-in-a-while, and help him as much as I can," promises Neal. He knows that he is going to see him the first chance he can find, after they get back home.

"That would take a big load off my mind Neal and I'm much obliged to you," replies Glenn as he turns to leave.

"Oh think no never mind about it," smiles Neal, still hiding the excitement he feels at a chance of getting his own place.

Once Glenn is gone, Clyde comes out of the court house, Neal helps him up on the wagon seat and they begin their trip back home.

"Neal you know Glenn Taylor is staying in the army don't you?" asks Clyde as he watches Neal guide the team out of the court-yard where several other wagons are waiting for their owners to return.

"Yes Sir, I do and we know that with him staying in, it gives me and Mickey a chance to get the Taylor place," answers Neal as the wagon keeps rolling toward home.

"Yeah, that's if Red can find a trade to get into that he can handle with his bad leg," reminds Clyde.

"You're so right Mr. Wilson. We've talked about this and if he can find something else to do, he will sell the place."

"I've been thinking about that and I've come up with an idea."

"You have! What's that?"

"Well Son, the one thing that Olive Branch needs and hasn't got, is a blacksmith shop," answers Clyde.

"Yeah, but most everybody shoes their own horses and repairs all their stuff themselves," complains Neal.

"I know that Boy, but the thing about it is, times are changing. Take Glenn for instance, he likes the army and don't wanta' farm. The young people don't want to farm, or do what their folks did. The army has taught them that there is a big world out there and other things to do," explains Clyde.

"So what you are saying is, that if Mr. Red were to open a shop he could make a go of it because times are changing and there will be a need for a blacksmith shop."

"That's it in a nutshell Boy," answers Clyde as the pair of mules pulls the wagon toward Canny Community.

"I hope you're right," says Neal. "And I hope that there is some way I can work it out to pay Mr. Red, if he does sell."

"Oh there will be a way. When we were mustered back there in the courthouse, they questioned me about my leg. It seems that since I was in uniform and under orders coming home, the action that took place where I was shot, was a act of war. That being the case, and my leg now being shorter, the government is going to give me a pension from now on."

"Really! How much?"

"I don't know, but I'll find out when it comes."

"That will really help you and Mrs. Wilson out, won't it?" says Neal as he turns the mules down Canny Road.

"Not only me and Rebecca, but it can help you and Mickey," smiles Clyde.

"If it does, don't tell the people in Washington that their money is helping a Reb," laughs Neal.

"I won't and that's a fact," laughs Clyde in agreement.

July 16, 1865

After the chores, Clyde and Neal journey over to Red Taylor's place. They find Red sitting on his porch when they ride up in the wagon.

"Good morning Neighbor!" greets Red. "I bet I can guess what brings you two over my way."

"Yes sir Mr. Red, I bet you can too," agrees Neal as he stops the wagon and helps Clyde down, then up the steps to the porch.

Once seated Clyde starts the conversation with, "Red, Neal here tells me that if Glenn stays in the army, you may sell your place to Mickey and him."

"That's right Clyde, but I need to find me a trade first. I also have my crops to worry about."

"Well Red," continues Clyde, "I think I may have thought up a trade that you would be good at. Now about your crops, Neal says he will tend them and harvest at the end, for a fourth of the selling price."

"Sounds pretty good about the crops Clyde, but what is it you got in mind that I can do?" questions Red, as he eases forward in his chair.

"Olive Branch ain't got no blacksmith. I know you could buy a spot on the edge of town and put up a shop and stable," explains Clyde.

"Yeah, I guess I am pretty good with my hands and town folks could use me," agrees Red.

"Not only them Mr. Red, but us farmers will buy plows from you that you can make, or pay you to fix-up our old ones. Some will even get you to shoe their mules and horses," explains Neal.

"You two sayin' that you would use me?"

"Yes Sir, ever chance we can," affirms Neal.

"Well I tell you what, I'll go into town tomorrow and see about setting up shop," promises Red. "If I can, I'll let you have the place."

"How much you gonna want for it Red?" asks Clyde.

"Oh, I don't know Clyde. What would be fair? Oh about seven or eight dollars an acre I guess, since it has the buildings on it," considers Red.

"Well could Neal use the quarter of the crop for one of the payments, and we say that you're selling it for eight dollars an acre?" asks Clyde.

"Let me see now, the crop should bring two hundred dollars and one fourth of that would be fifty dollars. Is that right?" questions Red.

"Yes Sir," answers Neal. "And if there's one hundred and twenty acres here, I'll be paying nine hundred and sixty dollars for it, but I'll need to pay you out, say over the next five years."

NEAL'S HOMECOMING

"The boy is going to get half of my crop this year and that should bring him about sixty dollars. We didn't get it all planted like we should have, but we got the staples, and the corn should sell. Of that sixty dollars, he can give you thirty. Then next year he is going to split my crop with me again, because of my leg, and have his own place as well. He should be able to pay you out with just the crops in the next four years," explains Clyde.

"That's right Mr. Red, I'll pay you somehow, even if I got to come into town and work for you for nothin, to help you build up your business. Once you get it goin' good and I've paid you off, you'll be doing good enough to hire somebody who needs the job," projects Neal.

"Well you two surely work good together, and I really like the idea of the blacksmith shop. I ain't one to think long on somethin' I like, so if you two will help me get started in town with a shop, we'll call it a deal," smiles Red as he sticks out his hand to Neal, to seal it with a handshake.

After the men seal the deal, Clyde and Neal go back home where Rebecca and Mickey are anxiously awaiting the outcome of their visit with Red.

As they ride in Neal yells out, "We got it! We got a place of our own!"

Mickey runs out to the wagon as it stops in front of the barn, jumps up on it, and hugs Neal. "We really did get it?"

"Yes Darlin' we did, but it is going to take a'lotta hard work to pay for it," explains Neal.

"Well I'm willing, as long as you are," smiles Mickey.

After putting the wagon and mules up, Neal and Clyde go into the house to explain it all to their women.

"Well when Red finds him a place in town, or even if he has to build a place, I'm gonna help him so we can pay our place off faster," explains Neal.

"That's wonderful," grins Mickey.

"Now we have to make plans about going down to Gregory's wedding," reminds Neal. "You know we'll be leaving the nineteenth."

"Oh I know that Darlin. I'm jes so excited about having my own house."

"You're going to have to be a little patient. We can't do anything to rush the deal through until Mr. Red finds what he wants."

"You're right, so let's make plans," agrees Mickey, still bubbling with excitement.

July 19th, 1865

Mickey and Neal finish their chores early so they can leave for the wedding. They want to get to the Bailey home before dark. Neal has borrowed a sidesaddle from Mr. White, for Mickey to ride on the second horse that Neal took from the raiders, who came to the farm. This animal is a medium size mare of mixed blood. She is a good natured horse with average spirit.

The couple put the extra clothing they are taking, in bags across the rear of each animal. Mickey wears a long green dress, to ride in, with laced boots and a wide brimmed hat. Neal wears his gray pants, a white shirt, and a gray hat. The pair of 44's are strapped around his waist in their reversed holsters.

"You two have a good time and be careful," instructs Rebecca as they mount the horses.

"Yes Mother, we will," answers Mickey.

"We'll be looking for you two back on the 21st," adds Clyde.

"Yes Sir," answers Neal, "We need to get back so I can keep an eye on the crops, and to finish our deal with Mr. Red."

"Aw'right then, have fun," calls out Clyde as the young couple heads off in a southerly direction. "Now don't worry Rebecca. They are two grown, married people and Neal can handle any problem that may come along," states Clyde, turning to go back into the house.

"I know you are right, but I can't help but worry," admits Rebecca as she turns and opens the door for Clyde.

The young lovers travel at a slower pace than Neal did when he made this trip a few weeks back. After a few hours they come to the spot on the river where Neal rested before and he pulls Outlaw to a stop. Then Mickey reins her mare in beside him.

"This is a good place to stop and rest the animals Darlin'," says Neal as he swings down out of his saddle and helps Mickey get off of her mount. Then he feeds the pair of horses and takes them to water.

While he is doing this, Mickey prepares some ham and biscuits for them to eat. After they've eaten, they lie back in the cool shade of a tree and watch the horses munch at the tall grass on the roadside, a short distance away from the tree.

"Come a little closer Luv," whispers Neal, holding his arms out to Mickey.

She smiles and slides up close to him, bumping her ribs on the handle of one of the pistols, which is still in place at his waist. "Here let me get these things out of our way," says Neal as he proceeds to unbuckle the belt, setting the pistols within arms reach, but out of their way.

"Well Darlin' you must have something on your mind," smiles Mickey as she kisses him lovingly.

"Now how could you ever have guessed?" questions Neal after the lingering kiss.

Some time passes for the newly weds who are enjoying each other's company, and they don't realize that the two horses have left off grazing, and have eased back up closer to them. Outlaw steps up right beside the lovers, and as if to give his approval, stomps his front foot. This action by the horse, gets Neal's attention and makes him aware of the time at hand.

Then Mickey says, "Darlin' don't you think we'd best be going if we want to get to Gregory's house before dark?"

Laughing, Neal agrees. "You are so right my sweet wife, let's go, even the horses are rested and ready to get on the road," he says getting up and taking Mickey's hand, he helps her to her feet. They both feel reluctant to leave this quiet place, but they're anxious to reach their destination before nightfall, so it's just another moment to remember, and they must be on their way.

Once they are on the road again, Neal asks Mickey, "Now what do you wanta name your mare?"

"I don't know, but she couldn't help being with those outlaws that came to the house, so we're not going to name her after that awful time, and she's a good mare," says Mickey thoughtfully.

"Aw'right Darlin'," answers Neal, laughing about her immediate defense of the animal.

NEAL'S HOMECOMING

"What do you think we should name her?"

"I guess Little Mama would be suitin' since ole Outlaw here, has already got to her," laughs Neal.

"Oh you men can never get enough can you?" laughs Mickey, "But that is a pretty name and I like it."

Little Mama and Outlaw keep a steady pace and just like the two riders, they seemingly enjoy each other's company.

The sun is getting low in the west when the McNair's get to Union City.

"You know Neal, this is the first time I've ever been outside the state of Illinois."

"No Darlin' it's not."

"What do you mean it's not? We are in Tennessee aren't we?"

Smiling, Neal tells her, "It's my fault, I forgot to tell you, back there on the river we were in Kentucky."

"We were?"

"Yeah, that town we went through right after we left the spot on the river, was Columbus, Kentucky."

"It was! And now we're in Tennessee," exclaims Mickey in astonishment. "My, my, I didn't know you could go so far in one day."

"Well jes' wait until you ride a train."

"Train! You mean I'm gonna get to ride a train?"

"Not on this trip, but you will when we go see my folks," explains Neal.

"When will that be?"

"Oh, I don't rightly know. I got to get us moved into our place when we get back, and farm two farms, plus work in town."

"I'm sorry that I pushed you Darlin'."

"You weren't pushing, but I am gonna need some help."

"You've got all I can give."

"I know that, and that's why I love you so," replies Neal as he leads the way to the Bailey home.

"You know Neal McNair, I'm really lovin' being married to you."

"Good, and I plan to keep it that way," answers Neal with a grin. "Well, here we are."

"Gosh! You didn't tell me they're rich."

"Aw girl, they're jest people like us."

"Good, I like people like us," smiles Mickey.

Neal dismounts Outlaw and is helping Mickey down from Little Mama, when Gregory walks out on the front porch to greet his guests.

"Look who's here! I'm glad to see ya'll got in before dark," says Gregory as he walks from the porch out to meet his friend and his new wife.

"We're mighty pleased to be here," answers Mickey, as she dusts off her dress and gets her hat repositioned.

"Yeah, you know we wouldn't miss your weddin' for the world," states Neal, "Even if we would'a had to ride all night."

"That's the way real friends are," answers Gregory. "Neal, you know where to stable your horses. I'm going to take Mickey in the house and introduce her to my folks."

"That'll be fine, I'll put the horses up and be in, in jest a minute," promises Neal as he starts leading the horses out to the barn.

Gregory carries Mickey on in, to meet his family and it's not long until Neal comes in the back door to join them.

"Gregory, help Neal and Mickey up to their room so they can freshen up before supper," instructs Mrs. Bailey.

"Yes ma'am," answers Gregory. "You two follow me. After ya'll have cleaned up or at least gotten some of the dust off from your trip, we'll eat supper. Then we'll go over to Teresa's house, and you two ladies can meet and get to know each other."

"I'd like to meet her, Neal has told me that she's very pretty, and a wonderful girl?" says Mickey, as she follows Gregory up the stairs, with Neal coming along right behind her.

After supper the three young people excuse themselves from the older Bailey's and walk over to Teresa's home. Neal leaves his pistols in the guest bedroom back at the Bailey's and as they get out on the dark street walking for a mile to Teresa's home, he misses them. He tells Gregory and Mickey, that he feels odd, being out after dark without his pistols. He further suggests that maybe he should go back and get at least one of them.

Gregory tells him, "They'll be just fine where they are, I have a tip-up Smith & Wesson in my belt, under my coat, just in case," he assures Neal.

"That ain't no gun Gregory. Heck that little twenty-two would jes' make somebody mad if you were to shoot 'em with it."

"This is the second model in thirty-two caliber," explains Gregory as they continue on down the street.

"Is that all you two have to talk about?" questions Mickey in a complaining manner. "Can't we talk about something besides guns?"

"Yeah Luv,' since Gregory ain't got much of a gun, I guess we can talk about somethin' else," laughs Neal.

"Not much of a gun! I mean, sure Mickey, we'll change the subject," snaps Gregory all in good humor.

The three walk on for about twenty minutes, then turn up a brick sidewalk to Teresa's house. "Here we are," informs Gregory as he leads them up the walkway to the front steps.

When they step up on the porch, Gregory moves forward and knocks on the door. Hurrying footsteps can be heard as someone comes to answer the knock. When the wooden door swings open, it's Teresa who quickly says, "Ya'll made it! I'm so excited about meeting you Mickey! Gregory has told me about this wonderful girl Neal married, and now here you are and I can see for myself." Teresa reaches her arms out to Mickey, and the two girls hug each other as if they both feel this is the beginning of a special friendship.

"That's for sure," agrees Neal, pleased to see the warm exchange between the two young ladies.

Teresa steps to one side of the door and invites, "Ya'll do come in."

The three visitors walk inside and Mickey admits, "I'm as excited about meeting you, Teresa, as you are about meeting me. Neal talks about Gregory so much, I feel that he's family and you will be too."

"Well thank you, I certainly hope I can be family," smiles Teresa glowing with excitement. Tomorrow is her wedding day, and she is so pleased that Neal and Mickey have come to share the happiness of this special day with them. She knows how close Gregory and Neal have become, and she looks forward to sharing this great friendship.

"Hello Teresa," injects Gregory. "I'm here too."

"Oh Gregory, I know you are here," answers Teresa as she reaches up and gives him a kiss followed by a big hug. "Now you just can't get jealous of us women talking. We've been looking forward to meeting each other, and we've got to talk now that we've met. That's right isn't it Mickey?"

"Sure is, that's cause we're women I guess, but these men enjoy talking too, don't they?"

"Hey, I was only picking," grins Gregory, glad to see the girls getting off to a friendly start so quickly.

"Ya'll have a seat while I go get Mother and Papa to come into the parlor to meet you," says Teresa, going out of the room to get her parents.

In a matter of minutes she's back to introduce her folks to her guests. "Mother, Papa, this is Neal and Mickey McNair, from up at Olive Branch, Illinois."

"Pleased to make your acquaintance," says Neal. Having risen from his chair when the ladies came into the room, he extends his hand to both Mr. and Mrs. Shaw in turn.

"It's a pleasure to meet you Mr. and Mrs. Shaw," agrees Mickey, holding her hands out to both of them.

The Shaw's shake Neal's hand, and they each take one of Mickey's hands as they acknowledge and return the McNair couple's greeting, with kind smiles and a warm welcome to their home.

Then the blond headed Teresa stands up and says, "Now you men visit here while we ladies go out to look at my wedding dress."

"Well you should be letting us look at it too," grins Gregory.

"No silly, you know that would be bad luck," laughs a bubbly Teresa, as she leads the way out of the room, leaving the men to themselves.

As soon as the ladies have gone from the room the men pull out their pipes, and begin to pack tobacco in them in preparation for a long talk.

During the conversation, the men conclude that the deep South will be hurt most severely by the war. Tennessee will be least affected by reconstruction, and southern Illinois will begin to prosper right off.

"I surely hope that all these predictions work out the way ya'll say, because when I get back, I've got to close a deal on a hundred and twenty acre place," adds Neal.

"You got the Taylor place, huh Neal?" questions Gregory, leaning back and drawing on his pipe.

"I sure did, and if times get good, I'll have it paid for in no time a'tall," answers Neal, obviously pleased about the matter.

"It's good that you are getting a place of your own," states Mr. Shaw, a man of about fifty.

"I thought so too Sir," answers Neal.

"You just going to farm it?" asks Gregory.

"I'm going to farm about half of it, and Mr. Wilson's place on halves, because of his leg."

"You got plans for the other half?" questions Mr. Shaw.

"Yes Sir. Gregory gave me the idea."

"I did? What's the idea I gave you?" asks Gregory.

"You did, when you came up to my wedding. When Tally and Outlaw got together," answers Neal.

"Horses! You're gonna raise horses!" exclaims Gregory.

"That's right," smiles Neal. "Outlaw has already serviced Little Mama, and if I can get me another mare, I'm on my way."

"You've got it figured out and I think it will work," agrees Gregory.

"I believe it will work too," adds Mr. Shaw. "The war created a shortage of horses and there'll be a market for them."

"Not only good horses, but who's to say that a Missouri mule can't come for Illinois," adds Neal.

"Oh, you are so smart," grins Gregory, about the time they hear the ladies headed back their way.

When the womenfolk's get back in the room, the men empty their pipes and the conversation changes to tomorrow's wedding. After the plans are all made and discussed at length, it's time for Mickey, Neal, and Gregory to return to the Bailey home.

When the three go out the front door, Gregory stays back on the porch to tell his wife-to-be good-night. Mickey and Neal walk slowly on ahead by themselves, their arms around each other as they enjoy the cooler night air.

After they've walked for a short ways, Mickey asks, "Shouldn't we wait on Gregory?"

"No Darlin' he and Teresa are making final plans and it may be a'while before he follows."

"Oh, I think I know what you mean," whispers Mickey snuggling even closer to Neal, as they walk on back to the Bailey home.

When they get there, they see that all the lamps are out, except one at the foot of the stairs, which was left burning for them. They use this one to see their way up to the bedroom. Once they are in the room, they quickly undress and get in bed.

"You got something on your mind Mr. McNair?"

"Yes Mrs. McNair, I surely do. I want to tell you that I love you very much, and I'm happy to have you here with me, as my wife," answers Neal as he holds Mickey close in his arms.

Gregory comes in forty-five minutes later and as he walks past their bedroom door, Mickey whispers to Neal, "I know just how he feels, don't you?"

"Yeah, I surely do darlin', but tomorrow the waitin' will be over for them," answers Neal as he draws Mickey up close and they fall asleep in each other's arms.

July 20th, 1865

Everyone in the Bailey household is up early making preparations for the wedding. Gregory walks past Neal's room, reaches in and knocks on the open door.

"Come in," invites Neal as he ties his string tie, in front of the mirror.

"I believe I will," replies Gregory, stepping into the room. "Where's Mickey?"

"She's gone over to Teresa's to help with the dress fitting."

"Oh. Well before I forget, take this ring and hold it for me until I need it at the wedding." He hands Neal a silver wedding band like the one Mickey wears.

"Do I need to ask where this ring came from?"

"No Neal, I thought it was so nice that you could make the rings for your wedding, and when I told Teresa about it, she too, was moved by the idea. We both felt that rings I could make would mean more than the rings we could buy."

"I think it's pretty nice too," agrees Neal.

"You two had better hurry up! We've got to be at the church by 10:30, and it's 10:15, now," yells Mrs. Bailey, from downstairs.

"Yes Ma'am!" answers Gregory.

"Well come on down, or you'll be late for your own wedding."

"Yes Ma'am, we're coming," answers Gregory. "Come on Boy! Let's go," smiles Neal as he hugs his best friend and then leads the way down stairs.

"You boys aren't wearing any guns are you?" questions Mrs. Bailey as the two walk down the stairs.

"Now would we do anything like that, Mother?" laughs Gregory.

"Yes you would," snaps Mrs. Bailey.

"No Ma'am, we're unarmed," assures Neal as they reach the bottom of the stairs.

"Land-a-goshen, that's a big relief. If the preacher's wife thought any of my people wore a gun into church, she would make us the talk of the town," explains Mrs. Bailey.

"Must be Baptist," states Neal with a grin.

"That's a fact boy," answers Mrs. Bailey.

"I learned 'bout the Baptist in Atlanta," smiles Neal.

"You did?" questions Gregory.

"Yeah, but that's a story for another time, right now we gotta' go get you married," laughs Neal, "before your mother dies of fright."

"Yeah, that's right. Let's go," agrees Gregory. Then the three of them join Mr. Bailey, who's waiting in the surrey, in front of the house.

Five minutes later they arrive at the church house. Gregory and Neal, who are riding in the rear of the surrey, get out first, and Gregory helps his mother down, while Neal goes to the front to tie the horse.

Mrs. Bailey goes up to the front door and is ushered in to a front pew, while Mr. Bailey, Neal, and Gregory go to the rear of the building. They wait there till the time for them to go out and take their places with the wedding party. The plan is for Mr. Bailey to walk in with Gregory and Neal, then he will continue on down the aisle to the first pew, where he will join Mrs. Bailey.

While the three men are waiting, the organist begins to play softly as the people fill the sanctuary. "Well, this is it Men," states Gregory, taking a nervous deep breath.

"It's gonna be fine, My Friend," encourages Neal, putting his arm around Gregory's shoulder, "I jus' got through the same thing two weeks ago."

"Oh, you are the smart one," laughs Gregory.

"Sh-h-h, you boys be quiet, you're making too much noise," instructs Mr. Bailey.

"Yes Sir," answer both Neal and Gregory, and then they continue laughing softly.

At a given time, a song is played on the organ, and the three men enter the sanctuary as planned. Mr. Bailey goes on down front to join his wife on the first row, when Gregory and Neal have taken their places.

When the wedding march begins, Teresa's bridesmaids come in at the rear of the sanctuary and march to the front, escorted by friends of Gregory, from the community. The organist increases the volume of the music when it is Teresa's time to come down the aisle, escorted by her father. She's wearing a long flowing white gown, trimmed in lace, and has a white veil which covers her head and shoulders. When she stops at the alter, she raises the veil back over her head and her lovely face can be seen.

This wedding lasts much longer than Mickey and Neal's, and he wonders if he can make it up to Mickey for his short comings in what is supposed to be the happiest day in a woman's life.

The ceremony is over at Twelve O'clock, and a dinner is given at the Shaw's home, for all the wedding party and guests. This is all in sharp contrast to the simple gathering Mickey had in the front yard of her home.

When the meal is over and everyone is mingling around, Mickey walks over to where Neal is standing and asks, "Darlin' what's bothering you?"

"Mickey, I'm sorry that I've not shown you all these niceties," answers Neal in a low voice.

"Niceties? You did the nicest thing that ever could've been done for me," says Mickey in a sincere, loving tone of voice, looking into his eyes as she reaches out and takes his hands.

"I ain't got nothing to offer to make it up to you, but all of my love, and a lotta hard work, for now. One day I will, I promise," declares Neal in a low voice, as he puts his arms around Mickey and holds her close.

"Don't be worried about all this show. I wanted you and you gave yourself to me, that's the nicest gift that can ever be given. I love you and you love me, what could ever be better than that. Now stop your worrying about showy things and be happy for us, and for Teresa and Gregory," implores Mickey as she stands on tip toe and kisses Neal on the cheek.

"Thanks darlin. I needed your reassurance, I guess. I feel much better now, but one day we are gonna do for our kids what has been done here today."

"Only if our kids want to do something like this. My guess is they will be fairly simple like us," answers Mickey as she kisses Neal again.

"Hey! You two are acting as if ya'll just got married!" exclaims a friendly stranger, as he walks by the affectionate couple.

"We have Mister, jus' two weeks ago," answers Mickey. Then she kisses Neal again.

The stranger smiles and moves on to visit with some of the other guests. Mickey tells Neal, "Now you go and have a good time. Don't worry about me, I'm going to enjoy being here but most of all I look forward to going back to our home with you."

"Aw'right, but only if you say so," replies Neal with a smile as he starts off in Gregory's direction.

The wedding party lasts the better part of the afternoon and it's Four o'clock before Mickey and Neal return to the Bailey house. It's not long before Gregory and Teresa come in and the two couples visit past supper and on into the night.

Gregory tells of their plans to go to Memphis for a few days on a river boat. Plans are made to visit back and forth between Olive Branch and Union City in the future and then Mickey and Neal retire to their bedroom, not wanting to put the newly wedded ones on the spot by waiting for them to call bedtime.

July 21st, 1865

The two young couples are up early, and after breakfast they leave headed in two separate directions.

Mickey and Neal stop at their spot on the river for some lunch and other activities. They make plans for the future and Neal tells Mickey of his plans for farming and raising horses.

"One day My Love, you won't have to work in the fields," says Neal while putting a straw he's just picked into his mouth.

"You mean you don't want me out there with you?"

"No, you know what I mean."

"Look Neal I jus' want to be with you, doing whatever you're doing, and if it's working the fields I'll be happy," explains Mickey.

"I know that Sweetheart, and that's the reason I love you so," answers Neal, leaning over and kissing Mickey.

Outlaw and Little Mama wonder back up close to the shade Mickey and Neal are enjoying together.

"You know, I'll bet those horses are wanting to get on home," comments Neal getting up on his feet.

"I suppose so," agrees Mickey as Neal helps her get up from the grassy spot where she's still reclining. "But Outlaw didn't catch us this time, did he?"

"He sure didn't," laughs Neal pulling Mickey into his arms for a kiss. Then he catches the horses and they start on home.

An hour passes, and then the sun is blocked out by dark clouds as a thunder storm moves in out of the northwest. "Whoa boy," commands Neal as he draws the reins tight on Outlaw. The big horse stops and Mickey reins Little Mama in right next to him.

"We're going to ride double the rest of the way. When the rain hits us, the road is gonna get slick and I don't want Little Mama sliding down, in her condition. She'll be more sure footed without a rider on her back," explains Neal.

"Sure, I'd like riding close to you," smiles Mickey, getting down from her horse's back ready to do as Neal thinks best, without question.

Neal dismounts, gets a slicker out of his bag, and ties Little Mama's reins to the rope that was binding the bag containing the slicker. He places the slicker around Mickey and she lifts the skirt of her dress up as he helps her mount astride Outlaw. Once she is up, she moves back behind the saddle, so Neal can get in his place. He mounts with the rope in his hand, to lead Little Mama. When he is mounted, Mickey adjusts the slicker around her shoulders and up over Neal. He holds the reins of Outlaw in his right hand, along with the rope leading Mickey's horse, and with his left hand he holds the slicker as tightly as he can. When the rain starts to beat down on them, a sharp clap of thunder rings out and lighting begins to pop all around.

"Time to go Big Boy," says Neal as he rubs the heel of his boot in Outlaw's ribs. The big horse begins moving and the rope which is tied to Little Mama tightens and she knows to follow when she feels the first tug.

The storm worsens and rain is coming down in sheets as they ride on toward home. Mickey pulls the slicker over her head and puts her arms tightly around Neal's chest, placing them just under his arms. Her hands are clasped and her elbows rest on top of the forty-four's on his sides. This way of traveling slows them down, since the horses have to move at a slower pace to keep from stumbling or sliding in the muddy road.

Finally, the couple make it to Canny Community and the Wilson Farm, about an hour after dark. Rebecca and Clyde have already gone to bed, but have left a lantern burning on the porch for them. Neal ride's up close to the porch and let's Mickey get off the horse, then takes the animals on to the barn where he feeds, grooms and stables them. This takes about forty-five minutes and then he goes to the house where he finds that Mickey has put out some supper for them.

When they have eaten and put the remaining food away, Neal says in a low voice, "Come with me." They walk out to the barn and quickly take a shower together, under the edge of the roof, where the rain is still falling softly, and the darkness of night provides them with complete privacy.

When they have bathed, they slip back into their room and as they are drying themselves, Mickey asks, "Where did you come up with that idea?"

As Mickey is drying her hair, Neal answers with a smile, "Me and my brothers used to do it back home when it rained. You get a'lotta water coming off the roof at one spot, and it really feels good."

"It sure does!"

The rain has set in for the night and the sound of it falling outside their window, is like music to the ears of the tired travelers. Neal blows the lamp out and they snuggle close to each other in the darkness. The falling rain has a soothing effect on the young couple, and their tired bodies are soon lulled into a sound sleep.

July 22nd, 1865

Rebecca has prepared a hardy breakfast of ham and eggs, and as the four of them are enjoying the good food, Clyde speaks while he sips coffee from his saucer. "Neal, Red came over yesterday and told me he's found him a spot in town and is ready to close the deal."

Neal is letting his coffee cool in his saucer also, and he answers Clyde before raising the hot coffee to his lips. "After I check the crops, I'll go straight over to see him and get the deal closed."

"Can I go too?" questions Mickey.

"Sure, why not?" answers Neal as he finally gets to slurp his coffee from the saucer.

Neal checks the crops and finds that the rain which came the day before, really helped them, and he's feels pleased with the growth he can see in the fields. When he gets back to the house, he finds Mickey ready to go to the Taylor place. She gets on the horse behind Neal, and in just a few minutes Outlaw covers the miles over to Red's house.

When the young couple find Mr. Taylor, who is out in the barn, they all go back to the house and close the deal, the way they had agreed to do, a few days before. For the next few days, Mickey and Neal work her father's place and help Mr. Red move to town. The furniture that he won't be needing in his new place, he gives to the newly weds to start furnishing their own house.

Once Red is completely moved, Neal starts working both the Taylor and Wilson crops. This is a lot of acreage for one person to work, but anytime he needs help, Mickey is always there to pull her share of the load.

Rebecca and Mickey rework the curtains in Mickey and Neal's new home, when they have finished moving. Then the two of them paint the inside walls with the white wash Neal has taught them to make. This gives the place a brighter look, which makes the hard work seem worthwhile and they are pleased with the job.

Neal stays busy in the fields of both farms plus working in town at Red's new shop. Clyde is still on crutches, but his leg is showing signs of getting stronger and he hopes to be able to help Neal with his farm in the near future.

The execution of the conspirators in the Lincoln assassination, finishes out the month of July. This in some ways pacifies those seeking revenge for the death of Lincoln, but it does not satisfy those who want to punish the Confederacy.

STRUGGLES OF FARM LIFE

• • • • • • • • • • • • • • • •

August 1st, 1865

Neal and Clyde are talking on the front porch of the Wilson home when Clyde comments, as he pulls on his pipe, "Son, it won't be long till the corn will be ready."

"Yeah, I've noticed that the ears are full and hard. They'll be turning soon, but it sure comes in a-lot later here than it does down home," agrees Neal.

"You got any idea how you're gonna get it out?"

"Yes Sir. Mickey can drive the wagon and I'll pull the corn. It's the only way."

"It's gonna be a-lotta hard work."

"Yes Sir it is, but I'll make it as long as Mickey drives the wagon," smiles Neal. "Besides, I gotta' few more weeks before I start anyway."

As August moves on, Confederate General J.O. Shelby, refuses to surrender and takes his army of about one thousand soldiers into Mexico. When they reach Mexico City, Shelby offers his troops to Maximilian, as a foreign legion. Shelby is turned down on the offer, but Maximilian provides a large track of land near Vera Cruz to the Confederates. Many of Shelby's men settle there.

Rebecca and Mickey are busy canning peas and beans from their vegetable crop, while Neal passes the time working for Mr. Taylor and keeping a close check on the crops.

August 15th, 1865

"Mr. Red, the crops are demanding more of my time and your corn will be ready for pulling in another week or two, so I won't be coming in as often as I have been."

"I knew you would be working out there sooner or later boy, so don't worry none about it," answers Red, seeing Neal's concern about not being able to help him in his shop, now that it's time to harvest the crops.

"I knew you'd understand. Thank you kindly Sir," says Neal as he slips a wheel back on a buggy.

"You gonna set into farmin' and horse and mule raisin' ain't cha' Boy?" questions Red, shoving a horse shoe back into the hot coals of his fire.

"Yes Sir, I am," answers Neal as he starts greasing another axle on the buggy.

"There was a man come through here yesterday on a wind-broke mare. He said all she was good for was a walk, and he needed to move on a little better than that. So I traded him out of her."

"You did? Where have you put her?"

"She's out back."

"How old is she?"

"The fellow that had her, said she was four."

"Young enough," answers Neal.

"That's what I was a-thinking too. She may make a good brood mare."

"How much do you want for her?" questions Neal.

"You'd better have a look at her first," advises Red. "She may not suit you."

Neal goes out back and checks the mare out, then returns in just a little bit. "You know Mr. Red, that mare makes Little Mama look good. Now, jus' what'll you take for her?"

"I'll take five dollars for her."

"Now Mr. Red, you know that mare ain't worth five dollars. I'll give you three."

"Three? I got more than that in her," declares Red. "But I'll take four-fifty, for her."

"Mr. Red, I'll split the difference with you. I'll pay three dollars and six bits, and not a penny more," offers Neal, with a final note in his voice.

Red having three-fifty in the mare, senses a chance to make a quick two bits, and says, "Three dollars and six bits it is."

NEAL'S HOMECOMING

Neal pulls every penny he has out of his pockets and comes up with four bits and six cents and says, "I'll get the rest to you when I come back in the next time to work."

Red takes the money and agrees to the deal saying, "That will make you owe me three dollars and nineteen cents."

"Right," affirms Neal. "Plus what I owe you for the place."

"The place can come later Boy, when the crops come in."

"Yes Sir," answers Neal as he goes back out to check on his little mare. She is a small quarter horse, or so he figures. Her coloring is a roan red, with a white spot in her forehead. "What should I call you?" asks Neal while he rubs the horse between her ears. "You're not much for riding, but I'll bet you'll be a good mama. Let me see now, think I'll call you Lot Mama, cause you can't get out and go like the other horses, so you'll be in the lot more than anywhere else. No, now that's too much for a little mare like you. Think I'll call you Lottie for short, I've already got Little Mama, and we could confuse the two of you. We'll jus' call you Lottie."

Lottie just stands there while her new master runs his hands over her body and legs, checking her out. It's as if she likes the gentleness of his touch and the softness of his voice. "No wonder your wind is broken!" (Wind broken: a horse that has been ridden too hard, without a rest, and is not in shape for harsh treatment. Something like a heat stroke, will never be able to do hard work or to run like a healthy horse.) Neal says as he finds scars from the use of spurs in Lottie's sides. He finishes his inspection of the mare and is ready to go back inside to finish his day's work. Each day that he works for Mr. Taylor is two bits off of his debt on the farm that he's purchasing from him. So far, he has worked off two dollars and fifty cents, in ten days of working at the blacksmith shop.

Red is crediting the two bits each day that Neal works for him, on the agreed price of the place and he now has his indebtedness down to Nine hundred Fifty-seven dollars and Fifty cents.

Neal is anxious to get the crops gathered for market. Since he is finishing out Red's crop for one fourth of the selling price, he is trying to make the crop as good as he can, so his share will amount to more. He is also doing the same on Clyde's place, knowing that the more money both crops bring in, the larger his part will be. The rains have been good for the growth of the crops, and the shortage of corn, will help bring a good price for the corn produced on both farms.

Red steps to the back of the shop and sees Neal still rubbing on his newly purchased mare and calls out, "What're you thinking about Boy?"

"Oh, about the crops and how I can pay off faster, Mr. Red," answers Neal, and he starts walking back to the shop.

"You got plenty of time to pay that off," assures Red.

"Yeah, I know that, but I don't like owing money."

"Sometimes you have to borrow to get started," encourages Red, "But don't get in a hurry. You ain't in Mississippi and these crops come in later than what they do down there."

"Yes Sir."

"Before you start pulling corn, or anything else, ask Clyde to check it with you, to be sure it's ready. It may be two or three weeks later than what you remember it being, down south."

"Yes Sir, you and Clyde ought to know, and I'll be sure to do what ya'll say," answers Neal, returning to his work on the buggy.

When his day's work at the blacksmith shop is over, Neal saddles and mounts Outlaw. He has put a lead rope on Lottie, and now he rides off leading her, to her new home. She slows him down considerably, and it's an hour later than usual when he gets home. When he comes up in the yard, he sees that Mickey is waiting on the porch for him.

"I was worried about you," she says as he rides up to the house.

"You shouldn't have been," replies Neal, with a smile.

"Well I was. I couldn't help it. It's later than your regular time to get in, who's mare is that?" She asks in the same sentence, taking her eyes off Neal to notice the strange animal behind Outlaw.

"She's ours. That's the reason I'm late. She's wind broke, but should make a good brood mare," explains Neal to his wife, who is still puzzled by the appearance of Lottie.

"Ours! We can't afford another horse."

"Yes we can. That corn crop is going to be good and besides, I didn't pay but three dollars and six bits for her. If ole Outlaw throws a good colt to her, we'll get ten or fifteen dollars for it when it's a year old."

"Oh, you are so smart," smirks Mickey, smiling as she sees the reasoning behind Neal's purchase.

"I hope so. If it works we will have horses to sell in a year and a half, when Little Mama drops her's, and after that Lottie's will be here," says Neal, planning ahead as he walks the two animals to the barn.

When the horses have been put up for the night and they've eaten supper, Mickey and Neal walk over to Clyde and Rebecca's house. During the course of the visit, Clyde tells Neal that the earliest time he can pull his corn will be mid-September. The Taylor crop was planted a week or two before Clyde's and should come in a little sooner.

As the month of August draws to a close, the Confederate Raider, C. S. S. Shenandoah, is sailing from the Bering Sea toward San Francisco, when it is informed that the war has ended, by a British ship.

September 14th, 1865

Clyde has begun walking on his leg, with the use of crutches and at the dinner table he asks, "Neal, you'll be starting on Red's corn soon won't you?"

"Yes Sir, I'm planning on starting tomorrow. I'm going to check the harness and move the wagon down there this afternoon."

"My leg seems a-lot better, and I believe I can drive the wagon in the field for you, then you and Mickey can both pull corn, and it will go twice as fast for you."

"Clyde, you know the doctor told you to be real careful with that leg," reminds Rebecca.

"Now you jus' let me be the judge of what I can and can't do Darlin'. The kids need help in getting the crops in. I can be careful and help them too, by driving the wagon," states Clyde, as he finishes his lunch and slides the plate to one side.

"Papa, we can make it. We don't want you to hurt your leg again now that it's doin' good," adds Mickey.

Agreeing with the women, Neal says, "They are right Clyde. It could be too much strain on your leg, and cause you to have to be laid up again."

"You three treat me like I'm a child or somebody that don't know how to take care of theirself. Now I said I could handle the wagon, and that's final," snaps Clyde, with the sound of authority clearly evident in his voice.

"Well Darlin', if you are going to the fields, then so am I, and we'll get that corn pulled even faster," informs Rebecca then starts clearing the table.

"That settles it, all four of us are going to the fields. The faster we get the work done, the more I believe you'll get for the crop," states Clyde, ending this discussion and pulling out his pipe he begins packing tobacco into it.

By the end of September, Neal with the help of his new family, has gotten all the Taylor corn pulled, hauled into town and sold. The crop has been a good one, and it brings Two Hundred and Seventy-five Dollars.

When Neal has collected on all the Taylor corn, he goes to Red's Blacksmith shop. Going in the front door, he announces, "Mr. Red, we did real good on the corn."

"How's that Boy?" asks Red, turning from his work to look at Neal.

"Here, you count it and see for yourself," answers Neal, handing him the money he's collected for the corn crop.

Red begins to count the money Neal has handed him, "Let's see, One Hundred, Two Hundred, Twenty, uh, Two Forty, Two Sixty, Two Seventy-five! I'd say you're right boy, this is very good."

Anxious to get the deal done, Neal asks, "How much of it will count toward the debt?"

"Let me think boy. Now a quarter of a-hundred is twenty-five and that makes a quarter of two hundred fifty. Now a quarter of fifty is Twelve dollars and four bits. Then a quarter of Twenty-five is half of that, or Six dollars and two bits. So fifty plus twelve and four bits, plus six and two bits, is Sixty-eight dollars and six bits."

"Who-oo-ee!" shouts Neal, "I didn't have that much in mind."

"Boy, you done mighty well and I'm proud to see someone take my place who really wants to work it."

NEAL'S HOMECOMING

"That I do. So if I take that Sixty-eight dollars and six bits away from what I owe you, let me see uh, Nine Hundred Fifty-seven and four bits, take away Sixty-eight dollars and six bits, leaves Eight Hundred Eighty-eight dollars and six bits. Ain't that right?"

"Neal, I thought you were better than that with your ciphering," comments Red, turning to go back to his work.

"Mr. Red, I did it on paper before I got here, and I think I'm right," affirms Neal, showing a little concern about Mr. Taylor's comment.

"Well boy, you made a mistake," states Red, with a smile.

"How's that Mr. Red?"

"Well Seventy dollars from Nine Hundred Fifty-seven dollars and four bits, is Eight Hundred Eighty-seven dollars and four bits."

"You took away too much Mr. Red," corrects Neal. "I didn't earn that much."

"Look Boy, I say you earned Seventy dollars, and that's that," insists Red. "You made me more than I ever thought could be made, so if I want to give you a dollar and two bits, I will." This ends the conversation with Red going back to work, and Neal remaining speechless for a few moments.

"Whatever you say Mr Red," grins Neal. "I have to be going now, gotta get back and start on Mr. Wilson's fields. Thank you kindly, and I'll be back to pay on that Eight Hundred, eighty-seven dollars and four bits."

"I know you will Son," answers Red, starting to pound out a horse shoe from some red hot iron.

When Neal gets the wagon back to the Wilson farm, he gets Rebecca, Mickey and Clyde together and tells them the good price he got for the corn, and the generous way Mr. Red dealt with him The family, especially Mickey, is proud of Neal in the way he's handled gathering and selling the corn. Also, they feel very grateful for the providence of God, and the kindness of Mr. Taylor in his show of appreciation to Neal. While they are still seated together, Clyde leads a prayer of thanksgiving, for all the blessings that have been bestowed upon his family. He concludes with, "At a time when our world is so torn and poor, from the pain and destruction of war, we're thankful for our home which enjoys the blessings of Thy love, and an ever growing love for one another. Thou hast blessed us with food, clothing, shelter and good friends like Red Taylor. For these and the many other blessings that we receive daily, we give Thee our thanks. We ask that Thou wilt continue to guide us, through Thy Word, and forgive us when we fall short of all that Thou would have us do and be, as we live from day to day in this world. Be with us always Father, we pray in Jesus name. Amen."

October 1865

The month begins with Clyde and his family working hard in his corn field. The crop is good and he along with Neal, hopes that it will bring a good price like Red's did.

President Johnson paroles Vice President Alexander Stephens, and four other high ranking Confederate leaders. These men have been in prison since their government failed and Johnson sees no reason to keep them there any longer.

By the end of the second week in October, Clyde's corn has been pulled and Neal takes it to be sold. As with Red's crop, it brings a good price of One Hundred and Sixty dollars. Neal takes out his half, which is Eighty dollars, and heads to the blacksmith shop. When he get there he pays Red Forty-five more dollars on his debt, leaving a balance of Eight Hundred Forty-two dollars and four bits.

"Neal, if you keep paying me off this fast, you'll have that place free and clear in no time," declares Red as he takes the money.

"That's jes' what I got in mind Mr. Red," answers Neal. "I best be going on back to Canny Community now, see you in a few days, to 'work'."

"That'll be fine Neal, see you then," calls out Red, as Neal gets back into the wagon, heading south.

Once he's back, he goes to the Wilson home and gives Clyde his Eighty dollars and tells the family about paying on the debt, and that he and Mickey now owe Eight Hundred Forty-two dollars and four bits on their home.

"I kept Thirty-five dollars for us to use through the winter Darlin'," explains Neal, looking toward Mickey and seeing her smile of approval.

"You two keep your money, we got plenty here to buy seed for both places, and to buy staples for the winter. We kept enough corn for the animals to winter, so we're in good shape. Jus' keep your money," insists Clyde.

"Thank you kindly sir, but we need to make it on our own," says Neal.

Leaning back in his chair, Clyde adds, "Boy, you did one good piece of farmin' this year and you'll have to do most of it from now on, so Rebecca and I feel like what's ours is yours and Mickey's."

"Well if you feel that way, I'll do the best I can by ya'll."

"We know you will Son," agrees Clyde.

"Mickey and me have got to figure out when the best time for us to go see my folks will be."

"When do you want to go?" asks Rebecca.

"Whenever it's the least busy around here, and at Mr. Red's shop," answers Neal.

Showing a little concern on his face, Clyde interrupts Neal and Mickey. "Neal, when you paid Red, did you and him set that down on record some place?"

"No Sir, but I trust Mr. Red."

"I trust him too, but it's best to have it set down in writing some place, jus' in case," states Clyde.

"Well, I'm going in to work for him in a few days and I'll check and see. If it's not already in writin' some place, I'll get him to do it then."

November, 1865

Mississippi makes laws to restrict the opportunities of the freed Negroes. The C. S. S. Shenandoah, surrenders to the British at Liverpool, England. The Commander of the Confederate prison at Andersonville, Georgia is hanged on charges of cruelty to Federal prisoners.

Neal goes in to work for Red at the agreed two bits a'day. When the two men break for dinner at mid-day, Neal starts the conversation. "Mr. Red, I don't want you to think that I don't trust you, but did you take my payments down some place?"

"I don't think nothing about you asking, it's jus' good business. Come here," orders Red, as he gets up and walks over to a stable, motioning for Neal to follow.

Neal steps into the stable and Red warns, "Now keep this to yourself boy." He rakes some straw back out of the corner, removes some dirt down to a wooden board, and pulls a metal box out of a dug out place in the ground. "Don't tell anybody about this," instructs Red as he opens the box. He then shows Neal the contents' which is a record of Neal's payments and balance on the home place, along with a little money.

"I won't tell a soul Mr. Red," promises Neal.

"Here Boy, I've even made you a copy of all our business. In the future, you can't be too trusting," smiles Red, handing Neal copies of the payments signed by himself; with dates on each payment.

"Yes Sir."

Neal works off and on through the month of November, and digs sweet potatoes to store for the winter.

Thanksgiving is a very good one at the Wilson home. The war is over and Clyde is home alive, and almost well. Mickey and her new husband have a place of their own, just two miles away and Neal is steadily improving the house and out buildings. What more could a family ask for? They feel that things could not be better than this, and their hearts are filled with thanksgiving. When they gather for the noon meal, Clyde offers a prayer of thanks for the blessings they have received and those they continue to enjoy as a family.

December, 1865

With twenty-seven states approving it, the Thirteenth Amendment to the Constitution (abolishing slavery) is formerly put into effect. Reconstruction is put in motion by the Republican controlled Congress.

Clyde is walking without crutches now, but it is difficult for him to get around still, since one leg is longer than the other. He receives his first payment from the government, for his disability in the amount of Two dollars and four bits.

"It says right here in this letter Rebecca, that I will be receiving this amount ever month, until further notice," quotes Clyde from the letter, then he hands the pay voucher to her.

"That's good Clyde, that's about half of what Neal makes in credit, working for Red. We could almost live on that."

"Yeah," answers Clyde rubbing his leg, as if he's thinking how lucky he is to be home.

Neal is hard at work in his barn on an old shoe of Clyde's. He plans to equip the shoe with a thick sole, which will help Clyde walk more normally. When he first started this project, he had Mickey to get one of her dad's old, worn-out shoes. She got one where the leather on the bottom was almost gone, he then cut the loose leather off and replaced the sole with several layers of new leather which he stitched into place with rawhide. He put the rawhide in wet, so when it dried, it would draw up tight.

As Neal was going through this first step of building the shoe, his mind wandered back a few years when Ruben, his youngest brother had a cobbler to make a large pair of shoes for his best friend.

When the rawhide has dried, the shoe is ready for the raised sole. Neal then takes a piece of two inch oak lumber and shapes the bottom like a shoe, smoothes the top off and shapes it the size of the shoe. He then takes a full piece of leather and shapes it the same as the upper smooth side of the oak, but leaves it one inch wider on both sides and one inch longer on the ends. Using pine tar, he glues the leather in place and tacks it down. Once this is done, he turns the ends and sides up and laces them to the exposed rawhide, with wet rawhide. He then takes another piece of wet leather and wraps the wooden sole and sides, lacing it up as tightly as he can. Now he is finished with the shoe and all that remains to complete the job is waiting for the wet leather to dry and shrink tightly to the form of the shoe.

Mickey walks into the barn where Neal has just finished building the shoe. "So this is where you've been all morning."

"Yeah Darlin, I've been right here," replies Neal as he sets the shoe up on his anvil to dry.

"That's my papa's old shoe, isn't it?"

"It sure is," smiles Neal, "And I sure hope it will work like I think it will for him."

"How's that Darlin'?"

"Well with that short leg, it's hard for him to walk about. I made this shoe higher and I feel that it will even out his walking and make it easier for him."

"Oh, now I see what you mean. The higher shoe will make his short leg longer and he can walk without limping so much."

"Yeah, that's the idea, I jus' hope I got the height of the shoe right."

"Well you probably did, Gregory was right. You are so smart," smiles Mickey, moving in close to kiss Neal tenderly, when he turns from examining the finished shoe.

After the kiss, Neal asks, "You got all your chores done in the house?"

"Yes Dear. Why?"

"Good. Come on to the house and I'll show you," answers Neal with a wink.

The weather turns from a cool fall to a cold winter, seemingly over night. Neal has to feed and care for his livestock and Clyde's. He feels that when he gives Clyde his shoe at Christmas, it will enable him to help more with the chores. However, plowing the fields will still be too difficult for him, because of the loose uneven soil.

On Christmas eve it begins to snow, and it continues to fall all day. When night falls, there is about four inches blanketing the ground in white.

Christmas Morning 1865

Mickey and Neal get out of bed and gather their gifts for Clyde and Rebecca. They have the shoe for Clyde, and an apron Mickey has made out of a flour sack for Rebecca. The gifts are wrapped in brown paper and tied up with a string. They are practical and simple gifts, yet they represent a labor of love, and are given from the heart by both Neal and Mickey. Excitement brightens their faces and they talk happily together, as they dress warmly, and walk over the snow covered miles to get to the Wilson place.

As they step up on the porch, they begin stomping the snow off of their feet. Clyde hears them on the porch and hobbles to the door, opens it and says, "You two come on in here before you catch yourselves a death of a cold!"

"Aw Clyde, it ain't that bad out here, I'm kinda enjoying it. This is the first snow I've seen, that I didn't have to sleep in," states Neal, remembering the hard times in the army. Being from the deep South and never having seen a snow before the army moved him up North, it was very hard on him and the others from the warmer climate.

"Well I'm glad we ain't got to do that no more," replies Clyde. "Come on in and take your shoes off."

Rebecca has breakfast waiting for them and they all sit down to enjoy it together. When they've finished eating, Neal slides his chair back from the table a bit, then pulls out his pipe, while Mickey goes into the front room and brings the wrapped gifts back.

Clyde and Neal are smoking when she returns with the two gifts and hands the one to Clyde saying, "Papa, this is for you from me and Neal." Then she gives the other package to Rebecca, and says, "Mama, this is for you from both of us and we love you and Papa very much. Merry Christmas!"

"You two ought not to have done this," comments Clyde, with a smile on his lips and moisture forming in his eyes as he looks lovingly on the two young people.

"Yes we should have, now hush and open your present," grins Neal.

"Open yours first Rebecca," orders Clyde taking a draw on his pipe.

Rebecca opens the package and pulls out the fresh white apron which is beautifully sewn by hand. With a look of surprise, she exclaims, "Oh my goodness! I really needed a new apron, but seems like I couldn't ever find time to make one. If I had though, it sure wouldn't have been this pretty." Having examined the apron carefully, she stands up, removes her old one, and ties the new one on, then proudly turns around for the others to see how pretty it looks. "Thank you both for my Christmas present, I do love you, and my new apron. Now it's your turn Dear," she says to Clyde, when she sits back down at the table.

Clyde pulls out his pocket knife, cuts the string and takes the paper from around the old shoe. He can't believe what he sees at first. Then with a puzzled look on his face he blurts out, "What! What in the world is this supposed to be?" He continues staring at the strange looking shoe, then he looks at Neal as if he's waiting for an explanation.

"Just put it on," says Neal, "Then we'll know if it's worth talking about."

Clyde removes the shoe on his bad leg and slides his foot into the old remodeled shoe. Once the string is pulled tight and tied, he stands up evenly on his two feet, for the first time since he was shot in the leg on his way home from the army.

"Try and walk Papa!" instructs an excited Mickey.

Clyde takes a step, stops and looks down at his feet, then he walks across the kitchen floor as smoothly as if there was nothing wrong with his leg.

"Oh Clyde, I'm so proud for you Darling," cries Rebecca with tears filling her eyes.

"I'm mighty proud too," adds Neal.

Walking back to his seat Clyde says, "Not half as proud as I am. I really thank you kindly."

As Clyde sits back down, Neal says, "Oh think nothin' of it, I was jus' trying to get a little help on these here farms." He then bursts out laughing and the others join him in happy laughter.

Still laughing, Clyde agrees, "Yeah, I bet you were, and this shoe surely will help." He walks about in his new shoe, looks at the way Neal has made it, and makes plans to do his other shoes the same way.

The family spends the day together and enjoy a delicious Christmas meal about mid-afternoon. After they've eaten and visited for a little while, Neal takes care of Clyde's animals, then he and Mickey start home to care for their own.

When they're walking back to their home and talking together, Neal says, "Mickey, I hope my family had as good'a Christmas as I've had."

"Maybe they did Darlin."

"I really want to go home now, but I'm afraid to."

"Why Darlin, it is because of me?"

NEAL'S HOMECOMING

"No, it's not you. It's jus' that I don't know what I will find when I get there. Sometimes I wish I still had amnesia, so I wouldn't be so worried, or scared."

"Why's that?"

"You know, I don't know if any of my brothers are alive or what's become of Mother and Pa.

"Well Darlin, that settles it. Now the first clear weather we get, you and me are headed south," states Mickey determinedly.

"We can't. What about the animals?"

"Papa can care for them now, since he has his new shoe, he can walk about to do things so much easier than he could before."

"Aw'right, when this weather breaks, we're goin' home, or I mean we're goin' to see my folks," agrees Neal.

When they get back to their home, Neal goes straightway to take care of the chores at the barn, and Mickey goes in the house, pokes up the fire and starts heating up the stove.

January 1st, 1866

Neal and Mickey are talking together in their home, as the first day of the new year ends. "Yes Darlin, Sixty-five was a much better year than Sixty-four," quotes Neal, as he rolls up in the bed.

"Now why would you say that?" questions Mickey, puzzled at this statement which seemed to come right out of the blue.

"Oh, ole Gregory told me back at Rock Island, that Sixty-five was gonna be a better year than Sixty-four. He sure was right about that in a lotta ways."

"Well Darlin', now I'm tellin' you that Sixty-six is gonna be an even better year, than Sixty-five for the McNair's."

"Really? How?"

"You jus' roll over here and I'll show you," orders Mickey with a little giggle.

Neal blows the lamp out and does as he's told.

The month of January is a cold and snowy month, and the produce from the large garden, pays off all winter for the McNair and Wilson families. The livestock enjoy the fruit of their labor as well, in the corn that Clyde and Neal put up for their winter feed.

NEAL AND NEW WIFE MAKE IT TO CHILDHOOD HOME

• • • • • • • • • • • • • • • • •

February, 1866

"You know Dear, sometime this month, we need to be leaving for your folk's home down south," reminds Mickey, as she's pouring Neal another cup of coffee.

"Yeah, I know Sweetheart. I think that we should be going about the middle of the month. Clyde is doing well on his leg, and he'll be able to take care of our stock for us," agrees Neal, reaching out and taking the cup of coffee from Mickey's hand. "We need to go into town and get us some new clothes to wear on the trip."

"You mean it? But darlin' can we afford to buy new clothes?" asks Mickey with both excitement and concern in her voice.

"Sure I mean it, and I've save a little of our corn money for jus' that, and you know there are some things we both need before we go."

February 10th, 1866

Mickey and Neal ride Outlaw double, into Olive Branch, since Little Mama is due to foal any day now, and riding her would not be good. Their plans are to get their new clothes and wait until Little Mama has her colt, before going south.

When they get to town, Mickey finds a simple blue dress which fits her slender figure nicely. It has a white lacy collar on it which gives it a soft feminine touch, and makes it dressy enough to wear for any occasion. They also find a good black suit, a pair of new boots, and a black hat, for Neal. They both try the new clothes on and get each other's comments and approval before finalizing the purchase. They are pleased with the new clothing, and feel they are now equipped to travel in style.

"Darling, are you sure that the dress is all you want?"

"Yes Neal, I can borrow some of my mama's shoes and a coat," smiles Mickey. "Besides, you need the clothin' more than I do, and if I don't spend anymore, we will still have some money left over."

"Oh, how can I be so lucky?"

"What makes you feel that you're so lucky?"

Neal smiles at the puzzled look on Mickey's face and says, "I have a wife who is happy with so little, doesn't ask for things I can't afford to give her, she loves me, and to me, she's the prettiest girl I've ever seen. Now that makes me feel real-down-right lucky, and I'll be proud to introduce you to my family, when we get back to my home in Mississippi."

"Oh Darlin,' you make me so happy I wanta jus' hug you and holler out to everybody, this is my husband and I love him!"

"We better pay for our clothes and get out'a here purtty soon," says Neal as he looks into the glowing face of his wife. He pays a total of Nineteen Dollars for all of their purchases. Then they start home with the new clothes wrapped in brown paper, where Mickey can hold it all, and still hold on to Neal, as they gallop away on the big horse.

Once they get back home, Neal checks on his mare and finds that Little Mama is just before giving birth. He puts the expectant mother in a stable where she can be alone to have her colt. The other animals are in the barn and the outer door is left open so they can go in and out at will. Most farm animals are usually nosy, and these too, are curious as to what's happening around them. Lottie and Outlaw are outside the stable door keeping a close watch on everything.

After a while, Mickey comes into the barn and asks, "Is Little Mama foaling yet?"

"Yes, Darlin, she is," answers Neal, with a sound of concern in his voice.

"I figured as much when you didn't come on to the house. Now don't worry, she'll be fine. You act as if this is the first colt ever."

"I can't help it, this is our first one."

"Well, I guess you're right then, we'll both stay out here so we can help her, if she needs us."

"You don't have to stay."

"I know that Darlin, but I want to," answers Mickey as she walks up to Neal and takes his hand.

Little Mama is turning about the stable with each pain, but she's not turning fast or in a frightened way. She seems comfortable with Mickey and Neal being there, and nature has it's way of letting animals know what to do in giving birth to their young. When the mare stops turning about, the contractions can be seen in the muscles around her stomach, while she's standing still. With a sudden gush, the colt's water is broken and pours forth, followed by the two front hooves. A few more contractions and Little Mama pushes the front legs and nose of the little one out, but she seems to be having trouble at this point.

"Come on Darlin, we gotta help her," says Neal softly to Mickey, as he walks up to the mare's head and gently places a steadying hand on her.

"What do you want me to do?" questions Mickey, a bit frightened at seeing that something is not going just right.

"You stand here, hold her mane, and rub her face," answers Neal, starting to the rear of the mare.

While Mickey strokes the mare gently about the face, Neal takes hold of the colt and pulls with constant pressure. The pulling of the colt, causes Little Mama to lean forward, and with the next contraction, the head and body of the baby horse comes rushing out followed by the afterbirth.

"That didn't take much did it girl?" comments Neal, rubbing the new mother and continuing to talk quietly to her. "I've had to do this with ropes and jacks, but you're a good little mother, and you was helping get your baby out and into the world."

Little Mama turns to her new foal and begins licking it's body clean. Neal and Mickey watch as she cleans up the little stud colt. She then starts nursing it as naturally as if she had been a mother before, and knew just what to do.

"I was hoping that the colt would be a mare," states Neal as he takes Mickey's hand and they turn to leave the stable.

"Yeah, it would've been better to use in starting a herd, if it had been a mare," agrees Mickey.

NEAL'S HOMECOMING

"Oh well we have to take what we get. Maybe I can trade it off for a mare. Gregory may even want him," says Neal, as he latches the door to the stable behind them.

"We can't worry about that now, besides, he may turn out as good as Outlaw," comments Mickey.

Walking on toward the house, Neal agrees with Mickey that the little stud colt, may turn out to be as good as his father. He decides to name him Trouble, in Outlaw's honor.

"That's a suitin' name Neal, I like it," remarks Mickey as she climbs the steps up to the porch.

"It does suit him," agrees Neal, while he's pulling off his shoes. Then he asks, "What's for supper?"

"You mean you can eat after seeing all that?"

"Sure. Why not?"

"Well I can't, but I'll get you something," says Mickey, turning up her lips in disgust.

The next few days are spent taking care of Trouble and Little Mama. Clyde has built all of his shoes up, and he's getting around well enough for Mickey and Neal to go south, for a visit with his folks.

Clyde and Neal are in Neal's barn, admiring the colt when Clyde says, "Yeah Neal, I'd say ole Outlaw marked him good."

"He did do jus' that didn't he? The more I look at him, the more I want to keep him around, but I need more mares if I want to get into raising horses."

"You can't get into that kind of business overnight. It's gonna take some time."

"Yes Sir, I know, but if I could trade him for a mare, I would."

"You can worry about that when you two get back from down south."

"That's right, probably be soon enough to think of horse trading, there ain't nothing can be done till spring anyhow," agrees Neal.

As the two of them start to leave the barn, Clyde asks, "Well jus' how are you and Mickey going to Mississippi?"

"We're going down to Columbus, Kentucky and catch a train, then we'll work our way south."

"That should be a thrill for Mickey, since she ain't never rode a train before."

"Yeah, she's been tellin' me that, and I think she's been excited ever since I told her we'd be ridin' the train," smiles Neal.

"Do you have plenty of money?"

"I got a little better than Fifteen Dollars," answers Neal.

"I've got a little that I can let you two have."

"No Clyde. Ya'll may need your money."

"No, me and Rebecca feel that you worked real hard this past year, to keep the family's head above water. Now we can let you have Ten or Twelve Dollars for the trip, and not hurt us none," answers Clyde as he stops to light his pipe.

"If you are sure, we'll take it, but I don't want to put these two farms in danger for next year."

"You won't boy. We got our seed, and we've got our livestock, so the two of us can farm these places just fine. Now Rebecca and me want you to go back home and find out how your brother's, and your mother and pa are doing. It'll settle your mind and help you to be more at ease in what you're doing here."

"Yes Sir. I think you are right about that. As it is, I can't help wondering if my brother's made it home, and if the family's still at home and well. Too, I'd like to let them know what all's happened to me since Franklin, specially how I met and married Mickey. I want them to know that she's from a good family, and that we've bought our own farm and plan to live here in Illinois." The two men continue to talk as they walk toward the house to eat the dinner Mickey's prepared for them.

February 15, 1866

As the sun is coming up, the Wilson's and McNair's are pulling out of the Wilson yard in Clyde's wagon. Since Clyde's mules have not been used for a quite a while now, they are full of energy and ready to get going. Neal has put a one by twelve board from side to side across the wagon bed, behind the wagon seat. This makes a second seat for him and Mickey to ride on, behind Clyde and Rebecca. They have placed their bags in the rear of the wagon.

"It's been some time now since I was on the move this early in the morning," comments Neal as the wagon begins rolling south.

"What'a you mean Darlin'?" questions Mickey.

"I feel the same way Neal. What he means Mickey, is when we were in the army, it seemed that we were always moving and especially, early in the morning," explains Clyde.

"Well you two ought not even think about the army! That's behind you now so let the past rest," interrupts Rebecca.

"They could, if they'd quit wearing their guns Mama."

"That's not so Mickey," answers Neal.

"You know it is Dear. You can't go any place without wearing those pistols," snaps Mickey.

"Now Mickey, Neal's right. I have my old pistol on, and I'll keep it on jus' to keep peace and not let anybody hurt us," explains Clyde. "Besides, you know if we were to run into the James Gang, we'd be mighty proud to have these firearms with us."

"Yeah, jus' the sight of them can keep somebody from attacking you, cause they see you are prepared to defend yourself," adds Neal.

"Mickey, your papa is right now, when the country settles back down, maybe then we can live without Clyde and Neal always needing to be prepared to defend us. As long as there are killers and thieves turning up everywhere, we need to be ready," instructs Rebecca.

"Well, I guess I never thought of it that way," says Mickey. "Maybe someday there won't be any ole gangs to worry about, and the world can live in peace."

"Yeah, maybe someday," adds Neal.

The team pulls the wagon along at a good clip, and the weather is cold and clear. As the mule's work pulling the loaded wagon, the moisture of their breath can be seen coming out of their nostrils. At a little past Twelve O' Clock, the family reaches the train station in Columbus, Kentucky.

After Neal has gathered the travel bags from the wagon Clyde asks, "Are you sure you've got plenty money to get down yonder and back?"

"Yes Sir, I believe we have enough, but jus' to be sure, ya'll wait right here until I get our tickets," answers Neal, heading to the ticket booth.

After a little bit, Neal returns with two tickets in his hand and a big smile on his face. He announces happily, "Here they are, two round trip tickets to Jackson, Mississippi and back."

"How much did they cost you boy?" questions Clyde.

"Nine Dollars a piece."

"That means we have Nine Dollars to spend if needed on the way, doesn't it Neal?" asks Mickey.

"Nine Dollars? Here take these Two Dollars Neal," insists Clyde, reaching in his pocket and coming out with two coins.

"No Clyde, you have already given us Ten Dollars," reminds Neal.

Appreciating the way Neal feels, Clyde tries to reassure him, stating, "I told you I could afford to give you Ten or Twelve Dollars. Now take it and I'll be giving you Twelve."

"Whatever you say Clyde," smiles Neal.

"Now you two will be back in three weeks from today. Is that correct?" questions Rebecca.

"Yes Ma'am," answers Neal. "If nothing happens."

Turning to Clyde, Rebecca says, "Now we have to be here to pick them up, so don't forget."

"Yes Ma'am," agrees Clyde, with a wink at Neal and Mickey.

"You two have fun!" instructs Rebecca from the wagon as they are about to start home.

"Do that, you hear?" smiles Clyde as he rolls the lines across the team's rumps, and they head back north, going home.

When Clyde and Rebecca disappear from sight, Neal and Mickey move their things on to the loading dock and begin their long wait for the train. After about two hours, the train pulls in, in a cloud of smoke and belching steam. When the engine stops, the conductor comes to the passenger car carrying a step, which he places on the ground for them to step up on and into the car. He then calls out, "All aboard!"

Neal gets their belongings and leads the way for Mickey to the car where the step has been placed. After the tickets are checked, they board the train.

Once they are seated, Mickey who is sitting next to the window, is as excited as a kid with a new toy. Reaching into his pocket, Neal says "Oh before I forget, I've got something for you," and he pulls out a small brown package.

Mickey takes the package and opens it to find a new scarf. It has a white background with red roses scattered about in a beautifully arranged pattern. She exclaims happily, "Darling what is this for? Oh I jus' love it!" She holds it out to look at it, then puts it around her neck, and kisses Neal on the cheek.

"It's a birthday present a'few months late Honey."

"You shouldn't have Darlin. We were so busy when I had my birthday I understood, and I really didn't expect a present. This is a real surprise and I love you for buying it for me. I'll feel really fixed up now with my new scarf, cause it's the prettiest one I've ever seen and I'm wearing it on my very first train ride. Thank you so much," says Mickey as she holds Neal's hand and looks into his eyes smiling happily.

"I know that you're understanding and never expect things for yourself, but I wanted to make it special. I thought this trip would be kind'a special and maybe the scarf would help."

"It sure does My Love," assures Mickey, as she bends over and kisses Neal just at the moment the train jerks forward.

"Here we go Honey," says Neal as Mickey turns to look out the window.

The train starts off slow and when it gets up it's speed Mickey turns to Neal and says, "Oh my! We must be going thirty miles an hour."

Laughing, Neal answers, "Yeah Darlin' I'd say we are, and I've heard that some place before."

"Really? Where was that?"

"Oh when me and my brothers were headed south on a troop train to Alabama," he answers, remembering a happy time that seems so long ago.

Mickey is wearing her new dress and Neal is dressed in his new suit, hat, and boots, with the twin forty-fours showing under his coat. The train is rolling along south when the Conductor walks through the car, looking his passengers over. When he gets to Neal, who is riding the inside seat, he stops and says, "Pardon me Sir, but could I have your name and destination?"

"Sure Mister," answers Neal. "My name is Neal McNair, and this is my wife Mickey." Then Neal holds out his tickets and adds, "As you can see we're headed to Jackson, Mississippi."

"Well thank you kindly Mr. McNair, you see we get nervous when a distinguished looking man such as yourself boards the train, especially when they're armed as well as you are," explains the Conductor.

"May I inquire as to why Sir?" Neal asks in a polite manner.

"Well it's like this. You are dressed up to fit the description of the members of the James gang.

"Well Sir, I've met the James boys once and we're not on the friendliest of terms. You see, they raided my pa-in-law's place back during the war when Quantrill was their leader. It was real messy and trust me, I ain't one of 'em," declares Neal with a smile.

"You two have a good trip," wishes the Conductor, as he moves on through the car.

"You see, I told you those guns were going to be a problem," grins Mickey.

"That wasn't a problem. He was jus' doing his job. Besides, if the James gang were to hit this here train, I'd bet the conductor would be glad to have me helping him out, don't you?"

"Oh, I guess you are right," smiles Mickey as she turns back to the window and watches the countryside go by.

The train rolls into Tennessee as the afternoon passes on, and the shadows are long from the setting sun when it pulls into Jackson, Tennessee. The Conductor comes through the car and tells the passengers they will have a two hour lay-over here. He suggests that they get off the train and take this time to stretch their legs. He also tells them there is a cafe in the hotel across the street from the depot.

"Darlin' we can get off and walk around a bit, but mama packed some sweet tarts for us if we get hungry." Mickey says, as she stands up and gets a package which is wrapped in brown paper and prepares to follow Neal out of the passenger car.

"That's good, but first we need to find a place to set down," replies Neal, as he leads Mickey out on the loading dock.

"Well that won't be hard Silly," laughs Mickey.

The couple go off the loading dock and walk up to the Town Square where they find a bench and sit down. They eat the sweet tarts which Rebecca prepared for them, and they talk about what they will find when they get to Mississippi.

When they've finished their meal, Neal and Mickey walk back to the train where wood and water is being loaded on the engine, and other passengers are purchasing tickets. "Let's get back on board so we won't lose our seats," suggests Neal, as he gazes over the crowd now gathering beside the train.

"Sounds good to me," answers Mickey, taking Neal's arm to walk back to the passenger car.

As they walk through the crowd, Neal spots two well dressed men with shoulder holsters showing through the sides of their coats. Seeing this, Neal unbuttons his coat to allow his pair of pistols to be in full view, when he walks past the two strangers.

When Mickey and Neal start up the steps to the train, the Conductor, who is standing by the door says, "Pardon me Mr. McNair, but did you notice those two distinguished looking men in the crowd?"

"Yes Sir, I did."

"Did you see those pistols under their coats?"

"Yes Sir I did, and when I saw them, I unbuttoned my coat to make my own weapons more visible."

"Well I'm glad you did because I may need your help if that pair of men are who I think they may be."

"Yeah, I figured you might, but I don't see a firearm that you can lay your hands on."

"I have a shotgun inside the door."

"Well get it and let it be seen," orders Neal. "At least they will know that if they're gonna take this train, there will be a fight for it."

"Oh Neal," butts in Mickey.

"Be quiet Mickey, it's gonna be aw'right. Now go on inside and take your seat."

Mickey goes inside and does as Neal has said, even though she is reluctant to do so. The Conductor goes in and returns with a double barrel shotgun which he leans up against the rail car. Neal backs away from the Conductor a few steps and watches the two strange looking men.

"All aboard!" yells the Conductor.

The crowd of people form a line and begin to board the train. The two men that are in question look at Neal, who has pulled his coat back behind his guns and is resting his hands on their handles. When they have looked Neal over very closely, they glance at the gun standing next to the Conductor. The line grows shorter and the two strangers quietly drop out of it and just walk away. Neal keeps his eyes on them until they reach a pair of horses, which they mount and ride north out of town. When the last person in line has boarded, Neal walks up to the Conductor and tells him, "Them two distinguished gentlemen we talked about, decided they didn't want'a' ride your train. I jes' watched them mount their horses and head north," smiles Neal, thoroughly pleased with their departure.

"Well that's fine by me. I think they may have been the Younger boys that ride with the James gang."

"Do you think they will still try to hit the train?" questions Neal.

"Not likely. They don't like to get into fights and if they can't surprise you, they don't usually hit."

"That's good to know," sighs Neal.

"Yeah, just the presence of our firearms may have saved a bunch'a lives today," adds Conductor, an expression of relief showing on his face.

"I certainly hope so, but I won't rest easy 'til we're twenty or thirty miles south of here," says Neal.

"I feel the same, so let's get this train rolling," smiles the Conductor. Neal comes aboard and the Conductor signals the Engineer to move out.

Neal is walking down the aisle to his seat when the engine jerks the train forward, and starts rolling slowly south. When Neal sits down Mickey says, "I didn't see the men that you were talking about come on board."

"No, they must have changed their minds about riding the train," smiles Neal.

"Do you suppose it was seeing those guns of yours that changed their minds?"

"We'll never know, but if I had my guess, I'd say you were right in what you jus' said," answers Neal still smiling.

In just a few minutes the engine has it's speed up and darkness has set in for the night. Since there is nothing to look at from the window, Mickey puts her head on Neal's shoulder and closes her eyes. She is sound asleep in just a matter of minutes, but Neal decides to stay alert for an hour or so until the train is far enough out of Jackson to feel sure it won't be robbed. After some miles and time have gone by, he puts his head on the side of Mickey's and goes to sleep.

Neal sleeps for over an hour as the train rolls south into Mississippi. He is awakened when the train starts slowing down, and as the Conductor comes through the car, he asks, "What are we stopping for?"

"This is Holly Springs, Mississippi" answers the Conductor. "We take on wood and water here, plus more passengers. Some folks will be gettin' off here, but you and your wife just keep your seats."

"Thank you kindly Sir."

"No need in ya'll gettin up, I know your ticket is to Jackson, Mississippi, and we should be getting there about 6:00 in the morning," informs the Conductor as he starts to the rear of the car.

The stop in Holly Springs is a short one of about thirty minutes. Once the passengers disembark and others board the train, the wood and water have been added on the engine, the trip south begins anew.

The next stop is in Oxford, twenty miles down the line. Since the train was watered and fueled in Holly Springs, the stop in Oxford is for only twenty minutes and they are on their way again. Mickey has slept through both stops and when the train moves out again Neal puts his head down and goes back to sleep.

Two hours later the train stops once again, this time in Grenada. Mickey and Neal rest uneasily through this stop while the water and wood supply is replenished, more cars are added, and the exchange of passengers takes place. After the switching of the cars the train is diverted south on another track. At this point Jackson, Mississippi which is the end of the line for Mickey and Neal, is only four hours away. When the train is up to full throttle again, a sound sleep for the tired travelers takes hold.

Through the rest of night the engine rolls south at a steady pace. When it starts slowing down, the change in speed awakens Neal and he raises his head to look out the window. He sees the early light of dawn and the Capitol of Mississippi coming into sight.

February 16, 1866

"Wake up Honey! We're in Jackson, Mississippi!" exclaims an excited Neal, to a sleepy Mickey, who is stiff from the position in which she's been sleeping. She sits up in their seat and looks out the window.

"I'm mighty glad we're here, I don't know if I could ride this thing much farther," she says as she yawns and stretches sleepily.

Smiling Neal answers, "I know what you mean, but in jus' a few minutes we'll be stopping, and we'll get out and stretch our legs. Then when we get loosened up a bit, we'll find some place to eat breakfast."

"Now that sounds real good to me," replies Mickey, perking up at the thought of moving about and getting some hot food.

When the engine stops, they gather their things and leave the train. The little city is just coming to life at this early hour when the two of them start to walk up Capitol Street to the nearest hotel that has a cafe serving breakfast.

"Neal McNair!" comes a voice from the crowd of men gathered together at the end of the loading dock.

Neal turns and stops, facing the group of men who have their wagons lined up next to the dock. The man who called his name comes out of the group and says, "Boy, we all figured you died up at Franklin."

"No sir Mr. Womack, I didn't. I was wounded bad and captured," explains Neal.

As the man of about sixty walks up closer to he and Mickey, Neal adds, "Mr. Womack, this here's my wife, Mickey. Mickey, this is Mr. J. H. Womack."

Smiling and extending her hand, Mickey says, "I'm pleased to meet you Mr. Womack."

"Nice to meet you too young lady," greets J.H., with a friendly smile and a handshake. He then adds, "I'd say you've been real busy since the war got over Neal."

"Yes Sir, a-lotta things have happened since then," answers Neal, adding, "Can you tell me if Melton and Ruben made it home?" He inquires with an anxious look on his face, knowing that the answer to his question may tell him of more empty chairs at the family table beside's Thompson's. He holds his breath and grasps Mickey's hand, waiting for an answer.

"I surely can. Melton made it home a few months before the war was over, and Ruben come walking in several weeks after Johnston gave up."

"That's mighty good news to hear," smiles Neal with a sigh of deep relief, as tears of gratitude well up in his eyes and spill down his cheeks. He looks at Mickey and she senses both his fear, and the consequent sense of being grateful to learn that two of his brothers are alive and at home. She holds his hand, gives it a firm squeeze, and smiles up at him with tear filled eyes. Her love and understanding clearly show on her face, and Neal returns these sentiments in his smile for her.

"I guess you know about Thompson don't you?"

"Yes Sir I do, but how is the rest of my family?"

"They are jus' fine, worried sick about you, but fine. Where have you been anyhow?"

"It's a long story Mr. Womack. If you will go eat breakfast with us, I'll tell you all about it."

"No Son, I need to stay here to get the freight loaded on my wagon."

"Are you gonna' be going down to Magee?"

"Yeah, as soon as they load my wagon."

"Can Mickey and me ride with you that far?" asks Neal.

"You sure can, and on the way you can tell me what's been going on with you this past year or so."

"Aw'right, it's a deal," agrees Neal, with a smile. "I'll tell you about it on the way."

"Fine, now you two go get something to eat, and I'll wait till ya'll get back before I pull out," promises J.H.

Mickey and Neal walk on up Capitol Street and find a cafe serving breakfast. He tells Mickey that Mr. Womack has a place about five miles from his pa's place, in Simpson County. He tells her they are good friends in the community even though they live in different counties.

After Neal has paid the twenty cents for their breakfast, they head back down Capitol Street to the depot. When they walk the two blocks, they find Mr. Womack's wagon parked next to a stockyard and he's waiting for them.

"Sorry it took so long Mr. Womack," apologizes Mickey, while Neal puts their bags in the back of the wagon.

"T'weren't long girl, I just pulled out here," answers J.H., as Neal helps Mickey up on the seat then climbs up next to her, and she slides over next to Mr. Womack.

J.H. gets the team moving, and Neal begins telling him what has happened to him since he was separated from his brothers at Franklin, Tennessee.

The trip south from Jackson to Magee is about fifty miles. There are several small towns to go through and Star Hill to cross, before the wagon is to be unloaded at Rankin's General Store in Magee.

It's Ten o'clock, when the travelers get to Star Hill, and the team labors very hard in getting the load over the hill. Neal and Mickey get down off the wagon and push on the rear of it, to help them pull the load. When they reach the crest of the hill, they get back in the wagon, next to Mr. Womack, who rides his brakes to keep the heavy load from pushing the mules too fast. At the bottom of the hill, he lets up on the brakes and the animals keep working at a steady pace.

At One o'clock, they go through D'Lo, and at Two, they are pushing through Mendenhall, the county seat of Simpson county. At Four in the afternoon, they pull into Rankin's store in Magee.

"You kids going on out to your folks tonight?" asks Mr. Womack.

"No Sir. We thought we'd meet them in the morning at church. Nobody knows we're coming and it would be very fittin' for us to meet at church," answers Neal.

"I'd agree with you about that Son, but where are ya'll going to stay the night?"

"Oh, we'll get a room in the hotel I reckon."

"Boy, I can't let ya'll do that! You two are goin' out to my house and stay the night. In the morning, you can walk over to Calvary to meet your folks. It ain't but three miles over there and we'll be up in plenty time for you to get there for the meetin'."

"Mr. Womack" starts Neal, but he's cut off before he can finish his protest.

"Don't argue now, ya'll are staying with me, so let's get this wagon unloaded and be on our way," instructs J.H.

"Yes Sir," answers Neal with a smile as he jumps down from the wagon seat.

When the wagon is unloaded, the three of them make the two hour ride out to the Womack place. It is well after dark when they get there and Mrs. Womack has supper ready. J.H. introduces Mickey as Neal's new wife, and Mrs. Womack extends them a warm welcome to their home and the supper table. She puts two more plates out and the four of them sit down for the meal.

Mrs. Womack says, "Neal we were all afraid that you were dead. What really happened to you?"

Butting in before Neal can answer, J.H. says, "Let it lay Mama, it's really hard for Neal to discuss it. He told me all about it coming from Jackson and I'll fill you in when we go to bed."

"I'm sorry Son," apologizes Mrs. Womack, "But I didn't know."

"It's aw'right Mrs. Womack, I've made it back home now and everything is gonna' work out good," replies Neal, reaching for the bowl of turnip greens.

The friends enjoy the good meal together, and when they've caught up on the time lost while Neal's been away, they learn a little about Mickey and her family in Illinois. After they've eaten and the women have cleaned up the kitchen, it's well past Eight o'clock, and Mrs. Womack shows the young couple where they are to sleep for the night.

When the good-night's are said, both the McNair's and the Womack's retire to their separate rooms. Mrs. Womack is anxious to hear what her husband has to tell about Neal. When he has finished the story, she understands the pain this boy has gone through and why it's hard for him to recall it.

Mickey and Neal get into their bed and soon after a loving good-night kiss, the two tired travelers fall fast asleep.

February 17, 1866

They are awakened by the sounds of Mrs. Womack building a fire in the stove and they hear Mr. Womack going outside to tend his stock. The night's sleep has been a quiet and restful one for both Mickey and Neal. She slips out of the bed first and dresses, then goes to the kitchen to help Mrs. Womack with breakfast.

When J. H. comes back from his chores Neal is up and dressed so the two families sit down for breakfast together. After breakfast Neal and J.H. go out on the back porch to shave since the sun is up now so they can see well enough not to cut themselves. The ladies clean the kitchen once again, then go to their bedrooms to dress for the morning church service. When the men have finished shaving themselves, they go back into the house to join their wives in getting ready for church.

When everyone has finished dressing, Mr. Womack goes out and hitches his mules to the wagon and brings it up to the house. Neal and Mickey bring their things out on the porch, ready to start walking, when J.H. says, "Ya'll put your things in the back, I'll give ya' a ride down to Calvary."

Neal puts the bags in the back of the wagon and when Mrs. Womack comes out of the house he helps her up on the wagon seat, then helps Mickey up to sit beside her. He then gets in the back and takes a seat on the side of the wagon-bed.

The four of them talk all the way down to Calvary and Neal tells Mr. Womack to let him and Mickey off at the bridge, under the hill from the church building. When they have traveled the three miles to Calvary, J.H. let's the couple off where Neal has asked him to stop. It's still too early for anyone to be getting there, so Neal and Mickey take this time to tell the Womack's how much they appreciate their hospitably, and that they enjoyed visiting with them. They thank them for the ride and say good-bye. The Womack's assure them they are very welcome, and that they're happy to learn that Neal is alive and well. Also, they enjoyed the visit and the chance to meet Mickey. They wish them a joyful reunion with Neal's family, the best of luck on their trip back to Illinois, and extend an invitation to visit with them again. They all wave good-bye as the Womack's leave headed to their church at Rose Hill.

Mickey and Neal hide their things in the woods, and sit down where they can see the folks as they cross the bridge, going to church. They wait quietly for about an hour before the first people start showing up for the service. While they sit there hidden from view, Neal can't hide his anxiety about seeing his family again from Mickey. She not only understands, but is a bit anxious herself.

"I wish they would hurry up and come on," declares Neal.

"What are you gonna do when they do walk by Dear?"

"I don't know. I'll figure out something," answers Neal.

Its not very long until Lilly and Hilton come walking across the bridge with Melton and Ruben. Neal views his family through tear filled eyes. His heart rate quickens alternately with the joy of seeing the four of them together, alive and well right there in front of him, and sadness at seeing how much the turmoil of the war years has aged them. This is the first time he has seen his parents in four long and pain filled years. The difference in their appearance is a shock that causes tears to flow from his eyes, and a physical pain in his heart, along with mental anguish for the brother who gave his life for a lost cause. He looks at Melton with one hand, and at his parents, who appear so much older than when he last saw them. He sees the lines drawn on their faces from the sacrifices and changes war has brought to them. Ruben no longer appears to be the carefree mischief prone young boy that everybody kept telling to grow up. Neal reflects to himself, "Looks like Ruben has grown up." The memories and thoughts rush through his mind like a fast moving stream of water, and his emotions are mirrored on his face.

Mickey sees how the sight of his parents and brothers effects him, and she puts her arms around him and whispers, "That's your folks on the bridge, ain't it Dear?"

"Yes Darlin'," answers Neal in a low voice, so as not to be heard by the people walking across the bridge.

The four McNair's go on up the hill to the church. "Darling they all look so different. Melton and Ruben are grown men, and mother and pa look so old," cries the still tearful Neal, leaning on Mickey, who continues to hold him in her arms.

She tries to think of the right words to say that will comfort him in this emotion filled moment which she is sharing with her heart. "Look Darlin', they had it rough too, but the sight of you is gonna change things for them, you'll see. Now let's go meet them," insists Mickey.

"Aw'right Sweetheart, I guess you're right, it's time to go," agrees Neal as he wipes his eyes with the handkerchief from his hip pocket.

They start walking out of their hiding place just as Norris Bryant is coming onto the far end of the bridge. When they step out of the woods, Norris, who was in Neal's Company during the war, sees them.

"Neal! Neal McNair! Is that you?" exclaims Norris and he starts running toward them.

"Norris! Yes it is! I've come home," answers Neal, almost choking with both joy at the sight of his old friend, and the tears that threaten as he remembers the last time he saw Norris.

Halting the painful memory, he says, "This is my wife Mickey. Mickey this is a good friend, Norris Bryant."

"Wife! But How? I thought your were killed up at Franklin, Tennessee."

"It's a long story Norris, and I'll tell the whole church about it, but first I want you to go up there and get Ruben and bring him down here," instructs Neal.

"Aw'right, I'll be glad to," answers the excited, almost unbelieving Norris, who strikes a trot up the hill.

When he gets to the church building, he finds that Ruben has already gone inside, but goes on in, walks over to Ruben and tells him, "I need to see you outside."

Ruben, thoroughly puzzled at the request, and at the look on Norris's face, follows him out of the building. The congregation notices the two leave and wonders what's going on, but no one asks. When they get outside, Norris tells him that he has something back under the hill that he wants him to see.

"Norris, church is about to start!" protests Ruben. "Now jes' tell me what it is you want to show me," complains Ruben, a bit impatient at this interruption by Norris.

NEAL'S HOMECOMING

"No Ruben, you've got to see this," insists Norris leading the way back down the hill.

As the two men start down the hill, Neal hears them walking and he takes Mickey's hand and they step back into the trees.

When they get down to the bridge, Ruben says, "Norris, this had better be good, cause I can hear them singing already at the church."

"It is, you'll see," smiles Norris just as Neal steps out of the woods.

"Neal!" yells Ruben, running to greet and hug his oldest brother. After a long quiet, hug, Ruben backs up with tears streaming from his eyes and says, "I knew you didn't die, but I still feel so bad about not getting you out of that ditch." Mental flashes of that scene race through the mind of both men.

"Little Brother, let's forget that. It was a long time ago and you would've gotten yourself killed trying to get me out," answers Neal as tears continue to flow from his eyes.

"I did try Neal, you know I did," cries Ruben, softly.

"Yeah, I know," assures Neal, as he puts his arms around Ruben once again, and they cry together. Now it's tears of joy they cry over just seeing each other alive, and being together again.

After a few minutes Mickey walks up and stands beside the two brothers, and Norris just looks on with a big smile on is face.

"Well?" interrupts Mickey.

"Oh I'm sorry Darlin'. Ruben, this is my wife, Mickey," Neal explains.

"Wife!" exclaims Ruben.

"It's a long story Little Brother," explains Neal, trying to get his composure back.

"But."

"No butts Little Brother, I'm gonna tell the whole church my story in jus' a little while," states Neal. "Now I want you to go there and tell mother that I've come home, and prepare her for me coming up there when church is over."

"Yes Sir Lieutenant!" smiles Ruben as he heads back up the hill at a run.

Norris, Neal, and Mickey, start walking up the hill together, talking along the way. Ruben gets there, goes into the building as quietly as he can because the service has already begun. When he walks into the back of the church, he sees his family on the third pew and walks down to them. Melton is sitting on one side of his mother, and his father is on the other side which is the outside, next to the aisle. Ruben steps past his father and mother and makes Melton move over, so he can sit beside his mother. This commotion disturbs the service, but after he gets Melton to move, Ruben sits down next to his mother, and the preacher starts speaking again.

In a whisper, he says to his mother, "I think Neal's coming home."

Lilly answers in a whisper, "Sh-h-h, don't be silly, just listen to the preacher."

Still whispering, Ruben insists, "No Mother. I know, that Neal's gonna come home!"

"What did you say?" questions Lilly, in a low voice.

"I said, that I know Neal's comin' home today," whispers Ruben quietly, with a smile.

"How?"

"I jus' saw him. He's coming up here when church is out," states Ruben softly.

"Praise God!" yells Lilly, to everyone's amazement.

The preacher stops his sermon, while Lilly is crying tears of joy, and inquires, "Sister is there something that you want to add to my message, or shall I continue on with it as I'd planned?"

"No Brother Craft, I don't have anything to add to your message," answers Lilly, then adds, "But Ruben just told me that Neal is going to be outside just as soon as you let us out."

"Now that's the best message I've heard in years," states Brother Craft, "An answer to all our prayers. Let me lead us in a prayer of thanksgiving, then we'll all go out and greet Neal."

After the prayer, which to some seems like the longest prayer they've ever heard, Brother Craft dismisses the service. The congregation let's Lilly and Hilton go outside first, followed closely by their two youngest sons.

When they get outside, the family looks at Neal, scarcely believing he's real. They all run together with hugs, kisses, and many tears. The tears shed by the family, and the crowd of people who have drifted out of the church, are all for the moment of joy they share over Neal's homecoming.

After a few minutes of greeting's and expressions of gratitude for seeing him again alive and well, Neal gets up on the steps of the church. He tells them all who Mickey is, and what's happened to him since he was captured. When he's finished telling his story, a lone rider comes galloping in from the North. As the horse slides to a stop, Dan Curry swings down out of the saddle and runs to greet his old friend and comrade.

"Mr. Womack told all of us over at Rose Hill about you coming home Neal," yells Dan as he runs through the crowd, "So I skipped church and jus' come on over here to see you!"

It's a touching scene, when the two men come together with so much joy in seeing each other again. Looking on, as they hold each other and cry unashamedly, more tears flow from the eyes of the the family, and those who are still standing around with them. After one more big hug from his old friend, Neal tells his story once again.

When he and Mickey have visited for about an hour, the families all go their separate ways, to their homes. As the McNair family walks off the hill from the church, Neal tells Ruben where his bags are, and Ruben runs up into the woods, fetches the bags and rejoins the family on their walk home.

Neal and Hilton walk along arm in arm, with Lilly on Neal's free arm Mickey is being well guarded by Melton and Ruben as they all walk the three-quarters-of-a-mile home.

When they turn down the lane to the house, Hob and Nob glance at the group. Seeing Neal with them, they start braying and run up to the gate of the lot. Neal is touched by the recognition of the animals and walks out to the gate to greet them. Hilton walks beside his son to see the mules while the rest of the family goes inside to put out the dinner Lilly cooked earlier.

"It's good, so good, to have you back Son," states Hilton with fresh tears welling up in his eyes as he puts his arm around Neal's shoulders.

Rubbing on the pair of mules Neal answers, "It's sure good to be home Pa."

"Hey, you two! Come on in and eat. I'm hungry!" yells Ruben from the porch steps.

Smiling, Neal says, "Just like ole time, huh Pa?"

"Yeah Son, almost," answers Hilton.

"I know what you mean Pa," agrees Neal, "But we got to go on, and make the best of everything."

"You're right Son. Let's go eat," smiles Hilton, as they each turn and start to the house. They walk close, with their arms around each other, as if they're afraid to let go, again.

April 1932

When the old man has finished his story about his brother Neal, Ethel exclaims with excitement in her voice, "Grandpa, that was a good story of Uncle Neal's homecoming! Did it really happen that way?"

"Yeah Girl, that's what brother Neal told me."

"How long did he stay down here with Aunt Mickey the first time they came?"

"Oh, just a few weeks. They had to get back to his farm."

"Did he ever come back?"

"Oh sure, you know he did. You saw him once or twice."

"That's right!" states Ethel, still showing excitement in her voice. "Did you ever go up north to visit him?"

"Yes Girl, I made that trip a-few times."

"Tell me about some of them times Grandpa."

"Aw' Girl, I'm all storied out for now, but I'll tell you some, another day."

"You know I won't let you forget Grandpa," comments Ethel, as she gets up and walks over, hugs, then kisses the cheek of her beloved grandfather.

"I was afraid of that," laughs Ruben, when Ethel starts out of the room.

"It's only cause you're the best storyteller in the whole world, and cause I love to hear about our family too..."